TRACKS

MOIRA KAY

For my family, who support me in reality whilst I live a fantasy.

THE WATCHER

She was there again. Hayes watched constantly whenever on patrol, hoping to catch a glimpse of her. He'd nearly missed her. She blended into the derelict buildings and the rubble in this part of town. Almost perfectly camouflaged, she was deceived only by the insistent wind in the streets today. The same gusts that sent the street filth into dusty eddies, were forcing him to wear his scarf bandit-style, and had coaxed escaped hairs into dance at the base of her neck. Briefly caught by the sun, they were a copper-toned signal flag, in striking contrast to the lifeless surroundings.

It was the third time he'd seen her and Hayes was once again hypnotized by her movements. Initially he had thought it was a child he had been watching. Small by City standards, she appeared young and delicate, but when she moved there was an obvious grace that came with age and her motions were anything but fragile. She was one of them, he was sure. A Dalton from the Valley.

Motionless himself, he kept hidden. She was fascinating to watch. Getting herself up and into the most obscure gaps in the structures, she entered buildings that had been intentionally blocked for generations. Her calculated leaps, twists and acrobatic maneuvers were completed with such apparent ease that it was difficult to believe she was human. Hayes didn't know what was inside that building, but he did know she would be taking something. They always took things.

Frozen on his perch, the defender watched the thief. He had many jobs – watcher, provider, protector; but Morrison 'Smiler' Hayes, the Enforcer was his role in this situation. He knew the job all too well, but found himself reluctant to carry out orders. Waging the same internal struggle with regard to this girl several times now, he still felt more of a guardian than a guard.

Supposed to capture all intruders and present them to the City Director for 'processing', Hayes had seen his fair share of interrogations and eradications and baulked at the thought of this beautiful creature being caught. Luther Derrick, the tyrant who ruled the broken city with intimidation, found grievous satisfaction in the emotional and physical torture of others and his passion was for the punishment of Valley folk. They were usually geographically out of his range of regular control and extreme examples were always made of those unfortunate enough to be captured within the City limits. If Hayes was caught being lenient to this girl, he too would be punished. Him *and* his family.

Sighing, he waited, not wanting to pursue her unless it was absolutely necessary. Soon the girl was back on the street, moving stealthily through the shadows. She was leaving his sector. Silently watching from his boundary, Hayes knew that his associate, Reg, was posted the next block over. Scanning the rooftops, he hoped that Reg was in his usual reclined and careless position, scratching himself with his ape-like arms.

No such luck.

Reg was leaning against the cement wall of a stairwell. Set slightly back from the roof's edge, he watched the street; alert. He leaned forward with interest, his hands tightening around his baton. Turning sharply, he disappeared into the stairwell.

Damn!

Hayes realized his body was already moving. Leaping from his hiding place, he missed most of the stairs between each landing, his internal panic rising. Reg would turn the girl in for sure. He might even have his own fun with her on the way. He was almost as bad as Luther Derrick – like father like son. If Reg got to her first, he might turn Hayes in as well, claiming he should have seen her go by.

Damn, he thought again.

Pausing in the street shadows, Hayes raked back his dark hair and assessed the situation. Reg was already on the street, engaging the girl in combat. Reg's shining black baton caught his eye. Some distance away, it had clearly been lost before it was useful. Hayes watched the scene unfold before him, sneaking closer to gain a better position.

She could fight! Tiny next to Reg, she was quick and appeared to be expertly dodging his attempts to get a hold on her. He threw his knife and she hit the ground as it flew overhead. Reg grabbed her ankle before she could rise. Spinning in his grasp, she delivered a surprisingly forceful foot to his face. Shocked, Reg lost his grip and she retreated out of range.

Looking for an escape, she was blocked in from three sides where she stood. Zipping to one side and boosting off a pile of rubble, she landed a flying kick to his head to get past him. Looking a little stunned and more than a little outraged, Reg pursued and grabbed for her again. Once, twice she dodged, but Hayes could tell she had misjudged Reg's long reach. One more swing and he had her.

Reg shook his head in what looked like an attempt to clear it. Closing a huge hand around her throat, he raised her off the ground and punched her in the side of the face. She'd struggled to make the hit difficult, but was so slight he managed all the same. Her eyes were wide and desperate, searching for something, anything. Hayes could see her fearful, defeated expression even from his distance and knew she was out of options. The small girl was powerless against the sheer size and brute strength of Reg. Reg knew it too. He shook her until she hung loose in his grip, like a rag doll.

"SMILER! I got one! ...SMI-"

Reg was cut off mid-cry by a blow to the back of his head that sent his eyes rolling skyward. Crumpling to his knees, he sprawled face down in the street. Hayes threw the piece of wood aside, cringing at the blood and hair sticking to it. Kneeling down, he scooped up the girl. Her body went rigid as she glanced around uncomprehendingly before lapsing again into unconsciousness. Pulling her close and rushing back to the building he'd just left in his own sector, he paused momentarily in the entrance to look back at Reg's motionless body on the street. Hoping that he wasn't seen and that he hadn't killed a fellow Enforcer, Hayes ducked into the stairwell with his precious cargo.

"Shit," he breathed out loud. "What now?"

Looking down at the girl in gray, he saw her eyes were closed, her face slack. Her chest was rising and he could feel a pulse beating in her neck. One side of her mouth was swollen and there was blood in the crease where her lips met.

Her face was covered with a grayish mud. Uncapping his canteen, he moistened his spare bandanna. Carefully, but with a sense of urgency, he started wiping away the camouflage. Her forehead revealed honey-colored skin and she had dark brows curving innocently as if in sleep. Her eyes, still closed, spread wide across her face and Hayes wondered what color they were now that he was close enough to see. Her nose ran straight, then sweetly into a slight ramp. Over its bridge, and smattering across each cheek, was a playful collection of freckles. One cheek now revealed a red angriness that matched her puffing lip.

Hayes tipped more water onto the dirty cloth and held

it to the inflamed side. He looked out to the street, straining his ears for any sound. Nothing…yet.

Looking down at the girl, he tried to gather his thoughts and slow his galloping heart. Now that he could see her face cleanly, he saw it was every bit as beautiful as the way she moved.

Shaking his head, he sighed and looked out to the street again. "Who sends the prettiest girl in school out to be a burglar?"

Turning his attention back to the petite form under his care, he started. Her eyes were wide open and staring at him. The brows, no longer innocent-looking, were drawn together in disbelief. Before he could recover himself, she drove the heel of her hand up into his nose, sending him off balance and backwards.

Squinting, Hayes ignored the taste of his blood as it ran from its throbbing source. Not yet fully healed from last week's fight, he knew his nose was broken anew. Pinching it to staunch the bleed, he blinked his vision clear. Physical pain made little impact these days. He was a seasoned fighter and had taken more than his share of abuse. He recovered more quickly than the girl.

Hayes watched as she held the wall to steady herself; her face ashen and her body swaying alarmingly. Rushing toward her, he caught her as she dropped, easing her slowly to sit on the stairs. Holding her steady, he moved in front of her. Their eyes aligned.

"I'm not going to hurt you. You need to pull yourself together and leave before someone else does."

Hoping he sounded reassuring but firm, he tried to read her face to gauge her understanding. Jaw set and mouth tight, she gave a small nod. Scanning the stairwell, her eyes came to rest on his canteen. Hayes offered it to her. She studied him with big eyes, obviously measuring his intentions. Hayes tried to make his face a portrait of integrity. It was difficult with half of it covered by a bloodied bandanna. Then again, the rest of his face wouldn't necessarily be helpful in this matter. After a moment's reflection, the girl took the offering and drank thirstily.

Hayes watched transfixed, as she set the water down and readied herself to stand. One hand using the wall as support, she stood wearily, squeezed her eyes tightly in a wince and opened them again with determination. Her plaited hair hung down over her shoulder, the end swinging softly. It was much darker than he'd first thought, but as she moved to be framed by the doorway, the sunlight surrounded her with an auburn halo. Twisting the braid up and tucking it efficiently back into itself, she turned to look for her hat.

"You need to go right now. Our patrol will come from the east. Soon," he said, handing her the thin woolen cap that matched her bodysuit. Again she stared incredulously at him.

"What?" he asked innocently. "You thought chivalry was dead? *Go.* We've been here too long already."

Tentatively taking the hat, she pulled it down firmly over her hair, tucking up the loose end that had betrayed her earlier. Wiping her hand across her forehead, she froze. Looking at her hand and then at Hayes, her dark brows drew together angrily. Storming towards him, she pushed him back a step.

Too stunned to retaliate, he continued to watch over top his scarf. Some water had mingled with the dust near his feet. Stooping to mix it with her hands, she smeared it over her face, grimacing as she covered her injured cheek.

"Girls and make-up! Willing to suffer to look good huh?" he said jokingly. Then seeing her face, Hayes diverted his gaze and cleared his throat guiltily. "Well, at least you're thinking clearly. You'd better ... wait, what's your name?"

She moved to the doorway and glanced left, right and then upward. Turning back to give a final disbelieving glare in his direction, she softened.

"Rori," she whispered. The corner of her mouth raised just enough to be considered a smile, and then she was gone. Hayes thought it was one of the sweetest thank you gestures he had ever received. Sighing to himself, he pulled down his bandanna, grateful for the surge of fresh air.

He'd done it. Risked it all. For a thief. A thief! And a *girl*? Of all the Daltons he'd been scoping for a trustworthy collaborator, he'd had to act this time? Instinct had driven him. If he'd had time to think it through properly, would he have made the same choice?

Running both hands through his hair, he exhaled roughly. He could only hope that Rori had the sense to stay gone and keep her mouth shut about being rescued by an Enforcer. Probably no-one would believe her, but Hayes couldn't risk even a seed of doubt. He had enough stacked against him.

Wiping away congealing blood with the back of his hand, Hayes investigated his nose. Tender and thick. Smiling, he silently thanked the girl for thumping him and inspiring the cover story he was about to need.

Picking up a rock from the ground he tossed it in the air a few times. Not to delay any further, he took a deep breath and hit the back side of his head hard. Warm blood trickled down his collar and he made his way quickly back to Reg.

"Reg! Shit Reg, you OK? Flying *Men*, my ass! They move like alien madness!" Hayes called convincingly. "I've never seen them team up like that!" Reg was still on the ground, but looked to be moving. Hayes bent down to help him up.

"I only saw one," Reg groaned.

"Who got you from behind then? I came when you called. I saw the guy that whacked you. Nearly as big as me, he was."

Hayes smiled inwardly, thinking it best to stay close to the truth. "They tried to run. I threw my baton at the big one's head to slow him down. Think I just made him angry though - got me some of your treatment, see?" Hayes pointed at his bloodied head.

Reg looked him over and spat the dust from his mouth. "Cheeky wankers! They can't have gone far. Let's join up with patrol and track 'em." He took a few shaky steps before finding his pace. Squeezing his eyes shut, Reg pressed his palms to his forehead for a moment.

"A *girl*! Can you believe it?"

Hayes shook his head and remained quiet.

"The Flying Men have lowered their standards to include whores now? I'm gonna love processing that one." Reg said, adjusting his crotch. Rotating his neck, he groaned and looked at Hayes. "My head hurts like a bitch and you look even uglier than usual!" Reg laughed to himself. Hayes laughed quietly in agreement and hoped for both his sake and hers, that Rori was gone.

THE THIEF

It takes every ounce of control I can muster to move slowly, clinging to the shadows. I can feel my heart pounding in my chest, my throat, my ears and the aching side of my face. An assembly of hearts beating in amplified unison. I can hear nothing past the noise of it, and have to trust I move silently. Every part of my body yearns to make a mad dash back to the tracks.

Thankfully, my brain functions enough to insist that would only draw more unwanted attention. Taking steadying breaths, I set my mind to putting as much distance between me and the City patrol as possible. After a few more blocks my heart returns to a manageable rhythm.

I need a moment to plan my retreat, but my thoughts are reeling. I've been caught and released. It seems impossible. Nobody survives capture in the City, and Citizens don't help Daltons. The risk is too great. Enforcers should help least of all and yet here I am having met one and I'm still breathing. Instinct tells me I'm still in danger, that this has been part of an elaborate trap to mess with me psychologically before I'm re-captured and the physical torture begins.

Some small voice in the back of my mind has a different take on it. It's the same small voice that usually gets me into trouble. Maybe, just maybe this is what I've been looking for. Something different. The sign of a change in City dynamics. A chink in the City's armor? Two Enforcers, one attacked as expected, but the other protected me - *a Dalton thief.* With more questions than answers, I need time to think.

If a patrol is coming I should get higher and off the streets. The buildings grow close together here. Tucked in an alley between them, I can touch two at once. Pressing my hands and my feet to the walls, I spider upwards to a second floor window ledge. Pushing off one side, I swivel my hips to sit in the brick frame. The bricks seem stable, but some of the mortar crumbles to the ground as I melt into the dark masonry. Bracing myself I judge my visibility from the street and feel satisfied I'm hidden.

Just in time too. Uniform footfalls pound the street. I watch between the buildings as a series of khaki guards file past in single formation. Lackeys. Each of them looks down my alley, but few raise their eyes above ground level. There are no doors there and the windows are high up. There are no ladders, no stairs or anything else to climb - there is no reason to think someone would be higher than the ground. I mentally thank Ari Li, my trainer, for drilling me on such things. The footsteps fade as the last sentry passes. I unleash my restrained breath.

Feeling safe for just a moment, I close my eyes and try to piece together my fragments of memory. Rubbing my neck, I remember it constricting and then nothing but darkness. Maybe moving or being held, a body on the ground? And then there was *him.* Who was he, with his wise cracks and reckless disregard for boundaries? He barely flinched when I broke his nose and he still helped me. He actually broke City laws to help me. Had he even hurt his own comrade? That's a strange thought. This was all deeply illegal. And worst of all, he has *seen* me. Seen my clear face, could recognize me – and I was stupid enough to tell him my name! Wrapping my arms around myself, I ache for home.

With much distance to cover, I need to go. Shuffling my feet beneath me ready to lean across to the opposite wall, I hear approaching footsteps, and talking. I freeze, poised on my toes in a crouch, trying to keep balanced. I shoot an arm upward to steady myself just as two burly, bloody-headed, leather jacket wearing Enforcers come into view. They stop right in the opening between the buildings as they talk. I recognize them both from earlier, the violent and the suspiciously attentive.

Glued to the spot, I'm forced to wait and hope they'll move on. The mean one is yabbering on about something, while the other nods thoughtfully. His warm eyes sweep the length of the alley, look at his feet and then casually float up the walls, scanning. Dammit! *He* seems to know I can climb them. How long has he been watching me if he knows that?

His eyes land on me, creasing in the corners as they meet mine for just a split second before they move on. Is he *smiling*? He definitely saw me. I strain to hear what they're saying.

"...patrol's been by too, Reg. Clearly they've moved on. Let's head to the Mess, get filled up and washed down – maybe Joanie will kiss your boo-boos!" He sounds like he smiles when he talks, but I notice it doesn't reach his eyes.

"Smiler, Dad's gonna skin us if we've let them escape! I'm heading to the tracks. You know those dumb-ass Valley snots need them to find their way home!" Reg spat venomously at the pavement. "Let's cut 'em off. It'll be a million times worse if we don't do everything we can to bring them in."

The aptly named 'Smiler' runs his hands through his dark unruly hair, flinching as he reaches the back of his head. He studies the blood on his hands briefly before wiping them on his pants. Exhaling audibly, he kicks at the dust, then speaks clearly and precisely – for my benefit, apparently. "Fine, we'll check the tracks. But don't you think *they* know that *we* know they need them? They might just as easily take the least expected option and cut through the marsh."

"That's the stupidest thing I ever heard! No guy the size of you, dragging some skinny bitch, would have enough cover through there! Besides, it stinks like shit and it's fuckin' freezing this time of year. No. They'll be making for the tracks. I think you're giving those thieving shits way too much credit. Now come on!" Reg urges as he turns, not waiting for Smiler to follow. Smiler glances down the alley, shrugs and moves after the bully.

"OK Reg," he sighs, falling in. "Your catch, your call."

He's helped me again. Clearly they are looking for two. The big guy and the skinny bitch? I'm the only one in the city today, that I know of. Only our Gophers visit the City on covert missions of thievery and we don't have any big guys doing that. We're called Gophers because we *go for* things, and we have to be small and strong to maneuver ourselves through the gaps and holes. Big guys can't do that.

I'm on my own here.

What else do I know?

They are heading to the tracks. Well it's the fastest way home, but not the only way. The marsh is definitely the least expected option – especially if they're looking for two. I know from previous escapes that there is cover enough for me to go unseen. That Reg is right though. It will be truly cold slogging through that stinking swamp.

My family is expecting me home tonight, but that is looking impossible to achieve. I stroke the thigh-length pocket that holds my maglev board, regretfully. It would be slower going through the marsh, but after a slight detour, I'll be back in the right direction for either entry to the valley. I could meet the tracks further along, or I could go higher and use the side entrance. A fluttering in my stomach reminds me it's been a while since I've made that entry. To distract myself, I think of Mickey, the water-trained horse I left above the grasslands beyond the halfway house. I hope his friendly face will meet me along the way, or it will be an awfully long, uphill trip.

Sighing in resignation, I fall forward and catch the wall to begin the vertical descent. The streets are quiet now and I know where the guards are headed, but I continue to move cautiously. The City is more than just soldiers after all. There is always the risk of being seen. Moving smoothly, I cling to the concealing gloom cast by the towering structures.

**

It's late afternoon by the time I hit the marsh, pausing at the edge under the cover of a half-submerged car. With the light beginning to fade already, there will be no chance to warm up on the other side. Shivering at the thought, I toe off my light shoes and shed my skin-like outer layer - a flexible, mottled gray, full body suit with assorted pockets.

My pockets are filled with the usual items: my maglev board for track riding, a fire starter, a collapsible canteen (empty now) and a small parcel of nuts and dried fruit. In every other available pocket is wiring. That was my excuse for coming today, but I've been doing reconnaissance for my own agenda too. That is what put me in the wrong place at the wrong time. I should have been more careful.

Rolling the suit contents, shoes and all, into a bundle, I wrap the arms and legs around it and shiver. I am left in underwear and the wrap I bind around my torso to strap my chest down. Unwinding that too, I tie it around the bundle. Using the ends to cross my forehead, I fasten the parcel at the back of my neck, keeping my hat firmly in place to conserve body heat.

The wind raises farms of gooseflesh across my skin and fills my nostrils with foul stench. I wade out into the muck and sink to my chest, drawing an involuntary gasp at its icy grip. With no time to waste, I rub marsh mud over my exposed shoulders to cover the pale beacon of my skin. Setting my sights on the junk piles at the far bank where I can leave unnoticed, I keep my mind busy trying to calculate my progress. Pumping my arms, both to keep warm and to help push through the mud I struggle deeper into the mire.

Trying unsuccessfully to focus on anything but what slid by my leg at step number seven, I shudder. I've never seen what lives in the marsh, but my imagination tells me nothing nice could survive here. Rationalizing to myself, I have to admit it's positive that anything lives here at all. Through powers of adaptation it has earned a place in the world when so much else has perished. I just hope it doesn't feed carnivorously.

My stomach growls loud enough to be heard over my chattering teeth. I doubt I'll be satisfied by my available food stores, but there's no helping it. It's not like there is anything to hunt or eat past here, and if I'm honest, I'd rather be hungry than add marsh creatures to my menu. I couldn't cook anything if I caught it either. A fire could be seen for miles, though I'd appreciate the warmth.

An unlucky step sinks me unexpectedly deeper. The stinking, cold mud slops against my chin, almost invading my mouth. Face contorted in disgust, I force my way forward with the enticing thoughts of a warm fire now replaced by those of a steaming bath.

Grabbing onto the rim of some ambiguous metal object, I drag myself from the sludge, making sucking noises as I pull myself free. I shuck the filth from my body and jog on the spot behind the trash to get warmer. Using my wrap to wipe most of the muck off, I struggle back into my jumpsuit, grateful for its meager warmth, and dig into a pocket for food.

Savoring the tang of the dried fruit and chewing the nuts longer than necessary, I try to fool myself into thinking I've eaten more. It's not a warm snack, but it is sweet and uplifting. I'd kill for a drink to wash it down, but I'll have to wait until I reach the clean spring at the halfway house. The sun is sinking lower and I'll have to hurry if I'm to see the marker rocks before dark. I can use the stars from there. At least, there are no clouds around.

Breaking into a run, I get underway. Useless relics from a time long past provide ample cover on this side of the marsh, hiding my movement. Piled high to create some sort of protective barrier long ago, the rusted carcasses of bizarre Citizen contraptions continue to stand sentry even though the threats have gone. Nobody has thought to clear them.

Making good time, I arrive at the marker rocks, just as the sun dips below the horizon. Checking the sky, I head north east under a rising half moon. There's light enough to see, but not so much as to be easily noticed. Quickening my pace, will make it easier to cover the distance while the ground is still flat and I should reach the halfway house in a few hours if I run most of the way.

The halfway house isn't exactly half way to the Valley, but time has reinforced its name beyond change. No one lives there. No one has lived there for well over a century. It's barely even a house anymore, having been left to the weather. I'll rest there, but not in the house – too obvious. If they're still hunting for me, I'll need to continue with the least expected options.

The house has a walled garden, with assorted nooks and crannies for hiding in. It's a sheltered rest stop on route to the Valley and is home to one of only two known uncontaminated water holes outside of the Valley. It's the clean water that has seen the garden's sturdiest plant-life survive the excessive sprays that were used to clear the lands last century. Over the years, certain species within the garden have recovered and taken it over. If I'm lucky, I'll find a hidden place to sleep and maybe even an apple or two.

This year has seen several tiny apples clinging to the gnarled old tree. It's the most success I've had so far. I claim the apple production success as my own, because I prune the tree and pollinate the blossoms each year myself. There are no bees out here to do it.

Running with the thought of apples in my head has my mouth watering. Slowing to a walk, I weave through the blackened stumps of the deserted Deadwoods. I travel silently through the grimly preserved tree cemetery, though I doubt there is anyone or anything around to hear me.

Maybe a wild pig or two? Descendants of those released in the re-establishment experiments, before I was born. If they survived out here, I've never met one. Signs of life only start appearing as you head toward the Valley, though I only ever see the occasional rabbit or mouse, and even less frequently, a snake. The rodents manage to live and breed outside the Valley before death catches them, and the hardened serpentine bastards have adapted to survive on them. Those are the only creatures I have seen living beyond the Valley. Aside from Citizens that is.

Traveling home from the Deadwoods, I don't even bother to check the stars, I'm practically drawn to the Valley; like a compass to north. My home is a picturesque and welcoming haven. Carved out by an ancient glacier, the Valley is nestled among the mountain ranges and completely surrounded by towering, sheer cliffs. Miles of rocks rendered the land around it naturally unusable in the before time, keeping it safe from contamination. A huge green oasis, roughly four miles wide and thirteen miles long, it was protected for years from the ugliness of the world by its remote location, and hidden from above by a cleverly projected image of rock, as if nothing existed there but an impassable mountain range. Not anymore though.

Just over a century ago, a huge storm hit and lightning set one of the Valley woodlots ablaze. The smoke was immense, filling the Valley and pouring into the sky. It was undeniable that the rocks were concealing something.

Citizens on the brink of starvation sent scouts to investigate. By that time they'd exhausted almost all of their own resources, as had their enemies around the globe. Unable to penetrate our rock fortress on foot, they were desperate enough to brave the river's formidable caves and found a land of plenty and new people to exploit on the other side. We've been linked ever since.

I strain my eyes in the dimness to gain my bearings. Seeing no landmarks, I pay attention to the land underfoot. To my relief, the ground is at last starting to slope upward. I've been waiting for this. Increasing my efforts, I power on. My legs don't have much energy left in them, but I ignore their nagging. The halfway house is at the top of the hill. I'll soon have a well-deserved drink and a sheltered place to sleep until morning.

When day breaks, I'll have a clear view of the tracks as they run by. If there are still soldiers after me, I'll be able to see them. From atop the garden walls, I can see from the barren wastelands outside the City, all the way to the rocky hills where the tracks disappear from view, winding their way onward to the corridor and the tunnel - the century-old channel blasted by the Citizens, through a mile of solid rock in order to repeatedly raid our Valley with their prized train.

Dark like my thoughts, the empty windows of the halfway house watch me as I approach. Ignoring their eerie glare, I walk to the huge rambling rose that stands guard. Trying as best I can to avoid thorns, I squeeze between the rose and the rock wall and into the garden. The spring is on the lower level, and I take care not to trip on the tangles of overgrown vegetation as I descend. Kneeling at the stone edge, I scrub my hands clean before cupping them repeatedly to slake my thirst. I splash the cold water on my aching face, trying to clean off some marsh mud and then lie back on the thick moss behind me, exhausted.

Comfortable as it is, the soft moss is too open and damp to sleep on. I reluctantly stand in search of a more cozy bed. A few steps and I just about trip over an old log with a bank of dry fallen leaves behind it. Rolling over the log dam and into the pool of leaves, I sink approvingly to the bottom of the autumn bounty. Sitting up, I unwrap my binding and open the material strip as wide as it will go, wrapping it around my shoulders like a shawl before lying down again. I snuggle further into the leaves, allowing them to cover me entirely with a thick layer, and let sleep take me.

LEAP OF FAITH

I awake with a start, but can't ascertain why. Listening from the depths, I hear nothing; smell nothing. Under my leafy blanket, I roll to my stomach as slowly and as quietly as possible - cursing myself for not thinking of how noisy dried leaves can be. Bracing my hands beneath me, I raise my head a little, waiting as a few leaves float slowly out of my vision. What I see chills my spine.

Much too close to my face, is a coiled rattlesnake, head raised and tongue tasting. The sun is only just lighting the sky. It should be too early for snakes. Shuddering internally, I realize I was probably sharing its bed, warming its blood with my own. I can hear something scuffling in the direction of the wall and hope the snake might be distracted by breakfast, but it doesn't leave, only moves its head higher and backward into a better striking position. Sickened and petrified, I don't move; can't move.

The blur of its rattle is all I can see now, as its warning drones in my ears. Another sound pierces my awareness - the whistling sound of air parting for high speed metal. In front of me the snake seems to jump into the air and tumble backward writhing and curling into itself around a glint of steel. I remain a statue as my mind races to assess what danger I might still be in. The snake is still now and clearly displays a knife protruding from its head. A newly familiar voice interrupts my thoughts.

"Got him! Reg, I got a rattler!" Smiler says, in a hushed but excited tone as he comes into view to retrieve his knife. Just as he crouches down to pull his blade from its new snake-skin sheath, he sees me. His eyes widen and he stands so suddenly he slips on the dew-damp leaves and falls over, crying out in surprise.

"What are you doing over there? Quit messing around! We're trying to be quiet!" Reg hisses at him from somewhere over by the stone wall.

"Thought it was still alive when I picked up my knife," Smiler replies without so much as a pause. "Scared the shit out of me! And anyway, there's no one here."

This guy is good at covering his ass. My ass. Three times in one day!

Stretching casually, the oddly helpful Enforcer scratches his jaw and looks around. "Why don't you check the old house again, in case we missed something? I can see some apples up a tree back here that we can eat on the way home. I'll pick them and meet ya round front."

"Fine," says Reg, sending rocks skittering down the steps. "Dad's gonna be pissed. We're half way to the damn Valley and there's been no sign. Scum could still be inside the City for all I know. We'll search the tracks to the corridor and head back if they're clear."

Reg curses his way back through the rosebush. Still frozen, I keep my eyes on Smiler as he's watching Reg leave. Turning back to me, he holds out his hand. Hesitating (probably too briefly), I take it, hauling my stiff body up. My hat, shawl and a cascade of leaves fall as I rise. His eyes widen as they travel down my body and up again. Quickly averting his eyes when he sees me notice, a blush grows in his cheeks. Grabbing my wrap, I hurriedly twist it into place, my own cheeks warming as I study him.

No bandanna covers his face this morning. He is quite

good looking, despite the swollen nose I gave him yesterday and the bruising under his temporarily evasive eyes. He brushes a hand over his mouth and strokes it down his strong, stubbled jaw, as he exhales. My eyes are drawn to the shine of a curved scar that travels from the corner of his mouth up to his cheekbone, giving him a strange, permanent smirk.

"*Smiler,*" I breathe, not really meaning to speak.

Immediately, I wish that I hadn't. His whole face changes. Dark eyebrows plunge together, his eyes harden and his mouth draws downward as he runs his thumb down the scar. Seeing my mistake, I drop my eyes and step back. "Sorry, I…" Stumbling back into silence, I look back up at him from under my brows. He is huge. Far taller than me (not that it takes much), and muscular too. Solid. His hand comes toward me in a formal gesture. Leaning closer, he quietly introduces himself.

"Hayes. Morrison Hayes. Please don't call me Smiler."

Taking his hand, I shake it carefully, leaning in and responding just as quietly. "OK. Hayes. We have to stop meeting like this. A girl's got to feel independent, ya know?"

The warm smile returns and I send a beamer back to him. His smile broadens to reveals two rows of straight, white teeth, lighting his face with an expression that makes me self-conscious. Abruptly dropping his hand, I remind myself he's a Citizen. Seemingly aware of my sudden change of heart, he hides his hand in a pocket as his smile fades.

"I gotta go. Reg'll be wondering what's taking so long. You'd better hide a bit longer," he warns. "Do *try* to stay out of danger. Though I have to admit," he says, smiling as he gently strokes his damaged nose, "It's been a pleasure to meet you."

"Wait… your apples?" I hint, sighing internally. I won't get to reap the rewards of my labor this harvest. "Just leave me one, OK? I'll need to pay my horse, when I find him."

Hayes nods as he tucks the dead snake into his belt and takes out a bag. Looking up into the branches of the apple tree, he then looks to me. "A little help?"

I give a small shrug. "It's the least I could do." He saves my life and I get him apples? Another thought strikes me. "Maybe don't eat them all yourself? A few should be alright, but I haven't had them tested yet. And definitely don't eat the snake."

He studies my face, his expression a mixture of confusion and amusement. Giving a small nod, he moves aside to give me better access to the tree.

Taking a moment to stretch my limbs and arch my back, I swing up easily through the branches. I had pollinated the higher blossoms, hoping to keep them out of sight from anyone browsing below. Throwing them down, I tuck the smallest one tightly under my wrap, before dismounting lightly at his feet.

Straightening from my landing I meet his awestruck expression. "You're very... talented, Rori," he marvels, reaching a hand toward my face. Surprised, I duck out of reach and he sharply withdraws his hand.

"Sorry," he says softly. "You have, uh…leaves. Thanks for the apples. Maybe I'll see you on Train Day," Hayes says in a rush. He half-smiles and turns away without waiting for a response, swinging the bag of apples over his shoulder and whistling loudly as he leaves.

Realizing this is my cue to disappear too, I re-submerge myself in the leaves, using his noise to disguise my own. Alone with my stunned thoughts, I listen to his whistling. It stops a while before starting up again; this time, slowly fading. They're moving away from the area.

Smooth. Hayes, you are a rare one, I think to myself, smiling.

***

I wait impatiently, trying my best not to fidget, but feeling restless as always. Finally I can't stand it anymore.

Drinking my fill at the spring, my stomach rumbles at its cheated impression of breakfast and my thoughts turn to home and bacon and eggs. Time to go.

Climbing the steps to the top level of the garden, I use the well placed trees to swing up to the crest of the high perimeter wall and perch at the top in what's left of the blazing autumn leaves. The tracks are clear in front of me and my eyes travel along them, able to make out the movement of the Enforcers in the distance still heading toward the Valley.

I need to get home before my family sends someone out to search the tracks for me. I can't risk them running into prowling Enforcers on my account. I need to leave in a different direction. Swinging down, I head to the opening and shed my gopher-suit, turning it inside out to change from grays to browns. Wriggling beneath the prickles and inhaling the crisp dawn air, I make my way out of the garden. Mickey should be somewhere near the next spring. He's trained not to stray far from his clean water source.

It's well over an hour on foot to his spring, but there is reasonable cover most of the way. Rocks cluster in large groups all over the next hills making it easy to disappear. Moving between hills, or across the great empty plains requires more skill. That's where my height comes in handy. The tall straw surrounds me and I stand comfortably below the surface of the golden sea. It makes for good cover, but an easy trail to follow unless you move like the winds. Gusts get wild out here and flatten big stripes into the open plains. If I keep within the patterns, my tracks remain unseen.

Stretching again, I ready myself to run a bit. Taking out the small apple from my binding, I take a tiny nibble to suck while I run. Safely stashing the rest I start to jog, lengthening my stride as my legs warm enough to forget the previous day's work.

Rounding the tallest rocky hill and slipping by two

more, I keep my eyes peeled for Mickey's spotty hide. The grass is getting greener and the rocks more numerous. They're ragged here, shooting out of the ground at odd angles, or stacked atop each other sideways like stone-slab pancakes ready to be eaten.

A rabbit shoots from the long grass and I inhale sharply, choking on my apple piece. After a period of coughing and spluttering, I'm able to compose myself and carry on. The noise must have drawn attention to me, because I hear a snort of enquiry from nearby.

"Mickey Boy? Guess what Rori's got for you… a juicy apple." I wait, hoping he is at least curious enough to come closer for a whiff of apple-y goodness. "You want some, Mick? It's good… see?" Bringing the apple to my lips I attempt an audible bite. "Mmmm." That does it. He is out of the rocks and heading straight for me. Jumping onto a rock, I brace myself, holding the apple behind my back. His soft muzzle sniffles invasively, searching. I try my best not to fall off the rock as his hot breath penetrates my suit, tickling me ruthlessly.

Giggling, I bring the apple around and hold it under his lips. Snatching it up, he chews with gusto, swishing his tail and twitching his ears. While he's distracted, I grab a section of his wiry mane and swing onto his back. He shuffles a few steps sideways in disapproval, but settles quickly. Without reins, I use my knees to urge him uphill, which he thankfully does without opposition.

"Good boy. I tell ya Mick, it's been a crazy day at work and I am so happy to see your face! Take me to the Split, bud."

The path widens, making travel easier and Mickey picks up his pace into a smooth canter, mane and tail streaming behind him. I love the sensation of freedom that Mickey gives me. The two of us in the great outdoors, racing the wind and pounding the earth. Hunched low, I tighten my hands in his mane, feeling his muscles respond beneath me as he surges onward. I close my eyes and enjoy the ride.

As his pace slows, I open my eyes and pat him fondly on his shoulder. The rocks are closing in again and the wind is rising. We will have to part soon, but I'm delaying it. Mickey's familiar and reassuring company is keeping me from freaking out.

My brain keeps puzzling over why Hayes, a City Enforcer, has risked helping me. I can't but wonder about his intentions and whether they might be malicious or benign. He doesn't come across as depraved; quite the opposite actually. Catching myself smiling as I recall his friendly and handsome grin, I scold myself and remember the grim relations between Citizens and Daltons. Sighing, I feel nothing but confusion about the whole business. What could he possibly hope to gain?

Mickey slows to a stop and the wind shoves me impatiently.

"I'll be back to get you soon, Mick. I'll bring you a bigger apple too," I promise, stroking his neck. Dismounting, I walk slowly in front of him and pat the length of his nose, planting a kiss where I stop. Mickey snorts at me in approval and saunters away, leaving me to find my land legs.

I pick my way up through the rocks to the Split, wary of each step. There are deep crevices hidden between the crags and boulders. Some are so deep that you can drop in a stone and listen to its ping-ponging descent for three full breaths before you can no longer hear it. Whether or not that silence means it's out of range or has reached the bottom, I couldn't say.

I huddle into myself in an attempt to brave the wind. The higher I go, the stronger the winds become. The force of them can lift me off the ground well before I reach the ridge. That's why I cut through the Split. As the name suggests, it's a split in the stone, a deep crevice that takes you through the rock safely as the winds roll dangerously over the top. Wide enough to walk through comfortably, it allows a safe shortcut to the inner cliff face.

Behind a series of large rocks, I slip into the hidden opening. Hints of light sneak through from above as I walk. The giddy sensation in my gut grows stronger as the daylight at the end of the passage strengthens. Stepping into the light, I let my eyes adjust. From the ledge, the Valley lies before me, almost two thousand feet below. Aside from my ledge jutting out of its face, the cliff is sheer. There's no climbing up or down without ropes and tools. Just inside the passage is a large metal case. Taking a deep breath, I open it up and pull out one of the cliff-jumping parachutes.

My fingers tremble as I fit my harness, checking three times at every clip; tightening. I complete another full check and count down from ten, mentally preparing myself to part with the comforting rock underfoot. At zero I take the run and fly out into the air, praying my 'chute is packed correctly. Spreading my limbs in flight, I track as far away from the cliff as time will allow, reasoning with the panicked voice in my head the whole time. I release my pilot chute from its pocket and wait the heart-stopping moments as it drags my main chute free and the colors run clear and rectangular over my head. The satisfying tug as the 'chute fills and lifts, signals me to start breathing again and with relief I direct myself well clear of the cliffs and glide gently downward.

Floating safely now, I guide the canopy out over the Valley and enjoy the view while I can. The river tumbles over the cliff at the far end of the Valley and snakes its way downhill, running through the woods and gridded farmlands, until it disappears into the cave near the tunnel. My home. A paradise, with stark cliffs entirely surrounding the lush greens in a protective wall and backed up staunchly by the bigger, snow-capped mountains beyond.

The Valley floor is dotted with wind turbines, huge glasshouses, log and stone buildings and, as I get closer, animals and people. There will be no sneaking in the back door today. That is the downfall of flying down under rainbow colors. Well, that and risking death with each flight.

***

Pulling up smoothly a few paddocks behind our house, I hit the ground running, letting my chute fall tidily behind me. Expecting company soon, I work carefully to pack the parachute safely away again for next time, assessing any stitching for damage as I go. I wonder who will come first. It's normally the kids that get places fastest. My nieces and nephews, in a big 'kid gang' tend to move places as one noisy mob.

Hearing the noise behind me now, I know my guess is right. I check over my shoulder and see a tall man, curly and blond, at the back of the mob and know my brother Aiden is herding them. Checking the collar of my suit covers as much of my neck as possible to hide any telltale fingers of bruising, I look quickly over my shoulder again. I don't want to scare the kids, or have to answer awkward questions yet.

Jack, his face flushed, reaches me first, just as I pull the last straps tight and sling the pack over my shoulder. I pull him in close with my other arm and give him a gentle squeeze.

"Good to see ya, Jacky-boy! You been keeping your crew in line?" I tease, releasing him to tousle his hair.

Pulling his head out of reach, he smiles at me. "You know there's no controlling those clowns, Auntie Ro!" he says, before firing a barrage of questions at me. "Whatcha get this time? Get that wiring Horse needs? Reckon he's been buggin' you about that for weeks. How come you flew in? Tracks busy? What's up with your face? You get in a fight? They ambush the tracks? How'd ya get away?"

"Well if you'd stop for a breath, I could tell you!" I take a breath for both of us. The others are arriving now – Aiden and Rae's brood: Evan, Hattie, wee Isla and of course, Jack, followed closely by my sister Lena's two girls

Tilly and Bryn.

"Another grand entrance Aunty Ro?" Aiden says as he approaches. "Glad you're home safe, but I wish you'd stop making your job look so glamorous and exciting to the wee folk!" Aiden laughs, but I know he's half serious.

"Well, if you think hitting your face on a window frame is glamorous, your ambitions are way too low," I reply, pointing at my face and knowing it must be turning colourful by now.

"Now Jack, you had a few questions, so listen up. Yes, I got wire for Horse. I flew in because there were Citizens around the tracks. No, I didn't get ambushed. I saw them and went the other way like a good girl and got a ride with Mickey to the Split, to stay away from any danger. Yes I hurt my face - I lost footing on a window ledge and my face got acquainted with the bricks before I caught myself. Now, can we go eat, 'cause I'm Starving!" I begin ushering little people toward the house, carefully avoiding Aiden's eye and further analysis. Sighing, he scoops Isla into his arms as he falls in behind.

Residual smells of breakfast greet us as we approach. Its late morning, but traces of bacon and toast float to my nostrils from the open kitchen window. My gastric booms are loud enough to make Jack look at me, eyes wide in alarm.

Elbowing him in the side, I laugh. "I'm not so hungry I'll eat *you*, don't look so worried." My pace increases uncontrollably just to reach food faster. Swinging open the door, I'm halted abruptly as I run into Rae. She folds me into her arms in a tight embrace then releases me to arm's length to scrutinize me.

"Rori, you look like crap! Here, sit down. I saved you some bacon. How many eggs you want, two? Three?" Not waiting for an answer, she looks me over again. "I'll do three." Nudging me to the table, she slides a plate of bacon under my nose as I sit.

I don't even use a fork, just shovel it into my mouth

with my fingers, taking the briefest moment to enjoy the salty tang and the satisfying grease. Rae busies herself at the stove. Trying not to laugh at my gluttony, she calls to Jack over her shoulder.

"Go run the bath for your Auntie Ro, Honey. She's stinking out the kitchen. You been in the marsh again, Rori? You'll catch your death of cold this time of year." She gives me a steady look. "I guess you had good reason." Giving me the kind of sweet smile that lets me know she's glad I'm safe, she turns back to the eggs.

"Rae-Rae, I'm glad you agreed to marry my brother. We would've had to kidnap you if you didn't come willingly." Rae kisses my head and slides eggs onto my plate. They stare up at me briefly before heading down to meet the bacon.

Filled to the eyeballs, I push my seat back and set my dishes in the sink, filling a glass with the water as I rinse them. Two glasses later, I belch satisfaction and rub my full belly.

"Charming!" Aiden and Rae say in unison, chuckling. I turn to them and give a dramatic flourish and curtsy. Heading down the hall, past the composting toilet, I follow the steam to the bath.

Emptying my pockets into the waiting basket, I peel off my gear, kicking the soiled pile away. Holding my breath I put them into the soak bucket and put the lid on. That done, I open the window to let in the fresh, crisp air and glide over to the tub, tugging my hair free from its braid.

Testing with my toe I find the water hot, but bearable, just the way I like it. The heat feels amazing and I slide right down, pulling my head under a while before coming up for air. Soaking up to my chin, the sleepiness sneaks up on me as the heat seeps into my tired bones. I look for some soap and find a pleasant lavender bar and fresh cloth.

Starting gingerly with my face and then scrubbing more fiercely, I cleanse myself of grime. Paying more attention to the dirt than necessary, I try to avoid thinking about my latest adventure and its implications. I'm too tired to think straight and it's a complicated matter. Finishing up by lathering my hair, I duck under the water again. Reluctantly pulling myself up, I cringe at the color of the water I've left behind and pull the plug.

Wringing out my hair, I let it fall to my waist, marveling at how the moisture puts a wave through it when normally it's dead straight. I'm the only one in our family with straight hair, or dark hair for that matter. Aiden and my four older sisters are all some form of curly blond, like Da.

My Father is Owen MacGregor, Chief of the Valley and Great Grandson of William MacGregor who had the leadership on the grisly night more than a century ago, when the Citizens invaded and the rules of engagement were made. They killed a third of our people and began a tradition of hostage taking to ensure our compliance. The reigning chief must deliver a hostage of significant value. A child of their own. Insurance of a bargain to be kept; 'supply or die'.

Taking the stairs slowly up to my attic bedroom, my eyes lift to the frames that cover the walls. Those closest to the bottom contain faded photographs. Some of them are of my ancestors. One of the photos is of a large group - the founders of Dale town, smiling at their genius for branching off from mainstream society and hiding in a valley while the world turned to custard.

Further up the stairs, the method of recording faces changes from photography to hand drawn or painted portraits. This wall is the MacGregor family history in picture form. I stare at the eyes of William 'Bill' MacGregor. Voted into leadership by his people, he must have been a wise and charismatic man. I can tell the picture was painted before the invasion, because Bill's eyes smile; untouched by the devastation inflicted upon his people.

Despite elections, nobody has volunteered to replace

the MacGregors as head family. The responsibility of leadership and the price of a child, is too much. We MacGregors have endured it without choice, for our people. To be born into the MacGregor family is to be cursed with a twisted cycle of management and loss. It isn't fair, and I'm not the first to think that.

I climb past the faces of my ancestors that fought for their freedom. Two unsuccessful uprisings is what I see in their eyes. Loss of loved ones, Dalton numbers knocked back to the minimum required to work the land leaving them no time to plan another rebellion. I don't linger.

After a few more steps, I come to the picture of my father and his younger brother Alex. Just children, they have matching golden curls and mischievous smiles. Alex was the last hostage. He died just over eleven years ago. Too young.

Another step brings another picture of my father. This time he is grown, draping an affectionate arm around my mother as she holds baby Aiden. My parents are young and smiling, but their eyes are etched with the burden of their responsibilities.

The next picture is of Aiden, my sisters and me. You can tell the artist has had to create the image of us sitting together over time by collating separate portraits, because some of our faces look a bit mismatched with our bodies. Probably we couldn't or wouldn't sit still for long enough. My youngest brother, Patrick isn't in the picture.

Painted separately, his picture has its own frame. The portrait is just his cherubic baby face. It sits next to a matching frame that contains Mama's face. My finger traces around her frame. It's like looking in a mirror.

I don't fully remember how she used to be. My memories mingle with the stories I've been told and the image in this frame. These days, my own reflection plays on those memories too. It must be hard for Da to have me around, parading his loss in front of him, even though it's unintentional. I can tell by the look in his eyes sometimes, that when he looks at me, he is seeing her; remembering her. I wonder if sometimes that stops him from seeing me.

Shifting my eyes from Mama to Patrick, I smile sadly and touch the tip of my finger to his little button nose. Patrick is in the City. He was taken before his first birthday to replace Uncle Alex as the hostage. It is usually the leader's youngest boy that is taken, and there would be no more in our family after the night Patrick was born.

I'd hated him when Mama died. I'd hated the way my father still held him as if he weren't to blame. I was glad when he was taken. I'd thought he deserved to be cast out for taking her from us. It was easier to think that way at the time. I was young and selfish. With him gone, I could forget that he'd ever existed.

I am older now. I understand the situation. Staring into his innocent eyes, I'm racked with guilt and shame for thinking the way I did. I am still angry, but now my anger and hatred are directed where they should be; towards *them*. The Citizens stole my baby brother and turned him into a bargaining chip with which to exploit us. The injustice of it all disgusts me.

For the moment, I'm forced to accept that I can live in safety, because Patrick sits abandoned in the hostile City. Protected by his enforced absence, we Daltons are able to enjoy a life of relative freedom as he cannot. It makes me sick thinking about the abuse of power the Citizens have used to bring this all about. One day I will find a way to repay them and my family will be together again. Patrick doesn't even know what he's missing, but I intend to show him, when I bring him home.

My fingers follow the curves of his golden curls. Touching my fingers to my lips, I press them to the cold glass that protects him. An apology and a promise.

Rushing past the rest of the pictures, I head to my room. Even when I'm trying not to think about Citizens, they invade my brain. Too often I find myself grinding my teeth or frowning into the distance. I try to keep the rage I feel toward the City down deep, but still it seeps into my daily life.

Being a gopher requires certain physical skills, but they were far easier for me to master than the restraint required to hold a position, to keep quiet or still and stay out of City business. Watching a hungry child being beaten in the City streets for taking a loaf of bread, and being unable to do a thing to stop it, grinds you down and creates a bottomless well of fury within you. Suppressing my natural instincts at work, has impacted my Valley life by significantly reducing my tolerance levels.

I'm always angry under the surface, and I'm quite sure other people know it. I can be terribly impatient and I'm usually pretty blunt with my words. My eldest sister Lena calls me 'abrasive'. Da suggests 'caustic' as a better term. Most people don't appreciate blatant honesty, they like things sugar-coated for easy digestion. That might be why I avoid most people.

Sighing over my brooding thoughts, I force them from my tired brain and shut the door to my room. Dropping my towels, I pull on fresh underwear and slide into bed. With my stomach full and my body still warm from the bath, sleep finds me easily.

THE SOLDIER

Hayes left Luther Derrick's office in a dark mood, rubbing his shoulder. It was aching where Fat Elmo had wrenched his arm behind his back. It was actually one of the more light-hearted interrogations Hayes had been present for, which made him all the more sour about how Derrick ran things. He figured the leniency was due Reg's involvement.

Reg was disturbing to be around, but Hayes suffered his company because he was the Director's son and life was easier for those that were close enough to glean some shelter from Reg's protective family connections. For Hayes that benefit made City life slightly more tolerable for him and his family.

Regarding the evasive intruders, Hayes felt he had managed to avoid endangering his rank or his family, and he was fairly certain that the clues to finding Rori were sufficiently murky to ensure her anonymity. The matter had not been dropped though. Such incursions were an intolerable offense to Luther Derrick's maniacal control. Hayes and Reg had been instructed to maximize their search efforts by working overtime whilst in the City domain and observe the Valley for signs of the small girl and her large male companion on their next Train Day

34

escort.

The descriptions were vague enough to be any number of the Valley folk. They were definitely not specific enough to incriminate any individual. Having visited the Valley numerous times, he knew he'd never even seen Rori. Certainly he would've noticed her, he decided, affectionately recalling the sprinkle of freckles under those magnetic, hazel eyes. Not the same greenish hazel as his own eyes; hers were a blend of grays and browns like aging metals. 'Gray-zel', he thought to himself, smiling.

Catching himself before he passed a soldier in the corridor, Hayes smoothed his expression in practiced automation. Only his sneer of a joking smile was acceptable as visible emotion around here. It would not do for anyone to know he had something to smile sincerely about. It would just be used against him some time, to control him. That's how things worked in the City. It was a cruel place. Hayes knew that better than most. His fingers absentmindedly rose to the scar on his face and he lapsed again into the memories he could never escape.

Nearly fourteen years old, big for his age but not yet a man, he'd been helpless. He hadn't known until then that his father had been raising a rebellion to bring down the Director. He knew Ethan Hayes as a strong and loving father, in a home that felt safe, despite his mother's troubles. He learned that day though, that a dangerous hierarchy existed in the city. He learned what it cost to cross paths with Luther Derrick.

He'd thought his father had been at work. There was a knock at the door, and as his mother opened it, it slammed into her knocking her backwards into Hayes and his little sister. Men seized his mother and dragged her out the door. Hayes had acted on impulse and tried to stop the attackers, trying to get his mother released. He wasn't big enough or strong enough, and they'd grabbed him and Iris too. They were taken to the Tower, to Derrick's quarters and were seated on one side of his office, under guard.

Luther Derrick had sat at his desk with a chilling smile on his face. Hayes could smell the wool in the carpet, wet with the rain brought in on boots.

His father had come in the door then, talking casually with his companion. When he'd seen them, his face fell before twisting into an angry cry as he'd leapt across the desk, hands out-stretched, grabbing for Derrick. He was dropped mid-flight by a blow to his head by one of the Henchmen. Two of them had pulled him up by his arms and held him as Derrick strode back and forth in front of him, dealing heated blows as he relayed Ethan's mutinous activities.

Morrison Hayes had listened in disbelief, held back, unable to get closer. He'd started to understand the situation, as his father defended his actions and accused Derrick of being inhuman, a disease; unfit to lead. Morrison could see for himself how Derrick maintained power. His mother, broken on the floor, clutched Iris to her chest. He felt the knife at his own throat to bring his father under control. The fear in his father's eyes, the glint of steel under the fluorescent light. He saw it all. It was abundantly clear that Ethan Hayes was not leaving the room alive.

"Any last words for your family, in case they don't need to follow you immediately?" Derrick had snarled as he pulled his own jagged blade and pressed it to Ethan's ribs. A red flower bloomed at it's tip as the knife inched inward.

Ethan had looked at them and squared his shoulders, raising his chin as the bloodstain grew on the carpet about him. He'd inhaled with difficulty and spoke, pausing for breath between each sentence to be able to say the next.

"Family is everything. I love you. Do what you must. Protect each other. We protect those we love."

Derrick's Henchmen tightened their grips then for the final drive of the blade. Hayes had rushed forward, enraged and blind to his inadequacies. The knife that had threatened his own neck had moved, but not out of the way. He'd run through it as it pulled into his face, without feeling it or the blow that followed. He remembered his blood joining his father's. The way it made the carpet soggy beneath him, while his mother screamed and the darkness crept over him.

Brought suddenly back to the present, Hayes let out a growl and unleashed his fists on the corridor around him. He hammered incessantly until he slid down the wall, heaving for breath. Glancing about, he hoped he was alone. These unwelcome flashes from the past tended to take him by surprise, and the response was usually a similar physical outburst. No-one had come to inspect the source of the noise he'd made. Quickly, he moved away before anyone came, grimacing shamefully at the battered wall as he went.

Hayes worried about the damage he caused.

He worried about his grip on his sanity.

STANDARD DELIVERY

Waking up in my own bed is wonderful. I stretch under the covers, arching my body into different positions and releasing them; relaxed and happy. It's cozy under the blankets and I don't want to brave the wooden floors, but I courageously trade my quilt for a huge sweater and leggings before heading to the door. As I open it, I'm blasted with warmth from the fires below. I leave the door open, letting the warm air invade my room the way the children would have if I'd left it open earlier.

Drying my hands on my pants as I exit the bathroom, I head to the kitchen. It's usually a hive of activity. Judging by the lack of noise and the light outside, I figure it's about mid-afternoon. They'll be out in the gardens. Two of my sisters sit uncomfortably together at the table. Neither of them live here. Lena and Freya raise their eyes as I come in and both smile with relief at my arrival.

Lena looks frazzled as always. Ever since Stefan died last winter, she's looked the picture of a grieving widow. We all try to help out as much as we can, taking the kids, helping her cook or clean their wee cottage, but it's much harder work shifting the sadness. She's slowly recovering from the loss, but does much better when distracted.

Coming around behind her, I give her a lingering hug, meeting Freya's eyes questioningly as I do so.

Shrugging innocently, Freya avoids my gaze. "Bad day at work Rori? You should put some of that salve I gave you on your face to help that bruising."

Freya's appearance is the complete opposite of Lena's. Always immaculate, her frizzy blond wisps are firmly pulled back and restrained in a staunch bun. She has one child with her partner Eldon – baby Ezra, but from the look of her, you'd never know it. Probably depressing Lena just by sitting there, she's even starting to bug me a bit. And she knows it! Rolling her eyes at me, she excuses herself from the table with a mumbled apology.

"I already put the salve on. Who's got the kids?" I ask, changing the subject and reaching for an apple from the fruit bowl.

"Eldon's taken them for a walk to the bridge to float leaf boats," Freya responds quickly from behind the kitchen counter, apparently eager to fill any awkward silences.

"That's very good of him." Eldon is usually far too distracted to help with the kids, but I continue before Freya takes offense at my surprise. "I have to make a delivery and I'd love it if you'd come too, Lena. It's a nice day out and the fresh air will do you good. I'll tell you all about my last trip. It's especially juicy…" I tease, hoping she'll take the bait.

Hooked, Lena looks up and evaluates my expression to gauge just how juicy my news might be.

"Oh I'm coming," she says, "You're buzzing out of your skin and you have finger marks on your neck. This should be good!" Observant as hell, is old Lena.

"Finger marks?" Freya pipes up worriedly, moving toward me as I'm trying to pull up my collar.

"I'm sure I'm mistaken," Lena dismisses, waving her hand at Freya. "Get a scarf Rori. Your sweater won't stay like that, and you don't want to scare people." She pushes back from the table and heads to the door. "Where are we off to?"

"Um..." Preoccupied with finding a scarf, I shoulder my bag with the wires stashed in it and hunt through the multitude of coats and hats on the hooks by the door. "I've got to get some stuff to Horse."

"That's miles away!" Lena starts. I cut her off before she can get going.

"I know, but Freya and Eldon won't mind having the kids a bit longer, will you, Freya?" Again I don't pause long enough for an answer, much to Freya's annoyance. "Wouldn't it be good to see your old work bench to make sure Horse hasn't claimed it with a pile of junk? Besides, it's totally scenic and as you may have guessed..." I wave a hand at my face, referring to the damage. "It's a long story." Finally finding a scarf hidden under the coats, I throw it on. Pushing Lena out the door, I smile sweetly back over my shoulder at a huffing Freya. She'll get over it. My intentions are good.

Once we're on our way and out of earshot, I let loose my harrowing tale of capture, subsequent rescue and the strange circumstances that saw me repeatedly delivered from harm since. Lena listens attentively, nodding encouragingly until I've finished my piece. Then she just watches me a while. I'm beginning to get a little embarrassed about being viewed so intensely, when she finally speaks.

"You like him! A City guy? And you got caught! They'll be hunting you and they know your face and your name! You're screwed... And you *like* him!" she accuses, incredulous. Staring at me, she's doing that thing with her eyebrows, where one scrunches down while the other one pulls so high it tries to join her hairline.

"I don't *like* him!"

Frowning at how unconvincing I sound, I shake my head. "He's a Citizen! Worse - he's an Enforcer! And I don't even know him. And *they* don't know anything about me. Only Morrison Hayes saw my face and only he knows my name."

"Yeah, and you just said you didn't even know him! He can't be trusted to keep you safe!"

"Well I'm pretty sure he's already passed that test three-fold, so I might give him a break. Anyway, he's in as much danger as I am if they find out. You know that." Her face tells me that she agrees that much. I think about the likelihood of actually trusting a City Enforcer.

"But you're right anyway," I continue, as that thought is pushed out by one far more likely – the trouble I'll be in with Da. "I'm definitely screwed."

We're nearly to Horse's workshop. I call it his underground lair, because although it looks like a shed from the outside, down the stairs in back, it opens up into a cavernous space filled with all of Horse's tools and machines and whatever experimental devices he's working on. I do a lot of my City runs collecting bits and pieces for his work.

Horse is a genius. He makes our farming gear and all sorts of other random helpful stuff – like my maglev board. It lets me hover on the tracks like the train and I can go almost as fast. We have to keep all this stuff out of sight when the Citizen soldiers come to town, of course. We keep them in the dark as much as we can. The small amount of power that we retain, comes from our secrets.

From the time we leave the classroom at twelve, until the day we can no longer perform, we are tasked to produce enough food to feed ourselves and our aggressors. Each Dalton works the land in addition to fostering their talents on the side. We feed their population under the guise of submissive slaves without hope. Beneath that illusion, we are progressive.

Our secrets and our thievery are a few means by which we keep our wills defiant, though it hurts to admit that some Daltons appear to have bought their own con; their spirits have been crushed too many times. Not me. I know a time will come when it doesn't matter that our numbers are a fraction of theirs. We will use what we do have - knowledge.

Each adolescent spends time in as many work placements as possible, learning the fundamentals of every system in the Valley until their talents become evident and their direction obvious. I've spent time doing everything from shadowing Freya and Eldon in the clinic, to working alongside Horse, spending time making new things and working out how to make the things we already have, run better. It was Horse who re-designed our power networks and keeps them maintained. Not by himself, he doesn't have enough time for that, but he's the brains of the outfit.

You'd think a guy that spends most of his time in an underground factory would look a bit troll-like or something, but Horse is actually pretty decent looking for an older guy. A large man, his nickname is more obvious than most. I think his real name is Arthur, but absolutely everyone calls him Horse. He's got one of those welcoming faces, where the frequent smiles are warm and sincere and make his eyes scrunch at the corners. He's always been nice to me, even when I was young. Maybe because he's good friends with my Da, or maybe it was because he knew he'd need me. I was destined to be a Gopher, with my small frame and gymnastic ability.

Arriving, I bang hard on the door and wait. Horse hates being snuck up on – not that you do it intentionally. Absorbed by his work, he freaks out if you're suddenly right next to him, especially if he's holding power tools. He reckons he almost chopped an arm off once. I don't know if he meant his arm or someone else's. It's just best to knock first.

The shed door opens and Horse beams one of his hearty grins at me. When he sees Lena with me, he doubles his efforts.

"Ladies! What a lovely surprise! Lena, so nice to see you on such a beautiful autumn day," Horse charms. "And

Rori, I've been hoping you'd be around soon. Your father said you were back. I can't get much further on my main project without those wires."

"I haven't even seen Da yet. He must've seen my parachute. What is your main project at the moment, Horse?" I'm always keen to hear where his creative genius will take us next.

"I don't want to talk about it until I know it'll work, so never you mind. And what's this about a parachute? You jump in today? What's wrong with your board?" Horse asks, concerned.

Meeting Lena's eyes briefly, I tell him about the attack and that I had escaped, but hadn't been able to use the tracks because they'd been searching them all the way to the rocks. Horse seems somewhat relieved when I assure him it had not been due to faulty workmanship on his account, but he still looks worried.

"I'm glad you made it out safe Rori, but I think you should stay away from the City for a bit. Until things cool down." He looks at me seriously. "It's a dangerous job, and we'd all hate to lose you. It's not worth risking your neck for a few wires. You're only seventeen for crying out loud! That's not a fair trade. I'll make do with what I've got. Thanks for all the goodies." Smiling, he pulls me clean off the ground in an appreciative hug. "Now off with you both. I'm going to re-home these little babies," He says lifting the bag of wires and smiling affectionately at it. Waving as he turns back into his lair, Lena and I are left staring at the shed door. Taking the hint, we turn back towards the river.

Lena looks down at me as we walk. "Da's going to say the same thing you know. He doesn't like you going there at the best of times."

"Yeah, I know. He'll probably accuse me of being reckless and find a way to punish me. We all know he hates me being a Gopher because he can't control what happens beyond the Valley. Two years I've been riding the tracks, bringing home the things we need, and still he treats me like a child. He's a control freak." I kick at a rock in the path. "And what the hell are 'the best of times' in that rat's nest anyway? Is that the time when they burnt half the books in the library? Or when I saw them beating a woman in the street, while her kids watched? There are no 'best times' in the City, Lena. Da knows that as well as anyone." Kicking another stone, I stoop to grab a few more and hurl them at the river with gritted teeth until I meet Lena's sad eyes.

"Sorry, Lena." Sighing, I let go of my angst. "I just get so pissed off at that parasite-ridden shit hole and being so helpless. Come on, let's go excite kids for entertainment. Reckon if we provoke them just right, Freya might publicly explode?"

A smile crosses Lena's lips in answer and we head home along the river track, kicking leaves out of our path as we go. We let the fresh air and crunching leaves lift our moods as we plan our childish attack on our uptight sister.

"What are you going to do on Train Day?" Lena asks quietly, returning to our previous conversation. Hayes had said he might see me then. He must be an escort. It will be Train Day in a week and the escorts usually stay overnight, heading back to the City the next day when the train is fully loaded.

As of old, our family hosts the escorts for a community dinner when the train comes. It's a show, of course. Letting them see how we can all 'get along' with each other. Everyone dresses nicely and speaks civilly and nobody challenges the way things are. It's all so fake and infuriating. I haven't been to a Gathering in a long while, and I certainly don't spend time with any escorting soldiers.

I shrug. "I usually avoid them. Train Days make me prone to angry outbursts, remember?" I remind her of the incident in the main hall at the last Gathering I attended. A few years ago, I stood on the head table, verbally abused the escorts, and the Ambassador, and dumped a plate of buttered potatoes over them.

Lena giggles at the memory and clears her throat to speak. "No, I don't mean the Gathering - you've managed to hide from those for years now. I mean, if you see him around the village - if you see Hayes."

"Well shit Lena, I don't know!" I huff, trying not to kick any stones. "What can I do? I'll have to talk to Da before then, and I'm pretty sure he'll tell me what I can and can't do. Though I can guess what he'll say." Putting on a deep, manly voice, I waggle my finger: "Stay out of sight and avoid contact at all cost."

"Yes, I know he'll probably say that. But I asked what you were going to do," Lena says shrewdly. "I thought that might be something different from what Da says, knowing you." A satisfied, all-knowing smile graces her lips. Lena knows me better than most, better than myself sometimes, and she loves it when she's right.

"I don't know what you might be suggesting, Lena," I play along innocently. "Owen's children are dutiful and obedient."

"Mmhmm," she agrees. "How shall we serve the buttered potatoes this time?" Openly chuckling now, she wraps her shawl tighter as we walk.

"I think I'll stay away from the food, and the crowd," I begin sensibly, but can't maintain it now that Lena's in a lighter mood. "Or maybe I'll go in costume? I could go as a calf or a sheep – I'll just get Orla to fashion something from the tannery – unless you think the guests will eat me, or pack me on the train?"

Lena puts her hand on my shoulder to stop me walking, literally doubled over. "Imagine!" she says gasping for breath, "When the actual meal on the main table …rises up… and starts yelling at the guests! Classic Rori!"

"Well I'll have to think about that Lena, I wouldn't want Da to spill the gravy down his pants again!" I snort, as the tears stream down Lena's face and we wander home, stopping between fits of laughter to catch our breaths.

POWER STRUGGLE

We are quite the spectacle. The whole family has come to dinner in true Sunday fashion. All up, there are seventeen bodies crammed into the dining space that is far larger than most. The ten adults and baby Ezra are at the main table, while six kids squirm expectantly at their own smaller table. Once a week, the family shares a meal at Da's house in an oddly enjoyable episode of bedlam.

There are five adults who actually live here. At seventeen, I'm the newest adult, and with the occasional exception (usually involving my overbearing father), that's how I'm treated. I live in one of the two attic bedrooms, my sister Orla - two years older than me, lives in the other. Aiden's family takes up all the first floor bedrooms except for Da's. My other sisters all have their own places and quite separate lives.

Watching the interactions around the table, I play a game for my personal entertainment. I try to read people while they're talking, and see if their body language matches what they're saying. I'm pretty sure I've got them all pegged. Da is the only one I ever have trouble reading, but everyone's actions fit with their conversations at the moment.

Keeping my mouth full to prevent myself from engaging, I let the conversations wash over me. I won't have to try too hard to avoid questions just yet. Those will come later, when the kids aren't around.

Aiden and Da are discussing winter feed for the stock. Aiden is a veterinarian/farmer and Da is a gardener, when he's not busy with his leadership duties. It is very typical for them to be discussing supply and demand. Aiden will likely be chief one day, and the productivity of the Valley is a constant issue with growing populations to feed both here and in the City. Things are already tight in bad years when crops don't yield what they should or fail altogether.

They've been talking about when we'll exceed equilibrium. Trying to predict when the finite land inside the Valley is at maximum production and only just satisfying the demand of the small, but dependent populations. It isn't yet, but they have been brainstorming options. Da will never let his people starve, and it's in the best interest of the City if we don't. Without us to supply the bulk of their food, many will surely perish, or at the very least, be severely undernourished.

Even though food production is a life and death issue, the Citizens have been reluctant to continue the work started before they found us, tearing down the abandoned district to get to the uncontaminated soil beneath its buildings. They've refused to do it for generations. We don't know if it's because they think they'll populate the buildings again or if their laziness is to blame. It appears they'd rather make it our problem than assume responsibility for themselves.

If they refuse to progress and continue to force us to produce, we will have no choice but to pursue riskier options. It seems likely that mostly crops would be grown in the sheltered Valley, and the livestock would have to move through the tunnel to graze for periods on the other side. The grasslands at the Valley end of the tracks are becoming safer, as the chemicals leach away. Regular stock rotation would be necessary to minimize toxicity, but our research shows that for now, it's still too dangerous. It's a shame that might be the only choice when the delicate balance changes.

It'd be alright by me if anything grown or grazed out there only went to Citizens. They'd have no-one to blame but themselves if they got sick. In fact, I don't know why we haven't started the process already. We could have been free of them by now. Da would never intentionally harm others though. Not if there was another way. If he can do it safely, he will, even if it means years of dinner table discussions and planning.

My mind boggles just listening to them. I want to remind them that shifting the balance of power and making the Citizens fend for themselves would resolve the issue, and that they should focus on that, but speaking my thoughts on the matter usually gets me into trouble and I am trying to avoid attention right now.

Sighing, I shift my sensors over to Ava and Orla engrossed in a discussion of textile dyes. Entertaining to watch, Ava's animated gestures as she speaks, make me smile. Orla is trying to take in the gestures and the information at the same time with apparent difficulty. The look of bafflement on her face makes my smile widen. Easily overwhelmed is our Orla.

She looks very nice in her new dress though. Orla always looks nice. Golden curls wave effortlessly down her back, and she swishes them every now and then to flaunt them. Her eyes are wide like mine, but an intense green that stirs envy within me as they flash about with her showy smile. A talented seamstress, she often models her wares. Of course, nobody else would look as amazing as Orla in them, with her long legs and curves in all the right places.

She drives me nuts with her flawless exterior. That and the fact that she is an outrageous flirt. Even now, I can see remnants of straw amongst her curls, evidence of her latest tryst, I'm sure. I don't think she even knows her affect on others. It's most annoying when we are hanging out with friends, having regular conversation. Before you know it we're all just looking at Orla.

I usually enjoy pushing her buttons by using words with more than two syllables. Well, she's not quite that dim, I just tend to focus on her undesirable traits. It makes her easier to live with. Lena says my problems with Orla are more about me than Orla. Lena's probably right.

Next to me, Lena's seen me watching and nudges my ribs with her elbow. When I turn to face her I almost choke on my mashed potato. Her eyes are crossed and she has a goofy grin. Straightening her face, she looks in Orla's direction and rolls her eyes. I agree by way of a smile and a quick shrug of my brows and shift my gaze along the table.

Freya is engrossed in discussion with Rae on assorted childhood issues whilst inadvertently demonstrating proper table etiquette and posture. For twenty-four, Freya is rather refined. She and Eldon run the Valley medical clinic attached to their house. Eldon is more than a decade older, but they make a sweet couple. Both are as intellectual and as tightly wound as each other. I guess being responsible for the health of the Valley population of some 768 people would make anyone uptight, but I find their general nerdiness quite reassuring.

I look back to Ava, holding Frankie's hand now, as she laughs with Orla. She's only a year younger than Freya, and if they didn't look almost identical, you would never pick them as related. Ava is an artistic, free-spirit who only ever seems to realize the positive aspects of life. Everything is 'the best' or her 'favorite'. Having a strong tendency for cynicism myself, I try to counsel her that every this or that can't be her favorite – what with the true meaning of the word being the preference of one above any other. Her usual response is to smile sweetly and reply something like: "You'll never be my *favorite* sister if you keep that up!"

Ava and Frankie live down by the school, where Ava

teaches art and music. Frankie is a stonemason. She's as tall as Ava, but almost twice as broad. I tried to arm wrestle her once and was shamed by the result. I like to think of myself as pretty strong, but I'm not even half as tough as Frankie. She didn't make me feel bad though, just challenged me to see who could do the most pull ups – I beat her by thirty-four. I said it wasn't really fair because I didn't have to pull up as much weight. She laughed and said it was about as fair as the arm wrestle. She's got a great laugh, Frankie. It's easy to see why Ava loves her.

As I finish up my custard and fruit, I'm pleased that I've managed to speak only when spoken to, and to ask for food to be passed my way. I look at Lena, next to me, and smile in relief. She smiles back and turns over her shoulder to tell the kids to finish their dinners, or Auntie Rori will eat all the pudding before they can get any! A chorus of accusatory whining erupts behind me and I kick Lena's leg under the table. Before I can turn around and defend myself, a throat clearance comes from the end of the table.

Only the authority of Owen Mac commands silence by clearing his throat. "Thank you for the lovely dinner girls, I look forward to Ava and I besting you next Sunday," he says, toward Rae and Freya. "Excuse us from the table. We have some business to discuss. Aiden? Rori? My study," he says, pushing his chair back and standing. Aiden follows suit immediately, but I hesitate a moment, preparing myself for what is to come. Already on his way to the study, Da pauses to deliver me a stern look, nodding me over with his eyebrows. I give a quick, support-seeking glance to Lena before scraping my chair back and dragging my feet to the study.

***

A chill runs down my spine, despite the warmth of the study and I close the door behind me. The house has a large main fire, but the study has its own small fireplace so that it stays warm if Da wants to conduct business in private. He lets out a long sigh as he sits in his big chair. A big man, he needs a big chair to accommodate him. He's not fat - nobody is fat around here, he's just tall and well-built, from working the land.

My father is a fair man with reasonable demands and legitimate concerns. He's a good man and a good leader. I know this, but I feel defensive whenever I'm around him. Being in his presence sends my anger bubbles writhing beneath the surface. I can't pinpoint why he affects me like this, maybe because I feel like he expects me to be someone I'm not, or that he's trying to keep me a child, despite the fact I've outgrown the position. Trying to understand why I feel the way I do generally causes me more frustration. I abandon the issue.

Instead, I regard Aiden, sitting in the chair closest to Da, as always. I slip into the other chair, nearest the door and watch him. Aiden sits at attention, leaning towards our father with a look of anticipation combined with obedience and adoration. I can't help but think of him as a lapdog, keen to please his master and patiently waiting for the word so he can climb up for a scratch behind his curly ears. I must be showing distaste on my face, because when I look back to Da, I see him staring at me, questioningly. I dismiss him with a brief smile and a nearly imperceptible shake of my head.

Busying himself by tidying papers on his desk, Da delays the talk, making me squirm. I search the room for distraction. Hundreds of books clad the room on shelves made from planks, held up by thick dowels driven into the wooden walls. The shelf directly over my head is the smallest. I can't read the spines of the books upon it from my seat, but I can see that one of its supporting dowels is coming loose from its hole above me. I hope Da doesn't yell during our little chat, or it might crash down on my head.

"Righto Rori, spill it," Da says as he leans toward me in a gesture of added pressure, meaning 'tell the *whole* story'.

Apparently he's guessed that I'd prefer to omit details.

"Um, well…" I stall, trying to order my brain to work so that I can at least control my expressions as I talk. If I let on that I feel even remotely benevolent toward a City guy, I'm toast. Such relationships are forbidden. Daltons loathe Citizens as a rule. The only exception is Train Day, when Valley folk must appear pleasant and accommodating to City visitors to keep up our image of subservience and avoid any conflict or potential harm.

"It *was* just another day at work." My palms start to sweat a little and I force myself to keep them still. "The ride in on the tracks was fast and unremarkable. I jumped off before the old station and went underground to the old district, got the goods and was heading back. I'd checked the streets, timed it between patrols and everything. But I must've been spotted, because the next thing I knew, an Enforcer was on my tail." Pausing for breath, I note Da and Aiden's eyebrows raised in concerned surprise. They could be identical if the years didn't separate them. Both are intent on the story, wondering how I came to be sitting in front of them if I met an Enforcer.

"I tried to run away, but he'd surprised me and was too close. I managed to avoid his weapons and had to deal him a few blows to get enough room to run - but he was huge, with crazy long arms. I mean really abnormally long! He grabbed me and held me up by the neck, punched me in the face and shook me like a milkshake. Next thing I knew, I woke up somewhere else looking into the face of *another* Enforcer. So I punched *him* in the face and tried to run, but I couldn't even stand up straight."

"And?" asks Aiden impatiently.

"And it turns out *this* Enforcer was actually *helping* me. Weird huh?"

"What do you mean by helping?" Da shuffles forward in his seat. "Specifics Rori, I need to know everything."

"You know, helping. Not just 'not hurting' me, but doing things for my benefit. I passed out at some stage, but I'm pretty sure he got me away from the other one and carried me to safety. And I don't know how he got me away, but I kinda remember the other guy on the ground, so I ... I don't know." I stop, wondering again how events had occurred.

Looking as confused as I feel, Da squints at me. "So what happened when you tried to run, but couldn't?"

"He told me that he wouldn't hurt me and that I should leave as soon as I could. He gave me a drink and when I could, I left. Oh! - And he'd cleaned my face. I guess it was bloody or something, but I smudged it back up again before I left." I pause again, knowing that I'll likely get a lecture for that one, even though it wasn't my fault. I'd been unconscious after all.

"He saw your face?" Aiden accuses, right on cue. "He'll be able to recognize you!"

"I expect so, yes. Not much I could've done about it though was there?"

"Hmm," agrees Da reluctantly. "So you left then. Rae said you came back stinking like the marsh. Why'd you go that way?"

I sigh, ready to hear Aiden's judgmental response to the next encounter.

"Because he helped me again."

Aiden's "Who?" competes for volume with Da's "What?"

"Aiden, try to keep up – the second Enforcer. I was hiding from a patrol – which he'd warned me about, by the way. It was a good hiding spot too, but for some insane reason, he managed to spot me. He wasn't alone, but he kept it to himself and hinted I should go through the marsh. His buddy - the one that beat me up, was dead keen on heading to the tracks to look for me, I mean *us*. He seemed to think he was looking for two of us."

"Huh." Da strokes his beard thoughtfully. "Carry on Rori - the rest of the story. We'll not interrupt again," he says, directing his words at Aiden.

I go on to tell them of the uneventful trip through the marsh and on to the halfway house, only to find myself rescued from both a snake and again from discovery. I told them how the Enforcers had continued along the tracks and how I'd had to go to the Split, because I didn't want to be caught, nor did I want any search party from here to meet up with them. This is all received in silence.

The quiet continues for a time after I finish. Da looks to be mulling over what I've said and Aiden looks like he wants to ask questions, but dares not speak until Da permits it. Da rubs the crease between his brows.

"Why do you think he helped you, Rori? Did he say?"

"I have no idea. He didn't say anything about it, as though it was nothing out of the ordinary. I was as shocked as you guys look now." I wait impatiently for the debriefing to end, but Da's thinking again.

"You know I don't like you jumping Rori," he begins, scolding. "You could have been more patient. You could have waited until they'd passed back the other way and then taken the tracks safely. There are no guarantees in surviving that jump. Next time don't be so reckless. It is a lucky escape you've had, and it's clear you wouldn't be here without the help you received." He pauses, clearly still perplexed by this unexpected behavior from a City Enforcer. "Did you happen to get names?"

"I heard him call the mean one 'Reg'," I start, preparing myself for saying the next name. Trying to keep neutral, I don't want my voice to give anything away, "…and the helpful one's name is Hayes." I check Da's face, trying to read it. He's looking at me in an odd way, trying to read me back.

"Hayes? *Morrison* Hayes?"

My eyes widen in shock. "You *know* him?"

Da looks at Aiden, then back to me. "He escorts the train. For the last year or so he's been in training for Head Escort – Ambassador Malcolm is grooming him to take over. He's the one we trade through!" Da sits back in his chair, eyes unseeing.

We sit in silence again, contemplating this information. My brain is straining to take in the fact that Hayes knows Da; quite well by the sounds of it. He didn't seem to know Owen MacGregor was my father though. I would've seen it in his face when I said my name. I don't suppose Da would have mentioned me when he conducts business, and I'm never at the Gatherings. My brain aches and I realize how tired I am. It's been a long day and my nap seems a distant memory. I make to excuse myself for bed.

Da looks up then and studies me a while before dismissing me with a nod. Thinking I've gotten off lightly, I sigh in relief as I turn to go. "Rori," he says as I'm reaching for the doorknob. "Hayes knows what you look like. Does he know your name?"

My cheeks burn in answer as I sit back down, raising my chin slightly in defiance. "Not my last name."

"You...?" Da works his mouth without words, momentarily speechless. His breath blows forcefully between pursed lips. Composing himself, he begins again in his 'I am your *Father* and your *Chief*' voice.

"I think it would be best if you avoid any further contact with Hayes and Reg, who by the way, is Luther Derrick's son and a right thug. You were *very* lucky to escape him." He visibly shudders. "No contact. Got it? If they learn who you are, all hell will break loose. It's hard enough to deny Gopher activity as it is. If they find out my own daughter steals from them, there's no telling what the penalties will be!" He pauses to check I'm taking his direction. Clearly he isn't convinced, because he follows up with a further stamp of his authority.

"I'm glad you are safe, but your thoughtless, reckless behavior doesn't just affect you. You've put others in danger, and as a consequence, you are on manure patrol for the next three Train Days. Understood?!" He continues before I can respond, clearly aware of my hackles rising.

"It will give you plenty of time to think about your

actions, just like the others you'll be working with. Being the Chief's daughter, does not mean you're exempt from Valley justice. It also means that I will know where you are. You'll be away from the house when Hayes comes to conduct business, and your identity will be protected because your face will be covered for the job." Da finishes his lecture with a look of satisfaction.

"Shit patrol!" I explode, outraged at being punished. As if being assaulted isn't enough! "I've had enough City crap today to last me a lifetime, and you want me to shovel shit on to the train for those life-sucking parasites!? You're unbelievable! I don't know why you don't just block the tunnel and let them all starve!"

"You'd have innocent people die, including your own brother, just because you think *you're* more important?" Da stands over me to emphasize how small and pathetic I am.

"You should have that power should you? You think they'll just sit back and starve? You think angry men can't just come and kill us in our sleep?" Red in the face and trembling, a droplet of spittle clings to his lip. I know better than to respond at this point. Staring at the floor, I ride it out.

"Go to bed Rori!" he orders, finger shooting out as if I need directions.

Stomping my feet on the ground as I thrust myself from the chair, I glare at him. I know it's childish to have a tantrum, and I fight to hold it in. Using my eyes to communicate my rage, I dare not unleash my words. Da is apparently aware of my internal conflict. A smirk has crept onto his smug face. I'm entertaining. Opening the door, I pause in the frame for just a moment in a final struggle with myself, but spite bests my reason. Still facing the hall, I grab the loosened dowel under the shelf and yank it out, leaving a cascade of books pouring to the floor in my wake.

As I storm down the hall, his voice thunders after me.

"You *will* shovel shit and you'll damn well love it, or

you'll be doing it all year!"

MAN OF THE HOUSE

Hayes never knew what to expect when he got home, especially if he'd been gone more than a day. Opening the door, he glanced around, wary. All seemed quiet, but not too quiet. Tidy, but not too tidy. He let go the breath he'd been holding and walked in.

"I'm home," he called, turning 'home' into a two syllable word. At first there was no reply. Then a door opened, allowing blaring music to escape and fill the apartment. Iris wandered down the hall, singing along and carrying an armful of clothes. She promptly dropped the laundry, her singing turning into a scream as she saw Hayes standing in the living room.

"Morrison!" she exclaimed. "You scared the bejeezus out of me!" Recovering the laundry she put it into the hamper in the hall cupboard. Closing the door, she leaned against it, looking him over. "You alright?"

"*I'm* fine," he said, staring at her. "What the hell are you wearing? Put some clothes on!"

"These *are* clothes, Morrison." Rolling her eyes at him, she straightened the flesh-hugging tube top to align with her skimpy shorts.

"Scraps more like. I can see your internal organs!" he

exaggerated, covering his eyes with a hand in an effort to avoid looking at the goodies bursting out of their wrapper to meet him.

"Some people like this look," she protested, managing to sound insulted.

"Some people should be medicated then!" he exclaimed, before catching the hint. Dropping his hand, he glared at her. "*What* people? Don't tell me you leave the house like that!"

"What if I do?" she challenged, her porcelain face glowering fiercely at his tanned one.

Hayes rubbed his face, dragging his eyes down his cheeks, his throat rumbling in exasperation. "Iris, use your brain! Do you know what guys think when they see you dressed like that?"

"I'm sure you'll enlighten me," Iris muttered, checking out her cleavage in the hall mirror before turning to examine her butt.

"Guys are horny as hell, Iris! All they want is to get into those tiny pants!"

"*You're* a guy," she countered, suggestively.

"What? I'm your brother!" Hayes deflected, feeling increasingly frustrated and confused.

"And as your brother, I feel obligated to tell you of the danger you're putting yourself in. You might think you like the attention, but what happens when you don't want it? Some guys don't take no for an answer Iris!" He paused, glancing at her outfit again. Meeting her eyes and trying to gauge her intent, he softened his voice.

"Anyone can see you're not a little girl anymore Iris, and if you put yourself on display like that, you're advertising an easy target. Please don't make me worry about you like that."

Hayes gave her a steady look of desperation, urgently wanting her to cover up and end this conversation. He was feeling very uncomfortable and was legitimately concerned for her well-being, should she leave the house dressed as she was. What's gotten into her? he wondered, thoughts whirling.

"You're right," she agreed, "I'm *not* a little girl anymore." With that, she disappeared back into her room, slamming the door behind her, muffling the music again and leaving Hayes baffled and alone.

He stood dazed. *What on earth is she playing at?* His mother had warned him that girls got crazy with hormones when they were teenagers, but until now, Iris had been reasonably normal. Hayes racked his brain trying to think of any boys she might have mentioned, but came up with none. He distinctly remembered her complaining that all guys were arrogant jerks. And why had she got flirty with *him?* Surely she wasn't fishing for him. The thought sent a disturbed shiver down his spine and he hoped it wasn't the case.

They weren't technically related. Iris had been adopted by his parents when she was two, after her own mother had died. Hayes had always thought of Iris as his kid sister and would never think of her as anything other than that. Another frustrated sigh escaped his lips and he flung himself onto the ragged old couch, flinching at its creaking protests.

He knew what lay in wait for Iris and thought it was likely responsible for her behavior. Two and a half years from now, Iris would be eighteen. She would then be expected to marry a consenting man of her choice. If not, she would be admitted into the pool of single women that 'serviced' the soldiers, until a man selected her. *If* a man selected her.

This was City law, decided in the beginning, and unchallenged under Luther Derrick's reign. Originally it was a method considered to assist population growth, in a group plagued by infertility. Some well-meant attempt to ensure survival of the human race. Apparently, by keeping women of child-bearing age in 'productive occupation', they'd hoped to survive long enough to outlast their competitors with the thought of eventually trying to fix the damage done to the land and its inhabitants. Hayes believed Derrick kept the rule for similar beliefs, but also because it allowed for easy manipulation of the Citizens. It helped to keep the soldiers happy and doing his bidding. It also kept half the population, namely women, weak.

Iris's mother had been one of those women. It would be Iris's worst nightmare to follow that fate. If she hadn't found a guy she liked yet - one whom liked her back, she might be getting anxious. Anxious enough to pursue her own brother? Hayes wondered. Maybe.

Hayes didn't want Iris fated to that life either, but had never thought of marrying her as an option. Marriages required consummation. He felt bile rising in the back of his throat at the thought of having to bed his little sister. No. It was not an option.

He had a plan or two up his sleeve, but none were guaranteed. Hoping to find a suitable match before she turned eighteen, he'd so far been hindered by his high standards. Hayes had been raised to have a healthy respect for women and value them as people. These kinds of ideas were not upheld by many in the City. Women were second-class citizens present to cook and clean, tend the gardens and bear children. He wanted someone decent for Iris; someone who would appreciate her.

Iris would make some guy happy, he was sure. She was (usually) sweet and compassionate with a distinctly sensible streak. She was alright to look at too, he thought objectively, trying to avoid the most recent images he'd acquired. Blond, Iris was tall and slim, and surprisingly strong – which had come in handy over the years, when the two of them had needed to deal with a few sticky situations.

Yes, Iris would be a good partner for the right man. Hayes made a mental note to re-check his list of prospective husbands again using a fresh eye. He didn't want to compromise too much, for Iris's sake. There was time. For now.

***

Iris came out of her room. There was no loud music accompanying her and as she passed by the couch on her way to the kitchen, Hayes noticed she had changed back into her usual jeans and sweater. Relieved, and not wanting to revisit the issue, he decided on a different approach.

"What do you feel like for dinner Eyes?" It was the nickname they used at home, a play on her actual name that also referred to her bright, cobalt blue gaze.

"I thought I'd whip up a big batch of pumpkin and bacon soup for the next few days." She checked the cupboards as she spoke, taking inventory. "There's not much else until you guys get back from the valley, unless you have time to come fishing? We've got enough flour for bread until then too, and some barley, a little cheese, but that's about it. Mom did say she was bringing home some greens from the gardens today though. It's her turn."

Hayes had noticed his Mom's absence, but had been too shocked by Iris's performance to think where she would be. Reminded, he knew that of course she was working in the gardens today. He had learned to commit his family's schedule to memory, so that he knew where they should be at all times. It was harder to make sure they were safe if he didn't know where they were. Vigilance proved exhausting, but worthwhile.

"Has Mom been drinking her tea?" he asked, worried about her adherence to the medication regime when he wasn't home. "Morning and night?"

"Yes," Iris sighed, "I've been watching her. She's taking it, OK? I care about it as much as you do Morrison." She seemed offended that he would think otherwise.

"Hey, I know you do. I'm just checking." he said, facing his raised palms toward her defensively. "I know she makes a fuss about it on work days, that's all. I think it's working though, don't you?" he asked, knowing Iris would think so. "She seems more stable and it's been months since her last episode." He stared out the kitchen window, thinking about it as Iris banged pans around the cupboard in search of the heavy soup pot.

Hayes had been impressed at the difference in his mother's mental state. Lu-Belle Hayes was troubled. The impact of her erratic moods led to constant efforts in order to maintain some level of normalcy. His Dad had dealt with it as best he could when he was alive, shielding the children from it as much as possible. Hayes remembered some fragments of the issue from those happier, naïve times, like the sounds that came from the white room when it wasn't empty. Mostly though, he had been largely unaware of his mother's problems, until he was the one left to deal with her.

After her husband's death, Lu-Belle had sunk into a long period of depression. She and the children had made it through, able to follow Ethan Hayes' final instructions by sheer willpower, and with the help of Mrs. Wilkie their kind elderly neighbor. It was Mrs. Wilkie that made sure they all ate and it was her constant appeals that eventually got Luther Derrick to provide the treatment Lu-Belle desperately needed.

There was a price attached of course, but at the time there was no alternative to end the dire situation. Lu-Belle was granted use of the electro-cranial cap as she required it, provided she worked off the debt to the director, with her body. Coerced, she 'agreed' to it out of hopelessness and concern for her young children.

With each session under the cap, her clinical depression lifted.

Sadly the realization of a future under such an agreement, became more abhorrent. Lu-Belle's life became a constant battle. She tried to keep her 'payment program' separate from home life. With a brave face she kept the children safely ignorant, but the perpetual stress and abuse was overwhelming.

It was impossible for Lu-Belle to maintain stability under such circumstances, especially when her mind was so vulnerable to begin with. The years that followed were bruised by frequent relapse. Episodes of extreme lows were over-compensated for and mutated into manic highs. A lack of motivation to even leave her bed turned into wild behavior – a trait that Derrick boasted about putting to good use.

The highs were the hardest to recover from. Hayes would take Iris to Mrs. Wilkie, before running to the tower to inform Derrick. The Henchmen would come to fetch the raving Lu-Belle and it was never a smooth extraction. Each time it happened, the strain on their small family grew, highlighting their dependence on Luther Derrick.

Hayes was grateful that both he and Iris had grown enough to deal with things their own way now. He said a silent thank-you to dear old Mrs. Wilkie, may she rest in peace. These days if Lu-Belle's mood showed signs of elevating, he and Iris would give her a sedative tea and put her to bed in the white room.

It was the smallest bedroom in the apartment, with only enough room to walk a thin path around the mattress on the floor. There were no windows, just two small peepholes from the hall, through which you could see the whole room. There was a small drawer that could pass from the hall into the room, where you could post things in or out. It was painted completely white, and on the outside of the door, were locks.

Hayes was getting so astute with his observations, that he was able to identify a slide in his mother's mental state in the early stages and act quickly. The last few times his mom had only needed the white room for a day or two. Mostly unlocked too. Her longest stint, he remembered, was nearly two full months, locked. They had all felt damaged after that episode. That was when Hayes had begun to seek alternatives.

Wanting to breakaway from Derrick-controlled medical

options, Hayes had tried to research natural methods of mood maintenance, but it was difficult to find much of use in the library. A lot of books had been destroyed and those left behind held little information on the topic. In school, they'd been told of huge databases that had existed long ago - in a world with functional computers. These databases had kept vast amounts of information on any subject you cared to search for. He wished such things were still available.

Hayes had all but given up hope of finding anything helpful, when he'd thought to try the Valley. A very informative talk with one of their doctors at a Gathering had led her to seek him out after the meal, suspecting there was more to his questions than he'd been willing to discuss at dinner. Freya MacGregor had listened patiently and without judgment, and had told him of a few of the herbs they grew that might be beneficial in such a case. The next morning, she had kindly given him a bundle, with written instructions on how and when they were to be taken. She had said that if he found them to be effective, she would fill a prescription each Train Day, with a view to providing seeds for the next season, so he could grow his own.

He had been so grateful, he'd hugged her. Dr. MacGregor had seemed somewhat shocked and had made an excuse to leave as she brushed her hands down her clothes. Hayes had wondered if she was trying to straighten them or remove any trace of his touch. Valley folk lived such different lives. Hayes often wondered what it would be like to live there, in a log or stone house and surrounded by all the green and the fresh open air, instead of in his stifling apartment.

The sun was streaming into the small kitchen and he instinctively turned his face into it, appreciating the warmth. He realized Iris was saying something, because when he opened his eyes, she was staring at him expectantly.

"What?"

"You're in the way!" she said, awkwardly holding the heavy pot. "Move your butt away from the stove!" He did so and she heaved the pot past him and clunked it down. She must have been holding it a while, he thought ruefully.

"Sorry, must have zoned out. What can I do to help? Fry the bacon?"

Iris looked thoughtful for a moment, then dismissed him with a wave of her hand as she glanced at the clock.

"No thanks. The kitchen is too small for you to help without annoying me right now. Besides," she added, avoiding his eyes, "Don't you have a date with Indi? Or was it Grace today?" She made it clear from her tone that she disapproved of his participation in the system she despised.

For her own safety, he let her believe the lie.

"Oh yeah," he confirmed, with what he hoped was sleazy enthusiasm. "I do have a date, but I think it's with Talia." Watching her expression turn to disgust, he chuckled. "You were right the first time, Iris. I'm meeting Indi. You know me better than to accuse me of whoring around too much."

Iris blanched at the word 'whore' and turned back to dicing. "Just go, would you?" Keeping her back to him, she turned her head to the side and sighed. "Will you be back for dinner? Mom will be expecting you."

"Don't worry Eyes, I don't take long!" he joked crudely, grabbing his jacket and heading to the door.

"Ugh! You're such a dick." She looked at him over her shoulder and smiled. "Girls talk you know."

Pausing at the door, he turned to face his sister. "Meaning?" he asked impatiently, figuring he would likely be laughed out of the club if she was going to spread around that he was an early finisher.

"Meaning that your reputation isn't as a, um… Quick Jimmy," she divulged, using language that until this afternoon, he would have assumed her too young to know.

"My reputation?" he asked, unable to hide the curiosity

in his tone. "What have you heard?"

"Oh… just things."

"What things?"

"Things that girls talk about. Like you being a 'gallant and generous man'. Spew. I do *not* want details! Just go already, would you?" Shaking her head, she turned back to her chopping.

"There are worse things, I suppose." Smiling as he went through the door, he called back through the crack as he shut it. "See ya later Eyes."

INDISCRETIONS

Men filtered slowly into the club in small groups. It was just after shift change, the usual time for soldiers to quench their thirst and unwind. Hayes ordered two pints at the bar and casually scoped the room while they were poured. The band was still setting up the stage, before the lights were dimmed. Some of the corners were quite dark already and he could tell by the way the shadows moved that the women were about their business.

His beer arrived and he moved to a small table by the stage to wait. Draining one glass, he eyed the other as it waited flirtatiously in the center of the table. Taking a sip, he raised his hand to order another. It arrived just as she did, and he nudged it toward her as she pulled out a chair.

Indi looked worn-out. She lowered herself into the chair carefully, trying unsuccessfully to stretch her very short dress, in an attempt to cover more of her bare legs. Smiling gratefully, she raised her beer to him, before downing it without a breath.

"Bad day?" he asked needlessly, as she rubbed her face and tried to tidy her unraveling hair.

"Hmm" she replied, tucking the last few strays behind her ears. "Not all of us can look as happy as you all the time, Smiler." She looked instantly regretful. "Sorry, that was rude. I'm just… yeah, it was a bad day. But it's getting better," she said with just the hint of a smile in her voice.

"Thanks. I guess." he accepted, graciously. "The kids?"

"I love those little bastards, but they'll be the death of me, I swear! Between ear infections and hacking coughs, I feel like I haven't slept a night this week." Moaning, she rested her head on the table next to her empty glass, closing her eyes in escape.

The band had started playing, and the line at the bar was growing. Hayes leaned down close to her ear.

"Let's do this quickly then, and you can get home to bed." Scraping back his chair, he held out his hand. "Care to dance?" Lifting her head, she rested her own hand on his, letting him pull her to her feet.

"You might be tired Indi, but you still look great." Tucking a loose strand back behind her ear, he kissed her cheek, before pulling her out onto the floor.

The music was upbeat and they moved rhythmically between the few bodies already on the dance floor, keeping their own bodies close together. It was important for Hayes to appear interested, but not *be* interested. Just as he felt the heat and his pulse begin to rise, the music slowed down and he drew Indi closer still. They rocked slowly to the beat and he nuzzled her neck, whispering in her ear, "Let's go."

Taking his hand, Indi led him away through the swaying shadows and down the corridor to the private rooms. The bouncer, Eddie, waved them through and pointed to an open door further down, before turning to record their names in his ledger. Evidently they were not the earliest guests this evening, Hayes noted, as they walked past two closed doors.

An elderly woman waited at the end of the corridor with her stocked cart of clean sheets and astringent cleaners. Hayes shuddered as they entered the stark room and were hit with the acidic stink of vinegar. He hated the smell, and though he knew it meant the room was clean, it barely masked the musky scent of sex. Taking a deep breath from the less potent corridor, he closed the door behind them.

Going about his usual checks, Hayes scanned the walls, floor and ceiling for any sign of tampering. Satisfied that they were indeed in a private space, he sat next to Indi on the bed, angling a knee behind her. He began to rub her shoulders, causing a low rumble of pleasure to escape from her lips. She tilted her head to one side and his hands followed the cue and massaged her neck.

"I've got good news, Indi," he began, trying to curb his excitement. "I think I might have found a Valley contact."

"You have?" Indi turned abruptly to meet his eyes, intent. "That's great! Is it that girl you were watching?"

Hayes had thought about Rori almost non-stop as he'd aided Reg in the search for her. He had liked her immediately, fascinated by the way she moved and how she'd behaved toward him. Though understandably hesitant in trusting him, she hadn't been afraid to display anger or push him and had even joked with him. More astonishing, she had warned him that eating the apples and snake would be bad for his health - as if she cared! He thought she might just be open-minded and bold enough to speak with him again.

Conflicted, Hayes wanted badly for her to co-operate with him, but also found himself with an unsettling attraction to her. A complication he would need to set aside; his plans were strictly business. Besides, a Dalton would have a tough enough time on platonic terms with a Citizen and with good reason. The sad reality was that he *would* be using her, whether she was willing or not. Either way, she would end up hating him. After trying to think of every angle, he had made his decision. What would it matter if one more person hated him? The people he loved would be free.

"Yeah. I've spoken to her," he said. "Not about

anything important yet. But she sort of owes me a favor or three, so I can probably persuade her to help us. Failing that, blackmail might be an option. I have her name, and I know what she looks like now."

He paused for a moment, burdened with guilt. Blackmail would be a last resort. It didn't sit well with him. It was more like something a Derrick would do.

"I'll try and talk to her on Train Day. From there I should be able to gauge which track to take. I'll be taking it slow to be safe though. We'll only get one shot. Don't get too excited, and don't go telling the others yet, OK?"

"Well it's hard not to be excited – this is almost the best news in my life so far. Sorry, no pressure," she added as an afterthought. "Feel like celebrating? I'm feeling generous – you could actually use this time like you're meant to." She stood, pulling the strings behind her neck and letting the dress puddle around her ankles, leaving her completely exposed. Raising her hand, she loosened her hair and shook it gently. Dark tresses flowed over her shoulders and skimmed her nipples. She looked to him, awaiting his response.

Hayes swallowed, eyes taking in the offering. He felt a definite response in his trousers. Indi noticed and pushed him back on the bed, setting to work at unbuttoning his fly, as he lay staring at the ceiling.

"I-Indi," he stammered, coughing a little to clear the lust from his throat. "You know my rule. I will not be a father in this place. Stop. *Please*," he gasped as she cupped the bulge. Stopping, she smiled down at him, shaking her head a little.

"I know your rule," she said playfully. "But there *are* ways to enjoy yourself that don't result in children." Not waiting for an answer, she resumed her work.

Hayes closed his eyes and let her, cursing himself for being such a pushover. He'd wanted to keep his meetings with the girls even and uncomplicated. His intention not to reinforce their position as sex brokers, but to empower them as individuals. Initially, his brain battled, but ultimately betrayed him.

You're only human, he thought. A man.

Indi was good at her job. Hayes kept his eyes shut tight, as if denying his participation in the activity. In the dark of his mind though, there were images inspired by the external deed, but they didn't involve Indi. Inconveniently on his mind, was Rori.

***

Hayes kept busy for the next few days, trying to give the appearance of being 'intensely dutiful'. Given his involvement in the loss of intruders, it was best to keep his head down and be present as much as possible. Today he was running patrols, leading a search and training youth recruits. Boys as young as twelve would attend regular sessions with the Enforcers in order to learn key skills for combat. The City needed its soldiers, and since uprisings over the last century had depleted the City's ammunition and weapon supplies, it was crucial to know how to fight without them.

Most boys *wanted* to become Derrick's soldiers. The role had perks. Aside from regular access to obedient women, a soldier received more trade tokens, better living quarters, and additional food rations. They were also entitled to more of the higher quality clothing and other items that had been salvaged and stockpiled when the City had been stabilized. Most of the boys pursued these incentives, hoping to make a better life for themselves or their families, just as Hayes had taken his career path to provide for his family.

There were other options of course, for those that failed to achieve the necessary standards, or for those who did not wish to be soldiers. Men were needed to maintain the power sources and desalinization plant, for fishing, butchery and heavy labor, and to take on any role of management.

There were a lot of things Citizens couldn't do. The kind of things that required specific training, but the skills or knowledge for which, had been lost with those who had possessed them. It was the things they couldn't do that had led them to become so dependent on the Daltons. It was the Daltons who had separated themselves from society early, before the end time, and had planned on advancing into the future in a self-reliant manner. They had chosen that path, had been prepared and had progressed with the knowledge and skill base they'd needed.

The original Citizens could have chosen to learn from the Daltons, and progress with them. They could have shared their City stockpiles, and could have traded goods for learning essential skills. Instead, they had used force to take what they needed. It was what they were accustomed to, in the wars they had been fighting. Whether their judgment was clouded by greed, power or fear, they left the work and therefore the skills to the Valley slaves.

Now the divide was much greater; the difference in knowledge vast. The survival of the Citizens depended on the Daltons. Having backed themselves into that corner, the City had to continue to use intimidation tactics to maintain supply. That was the main reason Enforcers continued to train soldiers. With an adequate army, you don't need to learn other skills. You can take whatever you want!

There were boundaries of course. Firstly, the Director's word is law, and all resources are managed by him. Killing women and children was prohibited. They were needed for the future of society. Equally important as those rules: the supply must not be jeopardized. This had required a certain amount of compromise with the Daltons over the years. One of the concessions made, was that the City would supply such goods as the Valley requested to maintain or further food production. Of course, these would only be granted if deemed appropriate by the City Director.

Another agreement, was that if the Daltons were providing the demanded food, soldiers were not to enter the Valley unless escorting the train. Presumably so they could preserve their culture and work in general peace, but Hayes realized that in doing so, Daltons kept their trade secrets tightly hidden, making themselves indispensable. Very clever.

The expanse between City and Valley however, was no man's land and anything out there was fair game. Since Rori's sighting and presumed escape from the City, patrols had been expanding their watch perimeter. Following recruit training each morning, Hayes had been leading six of his men on patrols out along the tracks, into the lands beyond the City limits.

Intermittently directing his men to branch off and search the surrounding terrain, Hayes would continue directly along to the next point on the tracks where they would meet up again. He did this as far along the tracks as he had gone with Reg – until the rocks closed in around the tracks and limited visibility. On the return trip, they used the same search technique, with the men exploring the opposite side to that which they had investigated on the way up, using fresh eyes to ascertain any recent activity on the land.

It had been a fine afternoon and Hayes had enjoyed the walk in the warmth of the autumn sun. He'd stopped with his men to refill their canteens at the halfway house. Most of them were shirtless, as he was, hot and sweaty from the exertion. They drank and splashed water at each other in that playful but competitive way that men do, which ultimately led to the smallest member of the unit, Paulie, being turned upside down and dunked head first into the spring.

"C'mon… guys!" Paulie spluttered between dips, trying to wrest himself free.

"That's enough now," Hayes laughed, after another series of submersions. "We'll head back down to the tracks and work our way home."

"Just a few more Smiler!" said Ray, who held one half of Paulie's inverted body, with Benno on the other side.

Hayes looked at Paulie's face, eyes bulging and skin deep red from the blood collecting there. Paulie had since gone still and quiet, intent on giving as little entertainment as possible whilst enduring his current position.

"I said enough."

Benno stopped at the order, making to release their victim. Ray however, held him firmly in place and eyeballed Hayes. Seeing the unspoken challenge, Hayes drew himself to full height and stepped in closely to Ray, glaring down at him.

"Yes Sir," Ray conceded, averting his own gaze. With Benno, he eased Paulie back to standing, and held him upright as he swayed a little, regaining his balance and his composure.

"Right then." Hayes changed the subject. "We'll head back. Paulie, you go with Benno, You can take the ground from here to the next bend. Ray, you're with Lee. Take the ground from the next bend to the one after that. Ditto for you and Joel, Nige. Scan a quarter mile out from the track, then walk along to the final group's rendezvous. Any sign of Dalton travel: report. Got it?" Hayes paused, taking in their nods of agreement before looking beyond them to the tracks. His gaze traveled back to the rocky area at the end of their search zone.

"It's faster for me going straight. I'm taking a closer look at those rocks before I join you. I want to see if there's any sign of Daltons using them as hide-outs. Now move out," he directed, pulling his shirt back on and moving off in the direction of the rocks.

Checking over his shoulder to be sure his men were on their way, Hayes jogged to the rocks. As he approached he skirted behind the first of them, scouting for evidence of human movement. There was a thin path to the rear of some rocks further on. It wasn't well traveled, the grass wasn't trampled or worn, but it was definitely a path.

He followed it as it wove between the rocks, taking him higher. Rounding a large boulder, he came to a stop. The path had ended abruptly and he was facing a wall of rock.

"Huh," he grunted, taking his shirt off again and using it to wipe the sweat off his face and neck before looking around. The rock wall looked sheer, with no obvious hand or foot holds. Disappointed, he turned back down the path and stopped again. Cut into the back of a big boulder, were several man-made notches. Hayes tucked his shirt into the back of his belt and fitted his hands into the first few notches and hauled himself up, motivated by a sense of discovery.

At the top of the boulder, he found more notches etched into another huge rock that leaned against it. He kept following the stone grips upward, until he could find no more. Finding himself on top of a tall pillar of rock, Hayes warily leaned into the solid wall behind him, bracing his quivering legs as he stood.

Slowly turning around, so as not to lose his balance, he couldn't help but look down. Far below, set snuggly into the groove between the stone walls and their scattered guardian-like monoliths, were the tracks. Down the line, in the direction of the Valley, the walls and rocks grew bigger and more densely.

As his eyes followed the parallel rails back out to the open grassland he inhaled sharply. From his high vantage point, Hayes commanded a view of the wide open country. He could make out the Halfway House and its garden walls. Its corners stood out from the naturally rounded landscape; its trees, the only ones in sight. He could see down the tracks for miles and could even make out the hints of movement that he knew to be the men of his unit. In the far distance he could see the buildings of the City, his home in miniature, sitting on the edge of the sea.

"We're not the only ones who watch then," he thought aloud to himself, amazed at the distance he could see. He leaned into the rock wall at his back and relaxed, just enjoying the sun and the image before him. A flicker of movement in his peripheral vision caught his attention.

Something was coming. From the rocky hillside to his right, out into the grass and headed in his direction, was a horse. It was small and far away, but he was sure that's what it was. Hayes had seen horses in the Valley. He'd even seen them walking along with people sitting on their backs, but he had never seen one running at speed. He was amazed at how quickly the horse was covering the distance.

As it drew nearer, his pulse accelerated, reflecting the sight of the horse's pounding hooves. He could see the horse had a rider. The rider was small, and crouched so low on the horse's back it appeared to be merging with the beast. Only by their colors could he tell them apart. The white mane flew in the wind created by their speed. Extending the mane considerably, was a long stream of chestnut.

Rori! Hayes rushed to climb down, losing his footing in his haste. Gripping the rock beneath him, he tried to calm the hammering in his chest, as he watched pieces of gravel come free and plummet to the tracks below, hitting the larger rocks as they went. Staring after them, he tried not to imagine what his body would feel like on the same journey.

Collecting himself swiftly, by focusing on finding the clefts in the rocks, he began the climb back down. By the time he reached the bottom, he could clearly hear the horse's hooves treading on the shingle between the tracks. Its pace had slowed down to a walk, and he could hear the occasional loud snort. Hayes stepped out from the rocks to greet them in a warm and friendly manner.

The horse however, did not take his surprise appearance as friendly. Baulking at the sight of him and rearing, he almost shook his rider free as she forcefully spoke a variety of colorful words at Hayes, with a side of soothing croons and touches to the horse. After a few backward paces and more gentle words, she was able to loosen her grip on the reins. Both Rori and the horse eyed him suspiciously as he stood dumbfounded, in awe of her control over the huge beast.

Hayes was again struck by her unassuming beauty. Her face already looked recovered from its injuries and the flush in her cheeks was reminiscent of a ripened peach. Hanging loose down her back, her dark auburn hair danced in the slight breeze and the natural fibers of her Dalton clothing flattered her sun-kissed skin. She radiated warmth.

"What are you doing here?" she demanded, in a tone far from warm, checking the rocks and the tracks behind her. "Are you alone?" Her eyes traveled his body and rested on his face.

Hayes realized then, he was still without his shirt. Wrenching it free from his belt, he yanked it down over his head and slid both arms into their sleeves at once, driving it down. Somewhat recovered from his inert state, he thought how to begin. He hadn't really expected to see anyone, let alone the girl he needed.

"Rori, hi. Yes, I'm alone at the moment. Sorry about the um... surprise. I didn't know your friend here would react like that. I... I mean we... don't have..." he stumbled, unable to operate his mouth properly.

"Articulate." She sighed, looking about again. "Look Hayes, I don't make it a habit of hanging out with the enemy. I don't know why you're here but I can't stay and chat, OK? Thank you for saving my ass, truly. But I shouldn't be anywhere near you. It'll only bring trouble." She lifted the reins and he saw a subtle shift in her body. The horse started to move around him.

Hayes grabbed the reins near where they attached to the halter around the horse's head. The horse stopped as he'd hoped, but promptly tried to bite him. Hayes leapt away just in time.

"Mickey!" she scolded, "Don't bite people unless I tell you to!"

"Yeah Mickey!" Hayes agreed, clutching his hand close to protect it from the crazed horse. "I thought horses ate grass!"

Rori snorted in disbelief when she realized he wasn't joking. Her laughter echoed off the surrounding rocks, creating the effect of many people mocking him.

Hayes stared at her, his cheeks burning. Now he'd given her the impression that he was an idiot. This was a mistake. Wanting to kick himself, he strode away, kicking the shingle between the tracks. After a time, she called after him.

"Oh c'mon! Don't be a baby! You're safe – he's full of apples!"

"Hayes!" she called when he kept walking. He stopped, but didn't turn back. She clicked at her horse and it soon came around him, blocking his path. Sitting atop Mickey, she looked down at him, a puzzled look on her face. Returning her gaze as coolly as he could manage, he peered into those intense metallic eyes, rimmed with charcoal lashes and found himself having to look back at the ground before he melted.

"Look," she said, sighing again. "I'm sorry for laughing at you. I know you guys don't have horses, and you've never spent time with them. They are herbivores, but they will bite you and kick you if you piss them off."

"I didn't mean to piss him off," Hayes countered quietly, still not meeting her eyes. "I just didn't want him to take you away yet."

He felt her eyes boring into him, but refused to look up. After an excruciating pause, Rori dismounted and stepped under his bowed head, making herself unavoidable. Looking straight into his eyes she held him there with a force he had not anticipated.

"Here I am, Hayes. What do you want?" Her tone was strong and demanding, as if she was ordering him. Not used to girls talking to him like that, he was reminded again of the immense differences between Daltons and Citizens.

What *did* he want? He couldn't find the words. Her long hair lifted on the wind and brushed his arm. She was too close to him and he couldn't think straight. How would he put into words what he wanted? Unable to tell her unless he was sure he could trust her, Hayes looked warily at Mickey, deliberating his next words.

She must have thought he was still fearful of the horse, because her tone softened when she spoke again.

"Mick's friendly really. He just has a mind of his own." She paused, viewing Hayes expectantly. Thinking that maybe she was talking about more than the horse, he nodded, waiting for her to continue.

"He doesn't take kindly to strangers bossing him around and Citizens are the *worst* kind of strangers."

Hayes stared at her, wondering if she was intentionally insulting him.

Her bottom lip disappeared into her mouth for a moment, before reappearing. "You have to prove to him that you're not one of the bad guys." Rori looked at him boldly and ran her hand down the horse's spotted coat. "Pat him like this, see? He won't bite you if he trusts you."

Again Hayes got the distinct impression that she was perhaps referring to herself and didn't doubt for a moment that she was capable of biting him. Slightly unnerved, he watched how she stroked along Mickey's neck. Noticing the horse shudder pleasurably under her touch, Hayes raised his own hand. Hesitating, his hand hovered in midair as he eyed Mickey's mouth.

"Oh for crying out loud! Here!" Rori impatiently grabbed his lingering hand and guided it up behind the twitching ears. Keeping her hand on his, she drew it gently down the length of the horse's muscular neck. She did this twice more before she let go and left Hayes to sweep his lonely hand down the soft hairs under the coarse mane.

"Thanks," he said quietly, putting his hands in his pocket and looking at the ground. "Rori, I want to tell you things, but I don't know how. We both know the line we're walking is a dangerous one, and I want to talk about even more dangerous things." He stopped, thinking about the risks he was taking. "Did you tell anyone that we, uh... met?"

"Of course," she said matter-of-factly. "I had fingerprints on my neck. There are few explanations for such things."

"And you didn't get into trouble?" he asked, skeptical as he looked her over for signs of a beating.

"Yeah, I got in deep shit!" She laughed, more to herself than at him, but she soon stopped, after seeing the look on his face.

"We have a different kind of justice in the Valley." She eyed him carefully, regarding his scar. "I know what stands for justice in the City. I've seen. Are *you* in trouble? For losing me?"

"Not too badly. Nobody suspects me of treason, and as long as I pull extra shifts and make an effort to be as dedicated to catching intruders as possible, I think I'll be alright. You'll know though, that if word gets out I helped you, the punishment will be severe. I have a family, and people depending on me. I can't let them be harmed by my choices."

"And yet, here you are." she said, her eyes narrowing.

"Here I am."

She considered him in silence with a look of genuine concern on her face. Sighing, she studied her feet. Toeing the shingle between the tracks, she looked up at him. "I've been ordered not to see you again."

"And yet, here you are," he observed, suddenly wondering why she hadn't just let him walk away; why she hadn't run from him the moment she saw him.

"Here I am," she smiled, showing her top row of white teeth, uniformly straight bar one. That canine stood proud from the rest, giving her an imperfect and very sweet grin.

"Maybe we have something in common," she said. "We both seem to want the best for our families. Sometimes that means taking a dangerous path."

The sun went behind a cloud and the light dimmed, reminding Hayes, that his time was not limitless.

"Rori, I can't talk more today, my time is never my own. Time with you is..." He broke off, unable to find the right words to express the freedom he felt. He wanted to hug her, grateful for her apparent understanding, but remembered her flinching when he'd tried to pull leaves from her hair at the halfway house. She was different from the City girls, who were accustomed to men touching them as they pleased.

"Can I find you on Train Day?" he asked. "Please?"

"If you can." She was smiling again. "I'll be hiding in plain sight. Might be that I find you first." She glanced around, looking for something. With a look of mild frustration, she turned to him and laced her fingers together.

"Do this with your hands," she bossed him, showing him what she meant. Seeing his confusion, she elaborated, "I need a leg up."

Hayes did as he was shown, holding his hands low enough to create a step. Placing her leather-booted foot into his hold, she pushed up, swinging her leg over Mickey's back. Adjusting herself, she looked down at Hayes.

"Later then," she said in farewell.

"Looking forward to it," he said to her back as he watched her ride slowly along the tracks into the rocky landscape. Mickey's behind swayed rhythmically as he walked, tail swishing. Rori looked over her shoulder at him, blushing as she smiled approvingly. Hayes turned and ran down the tracks to meet his men, his own lips curling into a reciprocal grin.

MOTIVES

I'd like to say that sneaking out isn't my style, but I'd be lying. Sneaking is my specialty. I know I shouldn't be in the City, and I know meeting with Hayes is a bad idea, especially considering he doesn't know I'm coming. After stewing about him at home, I've chosen to observe him on his home turf before I decide whether or not to proceed.

My gut tells me I can trust him, and I find myself wanting to, but the alarms in my head won't stop nagging at me. A Citizen can't be trusted.

On the other hand, this is the best opportunity I've had to penetrate the inner workings of the City. I need to find out exactly where they're keeping Patrick and the layout of the building. I need someone to tell me the truth without asking too many questions about why, but because of who I am, I can't let a Citizen know he's my brother.

Leaving the window, I walk the halls of the abandoned apartment building. Curiously, I don't think I've been in this building yet. I chose it tonight for its view. The street outside is one that the soldiers use a lot at shift change and I was hoping to catch sight of Hayes. That was easy enough. Not hard to spot someone that others look like they're trying hard to avoid. He's definitely high up in the ranks.

After some careful sleuthing, I've already discovered he'll be back on shift at midnight. I'm just killing time.

Trying the first door that takes my fancy, I find it locked. Taking the slim blade from under my hat, I jemmy the lock and walk into the dim apartment. The meager glow from the outside streetlights makes the room appear as stale as it smells.

The first thing I notice is the dark paint splashed across the pale wall. The message is old. No-one has lived in the outer City for at least a century. We know the people huddled in the inner grid, only able to keep that serviced with electricity and water. We don't know much about that time ourselves, only how devastatingly brutal it must have been for the survivors. They apparently thought their only course of action was to invade us. What kind of world inspires that? I stare at the dark writing.

'What have we become?'

The words resonate. The answer that comes to my mind is 'monsters'. As I stare at the words a bit longer though, I see beyond them to their meaning. This Citizen felt remorse for their actions. The words imply a degradation of human character. It forces me to consider my father's insistence that the City holds 'thousands of innocent people'. I understand that a whole City can't be evil, but when we only see the aggressors, it's hard to remember that there are others in the fold who aren't like them. I've assumed them to be the weak, the women, the voiceless few, but maybe there's more than I think. Looking for answers, I scan the room.

Like most of the abandoned apartments, the furniture is stacked neatly in one room. Opening a drawer, I'm not surprised to find it empty, the owner's belongings have been removed years ago in the systematic cleansing of the outer sector. All small items were taken and housed in the inner grid where they could be more easily distributed, or more easily guarded.

Some things got left behind though, if you know where to look. When bad things happen, people get worried about the things they value most. They try to hide them away. In the Valley, we value our people and our knowledge. It sometimes amuses me to find what some of the Citizens thought precious enough to hide. Sometimes I find bundles of useless paper money, sometimes jewelery, knives, documents. Once I even found a toothbrush hidden on a secret ledge under a sink.

Being well versed in keeping things hidden, I am adept at finding other people's secreted items. Searching the room now, I look for anything that strikes me as curious. An ill-fitted ventilation grate catches my eye, but I dismiss it immediately. Too obvious. Anything there has already been found. Hopefully the person who wrote the words knew a decoy would keep their real treasure safe.

My eye continues to be drawn to the window. One of its moldings is dented slightly. On closer inspection, I can see other small scars in the paintwork along its edge. Testing, I give it a wiggle. It stays firm. Glancing around, I can see no other oddities about this room. Before moving on to the next, I reach through a false pocket in my gopher-suit, to the knife on my thigh.

Working my knife carefully under the wood, I slowly prise it up. It comes away after some resistance, but I'm rewarded for my efforts. Stashed tight against the internal window frame is a small, plastic-wrapped package. Extracting it gingerly, as if it might disintegrate with my touch, I sit on the floor in the square of light from the window.

Thin slivers of plastic shed from the package as I tenderly unwrap it. Inside is a small, rectangular metal object and a notebook. Studying the metal object, I notice a split in its metallic skin and a tiny hinge on one side. Slipping my nail into the thin groove, I pry it open and stare into the eyes of the past. A woman and a girl, each in their own tiny frame. They have the same eyes. Gently lying them on the ground, I bring the notebook into better light.

'Legacy of Travis Becker', read the words inside the front cover. I look at the small faces on the floor and wonder who they were to him. His treasure, obviously. Opening the pages, the small, but tidy hand of Travis Becker tells me of his life and times. I assume the pictures are of his wife, Darnelle and his daughter, Monique, who feature heavily in his writing. It turns out, Mr Travis Becker was a Scout for the City, looking for clean land, fresh water and the promise of a future. As I read on, I discover that it was *he* that risked the river and found the Valley.

Angry at a ghost, I stare at his people, wanting them to explain. Their innocent eyes and harmless smiles implore me to read on. Looking back to the notebook, I soon learn that his discovery was abused despite his protests. Turning to the last entry, I read his parting message.

People ask 'what happened?'

As if it was just one thing! If only it were that simple. One thing might have been easier to undo.

We couldn't stop the weather changing. We knew it was coming, but we couldn't stop it. It was only natural that people would flee the heat, the droughts, the fires, the disease, the death. Gamblers stay, but the hungry follow the resources.

If your country is dying because it can't feed or water itself, you pack what you can and you move elsewhere. Others are sympathetic. You form alliances and for a while things are better, but then the land gets overused, the water gets tainted and you get more desperate. You and your new friends need more. You decide if you should be enemies, or work together to move others from their lands.

Fresh water, clean land. That's all that matters. You wage wars. You destroy their land when you can't take it, and they do the same to you. You spike their water supply, they contaminate yours. Together we poison the world.

You move north (or south or anywhere things are better) with your army, where you can defend a pocket of civilization as you try and prepare for the worst. You lose contact and you don't know if it's because they are dead or that they have taken out your last satellite.

You fortify your last resort, hoping to outlast the others. You don't have space for all the people who wait at the gates, begging for help or threatening to take what you have, because they have nothing. Desperate men do desperate things.

You do your best with the resources you have, but when you repeat mistakes and systems break down, your choices are few.

Hungry and sick and isolated, people make demands that can't be met. Anger is as infectious as the diseases. Your military morphs into a bizarre dictatorship in order to maintain control. Nurturing compliance, they weed out threats and eliminate them. And so it was for us. A defiant citizen, a sick child or a valley full of potential invaders… In the eyes of our leader, a threat is a threat. It must be neutralized before what little we have left is destroyed. His strength to commit depraved acts, stems from the fear of those around him. Our fears are our weakness. Fear of him, fear for our families, fear of what would happen if he didn't do those things that we can't bring ourselves to do. Trapped are we in this world. Kill or be killed.

It is human nature to survive. Our most basic instinct. We are human.

If we survive through inhumane means, do we remain human?

I see people walking about in a daze as they 'live'; repeating, over and over, 'What happened?' and 'Why?', as if they can't believe, or don't want to.

What matters more? What happened, or what we became along the way?

Is this how life should be? No. Is there another way? Not yet. But if we can learn from our mistakes, then maybe one day, when someone asks 'what happened?' the answer will be different, and what we will have become, is human again.

Putting the notebook down, I stare at it. I've never found anything like this. Bits and pieces from the time before, but nothing so profound; nothing that has impacted me like this. With trembling hands, I re-wrap the journal and its guardians. Tucking them safely back into their nook, I pick up the wooden framing. Aligning the nails with the holes in the wall, I push as firmly as I can, setting it back in place.

Assessing my work, I know it doesn't look quite as flush as it should, but no-one is likely to notice. Anyone who comes in here will be looking for a new desk or a chair, not at the window. I however, will be keeping this apartment and its hidden treasure in my memory for another time, when I won't feel as if Becker's words are talking to me, personally.

I look out the window, checking the street for soldiers on their way to relieve their comrades. None yet.

Sweeping up the skin-like flakes of old plastic from the floor, I hide them in a drawer. It must be getting close to midnight now. Pacing the room restlessly, I glance at the painted words repeatedly. Unsettled, I leave the room.

In the next room over, I stand a chair beneath the light fixture in the center of the room. Unscrewing the fitting with my knife, I lower it down and detach the wires. Tucking them back into their hole, I re-attach the light to the ceiling. Moving to the switch at the wall, I unscrew that, detaching the wires there and pulling them out. Watching the street as I skin it with practiced ease, I coil the length of wire tightly and seal it into a pocket. No sense in going home empty handed. Collecting the split casing, I coil a section of that and put it in another pocket, shoving the leftovers back into the wall and replacing the cover plate.

As I finish re-screwing the switch in the fourth room, I hear the City clock begin to clang out the hours. Deciding it would be cover enough, I return to give the window frame a few well timed thumps to hammer it back in place. Satisfied, I leave the apartment, closing the door carefully behind me.

***

Taking a gamble, I make my way through the shadows, toward the tallest building on the outer perimeter. If Hayes is still trying to make a good impression, the best lookout post will be up there. Hiding in darkness, I watch as he walks through the pools of light along the fence line, approaching the building. Holding himself tall as another soldier passes, Hayes nods cordially and watches over his shoulder as the soldier moves on. Bending to retrieve something from the ground, he slips around the building to access the fire escape, where his shoulders slump wearily. With effort-laden movements, he drags himself upward. I'll easily beat him to the top.

Retreating further into the alley, I begin to spider upwards. Near the top, I run out of building on one side and have to transfer onto the taller one. Using the shallow grooves of the brickwork, I climb the last level and pull my eyes just above the roof wall. A Lackey leans on the far wall, looking out over the wastelands. Surprisingly, he's singing.

Trying to suppress a smile, I swing myself quietly over the wall and creep behind the blocked cube that houses the stairwell. With a few soft steps, I catapult myself on top of it and lay flat on my stomach, pulling myself slowly forward until I can see the soldier more clearly. His foot taps out the rhythm as he croons. I don't recognize the song, but it sounds catchy. The man's got talent.

The metallic thudding from the fire escape makes the guy clear his throat and become silent. As Hayes comes into view, the Lackey gives the impression of a dedicated soldier, serious at his post.

"You're relieved Ray. Go get yourself a hot meal."

"Smiler?" Ray moves slowly as if unsure. "What are you doing on night shift? I thought I was handing over to Joel?"

"I've got it covered."

"But I -"

Hayes stands over him. "I've got it covered."

"Yes Sir. As you say." Tucking his tail, Ray heads for the fire escape.

"And Ray?"

"Yes Sir?" he asks, stopping in his tracks and turning hesitantly.

"I found a busted pair of sunglasses below. They yours?"

"Yes Sir. They were busted before I threw them over," he says defensively. "I'm entitled to a new pair this month, Sir."

"Entitled. Interesting choice of words. Don't try and climb too high too fast, Ray. You'll fall." Smiling falsely, his tone lightens. "Let's hope you're not as expendable as your property." Hayes turns out to the wastelands. "Dismissed."

"Yes Sir." Ray hastily makes his exit, the stairs thundering underfoot.

Not wanting to engage the prickly man in front of me, I begin to regret making the trip. Waiting for an opportunity to leave, I stay silently in place and watch him. Hayes stares out into the darkness a while longer and eventually his shoulders relax. Sighing, he walks toward the stairs and sits against the wall below me. Opening his jacket, he reaches inside and retrieves the broken set of glasses.

I watch as he removes and inspects the lenses in the moonlight. Taking something from another pocket, a cloth, he cleans the detached lenses and inspects them again. Wrapping them carefully in the cloth, he puts them in his pocket and turns his attention to the damaged frame. Taking out a knife, he uses the tip to unwind the tiny screws that hinge the glasses together. Dismantling the pieces, he replaces the screws, keeping them safe and puts the separate parts in his pocket with the lenses.

"Interesting," I say quietly from above

Jumping to his feet, Hayes spins around to glare at me.

"What the hell are you doing here?" he hisses at me,

before walking to the fire escape to check it's clear. He walks slowly back toward me, uncertain. "The City has a lot of eyes."

"So do potatoes, but they can't see in the dark either." Cringing at my dismissive response, I await his reaction.

Hayes stares at me, his dark brows flat and unimpressed. "How long have you been up here?"

"Longer than you, but not much." I prop my chin on my hands, and watch his rigid posture, waiting for him to relax. Hoping he *will* relax.

"And Ray didn't hear you or see you?"

Shrugging, I try to act calmer than I feel. "I'm good at my job. Him, not so much. Good singer though."

"Singer?"

"Sure. The guy can carry a tune."

"OK," he says, eying me thoughtfully. "How did you know I'd be here?"

"Maths."

"Pardon?"

"I *may* have been spying on you a little," I admit, looking away from his face. "You're working extra shifts, your rank is high and this is the best lookout. Maths, see?"

"I see," he says, not taking his eyes from me. "So you came to spy on me? That's why you're here?"

"Would you believe I came to steal things?"

He carefully considers my face. "Yes. It makes sense to combine work with pleasure if you're coming this far anyway."

"You think I'm spying on you for pleasure?" I ask, about to laugh.

Smiling, he scratches his cheek and lifts one shoulder. "I couldn't say. You did say *'interesting'* earlier, so maybe?"

Heat rises in my cheeks making me grateful my face paint is keeping them concealed. "You're mistaken. I merely thought it interesting that he threw the glasses away and you're preserving the pieces."

Hayes regards me from under his brows, his expression

too confusing to read. Almost sweet?

"So I'm *not* interesting?"

"Oh, as a specimen of Citizenship, you're very interesting."

His eyes turn cold. "Can you not call me a specimen, please?" he says, clearly offended. A little surprised by this, I keep quiet as we watch each other cautiously.

"Why are you here, Rori? I thought hanging out with the enemy was against your personal code and you were ordered to stay away? Don't tell me you've been ordered to spy on me now."

"I'm not very good at following orders," I say honestly. "I came of my own accord."

"That doesn't surprise me in the least," he says, shaking his head and looking out into the darkness of the wastelands.

"What's that supposed to mean?" I ask. "You think I'm some sort of ill-disciplined child or flawed character?"

His head tilts skyward as he exhales. "Whatever. My question was why?" Hayes looks at me impatiently, running his hands through his hair. When I hesitate, he sighs again, does a lap of the rooftop and another check of the fire escape before returning to stare at me questioningly.

"Why is a good question," I start slowly. "It's actually the reason I came. Why did you help me?"

"You didn't want me to help you?" he asks, confused.

"That's not what I said. We both know I'd be dead, or wishing I was, if you hadn't helped me. I'm quite glad to be alive. Why did you help me?"

"Because I did," he says, as if that explains it. Rubbing his forehead, he looks away. "If things had been different at the time, maybe I wouldn't have been able to. Maybe I would have been the one making you wish you were dead." Quiet for a while, he turns to me, his face serious. "Apparently I didn't want to do that."

"That's reassuring." Risking it, I slip down off the stair

enclosure. "Any other reasons? You said you wanted to talk about dangerous things."

Avoiding my gaze, he wanders over to the edge wall and leans on it. His restless, tapping fingers suggest there are more reasons, but he doesn't want to share them. Yet. It's almost laughable; a Citizen that's scared of trusting a Dalton. Strange to think that my reservations stem from the same concern as his.

My own fingers begin to fidget with my suit and I lace them together to still them. "I need to talk about dangerous things too. There's something I need to steal, but it's in an area I'm not familiar with. I need information. I came here to observe you in your own environment, to see if I could trust you. *That* was my reason for coming. An honest response about your motives would be conclusive to my research," I say, approaching him slowly.

His head turns to regard me warily as he chews the corner of his lip. "I need a contact in the Valley."

Narrowing my eyes at him, I consider his answer.

"Seems to me you have a contact. You're being groomed to be the next Ambassador. You have regular access to the best contact in the Valley - the Dalton Chief. He told me."

Hayes pales and a line forms between his brows.

"You talked to the Chief about me?"

"Who did you think I had to answer to when I got back late and all bruised up?"

"I don't know!" he cries, throwing his hands up. "Your Mom?!"

"Well that would be difficult. She's dead," I say, before I can stop myself.

His face softens. "I'm sorry."

Shrugging, I move my toe in an arc through the layer of dust on the rooftop, reminding myself to tidy up my tracks before I leave. "It's fine. She's been gone a long time now, but I like to think that she would've been supportive of my career and its… complications."

An awkward silence ensues and I fill it. "My father would rather I do anything else. I've had to fight him my whole life to get where I am." Catching sight of his raised brows, I unfurl my own. Shaking my head at myself, I get back on topic. "Talking to the Chief about you was unavoidable. Believe me, I would have gladly dodged it, if I could have."

His eyebrows lower slightly before his expression becomes serious again. "Owen MacGregor isn't exactly the kind of contact I need," Hayes says, sweeping a hand through his hair again. He takes a steadying breath. "The Chief is under obligation to return any refugees to the City. I need to get my family away from here, for good."

Staring at him, I attempt to process his words. Maybe I should have seen this coming. He wants to escape the City.

I wouldn't have thought an Enforcer would ever want to leave, they live high on the hog and it's their job to stop all the other rats from jumping ship. Citizens must stay in the City. If they leave, they and their families will be punished upon return. And they always return. There is nowhere to go. The only place within reach that holds the necessities of life, is the Valley, and the Dalton Chief must return all defectors or pay the price with Dalton lives.

Better them than us.

Things are more settled than they used to be. Years of conditioning have seen to it that Citizens behave exactly as the Director dictates. He wants them to stay put and do their jobs to keep the City running. Controlled by the fear of being cut off, beaten or killed outright, they stay and work. Only those in the upper echelons of the hierarchy (the soldiers) are allowed to visit with the train. They have the most to lose. Luther Derrick knows they'll return and help keep his project alive. Coercion is the way of life. So ingrained is the fear, that the Valley hasn't had to turn anyone away in two generations.

Wondering what kind of trouble Hayes' family must be in, I start to think I'm out of my league in offering any assistance in exchange for information. I'm certainly not helping troublesome Citizens hide out in the Valley, not that I could sneak them in or keep them hidden anyway. I'll have enough trouble trying to get Patrick in unseen when I steal him out from under Derrick's nose.

"So you want to smuggle your family out of here and into the Valley? You don't think the Chief would notice a few new faces? He knows everyone in the Valley. Intimately. We all do. If you're seeking anonymity, it doesn't exist there." Squinting at his disappointed face, I try to fathom what he's asking. "Why would you want to leave the City? Seems to me that you'd have it made, a high-ranking officer such as yourself."

Hayes scans the world below with sharp eyes.

"Things aren't always as they seem."

I scoff. "No shit!" The look on his face makes me wish I'd stayed quiet. "Sorry. Go on."

Hayes pushes off the wall and completes another circuit of the roof. I can't make up my mind if he's paranoid about being caught with me, or if he's pacing to let off steam. It soon becomes clear he's building up to say something difficult to share. The truth. Eventually he comes to a stop next to me, reminding me how tall he is. Meeting my eyes, he holds them with his own.

"The City is an awful place," he says. "For everybody. If we were allowed to leave, we would." Sinking to a crouch, he makes me the tall one. "It needs to change. I'd like to help bring about that change, but my hands are tied. As long as there are people I care about in the City, I can't do a thing without them paying the price. I need them out."

"Oh."

Pitifully, that is all I can say. I hadn't expected him to have integrity. Having assumed he wanted to escape too, I hadn't thought he'd have aspirations that aligned so readily with my own. Not for the first time, I find my usual beliefs challenged by this man. He is not a typical Citizen.

"Oh," he echoes, straightening back up and stretching his long legs. Watching me a minute, his forehead creases and he snorts quietly, looking away. "You thought I wanted to run. Does it surprise you that much, that my motives aren't completely selfish?"

"It surprises me more that your motives are similar to my own," I confess. "I've been looking for a way to change the system since I became aware of its existence."

"Is that right?" he asks after a pause. "What about you, then?"

"What about me?"

"How do I know I can trust you?"

"Because I'm very trustworthy?" I suggest lightly.

Hayes laughs quietly and I risk a small smile.

"You do as you please despite direct orders to the contrary. Unreliable, no? Seems to me, you're a rule breaker."

"Seems to me that you're looking for someone who breaks rules," I counter without pause.

"You're a thief," he says, his eyes smiling. "Not the most honorable profession."

"Maybe, maybe not. Ever heard of Robin Hood?" I ask, trying to think of a reasonable argument. Laughing again, he looks at me sideways.

"Are you honestly comparing yourself to Robin Hood?"

"I'm probably not quite as good with a bow," I admit quietly. Raising my eyes from my feet, I shrug. "I'm just suggesting that a thief can be honorable. It depends on the intent."

Trying to convince an Enforcer that I will be harmless is surreal. Their role is to harm, not mine. Hayes is still smiling at my Robin Hood reference. His kind eyes are creased in the corners in an authentic smile; not menacing or cruel, but natural and warm. Inviting even.

Stretching, he turns to display his physique and traps me with those eyes. "Intentions huh? And what *do* you intend to do with me, Rori?"

Again I feel my cheeks burn beneath my camouflage. My pulse soars. Our interactions suddenly seem a lot more dangerous. For all the wrong reasons.

I should leave.

Now.

"At this stage, I think our intentions align. We agree the City needs to change. You need a Valley contact, I need reliable City information. Sounds a fair trade. We'll work out details another time," I say in a rush, swiping through any of my footprints as I retreat to the far wall.

Hayes follows me, watching with interest.

"You OK?" he asks, his voice uncertain. "I didn't mean to scare you off."

"You didn't." I reply, probably too quickly. "The deal is on. I just need to be home before sunrise."

Hayes looks out into the darkness, his forehead crinkling. "How do you plan to do that? Fly?"

"Something like that," I say casually as I scan the dust for any other trace of my presence.

"Telling me you can fly doesn't instill my faith in you as a trusted ally," he says. "Seems dishonest."

Looking up, I can see he's trying to hold a straight face.

"Maybe I didn't mean it literally," I lie, smearing a print I just made and looking back at him. "What? Why are you looking at me like that?"

He gives a dismissive shake of his head. "It's just hard to know if you're serious with that stuff on your face," he says, yawning.

Momentarily stunned, I think how best to recover. "You can trust me. *I'm* not a Citizen. You're the ones with the power, remember? We might have a good spot for hiding in, but we can't make much trouble without a shit-storm hitting us."

"You think *I* have the power in this?" He gestures back and forth between us. "Whatever this is?"

"Of course you do. The Chief knows about your deeds,

but can't rat you out without implicating himself for having knowledge of Dalton intrusion into the City. You on the other hand could make him quite uncomfortable in front of the Ambassador on Train Day." Pausing a moment as he stares at me, I cross my fingers behind my back, hoping I've made the right call. "Will you?" I ask, afraid of what the answer might be.

"Will I what? Try to expose the Chief?" he asks, shocked. When he sees I'm waiting for an answer, his hand travels through his hair again. "No." He looks me in the eye. "You can trust me too. If anything, I need the man to like me. Probably can't do much without his support apparently," Hayes says, beginning to look more concerned.

"Guess we'll have to work on that then," I say, about to leap up on the wall.

"You hold sway with the Chief?" Hayes asks, staying me with a gentle hand. Surprised at my lack of repulsion, I note that recoiling from his touch is far from my mind.

"Not a lot of sway," I reply truthfully, looking at his hand on my shoulder. "But I can be quite convincing when I need to be."

Smiling slightly, he drops his hand and takes a step back. "I'm beginning to see that."

"You haven't seen anything yet," I say, smiling back. "Get some sleep Hayes. No-one else is coming tonight." Before he can say another word, I hop onto the wall and jump across the alley to the next building, rolling as I land. Returning to the alley-side ledge, I give him a quick wave before using both buildings to lower myself back down.

Two streets down, I slip through a hidden access into the old rail tunnels. There are no underground tracks anymore. They ripped them up and re-laid them in the direction of the Valley, leaving these tunnels plugged with debris to keep people in the City. Replacing the same rubble I move each time I pass through the blockades, I make it look as if I've never been there. Making my way under the City border, I travel through the old tunnels to the site of the collapsed station out in the wastelands. Taking my maglev board from its thigh pocket, I put my thin shoes in its place and seal the pocket up again.

Cautiously, I check the surface. No patrols. Raising my head a little higher, I catch some movement in the light at the City border hut. They'll be heading in at this time; back again in an hour. I'll be long gone by then. Keeping low, I dash to the tracks, taking little time to ready my board and fly home.

TRAIN DAY

Pulling on my lightest top and a pair of old shorts, I prepare myself for stinking, hot work when the train arrives. My trainer, Ari, had suggested I use it as a workout, and had gone easy on me during the week. I'd put any extra time to good use by helping in the gardens, returning my parachute to the box, collecting Mickey and of course, having a secret rendezvous or two with a remarkable Citizen.

A smile creeps onto my lips as I think of my meetings with Hayes. Unable to decide if my smile is because I feel one step closer to getting Patrick home or if Hayes himself is the cause, I try to put them both out of my mind. There will be plenty of time to think while I'm shoveling, and I'll need the distraction then. It'll take serious thought to decide how to handle the Hayes situation without getting on Da's naughty list permanently. Secrecy seems the obvious choice, but has its disadvantages.

My smile leaves, but the thoughts and the fluttering sensation in my gut remain. Anxiety or confusion? It's either about how Hayes makes me feel, or how he makes me think. Dangerous ideas about rescuing Patrick are escalating in frequency and my childhood dreams of raising a rebellion to overthrow the City have returned with a vengeance since meeting him too.

"Ugh. Enough."

Shivering, I pull a cardigan on and hunt for a kerchief to cover my face from the stench that will accompany today's workout. I know from experience that the manure is always pretty ripe, having encountered shit patrol as a punishment for previous behavior unbecoming of the Chief's daughter. Finding a threadbare scarf that should filter the smell without overheating me, I drape it around my neck and search the drawer again for my thick socks. I'll have to wear my farm boots today.

In the bathroom, I scrub my teeth and check my shabby, mismatched outfit in the mirror and decide that I could live without its components, should they need to be destroyed at the end of my service to the shit patrol. Splashing water on my face, I let it drip as I attempt to tidy my hair. Tying it up high, I plait it to the end and twist it up securing it in a bun, wondering all the while how I'll manage to grab a secret word with Hayes.

The face in the mirror looks a little too enthusiastic for shit patrol. *Well, Da did tell me to love it.* Rolling my eyes at myself, I splash more water on my face and try to even out my features. The blank expression is fleeting. I lick the water from my smiling lips, thinking of shirtless Hayes and the afternoon sun winking at me from his glistening muscles. My reflection rolls her eyes again and turns her back on me as I leave the bathroom.

The house is a-buzz with plans for Train Day. The discussions around me range from Da's order of business, to what food Rae is planning to take to the Gathering. The kids are always excited to watch the train come in as it levitates above the tracks. They're talking of what they can leave on the tracks to be squashed by the train when it powers down to rest.

"Stay away from that damn train you lot, or *you'll* be what's squashed," Rae warns, her implication purposely unclear as to whether it would be her or the train that would do the squashing.

"Yes Mama," comes a chorus of disappointment.

There is a knock at the door and I get up to answer it. Frankie stands outside in an outfit not that dissimilar to mine.

"Ready?" she asks, an exaggerated grin plastered across her face.

I laugh. "What do you mean?"

"I'm helping you sort your shit out," she replies before poking her head in the door and acknowledging the room, "Morning everyone."

Numerous friendly responses surround me as I walk my bowl to the sink to rinse it.

"What do you mean?" I ask again, more seriously.

"Well, it seems the Valley is short on miscreants this month - besides you and that Riley kid, that is. I know that's a good thing, but not when it comes to shoveling shit. I'm rostered on."

"Really?" I ask, wondering if Da has done that purposely. It would be typical of him to have someone watching me if he thinks I'll break his rules and talk to an Enforcer. I can't say his suspicions aren't warranted. "Well Frankie, I'm sad for you, but glad of the company. I was wondering why you looked as fashionably attired as me."

"Don't flatter yourself. Your outfit will look better *after* it's covered in shit. Now c'mon, I want the best shovel." Rumbling with amusement, she disappears out the door. I follow her with more laughter trailing from the crowd behind me.

We walk to the platform in silence, both soaking up the morning sun and the bustling life of the village. The packed earth road is always busy on the morning of Train Day. People are making their way to work in the fields or taking packed supplies to the platform to be loaded. Others move about their homes, hiding certain possessions. People are dressed in their work clothes, maintaining the illusion of poverty and insignificance. The air smells wholesome, like wood smoke, trees and fresh baking, but that will be replaced soon by something less appealing.

Walking through the village, we head toward the cliff face, where the tunnel breaks into the Valley. The platform comes into view. It's a series of split logs strapped together and raised slightly off the ground. Beginning at the storehouse, it stretches alongside the tracks to the tunnel, with the last log butting up against the base of the cliff. Next to the platform, at that far end and using the rock wall to help contain it, is a mountain of shit.

The mountain consists of manure from every type of animal farmed in the valley. On this bright but cool autumn morning, twists of steam are winding into the air above the pile, giving a convincing impression of stink lines. My nose wrinkles and I steal a glance at Frankie. She has clearly made the same observation; her face has screwed itself into a similar expression. Sighing, we walk on.

Some of the manure has started to rot, but most will continue to do so after it is shipped to the City. They don't get an adequate supply from the small numbers of chickens and rabbits they farm there - which is still more than they had before they met us. The Citizens had eaten every animal they could find in the before time, even the rats. Shuddering at the thought of being that hungry, I look at the mountain before me.

By sharing the animal waste, we are in fact encouraging the Citizens to supply themselves. They need the manure to replenish the soil in their indoor gardens, following their repetitive cropping. They still can't use the soil in the areas around the City, where the chemical concentrations are highest.

Frankie and I head to the small tool shed to claim our shovels. Riley is already there and I wonder what he's done this time. He's not really a bad kid, just gets himself in the wrong place at the wrong time too frequently. With his mother dead and a Dad like his, I reckon I'd spend as little time at home as possible too. Riley's father is a well-known ass, being fond of the drink and using his fists. It's highly likely that *he* is busy on some other Chief-directed punitive task right now.

I can sympathize with Riley. He doesn't have a great role model, and most of the town has already tarred him with the same brush as his dad. He's nearly twelve, and appears to have resigned himself to a life of nuisance. I'll be getting to know him better soon. Maybe I can find out what he's interested in and find him a mentor to keep him busy and out of trouble. Someone will be willing to help.

I give him a friendly wave. "Hey Riley. You ready to get this shit underway? Frankie and I will need your expertise to truly get the most out of the experience. You had a good breakfast?" Looking him over, it seems unlikely he's eaten this week. He is short for his age, thin and weedy-looking.

"Breakfast is for chumps." Leaning on his shovel, he gives me a leveling look. His hollow cheeks emphasize his set jaw.

"You can't do a hard day's labor on an empty stomach, Riley. Wait here," I say, walking to the storehouse before he can argue.

After a brief haggle with Bernie, the supply manager, I return to Riley and pull the shovel out of his hands, nearly causing him to topple over. He regains his balance and I hand him a small loaf of bread, a chunk of cheese and an apple.

"Go and eat." I point him over to a bench. "I'm not going to pull you out of the shit cart when you pass out and fall into it."

He stares at me a while, apparently trying to make up his mind about challenging me, but decides against it. Dragging himself over to the bench he proceeds to tear ravenously into the bread with his teeth. I will definitely make it a priority to find him some help.

Frankie is looking at me like she's enjoying a private joke. I frown at her.

"What are you looking at?"

"You," she says, smiling.

"What about me?"

"You're very sweet under that barbed exterior. All gooey on the inside, aren't you Rori?" She playfully pokes my side.

"I'll make you gooey on the inside," I mutter. She raises an eyebrow at me. Flinging a dismissive hand at her, I brush past and grab a shovel, heading to the shit. The train will be here any minute, and the sooner we start, the sooner we can finish.

The big tunnel door has been opened to reveal the dark mouth that allows the train to pass through the belly of the rock. A small light glints from the darkness. It's the signal that the engine is arriving, hauling its hungry carriages.

The train glides in silently, floating on air. It settles onto the track as a series of clicks indicate the electro-magnets shutting off. We have our scarves around our faces; ready. The door of the front carriage opens and eight soldiers walk out. I can tell by their size, the way they are dressed and how they move that there are four Enforcers and four Lackeys. Their backs are to us, but I recognize two of the Enforcers. Hayes and Reg.

Another man hops off behind them. Smaller and dressed differently from the soldiers, the train engineer has the same entitled swagger. The Ambassador does not come off the train, and I watch as the Enforcers talk with Bernie. Dipping into the bunk-rooms, they discard their gear. Hayes and Reg move off toward the Village and Bernie begins ordering his workers to start stocking the train. The other soldiers spread themselves along the platform to supervise the loading with dominating postures and matching expressions. The Ambassador has not come today. Frowning, I turn to the train.

Frankie opens the double doors of the last carriage. The shit carriage. The stink of stale crap smacks us in the face. Breathing through the scarf with my mouth, I step in and pull out the first cart, wheeling it closer to the manure pile. We get to work and lose ourselves in thought as we fill the huge crate.

With one cart full, we have worked an hour and are damp with perspiration. I head into the train to get the next cart, while the others hold their mouths under the tap of the raised-barrel, gulping water. Its stand is there purposely to provide refreshment after the thirsty work. I rearrange the big crates and roll another empty one out of the train before Frankie and Riley help me push the full one back in.

It takes all three of us to shift the resisting hulk and I can't help thinking how easy it would be to use magnetic levitation for this too. Da would never approve of that though. For one thing, it would lessen the punishment. For another, it would let the Citizens know that we use advanced technology. It would be one more thing they'd exploit or use against us. Best to keep quiet and push the shit manually.

There are five more huge carts to fill. Luckily the soldiers don't come down to the end of the platform much, preferring to stay beyond the stench. It's nice to be spared their involvement. Shit patrol would be a much worse sentence if you had soldiers standing over you while you did it.

After we break for lunch, we get to work filling the last two carts. We have eased into a steady pace, supporting each other. Riley turns out to be a hard worker, and is pretty funny too. We jolly each other along as we scoop and dump and the mountain gets noticeably smaller. Not all of it will go this trip, and more will be added to the pile before the train comes again. With deep chagrin, I think about the next round of shit patrol. My muscles are fatigued, my back aches and my clothes are soaked with sweat. To top it off, I can't remember what fresh air smells like, and a couple of soldiers are on their way down to laugh at us. *Capital punishment, Chief. Just great.*

AN INVITATION

Luther Derrick had insisted Hayes be intentionally late to meet with the Chief. 'Let him stew,' he'd said. Instructed to fill in time by stalking through the village with Reg, he was meant to conduct a search for the intruders whilst menacing the townsfolk. Hayes had no desire to do any such thing, and once Reg was out of sight, he strolled along the lanes, taking in the enviable sights and sounds of the small township.

Most of the Daltons were at the platform loading or out in the fields working. Hayes wandered along next to the fields that skirted the village, searching for any sign of the girl he couldn't get out of his head. Hoping to catch a glimpse of her hair in the sun, he scanned the heads as they bent over their crops, but saw nothing that made his heart race.

Any faces that rose to meet his quickly turned away, but not fast enough to hide the fear in their eyes. It was hard to be considered a monster and be unable to deny it, but that was the way of things. By turning their backs, the Daltons could pretend he wasn't there. That was how they lived; avoiding confrontation and delivering the demanded price of peace. Disappointed, Hayes plodded back to the village, stopping by the platform for a snack before heading to the Chief's house. He'd be working through lunch.

Knocking on the MacGregor door, he wiped his boots on the mat in preparation for entry. With Liam Malcolm, the Ambassador, taken ill, Hayes would be conducting business on his own today. He was looking forward to the opportunity to prove himself and was nervously excited about his new found autonomy, though the whole experience was somewhat tainted by his tardiness. Smoothing his hair down, he tried to project an orderly image.

Aiden MacGregor opened the door and smiled warmly at him.

"Mr. Hayes. No Mr. Malcolm today?" he asked, looking over Hayes' shoulder expectantly.

"I'm afraid the Ambassador is unavailable today, though he will be sufficiently recovered in a few days, I'm told. May I come in?" Hayes had been polishing his manners on the ride out to the Valley, hoping for an even interaction with the esteemed Dalton Chief.

"Of course." Aiden waved him in. "Father has been waiting in his study. Do let the Ambassador know that we wish him a swift recovery."

Hayes considered the Chief's son a while and decided he was sincere.

"Indeed. Thank you." Losing a bit of respect for the man, Hayes moved past Aiden and down the hall. The study was a warm room, but gave you the distinct impression that you should not feel too comfortable there. The walls were lined with books and maps of the Valley and its surrounds. It smelt dauntingly of knowledge. Hayes had often sat in the chair by the door, observing Liam's manner in business with the Chief.

The study door was open and Owen MacGregor sat at his desk reviewing a ledger and scratching notes on the paper in front of him. He didn't look up at the approaching footsteps. Hayes knocked on the open door and waited. Owen Mac raised his eyes from his paperwork and fixed Hayes with a measured gaze over his reading glasses. Carefully removing the glasses, he laid them on the paper, motioning Hayes toward the seat opposite. He stood then, exhibiting his full height and hovering a moment to accentuate it before closing the door and sitting back down to inspect Hayes.

"Young Morrison. Going solo today, I see."

"Yes Sir." Hayes affirmed, feeling as patronized as he was sure the man had intended by referring to him in such a way. "Mr. Malcolm sends his regards, but is regretfully unwell at present."

"I see." The Chief studied him again, a thoughtful look on his face. "Let's get down to business then. Here is the inventory list for this shipment," he said, handing over his piles of documentation. "These are our requests for the next time. Did you bring your requisition sheets?"

"Of course." Hayes exchanged the Chief's papers with Derrick's approved order for the next Train Day, wary that the Chief had made no mention of his late arrival. As Owen Mac put his glasses back on and ignored him completely, Hayes felt an overwhelming urge to express his regret.

"Apologies for being late, Sir."

"Really?" The Chief eyeballed him, his tone disbelieving. "It's not like it was your choice," he said, looking back to his papers.

More uncomfortable silence. Hayes tried not to sigh. He'd wanted to impress the Chief, hoping to eventually gain the man's trust, but Derrick's uncanny ability to foil such things without even intending to, was more than irritating. The Chief clearly regarded him as Derrick's puppet; which technically, he was. Feeling unable to salvage any shred of respect that the Chief might have for him, Hayes turned his mind back to business.

"When do you think this order can be ready for

retrieval? The Director wishes to be well stocked before the snows complicate travel on the tracks."

"Well stocked?" The Chief flipped through the pages gruffly. "There's nearly twice the expected amount requested here, even taking winter into consideration." He made a few quick calculations on his paper. "If Derrick wants all this, it will be another month. I could arrange most of it in three weeks, if he's feeling precious about it."

"I couldn't say precisely how the Director is feeling about it, but I'm sure he will want as much as can be managed as quickly as possible," Hayes said carefully.

Owen Mac, chuckled to himself. "Well put."

Hayes blushed a little, feeling his words may have betrayed some of his own feeling. He kept his eyes on the papers to avoid MacGregor's probing stare.

"Fine. Train Day again in three weeks. We should be able to get another load through following that too. Wouldn't want a little snow to bring an end to your town," he said, with just a touch of menace. Hayes kept quiet. He could hardly blame the man for being angry. The City held his son and his people worked endlessly to fill stores that were pillaged on a regular basis. It was bound to generate feelings of great displeasure.

"I assume some of the earlier provisions have been set aside for the winter?" the Chief continued, setting his glasses on the papers and rubbing his eyes.

"I can assure you, the stockpiling has begun," Hayes said evenly.

Owen Macs probing was uncharacteristic. During most exchanges with the Ambassador, strict boundaries were adhered to. Hayes sensed the man was testing him, to see if he could be a weakness to the regime. Indeed, he *was* a weakness to the regime. He was going to make the regime crumble if it was the last thing he did. But he would not show that 'weakness' yet. Not if it could be used against him. Waiting to see where the Chief was headed was the safest course. Hayes knew the rules. The Chief could easily rat him out to Derrick and have him tried as a City defector.

"Good. On my list there is something extra this time. I need more wiring. For the winter gardens. We run them through the soil to keep it warm enough to grow crops. With the rate Derrick's City is expanding, we've had to extend our season artificially to grow enough food." He watched Hayes expectantly.

Feeling scrutinized again, Hayes answered in a defensive but reasonable manner.

"I'm sure that if you have adequately explained the items on your list in writing, and said items are required to improve provision for our City, the Director will give them due consideration. I am sure you have thoroughly prepared such documentation as would be required Sir, have you not?"

"Of course." Looking mildly impressed, the Chief continued to examine Hayes through wizened gray eyes. After an uncomfortable silence, he pulled an envelope out from under his ledger.

"I have another item of correspondence." He passed the letter across the desk. "For my son. How is he Mr. Hayes?"

Hayes noted MacGregor's respectful use of his name and the amendment had him momentarily stunned. Had he made enough of an impression, or was MacGregor trying to appease him to obtain more knowledge? Hayes was unsure, but he would inform the concerned father regardless.

"Patrick continues to deteriorate. He is weaker than previously, though remains reasonably stable at this stage," Hayes reported solemnly.

"He is in no pain," he added in afterthought.

"Thank you."

A long silence followed and Hayes waited patiently for Owen Mac to break it.

"I knew your father, you know."

This was not what Hayes had expected and his face must have shown it, because MacGregor smiled kindly at him and relaxed back into his chair, folding his hands in his lap. Hayes stared at him not knowing how to respond. Thankfully he didn't have to.

"He was a good man. An honorable man." Owen Mac didn't break eye contact. "He was a good friend to my brother, Alex. They killed *him* too." Again they sat in silence, pondering the words left unspoken. Ethan Hayes and the hostage, Alex MacGregor, had been in cahoots. Eventually it was Owen again that broke the silence.

"I have heard of your recent activity in the City."

"I have many activities in the City, but I take your meaning," Hayes countered, knowing all too well the Chief was talking about his interactions with Rori. "What is your point?"

"I want to know if you, Morrison Hayes, are a *good* man, as was your father before you."

A loaded question, thought Hayes. He hadn't planned on openly admitting to the Dalton Chief that he was as keen on rebellion as his father had clearly been. However something about MacGregor's tone, when he had talked of his brother, had suggested to Hayes a possible ally sat across from him. Owen MacGregor would be a powerful and very necessary ally. Hayes chose his words carefully.

"It is difficult to say such things aloud. I am trying very hard to be a *good* man, but find myself challenged in the City. It is an ongoing process. I am myself, in search of other *good* people, but it is complicated in a place where *good* is discouraged." With a steadying breath, he took a risk.

"It would of course be helpful to have *other* good friends?"

MacGregor leaned forward, his elbows on the desk with hands laced together under his nose. He gave Hayes a long, hard stare, his face unreadable.

"The Valley is *always* a friendly place. But the level of

that friendliness is dependent on certain agreements between such friends."

"Do you care to share those agreements?" asked Hayes, trying his best not to seem too eager.

"Many are yet to be determined, this friendship being in its infancy," MacGregor replied. "However, there is one fundamental condition."

"Yes?"

"Leave her out of it."

The silence washed over them again. Hayes knew who he meant. Surprised by the Chief's intensity regarding Rori, he thought it best to speak honestly and inquire further.

"I find myself already friends with her. Is that a problem?"

"A big one. I suggest you sensibly trade one, very small friend for a larger, more powerful one - with access to many."

Hayes wanted to clear his head. He had a powerful urge to run hard in order to drain the nervous tension from his system. Overwhelmed by the potential this meeting had invited, and the fear of screwing it up, Hayes needed time to think.

"I'm sure you have other things to consider, as do I. May I suggest we sleep on it and reconvene tomorrow before I leave?"

"That might be wise. Will you be staying in the Ambassador's quarters in his absence or in the platform bunk-room, with your men?"

"I hadn't thought," Hayes replied, pausing to consider it. "The Ambassador's quarters would provide peace for deliberation. Yes, I believe I will stay there." Hayes had been to the small homely cottage in question, but had never stayed there himself. At the thought of it, he realized he was looking forward to its sanctuary.

"One more thing, Mr. MacGregor, if I may?"

"What is it?" asked the Chief carefully.

"I think better when I run. I know the agreement is for

us to remain in the village, but if you would permit me, I would appreciate wide open space. I am also meant to be conducting a believable search for a recent intruder and her fictitious companion. Access to a wider investigatory range would look good to my colleagues."

"I will allow it. A show of good faith." Owen Mac stroked his golden whiskers. "Just you. None of those other thugs," he said distastefully. "Stick to the river tracks. I'll not have you disturb the stock or frighten my people. Understood?"

"Yes Sir. Thank you." Hayes pushed back his chair and nodded respectfully at Owen Mac. "Shall we say tomorrow, ten o'clock?"

"Ten o'clock," the Chief confirmed. Shaking hands, they walked back through the house to the front door.

The door was already open, and Aiden's wife Rae was handing a pile of clothes to a tall, sturdily-built woman. She was dressed in an odd assortment of clothes and Hayes thought it kind that Rae was providing her with new attire. He turned back to Owen Mac to farewell him, but the Chief's relaxed expression had changed to one of concern.

"What's happened, Frankie?"

The tough looking woman eyed Hayes and returned her gaze to the Chief.

"She's OK, just had a little trouble with a couple of soldiers at the platform." She looked disapprovingly back to Hayes, giving him a clear idea of her opinion of his associates.

"What happened?" MacGregor asked again.

"Classic R-... regular stuff. There was an incident. One of the soldiers was harassing a young girl and she accidentally dropped the box of apples she was carrying." Frankie paused, but continued as the Chief waved her on. "The soldier pushed her around, yelling at her that if she thought she could send bruised apples to the City, then maybe she needed some bruises herself. Next thing I know, our little friend drops her shovel, grabs one of the fallen apples and scones him in the head with it, telling him the bruised apples work perfectly well, but we'd be happy to arrange an extra box of shit as replacement and… well. You know how she is. I tried to stop her, but…" Frankie trailed off.

"But she did it anyway. Yes, I know how she is." MacGregor sighed, rubbing his forehead, as if trying to erase the lines of worry there.

"How bad?" he asked.

"You won't want her in the house. I just came for some clothes and soap. A comb might be good too." Frankie grimaced.

Hearing that, Rae winced too. "That bad?" She went back into the house, presumably to find a comb.

"I'll have a word with my men, but if they were provoked as you say, their reactions would be understandable," Hayes said in vague sympathy, responsible for the actions of his men. They were encouraged to intimidate and undermine the Daltons, but were advised to be strictly hands off unless ordered by an Enforcer, who would usually have been directed by Luther Derrick. This incident was not pre-approved, but they were generally expected to stifle any act of Dalton defiance.

"If you'll excuse me now. I'll see you tomorrow Chief MacGregor. Good day." Hayes walked through the yard, hoping his men hadn't ruined his chances for him. Clearly they had thrown someone in the shit pile. A girl who lived at the Chief's house. Hayes hoped it wasn't one of his daughters. Please, be a maid, he thought.

He suspected Reg's involvement, but Frankie had said soldiers on the platform. Reg had been intent on snooping about the village, in hopes of spotting the City intruders. Hayes hoped he had stuck to his plan.

***

After speaking with his men at the bunk-room, he sent them back to the platform and took his gear to the Ambassador's cottage. Having packed no running gear, Hayes changed into his sleeping shorts and a t-shirt and took off his boots, opting for bare feet. The track was packed dirt and would be forgiving. Closing the door behind him, he sprinted toward the river, his thoughts racing with him.

Running until he had to stop for breath, Hayes looked about. Everything was lush and peaceful. He sucked in fresh air and felt himself slowly begin to calm. Ahead of him, the track divided. One track led further along the river and the other branch led across a bridge and along the other side. He jogged over the bridge, lost in thought.

It was a pleasant place. Unlike the City, there were many trees here. They crowded around, filtering the sun and waving their autumn foliage seductively at him. Relaxed by the movement of the leaves, he followed the willows along the riverbank until a small, grainy beach opened up. Watching his footing, he stepped into the shallows and watched the tips of the weeping branches move toward him with the breeze and the river current. Moving under the willow, he sat on the bank, dangling his feet in the cool water.

The water was soothing as it swirled past his ankles. He heard a small splash and looked up, but saw barely a ripple on the surface. There was an empty platform way out in the water that must have been anchored to the bottom, because it didn't move downriver with the current. Probably a fish, he thought, knowing the Daltons farmed trout and salmon in their untainted stretch of the river. Watching the vacant water surface a while before looking back to his feet, he thought about how his life was about to change. With the Valley people supporting him, he might just have a shot at success.

He had known he would need the Chief's help to shelter people in the Valley at some stage, but he hadn't thought he'd have a chance to talk with the Chief this soon, let alone have the Chief suggest an alliance. A big friend with access to many. To be able to talk with someone experienced and to plan properly hadn't been an option until now, and the fact that some of the Daltons would maybe join his cause? - If it came to that. He couldn't believe his luck.

Hayes wondered what Owen Mac's other conditions might be, and why he wanted Rori out of it so badly. She had some traits Hayes would consider beneficial to have in uncertain times. She was brave and intelligent, though obviously young. Maybe that was it? More likely it was that she didn't follow rules and the Chief couldn't rely on her, he thought.

As if his thoughts had materialized, Rori appeared. Pulling herself onto the pontoon easily and sitting with her back to him. He froze, unable to even close his eyes. He hadn't noticed the stones on the platform earlier, but she picked one up and scrubbed her skin pink with it. Perhaps it was pumice. She furiously scoured her whole body. A woman's body, Hayes noted. She wore only a halter and underpants, giving him ample to appreciate.

When finished with it, she threw the stone an anger-fueled distance downriver. Hayes wondered why she might be upset and looked around for clues. It hit him with unexpected impact when he saw a bundle of clothes nestled neatly into the long grass on the other side of the small shore. It was the same bundle that he had seen Rae give the woman at the MacGregor house.

Rori was the feisty girl who'd stood up to the soldier and been dragged through crap for her efforts. It made sense as soon as the thought occurred to him. He had been aware of her abundance of spirit since the first time they'd met and she'd broken his nose.

Hayes watched her with even more interest. Grabbing the second stone, she began rubbing it over herself. No, it was soap. She worked it into a lather over her body and up through her hair. Hayes found himself aroused by the sight and felt instantly ashamed at his voyeuristic behavior. Wishing he'd left or called out when he'd first seen her, he cursed himself, knowing it was too late to act now without shame. Not wanting to draw attention to his invasion of her privacy, he remained still, letting the trailing willow obscure his presence until he could leave unnoticed.

Rising to her feet, Rori leapt beautifully off the platform. The only evidence of her entry to the water were the bubbles left on the surface to float downstream. While she was under, Hayes stood up and hurried back onto the track before she could surface.

"Where are you going Hayes?"

He cringed.

Caught.

Turning slowly, he walked back to the beach to face her. Rori swam toward him and walked up the gritty bank, giving him an eyeful of her athletic, dripping physique. Tossing down the soap, she squeezed her hair, keeping her eyes on him. Taking a chamois from her pile of belongings, she proceeded to dry herself, raising an eyebrow expectantly.

Hayes swallowed. She was stunning. Her skin was still pink from her vigorous cleaning and those piercing eyes awaited his next move. He had no move. His cheeks burned with guilt.

"Turn around," she ordered. He did so immediately, relieved to hide from her eyes. Waiting patiently, he scolded himself again for not realizing she'd been there and for staying quiet too long.

"OK. Turn back around."

Hayes did as he was told and found her looking at him again, but fully clothed. Thank goodness, he thought. She braided her long hair down one side and tied it. The plait was almost black from the water and it still dripped slowly at the end. She crossed her arms over her chest and shivered.

"Shall we sit in the sun? You can tell me what you were running away from."

He opened his mouth to agree, then closed it in sudden realization.

"You knew I was there?"

"I did. But you looked deep in thought, so I left you to it." Smiling sweetly, she picked up her gear and waded back into the shallows. She walked in the water along the bank until climbing up into a sunny spot in the long grass.

"No tracks in the grass this way," she said over her shoulder. Following her lead, Hayes made the same trip into the sunlight.

"You knew I was there, and you… with your…" He gestured up and down her body, unable to articulate all he'd witnessed.

"Oh, did you find that distracting? Sorry."

"Very distracting." Clearing his throat, he shuffled his feet uncomfortably.

"Well it wasn't all for your benefit." She stepped closer to him. "Tell me, how do I smell?"

She had a naturally authoritative manner that Hayes felt compelled to obey. Bending his head to her, he inhaled.

"You smell like summer. Like flowers," he breathed, his voice catching a little. Clearing his throat again, he stood tall. He could escape her eyes with his height.

"Better than shit then. Good. Sit down and tell me why you were running. Your face looked like you'd been served a dose of MacGregor."

He looked at her appraisingly and did as he was told, the long grass flattening into a thin cushion beneath him.

"How did you know?"

"You had that look people have when leaving the MacGregor house. Like you had to swallow something unusual, but realized it was for the best."

Hayes laughed. "That's an interesting observation. And very close to the experience."

"You have a nice laugh," she said, almost shyly.

"Thanks, it doesn't usually come out like that."

"That's a shame."

Moving about restlessly, she looked around, as though someone might be watching. He hadn't seen anyone on his run and was about to tell her, when she yanked on his arm and pulled him down into the grass. Hearing the footfalls of someone running, Hayes sunk even lower into the grass. He hadn't meant to find Rori out here, and suddenly remembered that he was meant to be staying away from her, for more reasons now than ever. He'd have to tell her. Disappointed at the thought, he wondered how she'd respond to the news.

Although they hadn't known each other long, he was genuinely going to miss not seeing her. Rori was easy to be around. She was funny and spunky and he could see that maybe MacGregor thought so too. Maybe that was why he wanted to keep her from harm. He wondered again what she did in the MacGregor household.

Hayes studied her, as she held herself poised in the long grass, listening. She didn't act like a maid. He didn't even know if people had servants in the Valley. Maybe she was deviant and required the highest form of supervision? Surely the Chief wouldn't harbor a notorious criminal under that same roof as his grandchildren. No. A thief she may be, but not villainous.

Who else could she be? She wasn't tall and blond like the MacGregors. His train of thought was derailed as she moved her body smoothly across him. Bracing herself with one hand on either side of his head, she raised her eyes above the grass, hunting. She stayed there frozen for what Hayes felt was an almost infinite time as he lay tensely beneath her, breathing into the wool of her sweater.

The footsteps had slowed to a stop. Hayes could hear the coarse sand crunching underfoot as someone walked about the small beach. The sound moved further away and turned back into dull thuds on packed earth, fading back to where they had come from.

"Someone coming to warn me there's a big bad Enforcer heading this way," she whispered down to him.

Rori lowered herself back down beside him. Realization hit him like a brick when she relaxed next to him, so close her breath tickled his cheek. Smiling, she looked sideways at him. Her smile dropped away when she saw his shocked expression.

"What?" she whispered.

"You're his daughter!" he hissed, not wanting to believe it.

Scooting away from him, she sat up again, looking out over the river. Hayes shivered, his body colder without hers beside it. He sat up too, but waited for her to speak, not knowing how to approach this new revelation. They sat in silence a long time. The sky began to dim into early evening.

"So?" she asked eventually, still not looking at him. "Does that change anything?"

He thought about it. It didn't change anything. Owen Mac would only be his ally if she stayed out of it; daughter or not.

"Not exactly," he replied slowly.

"Good," she said turning to him, her eyes shining. "Because I like you."

Taken aback by her forward approach, he stumbled with his words and instinct took over his speech.

"I like you too," he breathed before he could rein it in. Her face lit up, a small smile of achievement touching her lips. He couldn't let it last though. The stakes were too high. The priority was getting his family and his people to safety and he needed Owen MacGregor for that.

"But Rori, I can't."

"Can't what?"

"Like you. I can't see you. I have to make a deal with your father, and I can't unless I leave you out of it. I'm sorry."

"Urgh! I knew if he got to see you alone he'd find a

way to keep me grounded!" she fumed. After a moment's thought, her brows unfurled and she spoke again. "This deal. Is it what you want? He'll help you?"

"I think so. We haven't confirmed the details, but I think it's my best option. There's a lot riding on it."

"Your family?" Before he could answer, the concern on her face was replaced with something else. "You don't have multiple wives and children or anything, do you?"

"What? No! Not married, no kids, no multiple anything." He stared at her, stunned.

"Don't look so shocked at the question!" she said, laughing. "I know being with only one person at a time is unusual for a Citizen." She studied him again carefully before turning her attention to wringing water from the end of her braid. "Maybe I'm glad you're shocked. Makes you seem more honorable. Monogamy is important. To me anyway."

Hayes raised an eyebrow. "Are you trying to tell me *you're* married?"

"Hardly," she scoffed, looking at him with those inquisitive and beguiling eyes. "How old are you?"

"Twenty-five," he said in a neutral tone, continuing to answer, because he didn't know how to terminate the conversation and the relationship. Or didn't want to. Rori moved on regardless.

"When do you finalize your deal?" she asked, looking at her lap.

"Tomorrow morning." Hayes watched her face as she struggled to hide her disappointment. He felt how she looked, but it was for the best. "Look, it's getting late. The Gathering will be starting soon. I don't suppose you'll be going?"

"You suppose right," she said, irritation in her voice. "I always avoid them, so don't think it's on account of you."

He ignored the jab. "The empty chair?" Hayes had always been puzzled by the presence of the extra chair at the head table. He had assumed it was placed there to make the Citizens feel guilty that the youngest son was a hostage in the City. Now he realized it was the chair meant for her.

She shrugged. "I'm welcome if I behave, but I find it difficult to maintain a friendly and subservient persona sometimes," she said, smiling a little.

He smiled back. "So I've heard."

"We'd better go. I'm starving and if I don't make it home in time to claim my food, it'll be taken to the hall and you assholes will eat it all."

"Like that is it?"

She gave him a deeply serious look and leaned in close to his face, their noses almost touching.

"It's always been like that, Hayes," she said quietly. "Until now, maybe."

Closing the gap between them she kissed him gently on the lips.

"Bye," she whispered to his mouth.

Before Hayes could pull himself together and respond, she had leapt out of the grass, grabbed her things and was bounding down the river path. He sat bewildered in the grass, the soft touch of her kiss lingering on his lips as the light of day faded.

HELPING HAND

The kids have nearly finished their meals as Rae spies me sneaking in. She opens the oven door and retrieves a pre-loaded plate for me and pops it on to the table alongside the others, smiling at me sympathetically.

"Thanks Rae-Rae. For the clothes and soap too." I sit down and dig in, joining the kids in their 'yummy noises'. Since I began boycotting the Gatherings, I have become the official family babysitter for the event. I much prefer the company of my gorgeous nieces and nephews to the arrogant Citizen soldiers.

The past few years of being a Gopher in the City have made me aware that male citizens appear to have little care for children. In all honesty, I think they feel about the same towards women. Well, the opinions of women anyway. They do appear to enjoy ogling and getting 'hands-y' with young women. Yet another good reason to stay away from them.

My mouth full, I wave as the adults leave the house toting plates of food to the Great Hall with them. I smile back at the kids as they scrape their plates to get every last bite. The young girls all look fairly worn out, but the boys are a bit older and still fired up. Clearing the empty dishes from the table, I stack them on the bench, delegating the washing up to the boys, who at seven and nine years old, think this is a fun activity. *Suckers.*

I turn the bath on and round up the girls while it's running. Tilly and Bryn will share Hattie and Isla's beds tonight, which means Lena will likely share mine. She likes to stay over when the girls do, so that she is there when they wake up.

By the time we have everyone's nightclothes ready, the bath is good to go and I pile them all in. They splash about loving the crowded tub, soaped up and slithering around each other like the eels in the river when they get trapped in the shallows. Hating to break up the fun, but knowing it will excite them too much for sleep, I hustle them out of the bath and into their pajamas.

The boys are loudly declaring that they've finished the dishes. Pleased at the good timing, I tell the boys to jump in the bath as I'm dressing Isla. Snuggling the girls and their dollies into bed, I tell stories of fairies and magic. They're all asleep before I finish and I kiss each cherub on the cheek as I tuck them in snuggly and leave to hurry the boys along.

Judging by the noise coming from the bathroom, it will be a while before the boys will sleep. Knocking on the door, I warn them they had better leave the bathroom in a decent state and be out in the hall in two minutes, or else. Disconcerting giggles reverberate through the door, but are thankfully accompanied by the sucking sound as the plug's removed.

As they burst out of the bathroom, I'm ready for them with my fake menacing expression plastered on my face. I inspect their cleaning job as they stand at attention in the hall, arms crossed over chests and holding their breaths to suppress giggles.

"Impressive work boys," I say, legitimately pleased. "I made it around the tub without slipping once and for that I'm grateful. Now who is up for a whipping at cards before bed?"

They jump up and down and race to their room. We often play a few rounds sitting on the big bed they share. They are both bouncing on their knees atop the quilt as I arrive in their doorway with a growly look on. They stop, becoming frozen statues in odd positions. Laughing, I lunge at them, with my tickling fingers finding their ribs and working them until they are a tangled mass of heavy breathing.

Winning two games of Speed and conceding three games of Go Fish, I pack the cards safely back into their steel box and tuck the boys in. They prefer bedtime stories of adventure and monsters. They live in a world full of both. I don't like to scare them too much before bed, so I opt for a tame retelling of the time I was nearly spotted in the City library and had to escape through the ducting system.

"What were you in the library *for* Auntie Ro?" Evan asks, eyes wide.

"To try and borrow a book, Silly! What else do you do at a library?" We laugh together and I tuck them in. "G'night boys, see you in the morning." Turning their light off, I close the door. Checking the girls again, I head to the living room to park myself in front of the fire with a book, I'm looking forward to escaping into someone else's life for a while.

I sit down and put my feet up. My fatigued body eases as it reclines, grateful to stretch out after the day's shoveling. Maybe I'll give the book a miss and just rest my eyes a little. It's warm by the fire.

The big clock chimes nine and rouses me from my doze. My body begs to be stretched, aching from the odd position I've slept in. Hobbling to the fire, I stack wood on the embers, sleepily watching the flames grow to engulf them. Closing the fire door, I reach for the ceiling and back to the ground, lengthening my spine before I head to the stairs.

On the next level of the house, I peak in at the sleeping children. The girls are fast asleep, and I tuck Hattie's dangling arm back under the quilt. The boys' room is quiet and the lumps in the bed are still, but as I creep back out the door, Jack rustles up from the covers.

"Auntie Ro?" he whispers. I turn back and crouch next to the bed. The light from the hall spills into the room and I can see a look of worry on his tired little face.

"What's up Jacky-Boy? Can't sleep?" I stroke his hair soothing him back under the blankets. "What's on your mind, Ratbag?"

"I was just thinking," he says, checking my face to see if I'm really listening. I nod and he continues. "I don't want Evan to go to the City. I should go. I'm faster and stronger and braver. He should stay home, where Mama can look after him."

"Your Uncle Patrick's in the City remember? No-one else has to go." I wrap my arms around him and feel how upset he is through the tenseness of his body. Giving him a squeeze, I leave a protective arm draped over him.

"Where has this come from, Jack? Nobody is going anywhere."

"I don't know, I was just thinking about how you go to the City and come back all the time, but one day Evvy might have to go and not come home. I think it would be better if I went instead. I'm older. Plus, I wouldn't have to worry about him if I went, because I'd know he'd be safe at home."

"Well you're definitely brave and I know you're tough too, but you and Evvy are staying right here. No-one is taking you guys anywhere, I promise."

His eyes are shining with tears, but he doesn't let them fall. Blinking them back, he looks at me, unconvinced.

"What makes you so sure?" he sniffs softly.

"Because your Auntie Ro is older and tougher than you, and she will *never* let it happen. Got it?" I am so forceful with my words that he shrinks a little. He nods submissively, his body relaxing under my arm. "Now get some sleep kiddo. I'm sure you and Evvy have adventures planned for tomorrow, and if you're tired he's gonna beat you in the race to get there."

"He'll never catch me." Jack smiles. "Night, Auntie Ro," he says, rolling over and nestling next to his brother as I pull the covers up under his jaw.

"Night, Ratbag." Tousling his hair, I smile down at the little lumps in the bed, marveling at the courage and thoughtfulness of this young boy. Turning back to the doorway, I follow the stream of light back into the hall.

Trudging up the smaller stairs and into my room, I change for sleep. The door stays open tonight for warmth and so I can hear the kids if they call out. Climbing into my own bed, I find myself lying on my back wide awake and staring at the ceiling, my thoughts busy. Poor Jack, already thinking about loss and responsibility.

At least Patrick didn't know any different. He'd be twelve now, not that much older than Jack. There were obvious benefits to having such a young hostage in the City. It'll be decades before they need another one, and surely I can change things by then. Not if Da has anything to do with it though. How am I going to get to Patrick now that the Chief has taken Hayes out of my range?

Feeling my anger rising, I dismiss the thoughts. Ruminating never solves anything. I'll just go back to waiting. I'm only getting worked up now because of Jack's worrying and he and Evan aren't at risk. I shut my eyes, but sleep won't come. The front door opens and shuts and I hop out of bed, pulling my pants back on. Probably Lena. She usually tires of gatherings pretty quickly and almost always leaves early.

I meet her on the bottom stair. She looks worn out. I smile and turn back up, linking my arm through hers. We silently check the kids again and go on up to my room. Lena slumps onto my bed, pulls off her shoes and flops back, leaving her feet on the floor.

"Good night was it?" I joke, poking her ribs for a response as she feigns sleep. She can't ignore my probes for long.

"Fabulous." She chuckles, pawing at my hand. "Our guests were a bit rowdier than usual. It seems some of them had an entertaining time at the platform this afternoon."

"Hmphf. Glad I could be of service. You know how hospitable we Daltons are. Entertainment and a hot meal. Anything to make a Citizen feel welcome." I lie next to her and we stare at the ceiling together.

"I watched your Morrison Hayes with new interest. I've met him tons of times before, but I didn't click when you mentioned his name. They all call him Smiler," she says, turning her gaze to my face. Rolling on to my side, I prop my head on my hand, waiting. She is keeping her face purposely blank, so I can't read it. I want to know what she thinks of him and to tell her about our meeting at the river. My stomach flutters as I recall it, but my brain shuts it down. *It's over.*

"He's not *my* Morrison Hayes. Da has made sure of that. From tomorrow, he'll be *his* Morrison Hayes, so long as I'm left out of the action. I've already said goodbye." I try my best not to pout. If Da wants to help him, that's his prerogative and it's good for Hayes. I hope it works out for him and I don't hold it against him that he's dumped me as a contact. Only a fool would turn down the chance of acquiring the Dalton Chief as an ally. I'd like to believe Hayes is no fool.

He must have told Da that his family needs protection while he changes things in the City. I wonder if Da would ever consider helping in a less passive way. Probably not. If his deal includes keeping me out of any action, I guess it's safe to assume we'll all keep hiding in the Valley.

Ultimately, nothing has changed for me. I'll have to wait for another opportunity to get into the action. An opportunity that doesn't involve Hayes. I wouldn't want to jeopardize his alliance with Da and I was beginning to like him too much anyway. That can only be a bad thing.

Closing my eyes, I try to chase him from my thoughts before Lena gets wind of my musings. It doesn't matter. I don't really know him. He could just be another stupid Citizen trying to fulfill his own selfish plots. Or not. Who knows? Maybe Hayes can successfully raise a rebellion while I sit on the sideline and wait. He can free the people and if he makes it through alive and single and is interested, maybe he can find me and we can get to know each other then. Simple. It could totally happen.

I've officially gone mad. That's the stupidest thing I've ever thought! The odds of me being able to sit on the sideline are about the same as Hayes being interested in me. Slim to none. Lena's looking at me as if she's reading my thoughts, one side of her mouth is smirking and the opposite eyebrow is on the rise.

"Ooh. You've got it bad," she teases. "He is pretty hot, I'll give you that. That crazy hair? It was adorable how he kept trying to smooth it down! And the way he carries himself, as if he can handle anything that comes at him? Very appetizing. I was impressed with his manners too," she said, with me hanging on her every word, nodding shamelessly.

"Does he like you too?" she asks, "He didn't look twice at Orla. You should have seen what she was wearing. The rest of them were practically drooling!"

"And he didn't even look? That might be his most attractive characteristic yet." I sigh. "I don't know if he likes me."

"Maybe he's gay?" Lena offers.

"I don't think so," I think aloud, reminded of how he'd acted at the river. "He would be dead by now if he was gay. They don't take man-love lightly in the City."

"Well most straight guys can't peel their eyes off a girl like Orla. Maybe you're more his type?"

"Oh yeah, what type is that? Short?" I ask defensively,

a little hurt at Lena pointing out what I already know; Orla is a goddess, casting a long shadow.

"Short in stature, short tempered, short on patience and in short supply. Yeah, maybe short is the right word. Look," she says, noting my injured ego and softening her tone. "You're gorgeous. You intentionally scare people away with your bite, but you're amazing." Pausing a moment, she looks me over.

"Maybe you don't really like him. Maybe you're just…*lonely*," she says diplomatically. "You haven't been with anyone since -"

"Lena! I do not just need a ride!"

She smiles at my phrasing. "You sure? Because I know Cyrus would throw you a bone."

I just about choke. "Cyrus the virus? Ew, Lena. That's *worse* than a Citizen!"

"What? He's nice! OK, so he has slept with half the Valley, but he isn't actually diseased!" she says in his defense. "And from what I hear, he's good at it. They wouldn't go back for seconds if he wasn't."

Shuddering at the thought I shake my head. "I'm not interested in being one amongst the masses. Thanks for filling my head with unwanted images."

Pulling a face at me, she shrugs. "So you're definitely hung up on Hayes then."

I don't respond.

"He might be just as smitten with you as you are with him. It's a shame you'll never know." She looks at me intently. "The curiosity is killing me, so I bet you're *really* feeling it."

"What would be the point, Lena? He was born at the wrong end of the tracks."

"Well sure," she says, jabbing me in the ribs. "Obviously it would be tragically doomed. That's what makes it a challenge! Being forbidden only makes it more appealing," she says, sighing dreamily.

Not knowing what to say or what to think, I stay quiet.

Despite trying to ignore it, I can feel the curiosity gnawing at me. I caught myself blatantly trying to tempt him down at the river. Dismissing it as teenage infatuation isn't working. It doesn't feel like that anyway. I've been *there*. Sighing, I roll onto my back and search the ceiling again. There's nothing there to help me of course. It's a lost cause.

"Why will he be Da's Morrison tomorrow?" Lena sits straight up and looks down at me, interrupting my wallowing. "What's happening tomorrow?"

"I don't know exactly. I think they're coming to some mutual agreement so that Luther Derrick can be overthrown and we'll all be saved, while I sit idly by. Nothing much," I say with a cavalier attitude, rolling my eyes.

"What? That's huge! Don't tell me anything. What I don't know, won't get me in trouble." Lena lies back on the bed and jogs her legs up and down restlessly. "You have to keep out of the action? No wonder you're all angst-y! This is your ideal opportunity going to waste!"

"I know. Da really knows how to rub it in."

We're both quiet for a while. The others will be home soon, done with dinner, drinks and dancing like puppets. I can't decide if I feel better or worse for having talked about all this with Lena. I definitely feel confused and jilted. Lena breaks the silence once again.

"So Da must like him too then." There is a hint of wonder in her voice. "And from tomorrow, they'll be working together? Without you?"

"Yes. That much is clear," I confirm miserably.

"And you're still here because...?" Lena prompts, but doesn't wait for me to answer. "Go see him! Maybe he can include you somehow. Whether or not he knows it, Hayes owes *you* for his alliance with Da. You might not get another chance, then you'll never know how he feels about you. Wouldn't you rather know, either way?"

"Not really," I say, thinking how horrible it would be if

he dismissed me for a kid, or worse, if he returned my feelings but we could never be together. I say as much to Lena, and she punches me. Actually punches me. Sure, it's a language I understand, but I'm too shocked to comprehend. Lena never hits anyone. Ever.

"Ow! What the hell, Lena!" I cry, jumping off the bed and staring at her. I rub my arm where she's hit me, to amplify my wounded response, not because it hurt. It didn't. "I can't believe you punched me!"

"That didn't hurt!" she says, challenging my act. "Would you get out of this funk, and get proactive? This guy is no ordinary Citizen! Even Da approves of him! I have never seen you sit on your hands so long. Are you *that* scared by your feelings? Go get answers!" she says, poking my ribs with each word of her demand.

Swatting her away, I pace the length of my room. "How? Just walk up to him and ask?"

"Maybe. If you don't get the answers from body language." Lena giggles. She watches me with that laughing smile and judging eyebrow of hers, as I stalk up and down in front of her.

"OK. So you think I should go and see him, and be like… Ooh Hayes, let me save the world with you and by the way, I think you're delicious. Wanna kiss me? You're crazy, Lena!"

I've stopped pacing, but I start again when she resumes her giggling.

"You should definitely *not* start the conversation like that!" she says, when she catches her breath. Wiping a tear from the outside of her eye, she attempts to compose herself. "I love you Ror, you have such finesse!" Clearing her throat, she watches me pace again.

I shake my head. "I don't want to ruin his chances with Da. He needs the alliance or he can't do anything. I'll find another way in."

"I know you will, you always do," Lena says plainly. "But you're avoiding the bit you're most annoyed about.

You want a chance to be with Hayes."

Staring at her, I say nothing. Turning away I tap my foot on the wall. Sometimes I wish Lena didn't know me as well as she does. I can't lie to myself when she speaks my truths. Giving the wall another kick, I turn back to her. Leaning on the wall, I raise my eyes to her in question. Her smile gets me pacing again.

"Tonight is your only chance to see him right? You'll want to be forward, but not comical. I was thinking wear something low cut, that puts the question out there, so you don't have to say it out loud. Then you can add words when you need to. What do you think?"

"I think you're older than me, and you should know better." I stop pacing and give her a long, hard look. "I also think you have a point." Pulling open the closet door, I look for something to wear. Lena leaves the room as I rummage. I can't find anything that would be considered sexy. My clothes are more sporty than flirty.

Lena comes back with an armful of clothes. She's raided Orla's closet. Brilliant idea. She throws them on the bed and together we rifle through them to find something that will fit. Between Lena and the mirror, we decide on my fitted leggings and Orla's short-sleeved wrap shirt.

On me, the shirt resembles a short, pixie-like dress, with the V-neck drawing attention to my bust. Lena makes me take it off while she works some magic with my boobs, strapping them in a way that creates even more cleavage. I shrug back into the dress and tie the cords at my waist. Finding my good boots, I pull them on and assess my reflection.

"I can't leave the house like this! What if someone sees me?" I spin around, glaring at Lena. I look very suggestive. There's no way to misinterpret this outfit.

"So wear your winter cloak over top. It'll be freezing out anyway. You'll blend in. You have to admit, you'll get definite answers with that outfit." She nods at my bust. "No room for innocent misunderstandings there."

"I can't believe I let you talk me into this!"

"What else did you have planned? Lying in bed all night not sleeping and not knowing? With me next to you, elbowing you in the ribs every five minutes? Live a little. You have one night, Rori. Make the most of it. You'll regret it if you don't."

All I can think is - what if I regret it when I do? Looking in the mirror again, I take a steadying breath. I feel better when my reflection puts her cloak on. As an afterthought, I grab my sheathed knife and strap it to my thigh, just hidden by the dress. You can never be too careful when Citizens are in town.

I'm almost mentally prepared when the noises start below. The rest of the family is coming home. Lena grabs the clothes off the bed and meets my eye. Her gaze flicks to the window and back to me. I nod and she disappears to Orla's room while I open the window and perch on the sill.

"Wish me luck," I say, when she comes back in.

"Luck," she smiles warmly.

Rotating on the sill, I grip it and lower myself down to the thin ledge made from the ends of the first floor ceiling logs. The framing of our house is made of split logs and their ends jut out through the stones of the wall. It is any easy house to climb in and out of; and I have, many times.

I shuffle to one side so I won't be seen through the window below, and lower myself to the next ledge by wedging my fingers into the crevices between stones. Shuffling back the other way to avoid the windows on the ground floor, I climb down to the ground and sneak under the windows of the first few houses. Moving down the lane, I head toward the Ambassador's cottage and potentially, emotional devastation.

AFTER DARK

Halfway to the cottage, I'm forced to duck into the shadows of the nearest house, as Horse and Da walk down the lane in my direction. Their heads are down and they speak in hushed tones, looking over their shoulders periodically to the empty lane behind them. Horse puts his arm around Da's shoulders, laughing as he thumps his back.

Da laughs too, relaxed. It makes him look a lot younger. They look like they must have in childhood. They've been friends that long. Sometimes it's hard to remember that there's more to Owen MacGregor than being the Chief and our Dad. I wonder what he would've been like if he'd been born into a different family. They move off down the lane and when they turn the next corner, I continue on my way.

The lane is dark, lit intermittently by the windows of the homes perched along it. There are fewer lights on now that the gathering is over and it's getting late. I walk along at a medium pace, one determined by my internal dilemma. I'm torn between racing to find possible reciprocation of my feelings of attraction and running back home out of fear of rejection. If I just keep my feet moving I'll end up somewhere.

I pull my cloak closer. With the chill of the night air and my stomach twisted with nervous excitement, I have to keep reminding myself to breathe. The wind teases my cloak and blows my hood back. Loose strands of hair whisk about my face, but I leave the hood down, finding the cold on my face diverting.

"Well what do we have here? Where do you think you're going little Riding Hood? Off to Grandma's house?" Reginald Derrick steps into the lane behind me, adjusting his trouser fly. I put my head down and keep moving, but he strides past me on long legs and blocks my path. I look about, but the lane is deserted except for us. Under my cloak, my hand moves instinctively to my knife.

"I *said*, where are you going?" His breath sends plumes of alcoholic mist into the cold air. Pinching the clasp of my cloak, he plucks it off as if it were a piece of lint. My cloak falls immediately, and he snatches it from behind me with those lanky arms, whipping it out of my reach as I grab for it. Exposing my outfit can only make this situation worse.

"I'm going to a friend's house. He's expecting me," I say in a firm and dismissive tone, trying to get my cloak back on the way past him.

He leers at me tastelessly. "I bet he is! You are a sweet wee thing!"

My mind races. This is Reginald Derrick. He doesn't appear to recognize me from our altercation in the City streets, but if I pull any moves, I'm bound to blow that cover. Using my knife would be equally unhelpful. Puncturing the son of the City Director will not bode well for me.

The best option is to take advantage of his drunken state, slip by him and make a run for it. I forget about trying to retrieve my cloak and wait for a gap to open up. He is keeping the way well blocked, but I feign to the left and take a quick wide step to the right, to avoid his extensive reach. Making the gap by a hair, I feel the rush of air on the back of my neck that he is grabbing instead of me. While he's still fumbling, I run.

Straight into the rock of a man that is Morrison Hayes. I stare in agitated disbelief at the effective roadblock. The look on his face is utter surprise, turning to shock as his attention is drawn to Reg.

"Smiler! Great catch!" He laughs. "Check out the rack on this one!"

Hayes looks at me, well, at my cleavage. A look passes across his face that I can't discern.

"Hard to miss, Reg," he says, managing a light-hearted tone through his clenched jaw.

"Says she's on the way to her *'friend's'* house," says Reg, making quotation marks with his hands. "We should warm her up before she gets there, don't you think? Seeing as it's such a cold night and all." He advances and I feel Hayes' hand on my arm. Stepping forward, he pulls me behind him and yanks my cloak from Reg's hand.

"This should help with the warming up, Miss. Apologies for my comrade here. It appears he's had a bit much of the fine Valley Ale." Hayes passes me the cloak and I pull it on immediately, feeling seriously exposed.

"Smiler, the killjoy! Shoulda kept her to myself! Piss off and let me at her! She's started something in my pants that I intend to make her finish!"

Reg lunges at me again, grabbing at my cloak. Hayes blocks him and pushes him back a step, causing him to stumble slightly and anger more.

"Trust me, Reg. You don't want to do this. Go back to the bunk-room and sleep it off." Turning to me, Hayes' eyes wash over my cloak with approval. "You should be on your way. I'm sure you have someone wondering where you are." His last words are accompanied by a raised eyebrow. I narrow my eyes at him briefly before I run off into the shadows down the lane.

Dipping into the dark between two houses, I circle back to take in the scene. Reg is seething. He circles Hayes with his shoulders hunched and his fists clenched. Hayes stands calmly in the middle, saying something too quiet for me to hear. Reg does not look as if he will back down easily. He circles in the other direction. Hayes changes his stance and stands his ground.

Suddenly, Reg lunges at Hayes. Ready for him, Hayes uses Reg's momentum against him and sends him sprawling to the ground behind him. Turning casually, he braces himself and waits for Reg to get up.

Reg charges again. Hayes places his hands strategically. With a swift movement, performed with more grace than I would've expected from such a large man, he turns Reg upside down, driving him into the dirt and pinning him there with a knee pressed into his back.

Hayes hasn't finished, because Reg continues to struggle beneath him. Yanking Reg's arm behind his back, Hayes rams his face further into the road. He lowers his head next to Reg's ear and says something to him that stops him resisting.

Slowly, Hayes releases his grip and Reg begins to rise. Hayes hold a hand, offering to help him up. For a long moment, Reg just stares at him. Eventually he takes the hand, pulling himself up and cuffing Hayes' head playfully. Hayes of course expertly dodges this and punches him back in the same jovial manner.

Stupid boys.

They head away toward the platform bunk-rooms and I sit in the dark a while, wondering if I should continue on to the cottage. The night has changed, but my gut is still fluttering. I know the only way to squash the feeling will be to confront Hayes, but I'm feeling even less confident now. He probably thinks I'm some hormone crazed teenager, senselessly roaming the streets at night.

Hell. Maybe I am.

Sighing, I stand up and carry on.

***

The small cottage is dark from the outside, but as I slip in the back, I notice that someone has drawn the curtains and lit the fire. The embers cast a dim glow around the hearth and I crouch down to feed them, not wanting to turn on the lights and give myself away. I'm still clinging to the idea I can hide or slip away unseen if I change my mind. As the flames lick the wood, the cottage brightens. I sling my cloak over a chair and look at my surroundings.

I haven't been inside the Ambassador's cottage before. It's open plan and the only room that's separate is the bathroom. You can see the little kitchen and the sleeping area, from the living space. My stomach knots as I look at the bed and I force my eyes elsewhere.

Where will I sit to wait? He is obviously coming back; his bag is here. I don't have the nerve to sit on the bed to wait. Turning back to the room, I consider the limited options. He'll probably come through the front door, so I'll wait opposite that, at the table. A table isn't too suggestive.

I look down at my chest, trying to work out how to un-create Lena's cleavage system, but snap my head up as the door swings open. He hasn't seen me. Slamming the door, he punches it before leaning his forehead into the wood.

"Damn it, Rori!"

"Present," I say quietly, wishing I had gone home.

Hayes whirls around, facing me with wide eyes. His mouth opens, but no sound comes out. Dragging both hands down his face, he expels air between his fingers as they descend. Closing his eyes, he runs a hand through his wind-tossed hair. Without looking at me he walks to the sink and pours a glass of water.

He stands at the sink, his back to me as he drinks. Filling it again, he reaches for another glass and fills that too. He carries them to the table and puts the second glass in front of me.

"Thanks." My voice is practically inaudible. Taking a sip, I meet his searing gaze. The only light in the cottage is the fire and I can see it burning in his eyes. Shrugging out of his jacket, he hangs it on the back of his chair, before sliding into it. Breaking the intense eye contact, he studies the water in his glass.

"I wasn't expecting to see you again Rori," he says, not specifying whether he meant the incident in the lane or my presence in the cottage. His tone has no detectable emotion to alert me to whether he is pleased or otherwise.

"I hadn't planned to see you like this either," I say evasively, hoping it isn't 'otherwise'.

Lifting his eyes from the water, he studies my face instead. His eyes roll downward and his brow furrows. That look again.

"Do you find my clothes offensive?"

Hayes pushes his chair back and leaves the table. He begins slowly pacing, reminding me of myself earlier in the evening when I was puzzling things out, and I can't help but smile a little.

"I just can't understand why a young girl would dress that way and walk the streets in the dark. I find it disturbing and risky, and I thought you had more sense than that. I hope you've learned a lesson this evening."

"Excuse me?!"

My smile is gone. I can't believe what I'm hearing. My face is heating; not from the shame he appears to think I should feel, but from the rage rising within me.

"You Jerk!"

I almost laugh at the surprise on his face.

"You think I was asking for it!" His expression turns evasive and I know I've got it right. "You're clueless! Do you know that? I'm gonna school you quick, before you *really* piss me off. First of all, I can dress however I like – which actually isn't like this." I gesture to my outfit. "But that's another story. Secondly, I would never have to worry about being attacked by anyone in the Valley but *your* so-called comrades, which is why I was covered with my cloak. And thirdly, I can go wherever the hell I like at whatever time I like and I am certainly not *asking* for someone to attack me on my way!" Really foaming now, I can't seem to stop myself. Hayes has been thrown into a stunned silence by this reprimand.

"And *you*! I had just managed to get past that drunken asshole without having to lift a violent finger, and there you were blocking my escape, making me feel pitiful and inadequate, like I need a savior! It's ridiculous. And I'll tell you about sense! I have more sense in my little finger than any of your dumb soldiers have in their whole stupid, over-sized bodies! Don't *ever* underestimate me."

I stop. Too worked up. Breathing heavily, I've advanced on Hayes while I was berating him, and have backed him up against the door. I step back, needing the space myself.

Looking at him questioningly, I await his response to my outburst. His eyes are on my chest, and I look down to find it heaving angrily in unison with my breathing. Groaning, I turn back to the table and gulp down my water.

"You deliver an effective education, Rori. Thank you for reminding me yet again of the different worlds we live in. It adds fuel to my fire," Hayes says to my back in a chillingly even tone. I turn to him, my eyebrow rising slowly, waiting for his next words.

"I apologize again for the behavior of my men." Pausing momentarily, he weaves a hand into his hair, massaging his scalp as if to encourage his thoughts. "I'm sorry you were interrupted on your way to your... friend's house," he says in a frustrated tone, glancing briefly at my chest again.

I'm going to strangle Lena when I get home.

"I could escort you there if you like, seeing as how my *comrades* will be in town until tomorrow," he says testily, scuffing the ground with his foot and avoiding my eyes.

"You're an idiot." I can't believe he hasn't realized I came to see him.

"Thanks. Shall I take it you're declining my escort?" Hayes clenches his jaw and meets my eyes and I can see his own anger fighting to be free. He thinks I'm on my way to see some boyfriend for a good time, and he's annoyed about it. My eyes widen.

"You're jealous!" I accuse, making sense of his hostility.

"I don't know what you're implying, but I'm sure your boyfriend is expecting you." Hayes opens the door and gestures for me to leave.

I walk forward. "I was coming to see you, Idiot." Grazing my arm past his shirt and pushing the door closed, I stare directly into his face, leaving no room for misinterpretation. "It recently occurred to me that you're not committed to my father until tomorrow. We still have tonight."

His startled face softens, the previous anger melting away. My heart starts pounding and he looks down at me so intensely, I feel myself drawing up to meet his face. The butterflies that fury had chased out of my stomach, return now with reinforcements and take up residence throughout my entire body, making it thrum with anticipation.

What little space there is between us feels alive. His hand moves hesitantly to my hair, and he tucks back the strands that have come loose during my rant. I close my eyes and enjoy the sensation. He likes me. I know now. His hand draws down under my chin and he tilts it gently upward.

Swallowing, I open my eyes, meeting his. Leaning in, Hayes hovers above my face, breathing the same air. Lifting my chin encouragingly, I ache to breach the final gap, but stand my ground. I want him to cover the distance, both in apology for his ignorance and as proof that the attraction isn't imagined.

After what seems an unbearable delay, he does. Gently at first, as if asking my permission. I give it wantonly and kiss him back with fervor. A hand grasps the back of my neck, sending shivers over my scalp as his fingers venture into my hair. My hands, that have been hanging limp at my sides, soar into action, sneaking under his shirt and running up his back. His skin is radiating heat, and I feel a flush rise within me as I trail my fingers back down his muscles.

My feet leave the floor and I'm spun around. The wood of the door is rough through my thin dress, as my back is pressed against it. My legs automatically wrap around his waist. Our lips break apart, and our eyes lock as we gasp for breath. His eyes are questioning as a hand glides up my side, pausing before it reaches a curve. In answer, I reach my hands around his neck and work my fingers into his hair, pulling him hungrily back to my lips.

Suddenly the door is gone and my back is supported by one strong arm, as a second arm presses my hips inconceivably closer to his. I travel through the air, my brain vaguely recognizing a change of location. The air is warmer; we're near the fire. Kicking a chair away, he makes room for us.

The angles of the world change as I'm lowered gently to the hearth rug with his bulk pressing into me. It's hard to breath and my hands push against his chest. Supporting himself on his elbows, Hayes watches me panting.

"Sorry," he rasps, making to move off me. Locking my feet behind his back, I travel with him as we topple over, leaving me straddled atop him.

"Don't be," I murmur in his ear, as I lean down to nuzzle his neck. Inhaling his scent, I emit a small sigh. He squirms beneath me as my breath tickles him. The roughness of his jaw grazes my neck and I shiver, pulling back and moving my hips against him. A groan escapes his lips and I fumble with his shirt buttons, trying not to appear too eager, but rushing nonetheless.

Firm hands run up my legs and stop suddenly. He looks down his body to see what his hand has found. My knife. Hayes raises an eyebrow at me and I give him a sly smile and move his hands onward for him. Giving me a squeeze where I placed his hands, his touch keeps moving. Deft fingers travel over my hips, and slide up my body following an invisible trail.

I watch in suspense as he slowly pulls a cord, unraveling the tie of my wrap dress. A strong finger sweeps it open and a gentle palm cups my breast, tentatively following its curve to the knot tied at the base of my cleavage. He deals with Lena's handiwork skillfully and unleashes my breasts from their restraints, pausing to devour them with his eyes, before sitting up beneath me.

Sliding the dress from my shoulders, Hayes leaves them bare. I shiver with pleasure again as coarse stubble scuffs my naked skin, raising every tiny hair to attention. Shallow kisses flow softly along my collar bone and down, circling. I gasp as he takes me into his mouth. His eyes look up at me and his lips curve into a smile and increase their efforts.

I want him. My hips tilt into him uncontrollably. Judging from what I'm rubbing against, he wants me too. Pushing him back to the floor, I work the fly of his trousers, but his hand closes over mine, stopping me. I look up to find him breathing heavily and squeezing his eyes tightly shut, shaking his head. No.

"Why not?" I ask, exasperated. "Don't you want me?"

His eyes open in shock and he sits back up. Folding his arms around me, he traps me against his solid chest so I can't see his face.

"Rori, I want you so badly it hurts. I'm literally aching to be with you. But we can't do this. I never should have kissed you. I'm so sorry." His breathing is erratic and he sounds panicked. I wriggle until I can see his face, but he looks away from me, getting his breathing and his appetite under control.

"We can't do this," he repeats, though his arms still embrace me like treasure.

"I know," I agree breathlessly. "You're an idiot Enforcer in Derrick's army. I should hate you. On behalf of all Daltons, I should hate you." There is no conviction in my words. It's too late to talk myself out of falling for him. With his heat against me, I'm beyond reproach.

"You should hate me," he says, finally meeting my eyes. They are filled with wanting, though it could just be a reflection of my own need. Leaning closer, he whispers in my ear. "I might be an idiot Enforcer, but you're a smart-mouthed, thieving rebel. I should kill you or be killed."

Quivering under the tickle of his breath and the truth of his words, I gasp as my body tries to move closer to his.

"Are those the only choices?" I whisper, hoping his flesh is as weak as mine.

Taking my face in both his hands, his mouth finds mine again and I lose myself under his roaming touch. My own hands search his body for something to anchor myself to. With a handful of his hair, I draw him closer still. Chest to chest, I can feel our hearts competing for top speed. Yanking himself away, he holds a hand to my heart, his eyes meeting mine. Placing my hand on his chest, I smile at him as I try to get my breath back. Hayes returns my smile, his eyes full of something that moves me deep within.

After a moment, his eyes become wary. Shaking my head, I pull him back to my lips. Returning my kiss, his hands stroke my hair, but it's different. He's holding back. I pull away, searching his conflicted face. Closing his eyes tightly, he bites his lip and exhales slowly.

"I can't," he says sadly. "I can't start an allegiance with your father after deflowering his baby girl. He'll never trust me," he says, reminding me how determined he is to challenge the system. I grudgingly admire his devotion. If he was lusting anywhere near as much me, he must be extremely dedicated to the cause.

Sliding off him, I readjust my clothes to cover up, self-conscious now that the moment has passed. Tidying my hair, I try to dampen my desire, which is hard when he is so beautiful. The fireplace illuminates his exposed skin and throws shadows across his body, emphasizing its lines. Sighing, I turn my face to the fire and stare at the flames.

"I could argue about your choice of words and your assumptions, but I won't." The term 'baby girl' is poor taste after what we were just doing. I hate being made to feel like a child, but I'll let it pass. "I want you to succeed. I want to see an end to Derrick's regime."

Sitting in silence, we both watch the flames get low. Hayes pokes the embers and puts on another log.

"It's good that we didn't," he says firmly, trying to convince himself maybe. "What would've happened if we had?" He means it rhetorically, but I answer anyway.

"I suspect I would have enjoyed it."

Looking at me with astonishment, a little hunger creeps back into his eyes. Shaking his head, he looks at the fire.

"I don't even know how old you are."

"Adult," I say, seeing a chance to argue his baby girl comment. "Seventeen."

"Seventeen!" He rakes his hands over his face, exhaling roughly. "What if you'd gotten pregnant?"

"I would've taken the herbs in the morning. I don't want a baby! I have a career that depends on my body being small and agile, and I love it. I'm not throwing that away!" A baby is the last thing on my mind. Is he crazy?

He's looking at me strangely.

"Do you even know how much power you have? To be able to choose like that?" he asks, his voice wistful. "There are no such herbs in the City. It's forbidden. Anything that inhibits procreation is punishable."

"But that's awful! What if a girl's not ready for children? Or is sick and shouldn't? Or has ten kids already?" I had noticed how poorly women were treated in the City, but I hadn't realized the extent of the predicament they were in. Until now I had taken birth control for granted. I've only known the possibility of choice and assumed it was my right.

Hayes shrugs and buttons his shirt. Standing, he holds a hand out to me. Taking it, I pull myself up and straighten my clothes. My body longs to be closer to his and I want to kick myself. Now that I know how amazing it feels to be in his arms, I don't want to be out of them. It's going to be torture every time I see him. Thankfully, he will be out of my sight soon.

"As I said before, I have people depending on me. I can't let them down by following my own selfish desires. No matter how tempting they might be," he says, glancing from the floor, up my body to my eyes. He lingers there, with a tenderness that surpasses physical yearning, and my heart begins to hammer again. I'm about to melt, and jump on him when he looks away.

"Besides, I don't need another person to worry about. I don't have the capacity to continually fear for your safety. I can't do that and everything else. I'll stay away from you, you'll be safely out of danger and that's how it should be."

Taken aback, I frown at the floor. I've lived a dangerous life since long before I met Hayes, and I enjoy the thrill of it. I know my family worry about me from time to time, but they trust in my abilities enough not to hound me about it. Never have I been offensively told that I'm an annoying concern. He's making me feel like I'm a hassle; as if I can't take care of myself. I'm too small and inept. Angry heat begins to rise again and I try to push it down, feeling like my emotions only come in extreme forms lately.

He spies my clenched fists as I fold my arms across my chest to hide them.

"What have I done now?"

"I can take care of myself," I snap. He shouldn't have asked.

"I told you, I don't need you to rescue me and I don't need you to worry about me! Do not use that as an excuse to stay away from me! I accept that you want to forge the alliance with my father. *That* I can tolerate. I'll even tolerate it happening without me - for a while, until I find a way in. I have a lot to offer, and I am tired of you assuming I'm some 'damsel in distress'. It's insulting!"

Hayes regains himself. "Rori, I've saved you more times in the last week, than I care to dwell on, and I was happy to do it. But I have never met someone who so frequently puts herself in jeopardy and it scares me. How can I *not* worry about you?"

He's running his hands through his hair again and the crease between his eyebrows is deep enough to sow seed into.

"You know what, Hayes? You don't have to worry, because you'll never have to see me again!"

Pushing past him, I grab my cloak, not stopping to put it on.

"Rori wait," Hayes pleads, putting a hand on my shoulder to stop me.

I can't help it. Instinct kicks in. Someone is stopping me from moving. I put my hands over his and reverse into him, bending and pulling him over my shoulder. He lands on his back with a thud. While he's lying dazed on the floor I thrust my knee into his chest and pull my knife from its sheath, bringing its tip beneath his chin.

"Do *not* underestimate me."

I stare down at him viciously, but as I do, his face changes. The look of shocked surprise vanishes and his eyes glaze over, unseeing. His body tenses and his breathing accelerates. I remove my knee and put my knife away.

"Hayes?"

I shake his shoulder trying to get his attention, but he's somewhere else. His hands are fisted and shaking. What the hell is happening? Is he having a seizure? Oh hell, I've hurt him! Feeling for his pulse, I find it racing.

"Hayes!" Shaking him harder, I search the room looking for something to help, thinking I should get Freya.

I see his glass on the table and grab it, splashing the water onto his face. That does it.

Shaking his head, he wipes his face, but he's not himself. That faraway look is still in his eyes. He immediately jumps into a fighting stance and I back up, putting the table between us.

"Hayes! Snap out of it! What are you doing?" My words fall on deaf ears, and I can't deny the stab of fear in my gut. This cannot be happening. I was set to become intimately acquainted with this guy only minutes ago and now he looks like he wants to kill me.

I watch as he pulls himself to full height, towering above the table. I am in trouble. Hayes lunges toward me. Ducking under the table, I make a run for the door. The damn thing opens inward and by the time I've opened it, he's crossed the room. I try to pull it closed behind me, but he takes hold of it and yanks it wide open, pulling me back with it.

He grabs for me and I duck under his reach, but lose my balance, falling. Going with the fall, I roll backwards, getting up so fast he doesn't have a chance to grab me. Catching a glimpse of his crazed face over my shoulder, I run. The door slams behind me, followed by pounding on wood and the splintering sound of shattering wooden furniture.

Running all the way home, I wait in the shadows to calm myself before making the climb back to my room. What the hell just happened? One minute he's normal and the next he's demented. What the hell is wrong with him? And what the hell is wrong with *me*? I pulled a knife on him for no good reason!

Sudden realization hits me and I sink to my knees.

I shoved a knife in his face.

His beautiful face with its tidy scar. A scar that tidy was made by a blade. I just did to him what *they* did to him. I've triggered some primal defensive reaction.

I'm as bad as them!

As I sit in the dirt, guilty tears roll down my face. Wiping my chin as they collect there, I lean my head back against the house. *Just breathe.* I can't be crying when I get in or Lena will make me talk. That's the last thing I want.

I just want to forget.

Taking a deep, shuddering breath, I stare up at the stone wall. At least Da won't have to worry about me getting involved. Even if I was brave enough to confront Hayes and apologize, I don't think he'd ever let me close enough to do so. What I did was inexcusable. I'm as much of an asshole as the Citizens I claim to despise. With that happy thought, I throw myself at the wall and climb.

"How did it go?" Lena asks, as soon as my feet touch down inside the window.

"As expected. Over before it started. I don't want to talk about it. Tomorrow? Or later, the story isn't going to change." Shedding my borrowed ensemble, I pull on a comfortable top and slide into the bed next to Lena. She wraps her arms around me in a hug. It's enough to make the tears well again, but I hold them back, swallowing the ache in my throat.

"I'm sorry it didn't work out, Sugar-Plum. It wouldn't have worked anyway, I guess," she says softly. "You'll feel better after a good sleep." She gives me another squeeze before rolling away.

I lie there listening to her breathing becoming deeper, wondering if I'll ever feel better again.

FALLOUT

Hayes sat in the dim light of the dying fire with his head in his hands, his back against the door and his brain aching. Next to him on the floor was the cracked leg of the chair he had thrown at the door. Looking at it, he sank further into his dark mood. He had lost it. He'd been ripped back in time again, tormented by the past he couldn't change.

Lowering his hands, he assessed the damage. His knuckles were bloodied and raw and he winced as he pulled out a lengthy splinter, uncorking a fresh rivulet of blood. Moving to the sink, he ran cold water over them, splashing some on his face. He opened the window above the sink to feel the chill on his face, collecting himself.

Drying his hands on the dish cloth and consciously refusing to think about anything but tidying, he switched on the light and turned to face to room. The pieces of furniture that weren't lying shattered on the floor, were strewn across the space haphazardly, their positions as upset as he was. Methodically setting them to rights, he moved them to one side of the room. As he lifted the table, a leg dropped to the floor and landed on Rori's cloak.

He put the table down and stared at the cloak awhile.

Finally, he lifted it and brought it to his face, inhaling her floral perfume. His hands tightened around the dense woolen fabric and his breath caught in his throat, constricted with emotion. Walking across the room, he laid it on the bed, and turned his back on it.

Finding a broom in the back cupboard, he swept the wooden and glass fragments to the kitchen before rearranging the furniture. Once he thought things were as he remembered, he took an inventory. Casualties included one dining chair, two glasses, the leg of the table and two buttons from his shirt. The door looked dented in places and hung slightly askew.

Pocketing his buttons, he looked for a screwdriver. Using a knife from the kitchen he tightened the screws on the door's hinges. Swinging it a few times to test its movement, he closed it, satisfied and grateful for the sturdiness of Dalton construction. City doors did not recover so well from his interactions. Putting the knife away, he returned to his collection of broken bits.

Salvaging the table leg, he noted that the table stood quite well in its absence. Without any means to reattach it, Hayes guiltily balanced it in its corner support and took a step back. As long as it wasn't knocked, it would look as if the table was whole. He rearranged the remaining chairs around it, making it less obvious that one was missing; that one could not be saved.

Carefully picking out all the wood from the pile of sweepings, he carried the pieces to the fire, using them to build it back up. He paused a moment to warm his battered hands. They weren't as bad as he'd thought. His skin had only opened in a few places, and if he could minimize any swelling, his injuries might pass unnoticed.

Sweeping up the glass, he put it in the bin. A broken glass or two could be an accident. Soaking the dishcloth in cold water, he held it to his knuckles as he surveyed the cottage. Switching off the light he heaped more wood on the fire before heading to bed. Throwing his bag to the floor, he sat and untied his boots, prying them off with his toes. Scooting up the bed, he pulled Rori's cloak with him. With his head on the pillow, he clutched her cloak to his chest and let the events of the night run through his head.

He'd been thinking of her all evening, since their meeting at the river, unable to get her out of his mind. When they were in the grass, the fibers of her sweater had tickled his nose as she'd moved over him, filling his nostrils with the smell of summer flowers. He'd had the urge to pull her to him then, but had been afraid of how she might react; afraid of rejection. It scared him most of all, that it had been *that* reason he'd remained still and not the fact that it would've endangered an alliance with the Chief.

When he had happened upon her and Reg in the lane, he'd had to restrain himself from dealing to Reg permanently. Hayes tightened his grip on Rori's cloak as he thought of Reg's intentions with a sickening shudder. He had only just managed to mollify Reg with threats of his father and the lure of more ale at the bunk-rooms.

He had been so worked up about the incident that when he got back to the cottage and found her there he'd blamed her for it. Not letting him get away with that, she'd let him have it too. She'd been right, of course, he'd been a jealous idiot.

When she had told him she'd come for him, with those alluring eyes and her figure-hugging dress, he'd been helplessly seduced. Unable to take his eyes or his hands off her, he'd been egged on by her reciprocation - and the noises she made! Everything about Rori, made him want her. Only years of experience had allowed him to stop when he had. He was a master of avoiding actual intercourse, but even so, he'd been at his limit.

Taking that in her stride too, Rori appeared to understand why he had stopped. He'd been surprised by her maturity, until she started yelling at him that is. That was his fault too, he realized. His mouth running off, before his 'idiot brain' (as she'd so aptly put it) was engaged. He'd meant what he'd said, but had said it all wrong. They could have parted on decent terms, but Hayes knew he had ruined any chance of that now.

Rori had proved she could handle herself, and he had lost all control. Hayes couldn't recall the moments after he saw the glint of the blade. There was a gap. The next thing he knew, she was running away into the night and his rage was all-consuming. He hoped he hadn't hurt her. Tomorrow would bring answers. Hopefully he hadn't ruined his chances with the MacGregors.

Pulling the cloak around him, he sought comfort in its enveloping warmth. He would have to return it inconspicuously, but couldn't bear to part with it just yet. Hayes closed his eyes against the thoughts that threatened to consume him and hoped for sleep.

***

My eyes don't want to open. I vaguely recall Lena climbing over me earlier and I wonder how long ago that was. The morning light is shining in my window and I suspect I've missed breakfast. Rolling over, my body chastises me with aching muscles. My back feels like a horse stood on it. Memories flood back to me from yesterday. My emotions feel just as trampled. Fair to class it as a shit day.

Stretching, I heave myself up and throw on some clothes for a run. My body always seems to recover better if I keep it going. Tying my hair into a pony tail, I splash water onto my face in the bathroom. The girl in the mirror looks better than I feel. That's comforting. I run downstairs to check the time.

As I approach the ground floor, I hear a familiar voice talking to Da. They are walking away from his study, so they must've been talking about a trip to the City. I jump the last few steps and spring in front of them.

"Jerome! You're back!" I pull his surprised body into a hearty embrace. "I thought you must have died! How was

157

it? Tell me everything. I'm so glad you're back!" I can hardly contain my excitement.

Jerome Marshall is my best friend and fellow Gopher. He has been gone three weeks, climbing in the snow-capped mountains to the north of the Valley. By himself. 'To think' he'd said.

Hugging me back, he lifts me off my feet, spinning me around before setting me back down.

"I missed you too, Twiglet." He grins at me through an untamed beard. "I hear you've been getting up to mischief while I've been away! Got yourself on a City ban. Ha ha!" Poking my ribs, he regards my clothes. "You going for a run? If you gimme a minute I'll join you and we can catch up."

"That'd be great. I'm just gonna grab a drink," I say, turning to the kitchen, where I see Morrison Hayes leaning against the bench next to Aiden. Unprepared, I stop in my tracks. I want to run away, to cry, to hug him, to apologize, but I can't move. An all too familiar lump begins to expand in my throat as tears prick my eyes. I clench my jaw, fighting them. It's Aiden that saves me.

Bringing me a glass of water, he exchanges a look over my shoulder, to Da I guess. Casually draping an arm over my shoulder, he guides me to the window, pointing out something the kids are doing. I can't see for looking. I drink the water to wash the lump down and set the glass on the windowsill before my trembling hand drops it.

Behind me, Da introduces Jerome to Hayes and explains that Jerome will be his contact in the City, receiving and delivering messages when needed, between Train Days. They exchange civilities and Da farewells Jerome, inviting Hayes down to his study. My eyes follow his back as he walks down the hall. He glances back over his shoulder briefly. In that fleeting moment, our eyes meet and he smiles. A smile so loaded with sorrow, it's penetrating my soul. I did that to him.

My chest aches and I can't breathe. Hot tears threaten

to burst their banks. Dropping under Aiden's arm, I race out the door, not waiting for Jerome. I run as the tears fall.

Running whilst crying makes it impossible to breathe and soon I have to look around for somewhere to hide. I'm down by the river, alone. Splashing into the shallows, I wade in under the bridge and reach for the cross supports. Pulling myself up, I sit shivering and sniffing amongst the triangles, guilt-ridden and grieving. Eventually my breathing settles and I mute my thoughts by staring at the water below, imagining my troubles flowing downstream in the current.

"Found you. Your turn to seek."

Jerome pulls himself into an adjacent triangle and sits looking at me, one leg dangling. I give him a weak smile and stay quiet. Reaching for my hand, he gives it a squeeze. I squeeze back, acknowledging his support and we sit together in silence.

When I'm ready I squeeze his hand again. Studying my face, he gives me a sympathetic smile.

"He seems like a good guy. Shame about his Citizenship huh?"

I nod, not ready to form words about Hayes. When I think about him, I see that sad smile and feel awful all over again. Jerome moves on without me.

"Don't feel too put out by not going to the City. Your Dad's got big plans for you in the Valley." He looks at me to gauge my interest.

"I bet he does," I say, conveying my annoyance. Da has never wanted me to be a Gopher. Encouraging every other option, he has maintained a constant desire to keep me 'safe' in the Valley. Trapped more like. Watching the water, my thoughts grow darker.

"I think you'll like what he wants you to do," Jerome continues. "I know you're disappointed about hanging up your gopher-suit for a while, but it won't be forever. And…" I look up at his pause, meeting his contemplative blue eyes. "Some distance might be good?" Frowning, my eyes drop back to the water, knowing he's not wrong.

His tone lightens. "A little distance, and maybe a change of perspective?" Jerome swivels on his butt and hangs upside down, his knees hooked over the support strut. "It's a different world down here. You should check it out."

I join him, the end of my ponytail dragging in the water. The blood travels to my head as I swing gently in thought. Seeing Jerome's reddening face, I stifle a laugh.

"You know down here smiles turn into frowns," he says kindly, swinging himself back up to sitting. He waits until I'm right way up again. "You still wanna go for that run, puffy eyes? I'll race you across the bridge and down to the cave?"

Not answering, I climb over him and swing down below the bridge support. Swinging as fast as I can across the river I splash down in the shallows on the other side. I race up the bank and am speeding toward the cave while Jerome is still swinging across, abusing me for cheating. He's faster than me, so I don't care. It feels good to run with him again, and I need to feel good right now.

He pounds the dirt behind me. The path will run out soon, and I need to get as far ahead as I can, because when we go off-road Jerome will kick my ass. The outcrop of rocks that signal the end of the track is up ahead, and I prepare for the transition.

By the time I've leapt up the first three rocks, Jerome is hot on my tail. Between rock five and six, his airborne silhouette blocks the sun briefly as he somersaults by me. At rock seven I catch a tree branch, and circle up. Pushing off that branch to one higher and further around, so I can swing onto the highest rock.

Jerome is already running along it to the first ledge. He's going vertical now, so I keep moving across. Lining up the gap in my mind, I throw my body across, landing just as I'd imagined and ready for the next one. I leap across three more gaps before propelling myself upward, groping for the crack I know is there. My hand holds and I keep the momentum going.

One hold after another, I swing up and across to where I'll meet Jerome at the overhang. I pull myself onto it just as he drops in from above. We look at each other and grin. We're both red-faced, panting and covered with sweat - and blood, I notice, putting a scuffed knuckle in my mouth.

"Tie?" Jerome asks. We shouldn't really be racing. Ari would be bothered by us misusing our skills, but it was just what I needed. I feel like myself again, confident and strong. Free-running does that for me.

"Tie," I agree, wiping sweat off my forehead. Together we walk to the edge of the overhang and sit down, hanging our legs over the edge. The river runs into the dark below us and we sit in comfortable silence.

We've always been able to do that. Jerome was ahead of me in school, but we had met at training with Ari Li, when I was four and he was eight. He'd been funny and kind to me, even though I was younger. Having him as a training partner has made me the best Gopher I can be. Jerome has never gone easy on me in a fight because I'm a girl; and we fight a lot! He has never made me feel incapable, just expects me to keep up. I have always loved him for that.

The train will be leaving soon. From our vantage point we'll see it disappear back into the cliff, taking with it the parasites and their cargo, like a double headed worm withdrawing back into its hole. Parasitizens. I can't bring myself to include Hayes in that category though. He refused to take from me what I would willingly have given. He has done nothing but keep me safe and give me hope - with the exception of last night's episode of bizarre aggression, for which I feel completely accountable.

I close the door on my thoughts, letting the distress of the situation leave with the train. It's over. He's gone. It's back to real life now. I exhale and feel the weight lift from me. Looking out, down the Valley, I break the silence.

"So who does Da want me to be now?"

REALITY CHECK

Hayes left the MacGregor house in a mixed mood. He was excited and heartened by his discussions with the Chief, but had been caught off-guard when Rori had appeared. She had seemed so happy before she'd known he was there. It must have been clear to everyone in the room that their friendship had terminated poorly. Owen Mac had reassured him, saying it was a good thing. He'd said that if Rori was upset she would be less likely to pursue further involvement through Hayes and had admitted that he'd been concerned that she might. He seemed relieved by her dejected reaction.

She hates me, Hayes thought, concerned by how much it was affecting him.

Sighing, he straightened himself and focused on the positives. He would be leaving. It was unlikely he would see her anymore, except maybe in passing on Train Days. He had a powerful new ally in his private battle against the City and he had completed his first successful interactions as acting Ambassador. Liam Malcolm might be impressed enough to let him come alone again in the future and he would be able to speak privately with the Chief again.

Standing on the platform with his bag, Hayes waited

for his men to board the train. Taking a last look around him, he breathed in the beautiful greenery. He felt exhilarated by a new sense of freedom that was so close he could almost taste it.

A flash of movement caught his eye across the treetops, by the cliff. There were two of them. He could tell she was one of them, he knew the way she moved. They sat down on a ledge partway up the cliff. He felt his heavy heart lift a little. She looked as free as he wanted to be. He stepped aboard the train feeling more confident. Rori was safe. She wasn't alone and she was free. That was all he could hope for her. Now he could focus on that for his own family.

Throwing his bag under a seat, he turned to his men. Reg was staring at him, but the others appeared relaxed as the electromagnets were engaged and the train rose up from the tracks, starting its journey back to the City. Hayes decided it was probably best to confront Reg before he said or did something impulsive or damaging.

"Can I have a word, Reg?" Hayes regarded his men. "We'll be back in a minute," he said, pushing through the doors to the next car. He walked between the rows of boxed vegetables and turned to face Reg as he arrived.

"What, Reg?"

"I thought *you* wanted a word with *me*," Reg said snidely. Hayes raised an eyebrow in answer and waited for Reg to come out with it. Reg advanced on him, his thick finger prodding Hayes in the chest.

"I've been thinking about what happened last night Smiler, and if you ever do that to me again, you will pay for it."

Hayes swatted the finger away.

"So I got a bit of dirt on your face, big deal. I'll tell you again what I told you last night. That was the Chief's daughter and your dad would've had your balls if you'd done anything to her without his permission. You could've screwed the whole system with one drunken mistake. I did you a favor. If you can't see that, your judgment is just as bad when you're sober."

"Whatever Smiler. You just like proving how tough you are."

Reg had always been jealous of Hayes' leadership and fighting skills. Since his father's death, Hayes had known he'd need to be as strong as possible to protect what remained of his family. It was his dedication to training coupled with his large frame that had seen him rise through the ranks, proving himself in fight after fight and earning the respect of others in the process. Reg lacked any such dedication and had gained his rank on the coattails of his father.

Hayes looked at his hard eyes and sinister smirk. Reg had an obvious deficiency of the moral fiber required for people to follow him. He was as malicious as his father, but he lacked the understanding of human nature that was needed to manipulate and bend people to his will. Or so Hayes had thought.

"If you *ever* try to belittle me again," Reg threatened, "I will stop your sweet little sister from marrying anyone."

The words hit Hayes like a sharp slap. He felt the shock register on his face. Reg went in for the kill.

"And once she hits the service pool, I'm going to do things to her that'll make you wish she was dead. It'll be so much worse than anything your crazy mom has ever had to do, and you won't be able to do a thing about it. Think about *that* next time you feel like pushing me around."

Reg turned and went back into the main car, leaving Hayes stunned. Filled with dread, he felt as though the oxygen had vanished from his lungs.

Managing to stay upright until Reg was out of sight, Hayes hurriedly scrabbled around groping for something to empty his guts into. He upturned a box of carrots onto the one below it as bile crept up his throat. He slumped to his knees retching, long after there was nothing left to bring up.

Eventually, he wiped his mouth and stood, holding the box-rail for balance. Nudging the box of puke to the side with his foot, he prepared to join the others. He pushed through the door and six concerned faces looked at him. Reg ignored him and looked out the window.

"Geez Smiler, you look like shit!" Griggs said, half laughing at him. "Reg said you had a rough night on it. Did you just hurl?"

"I've felt better, that's for sure," he replied honestly. "I think I might rest a bit. Just ignore me while I curl up and die, OK?" Hayes pulled his legs up on his seat and closed his eyes, playing along with the lie of being hungover for the privacy it afforded him. The conversations returned to normal and he relaxed a little, feeling sufficiently overlooked.

He still felt physically ill from Reg's warning. There wasn't anything he could do to prevent the threat from becoming a reality if that was what Reg wanted to make it. Not without getting rid of Reg anyway, which meant getting rid of his Father too. That was easier said than done. The Director had over-sized body guards, and an endless horde of soldiers waiting in line to take their positions and their benefits should they falter. It would take time to break down the barriers, and Hayes planned to work hard with Owen Mac to generate a powerful uprising and achieve their goals as soon as possible. Definitely before Iris turned eighteen.

He spent the trip back to the City with his eyes closed, running over tasks in his mind. After this morning's frank discussions with Owen Mac, it was clear there was plenty to do. MacGregor needed time. He intended to construct shelters for the potential influx of people and expand the Valley medical services. They would need time to grow, make and store the medicines and other supplies they might need. He'd said they'd been stockpiling some things for a while, but perishable items required constant renewal.

MacGregor also planned to instigate a military type

training program in the valley, to organize and ready his people for potential combat. He wanted them to be able to defend themselves, and if need be, to fight. The Chief had stressed to Hayes that his goal was to succeed with as few casualties as possible, on both sides. He was adamant that the majority of Citizens were victims of circumstance and were not to be held accountable for Luther Derrick's choices.

Hayes had agreed with him, thinking of the women and children in the City. There would be others too, men like him, who cared and wanted more for their people. It was Hayes' job to find those men, without alerting the Director or throwing suspicion on the cause. Most men he knew were soldiers. He didn't trust any of them enough not to turn him in. Especially if Derrick had something over them, as he undoubtedly did.

He thought about the Fish Barrel; the sector of town where the fishermen lived. They were an insular group with different values from soldiers. Maybe they would band with him. If they'd even talk with him, that is. They were very distrusting of all but their own. Even through school he'd had trouble penetrating their restrictive culture and now that he was one of Derrick's Enforcers, he would be even more repulsive to them. He'd have to work on that idea.

Support from the female community was assured already, via his contacts in the service pool, but he had to find a way to empower the women. No more talking about it. It was time for action. He would have to find a way to teach them combat skills. He'd already taught Iris, as his father had taught his Mom, but that was in the privacy of their own home. It would be harder to keep a mass training program under wraps. The women would have to maintain a facade of weakness and submission, but in reality be determined, confident and perhaps even courageous warriors. Strong in every sense of the word and in a position to help themselves.

When Hayes thought about how the women would need to be, he automatically thought of Rori. She had combat skills and fitness certainly, but it was her sense of self that was most significant. She knew who she was, knew what she wanted and wasn't backward about seeking it out. Hayes wanted to instill that kind of thinking in the women of the City. They needed to believe themselves both worthy and capable of the changes they'd have to make.

Hayes shook his head as if to physically remove Rori from his thoughts. He couldn't have her sneaking into his mind all the time. He had to focus on the future now. The train was slowing. Looking up, he saw that they were pulling into the station, the carriage doors aligning with their docking ramps, ready for the goods within to be unloaded.

Reaching for his bag, he swung it over his shoulder. "Right men. Good trip. See you at the training yard." He looked Reg in the eye. "See you in an hour. I have to go home first."

Almost walking out then, Hayes remembered the unpleasant box he'd left in the next car and turned back to retrieve it, not wanting some poor, unsuspecting laborer to unpack it with the other boxes.

"Gotta run home to check on your crazy Mommy?"

"Yes, actually."

Pushing through into the next car, Hayes picked up the offending box and walked out the doors, dodging the incoming laborers and any further comments from Reg.

He walked toward his apartment building. People brightened the streets with their colors and their noise, but he ignored them all. He always worried about what he'd be coming home to and today was no exception. If anything he felt more apprehensive, destabilized by Reg's threats.

Derrick Tower loomed behind him as he strode away from the station. He walked through the crisscross shadows cast onto the street by its transmitting antenna.

The building itself wasn't overly tall or tower-like. It was the pointed metal structure that had led to its name. Reg would be heading straight up to Luther's office.

The Tower, as it was more commonly known, was home to the Derricks, and housed their enterprises on the floors below. Luther lived on the top level, while Reg had the apartment one below. There was no Mrs. Derrick now, and the rumors of how she had died were many and varied.

Below their living quarters was Luther's office floor and two more apartment floors for his protective henchmen. The lower floors were occupied by military related spaces such as the club, the Mess, the medical center, the radio station and the gym. The ground floor joined right onto the train station. Derrick Tower was the center of town, with the rest of the population filling the surrounding buildings, spreading out in a neat grid-like pattern.

Inside the inner grid perimeter, where the buildings had functional plumbing and electricity, things were reasonably maintained. Beyond the limits, without enough people to revive them, the buildings lapsed into slowly decaying ruins. Hayes rounded the corner and walked toward his own building, the tallest in the City.

It was a sixteen-story beige monster, standing conspicuously above the smaller more streamlined grays, rusts and creams of the structures below. Made all the more unattractive by its false block fascia and bulky intermittent protrusions of ledges and balconies, it lacked the tasteful appeal of Derrick Tower. Ugly as it was, it was home, and the sight of it eased some of Hayes' tension.

He walked inside and was surrounded by the unusually comforting mash up of shining beige tile, cracked mirrored glass and more assorted distasteful tones of brown. Walking past the box-like shell of the broken elevator that sat motionless in its shaft on the ground floor, he followed the path to the stairwell. Even the path felt reassuring.

There was something comforting about the gloss of the tiles having been worn completely away by the traffic of the building's occupants over the years. They'd all carved the trail homeward.

It was a long climb. The Hayes family lived on the fifteenth floor, where they had always lived since Ethan Hayes had first been granted the apartment. Morrison's rank and therefore his level of accommodation had exceeded his father's, but he had chosen to stay put. He preferred his friendlier neighborhood and its distance from the Director.

Most of the other apartments in the building housed mid-level soldiers with families. It was a better environment for Iris. The apartment blocks closer to Derrick Tower, where higher ranking Enforcers lived, were less savory. Few of them ever married, preferring to live unattached and utilizing the service pool for sexual gratification, never acknowledging any of the children born to those women as their own. Hayes felt he had a greater sense of family than that.

Their's was a plain apartment, but his mother had dressed it with her creative flair over the years using color and texture to create a pleasant retreat from the dreary outside. It was home, and worked well for all of their needs. The white room that his father had built into it would be hard to recreate elsewhere these days. The levy on building supplies was ever-increasing.

Hayes came to a stop and reached for his keys, regaining his breath from the climb. Opening the door, he scanned the room, assessing it as usual, for signs of disruption. Everything looked as it should, and he could hear voices in the kitchen.

"I'm home," he called, relieved. Dropping his bag to the side and strolling to the kitchen, he swept his mom into a warm hug, kissing the top of her head. He smiled at Iris, who smiled back and nodded in answer to his unasked question. Things were fine.

"I can't stay long. I have to get back to work." Releasing his mother, he slung an arm around Iris's shoulders. "Did you miss me?"

"Always, Morrie," Lu-Belle gushed. "Look at you!" She dusted his jacket sleeve and reached up to tidy his wiry hair. "You look like you could use a shower. Do you have time?"

"Mom," he moaned half-heartedly, angling his head away from her fussing. He secretly enjoyed her motherly attentions, but felt it silly for a grown man to feel that way. "I'm about to clean up, I just wanted to see my girls first OK?" Lu-Belle smiled fondly at him as her hands swept him out of the kitchen.

Grabbing his bag, he went down the hall, tossing it on his bed and shrugged out of his jacket. Pulling a new set of khakis from his immaculately ordered drawers, he tucked them under his arm, looked around his room and felt calmer. Keeping his surroundings neat and controlled eased the anxiety that frequently plagued him.

Threats to his family were normally subtly implied to promote his ongoing compliance. It was the same for all citizens. It had been a while since a direct threat was made against his family and he feared for them greatly. He knew all too well what could transpire if the bully tactics became reality.

Hayes looked at himself in the bathroom mirror while the shower warmed up. Sighing, he tried to release the strain he saw on his face, not wanting to worry his Mom and Iris. He splashed cool water from the sink onto his face and cupped his hands under the tap, bringing the water to his mouth. It tasted stale and tainted, the way it always did after drinking the naturally fresh water from the Valley.

The shower was pitiful but hot and he let the heat soften his tense muscles as the water circled around the stained shower floor and down the drain. Washing in a hurry, and drying himself just as quickly, he dressed and combed his hair. He wiped the steamed mirror with his towel, revealing a tidy, well presented young man.

Confidence restored, Hayes left the bathroom. The apartment smelt delicious and his stomach rumbled, reminding him of its emptiness. Throwing his laundry into the cupboard hamper, he joined his family at the table.

"I thought you might be hungry, so I whipped up a meal." Lu-Belle nudged the plate in front of him. It was a steaming plate of vegetables and fish, big enough to feed the entire family. Hayes looked at their plates and noticed the contrast in portions.

"Mom, I can't eat all this," he said convincingly. "You know they feed us well in the Valley. I had a huge breakfast. Here!" Moving their plates closer to his, he evened up the servings with his fork. "Help me with this so it doesn't go to waste." His stomach rumbled in disagreement, but he ignored it.

Eating quickly, Hayes watched, satisfied as Lu-Belle and Iris finished theirs. Thanking them, he excused himself from the table to rinse his plate in the sink. Shaking the dust from his jacket, he pulled it back on, kissing his girls on the top of their heads before rushing out the door.

RAILROADED

Hayes' stomach was troubling him. He'd had to run to the Tower and his hastily eaten lunch was not sitting right. Being nervous didn't help either, he thought as he rode up to Derrick's office in the only functional elevator in town. The sensation of moving vertically in it always toyed with his gut and the compounding troubles from all these factors had brought the tension back into his shoulders.

He used his brief time in the elevator to prepare his face. He blanked his expressions, feeling the practiced mask slide over his features. He was Smiler now. Smiler lived to be an Enforcer. He conducted himself strongly and dutifully whilst easily dismissing emotion with sarcastic jest. Most of the young cadets thought Smiler was the nickname he'd acquired with wit and that his scar was a coincidence. The older soldiers knew the truth.

The elevator doors opened and Smiler stepped into the reception area of Luther Derrick's headquarters. Two very attractive young women smiled at him as he approached the polished wooden counter. Both sported invitingly rouged lips, boasting the rare and expensive luxury of make-up. Luther liked to keep the best for himself, flaunting the extent of his power. It reinforced the hierarchy he had created. When others saw what was available to those at the top of the ladder, they got motivated to climb it. There was an ever-increasing number of Lackeys set to assume the position of anyone who happened to fall from grace. Morrison Hayes had a long way to fall if he lost his grip on the ladder. Swallowing the thought, he ensured Smiler's grin was plastered onto his face.

"Smiler. Mr. Derrick is expecting you." She rose from the desk, giving Smiler the full view of her stylishly clad figure. Her name was Cynthia. She had been two years behind him in school and he recalled she had known back then that she was beautiful. The sound of her heeled shoes on the tiled floor accompanied them as he followed her teasing sashay to Luther's door, where she knocked and waited for a response.

"Enter."

"I'll take it from here, Cynthia. Thanks." He dismissed her as he opened the door, but staying in character looked behind him at her ass as she walked away, knowing the occupants of the office saw him do so. Closing the door, he walked in, shaking his head and making appreciative noises.

"Mr. Derrick, good afternoon. Beaumont. Elmerson," Smiler greeted the two over-sized henchmen standing intimidatingly on either side of him as he entered. He nodded acknowledgment to Reg who stood behind his father, his mouth warped in a disturbing smile.

"Smiler," Luther stood in greeting. His height was imposing to most, but Smiler was both taller and broader than both Derrick men, and did not find a display of height unsettling. What he did find unsettling, was Luther's stone cold glare and the lines of his face that emanated cruelty. With those steel eyes, he directed Hayes to sit. Smiler did so, resting his bag on his lap and rifling through it to retrieve the trading paperwork.

Luther sat down too, his chair creaking as he leaned

back. Hayes felt the weight of eyes appraising him and was not surprised to find Luther staring at him as he looked up from the papers he'd placed on the desk.

"Reg reports you managed the duties of Ambassador in Liam's absence. I assume you somehow managed to use this position to obtain other information." For a moment Hayes nearly lost his mask. Derrick couldn't possibly know what he and MacGregor had discussed. Holding his tongue, lest he implicate himself, he looked blankly at Derrick.

"My son informs me you gained access to an area outside of the village. Did you find the criminals who evaded you?"

Hayes sighed internally. Of course, he was meant to have been looking for the escapee Daltons whilst in the Valley.

"No sign, Sir," he lied. "I was able to access only marginally further than the village. If the culprits were in the Valley, they were lying low."

Luther begrudgingly digested this as he scanned over the paperwork. "Any reports of Dalton defiance?"

Hayes was about to say no, but remembered Rori's infraction. "There was an incident of a girl throwing an apple at a soldier, but she was dealt with appropriately, Sir. It'll take her a week to clean the shit off herself."

Smiling, the Director shuffled the documents and slid them into the sorting tray to deal with later. Sitting back in his chair, he steepled his fingers in thought as his smile faded. Normally, Hayes would be dismissed to return to patrol or training, but he sensed the delay. Noting Reg's increasing smirk as he stood at his father's shoulder, Hayes began to worry about what was coming.

"I find myself perplexed," Luther said, without alluding to the cause of confusion, forcing Smiler to inquire.

"Sir?"

"On one hand I'm pleased, but on the other, I'm deeply enraged. I thought I had made it clear, what I expect from you, Smiler. I didn't think you were capable of this kind of behavior after how well I've treated you and your family. Have I not been clear enough?"

Hayes felt his stomach drop. He held his mask, petrified of dropping that too. His heart hammered in his chest as he searched the faces around him for clues. Reg looked delighted. Beaumont and Elmo had stepped closer to him and looked prepared to pounce, merely awaiting Luther's directive. Luther himself looked mildly surprised, partially annoyed, but overall appeared to be reasonably composed. Surely if he'd caught wind of rebellion, Hayes would be tortured or dead by now.

No. This was something else. From Reg's behavior, it was obviously something to do with him. Hayes collected himself. He wouldn't know until he asked.

"I'm not sure I know to what you're referring, Sir. Do you have a complaint of misconduct?" he asked, unable to keep his gaze from returning to Reg questioningly. Reg gave him a menacing nod. Damn it Reg, *what now*?

"You don't recall?" Luther asked. "My, my. You must have had a lot to drink. Interesting how one's true nature can be unleashed by alcohol. I'd always thought you a bit too *nice*, you know, a bit much like your father. I've kept a close eye on you, kept your strings tight, in case you turned out as he did. I doubted you would, after we made an example of him in front of you, but I've always wondered if that lesson was enough to keep you in line."

Hayes was confused again. Luther's words were swirling around in his head. Derrick had suspected him of being like his father, but now appeared to be leaning the other way. Definitely not rebellion then. What was it he was meant to have done? Keeping his mouth shut, Hayes waited to be enlightened.

"Now I learn there is a dark streak in you," Derrick continued, "And it pleases me no end. However, I will not condone insubordination."

Hayes' continued state of confusion became disrupted

as he was pulled from his chair by Fat Elmo and Beaumont. He knew better than to resist and stood compliantly, waiting. Waiting for Luther to make sense, and for the beating he knew was coming.

"Next time you want to dip your stick, do it in the women provided. Do not attack them in the Valley streets." Hayes couldn't believe his ears. Luther continued before he could deny any such behavior. "While I applaud your choice of the Dalton Chief's daughter – Lord knows I'd love to see his face if that happened, you were lucky that Reg had the sense to stop you when he did. Do you accept responsibility for this incident, or do we need to involve your family?"

Hayes looked to Reg, who nodded again, his eyes amused, challenging Hayes to defy him. Thinking of the threat on the train, Hayes swallowed.

"I remember now, Sir. I accept full responsibility. I clearly overindulged and accept the repercussions for that. I was blinded by a hot piece of ass with a rack so inviting I couldn't help myself. It was an error of judgment and I apologize for any inconvenience it may cause," Smiler confessed.

"*Inconvenience?* Your actions could have threatened the arrangements we have with the Valley. You've endangered the supply and you will be held accountable. However, you have impressed me with this uncharacteristic display of aggression toward Daltons and I'm sure I can use that to my benefit. Should you survive your punishment, you will maintain your rank and title as Enforcer and continue to train as Ambassador." A smile grew on the Director's cruel lips. "And please do survive Smiler, because I am so looking forward to hearing stories of your interactions with the Chief following this incident." Chuckling to himself, Luther Derrick rose from his desk and walked around to stand in front of Hayes. Grinning in a disturbingly, pleasant manner, he jammed a fist into Hayes' stomach, causing him to double over and gasp for breath.

Still bent over, Hayes felt firm hands grasp his head by the hair, driving it down hard to meet the knee that came charging from below. His nose split across the bridge and his vision blurred, a blackness tinging the edges.

"Get him out of here before he makes more mess," Luther directed his Henchmen, before returning to his chair. Dismissing them all with a wave of his hand, he spun his chair around, laughing again.

Reg joined in the laughter, and it followed Hayes out the door as he was escorted to the room down the hall reserved for delivering Luther Derrick's justice. He moved mechanically with his captors, in a partial stupor. As they entered into the easy-to-clean room, he retreated into his mind, distancing himself from his body. Knowing he must survive whatever came, he waited for the real beating to begin. He barely registered the first blows. After that, he felt nothing.

***

Hayes became aware of noise around him. Pain shot down his sides as he tried to move. He ached all over. He'd survived then. Struggling to open his eyes, he found they were swollen shut. Tongue fat and tasting of metal, he tried to speak, but the words came out as muffled and clumsy grunts.

"Don't try to speak Morrie," his Mom's voice warned. "They did a real number on you. You're in Paulie's apartment. When they dropped you off, there was no way we could get you upstairs. Paulie was kind enough to offer his, and helped us get you to bed." Her voice was full of concern, and wavered as though she was on the brink of tears. It must look pretty bad, Hayes thought.

"Do you think you can take some medicine? We got some poppy serum from the clinic. It will help with the pain." Hayes felt something cool trickle past his swollen lips and had to swallow. It tasted awful.

"Water," he mouthed. The pain was less annoying than

the taste or his dry mouth. Again something cool touched his lips and he drank as much as he could. His head was throbbing and he wondered how long he'd been there.

"The doctor came by. He said when the swelling goes down he'll be able to assess you better. He said that your ribs are the most concerning at this stage, and that you have to breathe properly even if it hurts." Lu-Belle gingerly swept the hair from his brow and placed a cool compress over his eyes.

"Oh Morrie. Whatever it was, don't do it again. I was so scared we would lose you." She was openly weeping now. Hayes raised his hand, reaching out to her, as the pain shot down his side. She took it and he gave her hand a firm squeeze, trying to communicate what his injuries prevented him from saying. She sniffed and squeezed back. He listened as her breathing steadied and soon her weight shifted away from him.

"I have to get to work now Morrie. You rest and I'll come and check on you as soon as I'm done. Iris will be along after school and Paulie said he'd pop in on his breaks. Indi was asking after you too, but I told her to hold back a while. You're not up to dating in your condition."

Hayes would've laughed if he could. His mother squeezed his hand again before she left.

Wishing he could see, Hayes wanted to take stock of his wounds, to gauge how long he would take to heal. The longer he was down, the less protection his family would have. His brain started to tingle around the edges and his pain ebbed slightly. He fought sleep, but the medicine overpowered him. He slept restlessly, plagued by bizarre dreams and pain when he lashed out.

When he woke again with some clarity, he was alone. It was light. His eyes told him that much as he strained to open them. Slowly the room came into focus through the thin slits he could manage. He moved a hand toward his face, but gasped as his ribs reacted to the movement. Wary, he slowly moved the other arm instead. While uncomfortable, it was more manageable and he was able to run his fingers lightly over the contours of his tenderized face.

His fingers didn't recognize what they were touching. His nose and eyes were puffed out, the skin pulled taut in an attempt to contain the swelling. Both eyebrows had been split and he could feel the bristles of several stitches. Tracing his jaw, he was pleased to find it tender, but intact. His mouth was swollen and a tooth was slightly loose. It must look worse than it really is, he thought. He would heal. Falling asleep again, he slept heavily.

***

He could hear Iris's voice, but she wasn't talking to him. A man was responding to her and she laughed. Hayes wondered who it was, his thoughts still scattered from sleep. Opening his eyes, he couldn't see anyone, only flowers. It didn't make sense. Forcing his brain to focus, he stared at the identical daisies, growing in their uniform rows. He was staring at a wall. Paulie's wall. It was coming back to him. His body felt as if it'd been thrown into a washing machine for the spin cycle. He knew rolling over would bring more pain, so he stayed where he was and listened.

There was something about the way Iris had laughed that made his hair stand on end. It was a flirty laugh. Hayes presumed she wasn't talking to the doctor. Dr. Wilson was a slimy old weasel, with bad breath and a pot belly. Iris would not be flirting with him. Who else could it be? Paulie? It was Paulie's apartment after all.

Hayes listened intently, trying to catch familiarities in the masculine voice. Yes, Paulie. Straining to hear what they were talking about, he caught words that sent chills down his spine.

"…shouldn't be able to do this." "…kill them and set us all free."

They were talking treason. Openly.

"Iris?" It came out in a rasping exhalation. Hayes coughed a little to clear his throat and immediately wished he hadn't. Stabbing pain radiated from his left side. Despite his high tolerance, the pain took his breath away. He waited for it to subside. It didn't, so he figured he might as well move into a more comfortable position. It hurt like hell.

"Morrison?" Iris hovered over him. "Here, let me put something cold on it. The doc said that would help." She wrung out a cool cloth and lay it over the offending ribs, loosening his arms to do so. "The doc said deep breathing and coughing now and then would help keep your lungs clean, but you should take pain relief first."

She sat next to him, leaning over with concern. "They really messed you up this time. Your face looks terrible."

"Thanks Eyes, always nice to get compliments." Cracking what he hoped was a reassuring smile, he split his swollen lip. He tried to suck it into his mouth to stem the bleed, but couldn't manage it. Iris brought another cool cloth to his lip and held it in place.

"Don't joke, Morrie. We were really worried. You wouldn't wake up for hours. What if you'd been turned into a vegetable?" She stopped, choked by emotion.

Hayes put his hand over hers and squeezed lightly. It upset him to have his family worry like this, but it was far better than the alternative. He could heal from a beating, but he couldn't heal from causing them to needlessly suffer alongside him.

"I'll be fine Iris," he said, meeting her red-rimmed eyes. "It's not as bad as it looks. I'll be better in no time. Derrick wanted me alive so he could make me squirm some more. You'll see. If he wanted me dead, that's where I'd be."

Understanding flashed across her face. She knew it to be true. Her mouth tightened to a thin line and she nodded, wiping a stray tear from her cheek. She watched him awhile, fiddling with the wet cloths and checking his wounds repeatedly.

"What do you want to ask, Iris?"

"What did you do?"

Hayes studied her face and thought about the partial conversation he'd overheard. He couldn't risk her getting involved in that kind of discussion. She was too young to understand the potential fallout of a throw away comment.

"I didn't do anything Eyes. I had a disagreement with Reg, which lead to this." He gestured vaguely to himself with his free hand, leaving the other firmly at his side. "It's over now. He's had his revenge."

Iris looked intently at him. "Are we still in danger?" she asked, assuming he'd taken the beating on his family's behalf. She didn't shift her gaze, giving him no leeway. He sighed painfully, wincing again on the following inhalation.

"Iris," he said steadily, "you are always in danger. Never assume you are not. Never assume no one is listening to what you say." Pausing, he darted his eyes to where she had come from. His eyes locked onto Paulie's, who bashfully acknowledged his part in the discussion, by blushing and nodding in agreement.

"Now help me up. I'm busting for a piss and I don't want to swim in it," he said light-heartedly, easing the tension in the room. He was satisfied they had heard his warning.

Iris showed him how to move clutching a pillow. Hayes was surprised at the pressure it relieved, making movement moderately less painful. Once up he was able to move slowly, but unaided to the bathroom, where he closed the door on Iris and Paulie, to afford himself the privacy to check out his injuries.

He wasn't surprised to see blood in the bowl as he painfully emptied his bladder. His kidneys had been pummeled. Flushing it away, he stood in front of the full length mirror.

Able to see better each time he'd woken up, Hayes knew the swelling around his eyes was going down, but it was a shock to see the dark colors marbling his distorted face. He ran his fingers over it again, seeing each area as he did so. It was fairly superficial, he decided. When the bruising cleared up he would have a few more scars, but he was beyond caring about such things.

His eyes traveled down his reflection. Wearing only shorts, he had a full view of his damaged body. It was a calico patchwork of blooms ranging from inflamed reds to blacks. There were more stitches, where skin had split with the impact of the blows he'd received. It hurt too much to twist and see his back, but he expected it was just more of the same; it felt like the rest. He left the bathroom in a hopeful mood. Apart from maybe the ribs, his injuries should heal over the next few weeks.

A delicious smell greeted him as he returned to the room Paulie had lent him. Iris was holding a bowl of steaming stew and had propped his pillows so he could sit to eat in bed. Hayes eased himself down, hungrier than he could ever remember being.

"Thanks Eyes, I'm starving. How long have I been out of it?" He tentatively accepted the cloth wrapped bowl and nestled it into the crook of his left arm, using his right to raise a heaped spoon to his mouth. Blowing on the hot, meaty contents, he greedily shoveled it into his stiff mouth. His hunger trumped his pain.

"It's been two and a bit days since you left home to go to the tower." She set a glass of water on the table by the bed, next to a small, nearly empty medicine bottle. "The doc said you should keep up your fluids and your strength. He wants you up and about as soon as you can, but no twisting, pulling, pushing or reaching." She repeated the instructions sternly as if she was the authority on the matter.

"Yes Dr. Iris." Hayes smiled, scraping the last of the stew from the bowl.

Iris scowled at him and traded his empty bowl for the glass. He drank it dry and watched Iris reach for the little bottle. Holding it close to her face, she swilled the liquid and frowned.

"No more poppy serum," Hayes said, guessing her thoughts. "We can't afford it."

"But -"

"No more."

Nodding sadly, she gave him the last of it and made him drink more water. Iris cleared away the dishes and set up a fresh bowl of cold water. Making him lie down, she applied cold compresses to his side and face again.

"Now get some more sleep," she ordered. "I'm going upstairs to keep an eye on Mom. You know how she gets if her stress levels rise. I've got it covered though, so don't worry," she added, before he could interject. "Paulie's here overnight if you need anything. Other than that, just get better, OK?"

"I'm on it, Eyes. Thanks. For everything," he said gratefully. "I'll be walking up the stairs by the end of the week, you'll see." His voice faded as the medicine dragged him under again.

DALTON SQUADRON

When Da banned me from returning to the City, I thought he'd just have me doing what I normally do during my downtime in the Valley. In winter especially, when the tracks are covered in snow and the way to the City is blocked, I fill in gaps. Whenever someone is short of a hand, I lend it. I quite enjoy doing it. Each day is different and I get to learn all kinds of crazy stuff.

I love working with Horse on his inventions and roaming the foothills shepherding stock with the farmers. I enjoy spending time mixing herbs with Freya, teaching gymnastics to the kids at school, or spinning wool with the old biddies. I can do almost everything there is, to some basic degree. In fact, the only thing I don't do very well, is cooking. Rae says I excel equally at burning and over-seasoning.

This winter will be different. Da wants me to run a training program with Ari and Jerome. We are going to train an army. I'm so excited I don't even mind staying away from the City. We are doing it quietly, as we Daltons do best.

Men and women over sixteen will volunteer for the program. We will get them fighting fit, teach them self-defense and weapon use. Da says we should prepare for the worst, but hope for the best. I've never known him to be like this. He has never even hinted to me that he's had thoughts of overthrowing City rule and has always chastised me for flaunting my opinions on the matter. Having dreamed of an opportunity like this, I can't wait to get started.

We have been designated a back field and can use the Great Hall when the weather turns bad. Training will occur each morning at dawn, before the work of the day begins, and before children are set loose outside. The last thing we need is for some kid to shoot his mouth off around an Enforcer on Train Day.

We've set up archery targets along one side and have developed an obstacle course with which to build fitness and strength as well as confidence. There are areas for practicing skills for defense and hand to hand combat, including a designated fighting area. Most Daltons are strong and fit from working the land, but it will take time to get them in shape for an uprising.

Jerome and I view our set up with grins on our faces. Ari appears more thoughtful and serious. He of course is older, and wiser. He knows better than anyone, the path ahead will be paved with blood, sweat and tears. Ari has been training Gophers for two decades, and has lost good men and women to the City. His own son Neeko is in Gopher training, and at fourteen, is almost ready for his first trip to the City.

"Here we go again," Ari says under his breath. I stare at him in disbelief. Giving me a tight smile, he turns away. Of course there have been uprisings before, but I've never heard of any recent enough for Ari to have been involved. My thoughts reel and land on one conclusion. Da would have been Chief then too.

He's tried it before. Unsuccessfully! Being kept in the dark is fruitless. I need to talk to him. If he wants me to be useful, he owes me the truth. I don't want to fail.

I make a firm decision to find Da after training and have a serious conversation. It's too late to find him to talk now that we're on the field and waiting to see how many people will come to the first session. The word has been quietly put out among the target population, stressing the need for secrecy. People start arriving as the sky begins to lighten.

Over two thirds of the Valley's able men and women assemble on the field. A staggering turn out. They are all familiar faces, some from the village I see regularly and some from the far end of the Valley that I see less often. All are dressed appropriately for the task ahead, including the looks of determination on their faces. So many willing to take a stand, I can feel my heart swelling with pride. My people.

Da makes his way through the crowd and climbs up on our makeshift hay bale platform to stand before them. A hush descends. Owen MacGregor is their respected leader. If he speaks, they listen. He sweeps his arms wide in welcome.

"People of Old Dale Town. Daltons of the Valley. Friends and family. It brings me great joy to see so many of us dream of the same future. A future free from slavery and persecution." Da lowers his arms, pausing dramatically. I find myself enthralled, waiting for the next words. I have never seen Da address his people like *this*.

"There is a time fast approaching, when we may have to fight for that future. This time, we will be ready. We are preparing for a potential hostile situation. Every one of you should be prepared to defend yourselves and your families should it be necessary."

Another pause allows the weight of the words to sink in and mutterings rumble through the group. Da raises a hand and silence falls upon them once again. Ari, Jerome and I still stand on the platform, to the side of my father and I cast my eyes over the crowd from my raised position. All eyes are fixed on the Chief.

"I want to make it clear to you all right now. Your lives are too important to throw away in battle. Our numbers speak volumes here, but are a drop in the river when compared to the City. We cannot win that way, and we will not try. We are smarter. We will rely on strategy. We will train to survive."

I'm hanging on every word, like the others. He's right. The City would overpower an army this size in a flash. They have at least five times the manpower, trained and ready.

"If we use our brains and retain our lives, we live to fight another day. Some of you will remember meeting like this before. Things didn't go as planned then, but today is another day. Today is a new beginning!" His voice booms over their heads. The energy in the crowd is electric.

Da thrusts a fist to the air and shakes in emphasis with his next words.

"We will try again and we will keep trying, until we are free!"

The roar of agreement erupts from the crowd so loudly I can feel the vibration in my bones. People are clapping and stomping and whooping. The noise is tremendous in the early morning air. Da raises his hand again for quiet.

"These three remarkable people will be in charge of our training program." Gesturing to us, he still faces the crowd. "I am sure you have all seen them in action before and are in as much awe of their talents as I am. They achieve more with their bravery and sound decision-making than many of us could hope to in our lifetimes. They are the reason we progress as we do. Take it away Gophers."

He meets my eye before he leaps back into the sea of people. The look of pride is unmistakable. My knees feel weak and I feel suddenly overwhelmed that a third of the Valley is watching me as I realize for the first time that my father knows exactly who I am. Before now I have assumed he thought of me as a reckless pain in his ass.

It's difficult to find words, and I'm eternally grateful as Ari begins to explain what will be expected throughout the training program.

***

We Gophers sit together around the table as Jerome's Mom dishes out hot biscuits with cream and jam. Loading up a biscuit, I shove it in my mouth, starving now that training is over. Mrs. Marshall clicks her tongue, tutting at my manners. Stretching an apologetic smile over my bulging cheeks, I thank her graciously when I've swallowed, complimenting her baking abilities as I help myself to another.

"You won't be that size forever if you carry on like that love," she warns. "One day it will find your hips and stay there, you mark my words."

Jerome cracks up. "Might balance out your boobs then, ay Rori?" he says, waving his mother away as my cheeks redden. She chuckles off back to her stove, her own wide hips swaying as she goes.

"Stop talking about my boobs at the breakfast table Jerome," I say between bites. "Don't you have any class?"

He raises his eyebrows at me. "I should wait until lunch to talk about your boobs?" We both laugh, while Ari and Mrs. Marshall exchange eye-rolling glances. Ari clears his throat in his serious teacher-like manner. We snap to attention.

"Tell me how you're spending the week, so I can plan," he says, swiping a biscuit through the whipped cream remnants on his plate.

"Da's got me working with Horse today, then out for the muster tomorrow. The gardens fill all the in between times as usual, but I'm free for training every morning and whenever I'm needed. The muster is an overnighter, but once I'm back, I'm available," I say in a rush. I want to add that I'm very enthusiastic about the training program and am well-psyched by Da's speech, but I know the words are redundant.

Ari nods and looks across to Jerome. Cool and collected, Jerome is suppressing his excitement like a pro. The rugged beard and shaggy blond hair that accompanied him back from the mountains have gone. With his hair cut short, it looks darker and he looks more serious. The dimple in his left cheek still makes an appearance when he smiles though. I like that dimple.

"I'm heading to the City this morning. I might come with you to see Horse before I leave. I want him to check my board before I go. Rori?" He waves his hand in front of my face to bring me back from my thoughts.

"Huh?" I push his hand away. "Why so soon? The train only left a week ago. Has something happened?" A sense of dread begins to build low in my stomach. Had things gone badly in the City? Was it all over before it could start?

"How would we know? That's why I'm going, remember?" Jerome looks at me as if I've said something colossally stupid and out of character. I guess I have. Sitting quietly, I wonder where I left my brain. His look changes to one slightly resembling pity and he explains himself further for my benefit.

"Your Dad thinks it would be best to check the lay of the land early. He believes if our contact were to turn on us, it would happen earlier rather than later. He doesn't want any nasty surprises on Train Day." Jerome watches my expressions for information, so I keep my face perfectly blank.

"I know for a fact, the contact is committed to the cause, but I understand, thank you."

"For a fact?" Jerome prompts, his eyebrows raised in question. Avoiding his eyes, I plan my response. I'm not about to tell him that Hayes is so committed that he stopped in the throes of passion to maintain an alliance with my father that hadn't yet been confirmed.

"He has family to think of and he has suffered at the

hands of Derrick before."

"That sounds like every Citizen ever. Got any other proof?" Jerome probes suspiciously.

Dammit. I narrow my eyes at him. He knows there's more I'm not saying. Well, I'm not going to tell him.

"Where's your dad this morning?" I ask, looking around for anything to distract from his current line of questioning.

"Stalking Aiden's prized stag that escaped to the back forest lot. Don't change the subject."

Another moment passes and I become aware of Ari's added scrutiny. I can't stand it. Excusing myself from the table, I thank Mrs. Marshall for breakfast and walk out the door.

Hitting the road, I head home, wanting a word with Da before I go over to Horse's lair. Jerome trails behind me. I recognize his swift, light-footed gait by sound.

"What?" I say before he reaches my shoulder.

"You don't want to talk about it. I get it. But I need to know if you are going to compromise any of this with your…" He pauses, searching for the right word. "Emotional investment."

"My emotional investment? Are you serious? We are all emotionally investing in this," I point out, ignoring what he is actually asking.

"You know I don't mean that, Rori. I mean us working with your boyfriend."

I stop dead and stare at him.

"He is *not* my boyfriend," I growl at him, skirting my eyes about the lane for anyone who might be listening. "You call him that again and I'll deck you." I storm on toward home, leaving Jerome in the lane thinking whatever he likes.

***

Disappointingly, the study is empty and Da is out. The shelf I'd collapsed still leans against the wall, next to the stack of books that once sat upon it. Picking up the troublesome dowel, I insert it into its empty wall socket. It swivels around loosely and I take it out again, putting it into my satchel. Grabbing some fruit on my way through the kitchen, I head back out.

Closing the door behind me, I begin my walk to Horse's lair. Jerome peels himself off the wall where he has been waiting and falls into step beside me. We walk in silence along the river track. The trees are really starting to lose their leaves now. I pull my jacket closer, noticing the chill in the air. I'm too stubborn to start the conversation, but Jerome isn't going to drop it.

"Look, I've been away, and I've clearly missed something," he starts, testing the waters. "The first I know of anything is when you see him and run crying from the house. I need you to help me understand, Rori. Did he do something to you? Did he hurt you?" The look of concern on Jerome's face is intense. Behind the worry in his eyes is a suppressed anger that catches me off-guard.

"You think he hurt me?" I ask stunned. "He didn't. He didn't do anything." Jerome visibly relaxes. I could leave it there, but he'll be back with more questions soon if I do.

"I was upset, because I did something terrible to him. I acted like one of them. I was trying to prove a point and it backfired. Big time. I hadn't expected to see him the next morning, and I was so ashamed of what I'd done." I pause to calm myself as the feelings rise back to the surface. Swallowing them down, I gesture to Jerome the reason for my inability to speak. Nodding, he waits patiently until I have it under control.

"I owe him an apology, and I couldn't deliver it. Couldn't even look at him without," again the emotion cuts me off, illustrating my point. With a shuddering sigh, I continue. "I feel awful about the whole thing, but I doubt it will have any impact on future interactions for you guys. It will serve Da very well by distancing me though. Satisfied?" I ask, my breath catching as it comes out.

Jerome puts an arm around my shoulder, squeezing me into him briefly, as we keep walking. The wind swirls around us, bringing a blast of cold from the mountains. I huddle under Jerome's wing and feel his chest shake with quiet laughter. I look up at his face, for an explanation.

"So all it takes is cold weather to get you closer to me?" he jokes. I jab him in the ribs and he flinches. "Ow! Geez Rori, can't a guy just enjoy himself a little?" I make a face at him as he rubs his ribs.

"Some guys enjoy themselves too much," I say, snuggling back in. "Can't a girl just warm up in peace?"

"Not a girl as fine as you, Rori." Stopping suddenly, he turns towards my confused face. "Hearing you talk about someone else with that kind of emotion is… I don't like it. I only want you to feel that strongly about me," he says frankly. "Is what we had so easily forgotten?"

"Forgotten? You slept with my sister! You tell me how easy it was to forget what we had!" Pushing him away, I march on. He catches up, but wisely doesn't speak. Horse's shed appears in the distance and I stop, wanting to sort this out before we get there.

"Look Jerome. We're better as friends. What we had wasn't real. We spent too much sweaty time together and it was bound to happen. It was great, but it was hormones. You and Orla did us a favor by highlighting that. I'm over it, and I thought you were too. You've had a string of conquests since then, and it hasn't bothered me. Now, suddenly, I'm briefly involved in an impossible, *inconceivable* non-relationship and you drag this up?" I see him about to respond and I cut him off with my hand. "No. I put it behind me to preserve our friendship. Now I'm asking you to do the same, because I need *you*, not your bullshit. You're amazing and I love you and once I thought I was *in* love with you, but I'm not now. Please, don't mess with my already confused head. I'm not interested. Got it?"

Jerome stares at me, clearly weighing up his argument. Opening his mouth, he promptly closes it again and looks to the ground, searching for his answers there. Folding my arms over my chest, my feet shift impatiently. We both know I'm not going anywhere until it's sorted. Eventually he meets my eyes again, his decision made.

"I get it Rori. I'm not jumping for joy about it, but I understand," he says. "I can't say it doesn't hurt though."

"I'm sure you'll live."

Starting on my way again, I pat his shoulder as I pass. I'd expected a little more dramatics, and I'm glad he didn't embarrass himself by doing that. Things will be a bit awkward between us for a while as it is.

"Yeah, I'll live," he laughs. "Hey, you want me to pass on any messages to your boyfriend when I see him?"

Whirling around, I fix him with a fiery glare. "You're being a real jerk, Jerome!" Walking back to confront him, I push him in the chest. Stepping back, he knows what's coming. I've already warned him. Pushing me back, he readies himself as he would during any of our fight sessions. He dodges the first punch, grinning. That only spurs me on.

Faking to the left, I slam my right fist under his jaw, sending him backwards. Stumbling on a tree root, he lands on his ass. Turning my back on him, I stride to Horse's door, banging on it angrily.

Horse opens up, takes one look at my face and looks behind me. Jerome has pulled himself up and is rubbing his jaw.

"Trouble in paradise?" Horse asks, trying not to laugh.

"Can you check his board now, so he can leave please?" I ask, wanting him out of my sight. Horse takes the board from Jerome and I walk around him, into the workshop.

"Careful at work today, Jerome. Be sure to make it back, because I'm not finished with you!" I yell over my shoulder.

"I'd be disappointed if you were," comes the reply.

Walking straight to the back stairs, I follow them to the

cavern below without looking back.

COVERT AFFAIRS

Hayes pulled open the heavy library door with difficulty, nudging it wider with his hip. Pain shot through his side from the effort, immobilizing him until it subsided. Edging his way carefully inside, he took slow, calculated steps. The walk up to his apartment yesterday had nearly wrecked him. It had been enough to convince him to stay on at Paulie's for a while longer.

Doctor Wilson had written him off duty for the next two weeks. It was both a blessing and a curse. Hayes was in no shape for active duty and had little desire to see the Derricks, or their men at this time, but no work meant his rations had been cut back to the minimum. It wouldn't have bothered him so much if he was able-bodied. He normally took out the rowboat and caught fish to supplement their family allowance, but in his condition, he couldn't haul a fish or row the boat.

He thought maybe Paulie would help Iris to do it, but was loath to ask for more help from the young soldier, who'd already been so accommodating. It didn't pay to be indebted to others. Hayes didn't like the idea of Iris out on the boat alone with him either. The blossoming of chemistry between them over the last week was clear, and although Paulie seemed a nice guy, Hayes was reluctant to condone such a relationship. Not until he was able to explore Paulie's intentions, could he be sure of Iris's safety. He also needed to find out where Paulie's loyalties lay. The earlier comments he'd heard them make, left him uneasy, but also curious. Maybe Paulie could be of use.

Hayes wandered slowly between the aisles of books, craning his head to see who else might be there. After a silent review, he saw a solitary figure. Tucked beyond the table at the far end, almost out of sight, was a dark-haired girl, hunched over an open book. He recognized her immediately.

"Grace?" he called, moving toward her.

The girl jumped and swiveled so suddenly on her chair she nearly fell off.

"Morrison! You scared me. I thought I was alone." Closing the book, she clutched it to her chest and walked into the aisle. Stretching up on long legs, she slid it between the books on the highest shelf.

"It's good that you're reading," he said, brushing his hand along the spines of the books. "You should whenever you can. People hardly come here, so you're not likely to get caught."

"As long as no one sees me." She nodded. "I don't know why they bother teaching us to read if we're punished for wasting our time on books. Derrick says our time is better spent lying on our backs, but I think he's scared of what we might learn if we're given the chance to find out."

Sighing, she moved in close to Hayes, running her fingers gently down his face. The swelling had gone down, but his bruising was still nasty to look at. Citizens were accustomed to such sights however, and Grace's expression showed little reaction.

"Indi said it was bad," she said quietly. "She saw you when they dropped you off, but your Mom wouldn't let her see you up close."

Hayes laughed a little under his breath. "Yeah, Mom told me. I think she was worried Indi might jump my bones and break more of them. It's not too bad. The ribs are the worst, but I'll be better soon enough. Are you going to see Indi today?"

"I'm working at the club with her tonight," she said, looking at the books longingly. "That's why I come to the library. I like to get something else in my mind to think about. You know, *during*. Makes it easier."

Hayes drew her in close on his good side, giving her a light squeeze.

"I'm so sorry Gracie," he breathed across the top of her head. "It won't be for much longer." He moved her back to arm's length so he could see her face.

"I've got good news. It'll be hard work, but if we can pull together there's hope. Tell Indi and the others when you can. I don't need to tell you to keep it quiet, but make sure the kids are all away and you're safe to talk. We need to start planning. For real."

Grace's eyes went wide.

"Are you serious? It's going to happen?"

"We're going to make it happen." He smiled, settling his hand on her shoulder. "You guys need to start training for it. I'll have to show you some things to work on, but," he paused, reviewing himself with disappointment. "I guess I'm going to have to wait until I can open a door properly. Sorry."

"Don't you dare apologize!" Grace scolded. "You're a good man Morrison Hayes, and you deserve better. You concentrate on recovering, and when you're ready, we'll be ready too!" She reached up on tiptoe and kissed his cheek. "I gotta go."

She hesitated, looking up at him with what might have been adoration. Hayes raised an awkward eyebrow at her and she quickly suppressed whatever it was he had seen there. Giving a polite nod, she scooted around him toward the exit. Exhaling roughly as the door closed, Hayes perused the shelves for something to read while he waited.

"Pretty. She your girlfriend?"

Hayes winced as he jerked in the direction of the voice. It came from above him, and Hayes had to take three steps back, before he could comfortably see Jerome Marshall. He was stretched out atop the ventilation ducting that was suspended from the ceiling. Looking very casual for such a feat, he propped his cheek on a crooked elbow, a bored expression on his face.

"How long have you been there?" Hayes asked, ignoring Jerome's question.

"A while," he said evasively. "You look awful. You fall down an elevator shaft or something?" Jerome moved himself to a crouch and tumbled off the ducting to land gracefully on the shelf next to Hayes. He slung his legs over the edge and sat, waiting for a response.

"A case of appeasing a blackmailing Derrick," Hayes said slowly. "Reg told his Dad that *I* drunkenly attacked Rori in the street, when really it was him. I could either confirm the story and take a beating or deny it and have my family beaten instead. No choice really." Hayes studied the Dalton's face. "You?" he asked, nodding to Jerome's swollen jaw.

"Ah. That would be Rori. I called you her boyfriend. She wasn't impressed."

Hayes laughed. Grimacing at the pain it triggered, he grabbed his side. "That sounds about right."

"You think you know her?"

The hairs on his neck bristled at the Dalton's tone. He would need to tread carefully. Staying professional was the best way to continue, but he needed to dispel any ideas Jerome might have of his feelings towards Rori. Hayes immediately regretted his laughter and over-familiar comment.

"Not as well as you," he conciliated. "But I'm sure after my behavior last week, there could be no worse insult to her than referring to me as her boyfriend." Hayes spoke honestly. Being crazy was not a characteristic girls looked for in prospective companions.

"Mm," Jerome mumbled in a noncommittal manner, studying his knuckles as he made a fist and unfurled it again. "She seems to think she owes you an apology for *her* behavior."

"If anyone should apologize, it's me. She told you what happened?" Hayes asked warily.

"She didn't. Seemed pretty cut up about it though. Deeply ashamed of herself, she said." Jerome frowned down at Hayes.

"She needn't be. It was my fault," Hayes stated firmly. "Anyway, enough of Rori. Let's talk about what matters - what you're here for," he said, hoping he could throw Jerome off the matter with a change of subject.

"I just came to check in, as agreed. The meeting place seems appropriately abandoned. No surprises there," Jerome scoffed.

"What do you mean by that?" Hayes narrowed his eyes, not caring for Jerome's judgmental attitude.

"Dumb City slickers stay dumb, because they don't use the information sitting right in front of them. Geez, I thought maybe *you'd* have read a few of these," he said rudely, gesturing to the shelves.

"It's not as simple as that," Hayes said evenly, careful not to bite back. "But yeah, that's the reason I suggested the library. It's often empty and can be accessed by your kind easily enough." Moving on, he indicated his injuries. "As you can see, I haven't achieved much since my return. You've just witnessed my first contact with my network, so you can see there are others willing to build a resistance. That's all the news from this end. Do you have any messages to deliver from MacGregor?"

"None for now." Jerome stood and began walking away along the top of the shelf.

"Oh. Just checking I'm legit then?" Hayes called after him, sure he had guessed correctly. Jerome stopped and

Hayes stared at his back. "I assure you, I'm committed to the cause."

"I'll let him know." Jerome looked over his shoulder. "This is going to be fun. I can tell," he said sarcastically, continuing along the shelf. He acrobatically leapt to the wall, swinging himself up to perch on one of the high windowsills all in the same skillful movement. Hayes watched as Jerome paused briefly on the sill, viewing the scene outside the window before pushing it open and sliding himself through. Just before he pushed it closed, he leaned back in, a sly smile on his face.

"See you on Train Day, Casanova."

With that, he disappeared from view.

FAMILY HISTORY

The light began to fade into evening as I walked back from Horse's lair. He'd been showing me how to calibrate the upgraded maglev boards to account for the extra weight of the materials we bring back from the City. Extra often slows our travel, which is risky if we have to make a fast getaway. Horse has created a new system to ensure the board still sits the optimal distance from the track for top speeds.

It's a shame I won't be able to ride the tracks far enough to hit top speeds. My new boundary is the lookout on the other side of the tunnel. With my new and improved board in my satchel, I find my hand brushing against it, pining. I'm sure I'll get back out there sometime.

The house is quiet when I get home. Everyone is still at school or slaving away in the fields for the parasites. I wander down the hall to Da's study. Still empty.

After lighting the small fire in the study, I open my satchel and retrieve one of Horse's hammers and the new dowel I have made for Da's shelf. Setting the peg at the hole, I whack it in tightly. It holds firm as I wiggle it roughly, testing. The second dowel gets hammered home too and I put the shelf back up, stacking the books tidily, before finally taking my bag up to my room.

When I come back down, Da is waiting for me at the bottom of the stairs.

"Want to talk?" he asks, when I'm still at eye level, a few steps up. Nodding, I join him at the bottom. Putting his heavy hand on my shoulder, he looks down at me, transmitting stiff affection via this small gesture. We walk together down the hall. Closing the door behind us, he sits in his usual chair, behind the desk barrier. I assume my usual seat by the door, ready for a quick exit.

"Thank you for the apology," he says, glancing at the newly re-instated shelf. I give a small nod of acknowledgment. We both know I'm unlikely to emit the actual words of remorse for my behavior. Besides, 'actions speak louder than words' as the saying goes. Behavior always tells the truth and even when words come out right, they aren't always enough. My words rarely come out right. I usually end up provoking some other issue.

"What do you want to talk about, Rori?"

"Everything," I say, before I can stop myself. It sounds like a childish answer, but I realize I mean it. "Tell me everything. This is something I've wanted for ages, but you've always discouraged me - you never let on that you felt the same way! What happened last time? When was it? Why try again now? What's the plan? *Everything*." I fence him in with my eyes so he can't evade my interrogation.

Taking a deep breath, he lets it out slowly. He gets up from his seat and I start worrying he'll dismiss me, but he moves out from behind his desk and sits in the other chair, turning his body to me conversationally. The barrier is gone.

"The last time," he starts carefully, his eyes glazing over in memory, "Was around the time that Patrick was born. Throughout your mother's pregnancy, she had difficulties, and we decided the child would be our last. We didn't know how right we'd be," he says, grief shading his face. I wait quietly for him to carry on, feeling my own grief trying to climb out from the pit inside, where I keep it trapped.

"We had talked about ways to protect our children from the perils of the City. We loved you all so much, we didn't want to lose any more family to the City. My younger brother, Alex was the hostage at the time. I was nine when they took him. He was seven. The same ages as Jack and Evan now." He meets my eyes. "We were just as close."

"With no other successors in the Valley, we knew it was our duty to provide the next hostage. Damned if we weren't going to fight it though." Da's teeth are gritted as he speaks. I've never seen his anger so near the surface. I'd assumed he had somehow made peace with the system and was doing his best to help his people live with it. He's kept his true feelings hidden from me so well that I had come to believe that my own anger in regard to the situation was irrational. Butting heads for years, I see now that we are not so different.

"Of course you realize the Daltons know of the life they could have without the oppression of the City. Our people lived it before the Citizens came. Daltons will always support an endeavor to regain the freedom that is rightfully ours. The City is different. The hierarchy there, keeps the weak obedient and the strong in power. That is how they've managed to survive - by strict controls at a time of global devastation. The years since have just reinforced the regime. Strengthened it even."

I nod, having learned this from history lessons in school, from first hand observations in the City and from Travis Becker's journal. With a history steeped in military power, the citizens were conditioned to follow orders from the strong. They were taught they needed to be controlled in order to survive. History had proved it. Control had seen them live when so many others died.

Citizens lived in a pecking order then and they still do. The lower your rank, the less you receive. It is almost impossible to move up ranks, if you don't have the nutrition, health or support to do so, but it doesn't stop them from trying. They can't leave, so they might as well do the best they can to make it easier on themselves. Da is right to say the regime has strengthened over time. Soldiers rank higher than the rest, and each year there are more soldiers than the year before.

"We knew the Valley was behind us," Da continues, "But we needed people we could trust in the City. I wrote to Alex all the time, just as I write to Patrick now. But Alex and I had codes we had made up as children, so it was easy to communicate with him properly, despite the interception of mail. He told me of life in the City. We began to write of rebellion before Patrick was born.

"We began developing a plan to overthrow Derrick and his minions, to liberate the other Citizens and ourselves. Alex was going to create a council to take over leadership in the City and show the people the option of living another way. With our help, they could learn to provide for themselves and the Dalton-Citizen relationship could be a peaceful one, maintaining trade and support."

Da stops, pinching the bridge of his nose, as if he has a headache. Massaging his brow, he smiles sadly at me from the shadows under his huge hand.

"What happened?" I ask quietly.

"What can always happen when you have to trust others," he answers, just as quietly. Dropping his hand, he gives me a leveling look.

"Betrayal."

"Alex had a few trusted contacts in the City - Ethan, his best friend and two other soldiers that had some sway among the men. I'd met them over the years, during Train Days and such. I'd trusted Ethan and Martinez. It was the other one, Taylor Stevens. I got the wrong feeling from him at the start. He just didn't feel right to me. It was too late to change things though. Alex had already let him in on our plans, and we couldn't risk him leaking information if we expelled him from the group. We continued cautiously, but soon enough Stevens caved under the pressure."

"What did he do?" I ask, literally sitting on the edge of my seat. Shuffling back, I pull my legs up, folding them in front of me.

"It wasn't really his fault, I guess." Da sighs. "Derrick had become suspicious of the relationship between the four of them and had started watching them more closely. Alex informed me they would be spending time apart, until it was safe to resume contact. I suppose hope appears obvious on faces in a place where such a thing is unheard of.

"The last I saw of them, was Martinez. He managed a quick word one Train Day, a few months after your mother had gone. Barely holding himself together, he'd told me that as he'd boarded the train that morning, he had seen Stevens being dragged into Derrick's building. Said he didn't know what to think, but I knew," Da says, his tone turning bitter, as if the words taste bad in his mouth.

"I knew as soon as he'd said it that Taylor Stevens wouldn't hold up under interrogation. I can only assume Derrick threatened his family, as is his way. I knew that when Martinez returned, he would find both Taylor and Ethan killed. I could tell he knew it too by the time it came for him to go back. I offered to hide him, but he boarded the train. He had a wife and children and he wasn't about to let them take his punishment. I never saw him again. I feared the same fate for Alex."

Da stopped talking and moved to the fireplace to put more wood on the dying fire. I hadn't known how my uncle had died. I'd assumed he had died of some illness or accident, because he was still quite young.

"That's why they took Patrick when he was so young? Because they *murdered* Uncle Alex?"

Da nods.

"I wasn't prepared. We weren't ready. The City contingent was dead. Your mother was dead. They demanded a hostage. Derrick presumed I had something to do with the rebellion, though he never openly came out and said it. He came to the Valley himself to collect Patrick," Da says, looking directly at me with raised brows as he sits back down.

Luther Derrick does not frequent the Valley. I gather from Da's expression it had been a purposeful visit. His purpose was to threaten any further ideas of rebellion out of the Dalton Chief. I close my eyes and clench my jaw.

"What did he say that made you drop it?"

"He told me of my brother's conspiring and his intentions to terminate the threat as outlined by the rules of engagement. I was reluctant as we talked terms for the future, hoping to buy some time for my brother. I was trying to piece together an attack on the Director and the soldiers he'd brought with him to the Valley. I had Patrick, upset and squirming in my arms. You and Orla ran past us, playing. Derrick commented on how happy you both seemed, as if you didn't know that death could find you at any moment. It was a thinly veiled threat," Da says distastefully.

"He singled you out, Rori, noticing how the others looked like me. Even Patrick had a head of blond curls. He asked if you took after your mother, and only had to see my face to know you were the spitting image. He told me it would be a shame to lose two so beautiful. I agreed and passed him Patrick. Just handed him over. A *baby*."

A tear escapes the corner of Da's eye and travels into the forest of his beard.

"Oh Da," I breathe, untangling my legs. They shakily carry me to my collapsing tower of a father. Standing behind his chair, I wrap my arms around his neck, resting my face against his, cheek to cheek. Our tears merge, falling together.

One big hand comes to rest over my two. We stay that

way a long time, sharing; grief, anger, love.

Eventually my legs become restless, grounding me in the present again. Da feels it too. His hand gently pats mine and I move slowly backwards to my seat. Da wipes his eyes and pulls a hankie from his pocket. I giggle a little as he intentionally blows his nose loudly. He winks at me and re-pockets his hankie.

"So why now?" I ask. "What's changed?"

There is a weighted pause and I study Da's pensive expression. Why doesn't he just come out and say it? He looks at me. I know that look. He's wondering how much to tell me. Keeping information from me, as always, if he doesn't think I need to know it. Sighing, I wait for what I'm allowed to hear.

"Until now, I haven't found another Citizen I trust," Da states plainly.

"Hayes? I know you can trust him, but how do *you* know you can?"

Da looks at me quizzically and inhales deeply, his shoulders rising substantially with the effort.

"You mean apart from the fact that he has protected you, when he could have left you to be processed? Or could have joined in?" Da raises his eyebrows at me again. "You mean apart from the fact that in all the interactions I have had with him when he's been escorting the train, he has conducted himself with the integrity of an honorable man?"

"Yes," I say, narrowing my eyes. "Apart from those things."

"We share a common interest." He smiles at me oddly. "We want to protect the ones we love from harm. Is that enough?"

"I can see there's something you're not telling me."

Da pauses a moment, as if he's trying to decide whether or not to tell me something.

"Your Uncle Alex's best friend," he says slowly.

"Yes, Ethan. I was listening. What about him?"

"Ethan Hayes had a family too."

I open and close my mouth around silent words that refuse to form, at last, grasping the only word that means anything.

"Hayes."

It's no more than a whisper, but Da hears it and mumbles confirmation.

"So now you know why-" He is cut off mid-sentence by a knock at the door.

"Who is it?" he says gruffly.

"Jerome," comes a slightly nervous reply.

"Come in Jerome." Da looks at me and I lean back in my seat. Jerome enters cautiously. I wonder who he was expecting to see in Da's study, because from the look on his face he didn't want it to be me. Expertly wiping the shaken expression from his face, he closes the door behind him, without asking me to leave.

"Sir. Rori," he says by way of greeting. "Sorry to interrupt. I just got back and thought I would pass on my findings before heading home."

"Glad you're back safely, Jerome. What happened to your face?" Da asks, noticing the swollen mark I left on his jaw.

Jerome doesn't miss a beat.

"Just a rough dismount. Nothing to worry about."

"Right then. Rori and I were just discussing a few family matters. Do you have anything urgent to report?" He looks seriously at Jerome, flicking his gaze briefly in my direction. So briefly, it's almost negligible, but I catch it. It's a reminder I'm in the room; a warning for Jerome to mind his content. I huff a disgruntled sigh at their 'covert' behavior.

"Just talk," I say angrily as they turn their attention to my noise. Jerome of course awaits my father's nod of approval before he speaks.

"Our contact appears committed," he begins, not mentioning Hayes by name. "He also appears to have other -" Jerome breaks off briefly, appraising me before he continues, "*Parties* with similar interests, but I'm not sure how useful they will be. Time will tell."

"What do you mean, *parties*? Why not just call them women?" I suggest, guessing at what he means. I can see I'm right by his expression. "You think it's a problem to discuss it in front of me?" Leaning around Jerome to meet Da's eyes, I give him the eyebrow.

"Unlike you to get nervous around women, Jerome," I say, returning my attention to him. "Please, carry on. I understand the women of the City would be very motivated to overthrow the powers that be. They are treated like garbage and are unlikely to enjoy it. I couldn't think of better allies to have. You're not underestimating women are you?" I smile sweetly, as he tries to regain his footing. Eventually he manages to utter a few words.

"Of course not. And yes, he seems to have taken a few women into his confidence. He had only just made contact with them for the first time when I was there. I arrived early and witnessed the whole interaction. It seemed genuine."

Da's forehead creases. "Interesting it took a week before he did so. Did he mention his reasoning?"

Jerome tosses me another brief look. Sick of it, I throw back daggers from under surly brows.

"Get on with it, Jerome Marshall! I'm not made of glass and I promise I won't break any. I'm sure I can handle anything you have to say, now spit it out!"

Jerome raises his hands defensively at me and talks to the Chief instead.

"He was immobilized upon return to the City. Something unrelated and apparently fictitious caused him to receive a beating shortly after he arrived."

"What?" Da and I exclaim in unison.

"Maybe we should ask *you* about it, Rori? It seems you were the cause."

Again. "What?!"

"He said the other Derrick - old 'what's-his-name' - Reg attacked you in the street. When he got back to the City, Reg told his old man it was Hayes that did it. Not very friendly." Jerome stares at me. "Why is that, do you think, Rori? What the hell happened?"

Two sets of steely eyes nail me to my seat. Sighing, I look away.

"In my defense, it was unintentional. It was a case of wrong place wrong time, for all of us."

Still looking at me.

"I wanted some air, so I went for a walk. It was after the Gathering. Reg snuck out from behind the Kahn's place - he was probably peeing on their house. He pulled my cloak off and was trying to grab me. He was pretty drunk."

They're still staring at me, in alarm now.

"It was easy enough to get around him, which I did, but I ran straight into Hayes. True to form, he played the hero card - I didn't need him to. Anyway, I left and hid so I could watch what happened next. Reg got his ass handed to him, and Hayes made it look embarrassingly easy too. They seemed to end on friendly enough terms though. Hayes helped him up and they left together."

I shrug, trying unconvincingly to minimize the incident. Da and Jerome aren't fooled. Clearly there was more conflict between Reg and Hayes than any of us had known about.

"You didn't think it was important to mention this to me?" Da asks with a tight jaw. His balled fist thumps his desk. "My own daughter! Attacked in *my* streets?"

"Well, come on. 'Attacked' is a bit too strong a word. He was drunk. Rudely approached would be a better description. Besides, it seemed to have been resolved. How was I to know Hayes would be punished for Reg's misbehavior?" I stop as soon as I say it. "Yeah, that does sound about right," I conclude, unable to retain the spite from my tone. I change the subject to one which seems more important.

"How is he? What did you say before? Immobilized?"

"Calm down," Jerome says, unnecessarily. "He was walking when I saw him, but the guy looked like crap. His face was a mess of bruising and stitches and I'm pretty sure he's got some damage to his ribs. He didn't really go into it."

"He'll be alright though?" I ask, a little too eagerly. Da and Jerome both look at me worryingly. Dammit. My thoughts are open for viewing.

"I'm sure he'll live." Jerome stings me with the words I threw at him this morning.

"That's all to report Sir," he addresses my father, asking to be dismissed.

"Thank you Jerome. We'll talk again soon. Say 'hello' to your folks for me." Da pretends to organize the papers on his desk, waiting politely for Jerome to leave before he begins his lecture.

As Jerome passes, I try to catch his eye, but he purposely avoids my gaze and strides out the door, closing it roughly behind him. Well, I knew it would be awkward between us for a while, but now it looks worse than I'd thought. Turning back to face Da, I find his eyes boring into me.

"Rori Lauren MacGregor," he says, slowly and deliberately. I shudder a little, suddenly craving just a hint of the warmth from our earlier exchange.

"I want to give you what you want. What you would excel at. I want you to help, *but* I want you to be safe! I am giving you opportunities in the valley to aid the effort, but I cannot keep you involved at even a minor level if you continue to jeopardize relationships before we have even started. Do you understand?"

I nod miserably, knowing I have singlehandedly managed to hurt people and help complicate the pathway to a rebellion still in its infancy. In the space of a week! I need to be grounded.

"I understand Da. I'm sorry. The last thing I want is to stop this from happening. You know that. I'll stay in the Valley. I'll stay away from *all* Citizens. I'll even stay away from the village if you'd like? I'm going on the muster tomorrow, I could ask the Browns or the Johnsons if I could stay on the farms with them? Until we sort something more permanent?" I suggest, hoping he'll still let me be part of something, but knowing I must seem like poison. I don't want to be our downfall. "I'll stay away. I don't want anyone else hurt because of me. I'd still like to help at trainings and to be kept informed, if you think that would be alright?" I ask tentatively, not brave enough to ask the outright question - 'if you trust me to do a good job and not to act recklessly regarding any information'.

"We'll see, Rori." Da drags a hand over his face and strokes his beard thoughtfully. "I think it would be a good idea to ask around tomorrow about accommodation away from here. There is too much coming and going in this house and there will only be more as things progress. It'll be too hard to keep you out of it without locking you in your room. Not that a locked door would stop you!" He smiles briefly, chuckling under his breath.

"I know you'd rather be out in the air than trapped inside, and anywhere in the Village will be too close not to tempt your curiosity somewhere along the line." He meets my eyes. We both know that's the truth. "The farmlands is a good choice. I'll even give you a pass on shit patrol, so you don't need to be back for Train Days. I'll still need you at trainings. We can talk then if we need to." He nods in conclusion, approving the plan. It's what he's always wanted. "Maybe start packing now, if you are off down the Valley tomorrow. We both know no one will leave you out in the cold."

Deflated, I rise from my chair, conceding to my father's wishes. My attempts to be at the forefront of the rebellion effort have been disastrous. Apparently I have less to offer than I thought. Despite good intentions, I'm a liability. I'm hurting people on our side before we've even started. Cutting myself out of the equation is the right thing to do.

"We'll miss you around here Rori," Da says remorsefully, but continues with a teasing smile. "Who else is going to eat all the food and keep us in check with her sharp mouth?"

"A dog could do that," I reply quietly, walking out the door.

CHANGE OF SCENE

The material sum of my life fits into one bag. It sits patiently next to me on the bed as I gaze about my room, which is as bare as the ceiling I've stared at every night before falling asleep. Dragging the bag over my shoulder, I pull the curtains open. Still dark out. Turning off the light, I head downstairs.

Most of my family are up and waiting for me. They hug me and say ordinary things in ordinary ways, like 'take care' or 'see ya soon'. It doesn't quite feel like enough. I know I'm not going far, that I'll still see them at training or when I stop by. But this is the first time I've left for longer than a week or two. It's more permanent. I'm leaving home.

Feeling misplaced and awkward, I rush my goodbyes. Only Rae displays any sign of recognizing the gravity of the situation, but she quickly brushes the tear from her eye as she turns away. She has given me a second large bag to carry. It's full of food to take with me, for the muster and to aid the family I will be staying with. Maybe I'd feel better if I knew for certain which family it would be.

With a final farewell to all, I leave by the back door to where Aiden has hobbled Mickey for me. Snorting at me in welcome, Mickey snuffles me as I strap my bags together. He quivers as I sling them over his back, one each side. Attaching my bed roll in between, I give the cargo a quick tug to check it's secured.

About to climb up, I have to take one more look at the house I grew up in. The porch light is on and something gray catches my eye. My Cloak. It's hanging on one of the pegs at the back door. My mind goes back to the night I abandoned it at the Ambassador's cottage. I hadn't been able to find it when I'd stolen back the next day, after the train had gone.

Retrieving it, I roll it into a ball and stuff it into the top of my bag. Tossing Mickey's reins over his head, I swing myself off the mounting block and onto his back. Circling the yard, I walk Mickey out the gate to the lane. It's a small comfort knowing everything will run more smoothly and people will be safer with me out of the way.

Lost in self-pity, I direct Mickey down the lane towards the edge of the village. Just past the last house, where the space opens up to fields of crops, I'm joined by Jerome on his mare, Danni. The horses fall into step as he rides beside me in the half-dark of pre-dawn. Danni has saddlebags too. I look up to find Jerome smiling at me with an overstretched, clown grin.

"*You're* coming on the muster?" I ask, in a tone that is obviously less than impressed. "Don't you have some top secret espionage to attend to?"

"And miss all the fun?" he asks, laughing. "Why risk my life in the City, when I can get tortured daily by a beautiful girl in the comfort of my own environment?"

"Yeah. *I'm* tormenting *you*."

Urging Mickey forward, I leave him behind, but he soon trots up alongside, ready for round two. I shoot him a warning glance and his face softens into an apologetic smile, his look almost angelic. Rolling my eyes in vague acceptance, I give him a thin smile in return and we ride together in peace a while.

"You've got a lot of gear for an overnighter," he

observes, nodding at my loaded bags.

"I'm dropping some off before we head out," I say evenly.

"Where?" Jerome asks, his interest piqued.

"The Brown's or the Johnson's. I don't know yet. It depends who wants a house guest for the next season or two."

"You're moving?"

I nod.

Jerome looks at me in disbelief. "Punishment? Your old man kicking you out?"

"It was my decision actually," I reply, giving Jerome a small half-smile. Looking ahead, I relay the plan, talking as much to myself as to him; strengthening my resolve. "Da agrees. I need to leave the village. I should have left after I was caught in the City. Just can't seem to keep myself out of trouble and we can't risk any further incidents. I refuse to be the reason a revolution fails and I will *not* to be the reason anyone else gets hurt." I pause for a moment, thinking of Hayes receiving a beating due to my involvement, after I had already inflicted my own damage the night before. "It makes sense to leave," I state firmly, in a lowered voice.

"Sure you're not just running away?" Jerome asks after a while.

"Running from what?" I ask, surprised. "I'll still be at trainings and doing my bit to advance the movement. If that's all I can do to help, then I'll be as much help as I can. Can we stop talking about why I'm leaving? I need your opinion on something else," I say, blatantly changing the subject. "I need to stay somewhere. Who do I visit first, Browns or Johnsons?"

"Well now, that's a tough one," says Jerome sarcastically. "The Browns have three grown, well-built boys, and the Johnsons have three pre-teen girls. Are you asking my honest opinion?" He can hardly stifle his laughter. "Twiglet, I can't even believe your old man would sanction the Browns! What was he thinking?" Openly laughing now, he adjusts himself in the saddle. "That's just out of the frying pan and into the fire! Johnson's. It's a no-brainer."

"Yeah, I thought so too. Da must be pretty desperate to get me out of town. I swear, he didn't even bat an eye when I mentioned the Browns!" I can't help but laugh myself as I spur Mickey onward. "To the Johnson's!" I cry, a dramatic fist raised skyward as Mickey picks up his pace and we speed off down the road, Danni and Jerome at our side.

***

The Johnsons welcome me warmly into their home at sunrise. It seems I will be no trouble, and sharing a room with Juniper Edith Johnson, or as she is more commonly known, Grannie. She is the great grandmother, of Lucy, Sarah and Bess, who share the room next door. Their parents Bill and Liza Johnson have the other bedroom in the compact farm cottage. Nestled into the foothills at the far end of the Valley, their's is a cozy, family home and would feel quite comfortable were it not so oddly decorated.

It's going to be like living in a craft festival. There are countless displays of knitting, quilting, needlework and other assorted haberdashery. A house full of such… talent. I hope they don't expect me to join their sewing circle this winter. I'm only marginally better at sewing than I am at cooking. Walking through the house, it feels like something out of the fairy stories I tell my nieces at bedtimes. Actually, it's more like a fairy threw up in here. I wonder if Bill Johnson gets teased by his friends.

Leaving a small amount of the food in the bag, I give most of it to Liza, who gratefully eyes up Rae's oatmeal cookies. I follow the excited and giggling girls to Grannie's room to stash my gear before the muster, tucking my clothes bag under Grannie's bed, on the trundle that will be mine. We'll only be gone one night, and I have plenty of layers. Pulling on my woolly hat, I thank the Johnsons and bid them goodbye.

Jerome meets me in the yard, ready and waiting. I mount Mickey from the fence and we race to meet the others at the Browns' place. The procession is just starting out as we arrive. Calls of welcome travel above the noise of yapping dogs and farewells from the homestead. Jerome and I look at each other and grin. The atmosphere is full of infectious excitement. We wave to the house and join the departing cavalcade.

As our horses travel up into the hills, my gaze rises beyond, to the tallest mountain in the Valley. The waterfall drops down the cliff to meet the mountain peak and it reminds me of an egg timer, as the sand flows down to pile into a pyramid at the bottom.

The mountain isn't a pristine pyramid, it's more of a grooved, inverted cone, cut in half by the cliff at its back. It has deep gullies pleating its face, and running down to the rolling hills at its feet. There are rocks jutting out in strange directions and wiry patches of shrubbery cloaking it as the river tumbles roughly down the middle.

I have been on the autumn muster before, and so has Mickey. I trust him with the climb and the descent, which can be pretty hair-raising in parts. It all adds to the thrill. It's great fun to be out in the fresh air and beautiful scenery with a bunch of happy-go-lucky farm folk. There are always stories, drink and laughter by the fire at the end of the day and that usually makes up for any soreness accumulated on the job.

Every autumn the high country merino sheep are brought back down to the Valley floor. When the snows come, the hills get the worst of it, burying any available food. Bringing the mob down means they can be fed easily, the young can be weaned and the meat stock can be shorn before they're slaughtered for the winter stores.

At the base of the hills, Chris Brown and his strapping

boys give us our instructions. We will climb to the top today, searching for the positions of the sheep on the way. At the top, where the mountain meets the cliffs, we'll camp and at first light, we'll spread out, making our way slowly back down pushing the sheep in front of us.

Two of the Brown boys, Hadley and Kirk split off from the group and head in opposite directions. Reconnaissance. They'll meet us at the top having scouted the mountain's flanks for sheep. As they branch off, the main contingent begins the climb, giving the impression of a column of horses growing up the mountain in front of me.

Dogs weave in and out of the column, disappearing into the shrubbery, following different scents. Every now and then I catch a glimpse of one rejoining the group or crashing through the undergrowth chasing rabbits. It's a steep climb, but the horses manage by zigzagging up the mountainside using the tracks grooved into it by the sheep.

We break for lunch over halfway up, on a small plateau. The horses rest and graze the short grass as we sit around socially, eating and talking. The group is made up mainly of men this autumn, with the exception of myself and Tessa and Janna Brown (cousins to the Brown boys). The break allows Jerome and I time to catch up with the others, after our late start. I watch Bill Johnson a while, wanting to know him a little better. I've met him several times before, but now that I'll be staying in his house, I figure I should make more of an effort.

A tall, lean man, Bill looks almost out of place as he hovers quietly around the shorter, stockier men. He speaks sparingly and laughs politely at their obvious jokes. I notice his jokes are quieter and drier, but the laughter that follows them is the loudest. A broad brimmed hat covers his thinning hair and he has the deep crow's feet etched into the skin around his eyes that most aging farmers tend to wear. The ones formed by both laughter and worry, and deepened by the weather. Right now they are creased in amusement. He appears to be enjoying the respite from his gaggle of girls.

Chris lets out a piercing whistle and circles a raised finger above his head like a lasso. Feeling a bit like working dogs, we collect our gear and horses to get moving. Onward and upward. The parade starts again, snaking uphill. The view out over the Valley becomes broader and more breathtaking as we go, but it's nothing compared to the majesty of the view from the top.

We don't have much time to enjoy the view when we arrive as we race to set up camp in the setting sun. It's taken all day to reach the summit and my legs are aching from constantly gripping them around Mickey as he's traversed the steep tracks. Taking in the fading view, I tend the horses and tie up dogs with Jerome. Others move about pitching basic tents, fetching water from the river and firewood for the big cook fire in the center.

Hadley arrives with a gutted sheep across the back of his horse, which he promptly skins and begins to butcher. Dinner for us and the dogs. A few water-filled pots are clanked down near the fire by Janna, Neeko Li and Josef, the youngest Brown. They have clearly assumed the role of cooking tonight. Neeko sets the pots in the embers, to boil. Skewering several portions of meat, Janna sets them above the flames.

I walk to the river to wash up and fill my water pouch before it's too dark to find my way. Shivering as I arrive back, I tuck myself between Jerome and Josef. Jerome hands me a stick with a slab of meat stuck on the end, already crisping in the fire. I gratefully accept it, the smell of roasting lamb assailing my nostrils.

A medley of vegetables has been rounded up from everyone's kits and thrown in the pots. Boiling now, the water spits occasionally over the sides into the fire letting out feisty hisses as it turns to steam. I'm famished. Handing my skewer back to Jerome, I rummage in my ruck behind me, finding a package of Rae's cheesy crackers. Cramming two in my mouth, I pass them around the circle while our dinner cooks.

"Geez Rori," Jerome teases, handing me back my stick. "Can't you wait five more minutes?"

I shake my head, smiling, my mouth still stuffed with cracker.

"Nothing wrong with a healthy appetite," Josef interjects, nudging me in the side playfully. "How else will she ever grow tall enough to look a bellybutton in the eye? Right Rori?"

Choking a little on my cracker, I try to swallow it down fast enough to defend myself. The boys just laugh and take advantage of my enforced silence.

"There are plenty of things to keep a girl busy below a bellybutton!" Jerome cracks. They laugh harder.

My mouth still full, I assess my options. We've drawn attention from others now. The boys are trying to regain composure so they can launch into more lewd comments. Reaching out, I grab each one by the back of the head, clunking them together as I lean out of the way. The rest of the circle erupts into laughter as Jerome and Josef rub their temples, cursing.

"That's no way to talk to a lady, boys." I smirk, finally regaining speech.

Jerome eyes me warily, rubbing his head as Josef tries to recover the steak he has dropped into the fire.

"Lady!" Jerome laughs. "Good one Rori!"

More laughter from the crowd.

"I see my reputation precedes me," I say, laughing too.

We ravenously tuck in to our hot meal. The cold has set upon the mountain and I can feel the warmth of the food as it travels down. After dinner the old boys pull out their whiskey and pass it around the group. Enjoying the way it warms my innards, I happily have a few swigs to fortify myself against the cold.

Warm and replete, I pull a flaming branch from the fire for a torch and collect some pots to wash. Tessa grabs the ones I can't carry and follows me to the river. At the river's edge, I stack a small bundle of kindling and light it with my torch, leaving it to burn and provide light while we tend the dishes. We perch on the rocks, rubbing the pots down with the coarse river sand.

"I can smell rain coming," says Tessa.

Ceasing my scrubbing, I scent the open air.

"I smell it too. No stars anymore either," I add. "The clouds must have rolled in after dark. Hope it's not too heavy. Nothing worse than working in the cold when it's raining."

"Agreed. You almost done?" she asks, rinsing her last pot.

"Yeah, just working on my last. You might wanna start heading back, before it hits." As if to laugh at us, a huge thunderclap resonates from the heavens, unleashing an instant shower of heavy, stinging drops.

"Dammit!" I yell, as the small fire sputters out with a sad hiss, plunging us into darkness. I scramble for the pots around my ankles. Tessa scoops up hers from next to me, knocking me down as she does. I splash into the river. Jumping up cursing and dripping from head to toe, I dance around in shock, my pots still clasped in my hands. Slipping on the rocks, I fall again and lose a pot. Floundering around for it, my fingers find its smooth handle and I haul myself out.

"Rori! Sorry! Are you OK?" Tessa's voice cuts through the dark in front of me.

"Shit that's cold! Yeah, I'm OK. Got your pots?"

"I think so. You?"

"Yeah, let's go. Can you see the camp fire from here? Or did the rain get that too?" I ask, trying to wipe my eyes with a sodden sleeve and beginning to shiver. The last thing we need is to fall down a cliff in the dark.

"I think I can see a faint glow," she replies, groping me with her spare hand. "We'll stay together, yeah? No sense in getting lost and freezing to death."

"Agreed," I say, through chattering teeth. My wet clothes are clinging to me and the rain whips my face relentlessly in the wind. We stumble through the dark, tripping on rocks and scraping through bushes on what must surely be the longest possible track back to camp. The fire has died right down and dull embers spit with the rain.

Dropping the pots by the fire, we seek shelter in our tents. They can barely be seen in the dim. I'm sharing with Jerome in the compact tent he always takes into the mountains. It's smaller than the others, and its vague outline is easy to pick out. Under the shelter of the evergreen above it, I pry off as many wet layers as I dare. Wringing them out as much as I can, I throw them over the lower branches, cursing myself for not bringing another change of clothes.

"Rori?" Jerome's voice calls out from the tent.

"Yeah," I call back. "I got a bit wet. Just hanging up my clothes."

I crawl in through the flap, shivering uncontrollably, my frozen fingers fumbling with my bedroll. Jerome reaches out for me in the dark. His hand finds my arm and his touch feels hot enough to burn my skin.

"Rori! How wet did you get? You're frozen!" He folds himself around me, but pulls back with a gasp.

"What are you wearing? You're still wet!"

"M-my wrap," I utter, shuddering with cold.

"Take it off. You'll never get warm like that. Take everything off."

"J-Jerome!" Undressing, I crawl into his vacant bedroll. "I'm s-stealing your bed. It's w-warm r-right?"

"Take it. How did you get that wet? It only just started raining!"

"F-fell in the r-r-river."

"Shit Rori! That's straight off the mountains! No wonder you're frozen!"

Unrolling my blankets, he piles them on top of my

shivering body and climbs in next to me. Twisting my wet hair up out of the way, he spoons me with his warmth. My teeth feel like they're trying to shake themselves loose from my jaw and I clench down hard to stop them. Jerome's arms fold around me, trying to restrain my quaking body unsuccessfully. Sighing, he sits up and takes his own shirt off before cuddling back in against me.

His chest sets my back aflame. How can two bodies be so different in temperature? My body can't help but mold into his, drawn to the warmth. Nestling closer to Jerome and further under the covers, I mumble thanks amid my violent shaking.

"You're welcome, but don't try to get any closer OK? Between your constant shivering and close nude proximity I'm about at my limit." There is a smile in his voice.

I stiffen. I'm not the only one.

"Jerome!" I scold, "Roll over!"

We roll the other way and I fold myself around his back, relishing the new warmth on my front.

"Yeah," he mumbles. "This is much better. Having your boobs press into my back feels awful."

"Jerome! Am I going to be able to sleep in peace? I'm cold and tired!"

"Fine, fine. Roll back the other way. I'll be good," he chuckles. "I'm still wearing pants."

"Mmhmm," I mumble, unconvinced.

We roll back and I get comfortable as Jerome's heat radiates around me. My shivering lessens over time and I drift into a restless sleep.

I know I must be asleep, because I'm dreaming. The arms around me belong to Hayes. The breath on my neck is his. I shiver, and know it's not from the cold. Turning my head to stare into his hazel eyes, he smiles at me and kisses my waiting lips.

Kisses trail across my cheek, tickle my ear and move down my neck. Shivering again, I moan encouragingly. His warm mouth trails kisses down my spine as his fingers travel up my side in the other direction. I feel his warmth behind me as he moves against me, pressing me close as fingertips lightly brush my chest. A large hand closes around my breast, his thumb caressing the taut nipple.

Another groan escapes my lips and my hips move into him, wanting more. The hot breath by my ear releases its own hungry sound and his hand leaves my breast. Gentle fingers run down my belly, toward the growing heat. They barely arrive before I shudder with pleasure.

I sit bolt upright, breathing hard. The pulsating sensation below is still subsiding. I can't believe myself. How is it possible to do that in your sleep? Lena's right; I've got it bad. Even unconscious I can't escape him. I'm doomed.

"Rori?"

Jerome's voice snaps me back to reality and I shiver anew as the cold nips at my bare skin. Shuffling back under the covers, I lie on my back, staring up into the dark. Jerome's back is to me and I say a silent thanks that he wasn't still spooning me while I was dreaming.

"I'm fine," I say dismissively, turning onto my side away from him. "Just a dream. Sorry if I woke you."

"Must have been some dream. You were moaning like…" He hesitates, as if he's not sure he should say. "You know, like you were having a good time."

"Was I? Weird. G'night Jerome," I reply, hoping he won't pursue it further. We lie in silence, facing away from each other.

"Were you dreaming about me?"

How do I answer that? Do I deny such a dream or admit the dream and hurt his feelings by telling him it wasn't him? Squirming uncomfortably, I think of a response.

"Jerome, would I have to dream about you? Couldn't I just roll on top of you and get started if I wanted to?"

His body shakes with laughter next to me.

"I'd like to think you'd ask first. It's only polite."

"Fair enough. You can rest easy, I'm not a predator." I pull the blankets tight under my chin and scold myself. "It was just a dream. Dreams don't come true."

"Wow. You should do inspirational story-time at the school," Jerome says, laughing a little. "You sound a little disappointed. You want me to use my magic wand to make your dream come true?"

"Would you quit it Jerome? Just go to sleep." I sink further under the blankets, my cheeks blazing. "Before I kick you in your magic wand!"

He chuckles, turning his back to me again and adjusting the covers. "Goodnight Rori."

"Goodnight Jerome," I say with finality, trying not to smile.

Sleep stays elusively beyond my grasp. Every time I close my eyes, I'm reminded of the dream; Hayes' touch on my skin, the heat he stirs. I shuffle around restlessly. Do I allow myself to keep feeling this way? The dream might be amazing, but the reality is anything but. It's not enough to be physically away from him. I need to banish him from my thoughts as well or it's too hard to deal with. Sighing, I roll over again.

"Scared you'll have another dream?" Jerome asks through the darkness.

"Sorry," I apologize, not admitting he has drawn the right conclusion. "I don't mean to keep you up. I'm just having trouble getting back to sleep."

Rolling over, he props himself on an arm, his face close enough that his breath feels warm on my cheek.

"Bedtime story? I didn't finish telling you about my time in the mountains."

"Couldn't hurt," I say, pulling the covers closer and trying to get comfortable.

"Well, I was doing a lot of thinking," he begins slowly.

"About?"

"Lots of things. Farm work, thieving, the City, growing up -"

"Growing up?"

"Sure. We won't be able to do what we do forever, you know. Sooner or later we'll have to retire our gopher-suits, be it from injury or old age. Haven't you ever thought about what you want to do after you're done thieving?"

"Not really," I reply honestly. "I guess I want the world to change before then so I'll know what my options are."

Jerome laughs. "I'm as committed to overthrowing the Citizens as the next Dalton, but I'm not pinning all my hopes on it turning out for the best. It's been tried before and we're still here working our guts out for them."

Sitting up a bit, I stare into the black space where his head should be. "What are you saying?"

"I'm saying that if things are going to carry on this way for another century, I've been thinking about the life I want to live."

"And?"

"And after much deliberation, at some stage, years from now, I'd like to follow in my father's footsteps. I'll be a tracker and work the land and watch my kids grow."

"Your kids? Really?" I ask, just about snorting in disbelief.

"I know. I never thought that would be exciting enough for me. But while I was away, I realized it was important to me, and that it would be the most exciting adventure of my life, if I was with the right girl."

"Who'd you have in mind? You're not seeing anyone at the moment." Frowning into the dark, I cut him off before he can speak. "Are you thinking of trying things with Orla on a deeper level?" I laugh a little at the thought. "Orla's great, but you might be overestimating the depth or existence of levels there, but if that doesn't worry you, I think your children would be gorgeous. And if they had your brains, they'd be unstoppable. Definite warriors for a rebellion. Can I babysit?" I ask, actually excited by the idea.

Jerome sighs at me. "The right girl is you, Rori."

"Jerome, I…"

"You don't need to say anything now. I know I messed things up. I just wanted you to know where my head is at, and that one day, I hope you'll let me try again."

Quiet for a while, I try to decide if he's serious.

"This kinda sounds like a play to make the most of me being naked next to you," I say, testing.

"Dammit Rori! I'm trying to tell you that I love you and I want to be with you!"

Stunned into silence, I try to digest his words. Of all the men in the Valley, Jerome is the only one I would consider being involved with. Apart from Lena, he understands me better than anyone, but thinking about us together makes me uncomfortable. Maybe that's because I still have feelings for him and maybe it's because I trust him with my life, but not my heart.

I thought I'd forgiven him for going with Orla, but maybe I'm wrong. Before thinking about how cute their kids would be, the idea had annoyed me. Wouldn't that mean I *do* still feel for him? Trying to un-muddle myself, I think about what he is asking. One day, not necessarily right now.

Being with Jerome is a smart choice. We have a lot in common and I like him - to look at and to spend time with. He's a hard worker and has a nice family, and he isn't intimidated by me or my father. And he's a Dalton. Unlike Hayes. Starting over with Jerome could be a good idea. Even if I'm not sure about it now, it could grow into the long term lifestyle that he's suggesting. Life would certainly be easier if I fell in love with him again. I picture us falling into our old habits, falling into his bed again. He knows what I like, but is it enough? Sighing to myself, I realize I don't know how I feel.

I haven't spoken for a while and he must be stewing. I shuffle toward him. "So… You want to try *us* again?" I ask, clarifying.

"Yes."

"Now?"

"If you like!" he says, sounding exasperated.

"Alright. Let's try."

"You're sure?"

"Sure?" I shake my head in the dark. "No. I don't know how I feel. I need you to show me."

"Oh." He sounds displeased. I wish I could see his face.

"So… You *don't* want to try?" I ask, trying to read the darkness.

"It's not that. It's just that I thought you'd know if you loved me or not."

"I do love you. Jerome, you're my best friend. I just don't know if I can love you like *that* anymore. I haven't thought about it for a long time." Taking a breath, I admit something to the both of us. "There was a long time when I *couldn't* think about it."

"Oh." His tone reflects more understanding. "I want you to know that I'm not that guy anymore. All I want is your happiness. Even if you don't find it with me."

"You mean that?"

There is a pause.

"I'm pretty sure I do, but can I see if I make you happy first?" he asks, making me smile.

"Go ahead," I reply, releasing my grip on the blankets. Jerome hesitates.

"What are you waiting for?"

"I wasn't expecting you to let me. Not yet, anyway. It's a lot of pressure, and you're already naked and-"

"For goodness sake, Jerome! Just kiss me."

He moves closer in the dark. Our heads bump into each other and we both laugh nervously. Scouting fingers brush down my cheek and raise my chin. Jerome's lips find mine, kissing softly at first, then more insistently.

Leaving my mouth, his kisses stray down my neck, where he breathes into my hair, sending shivers through my body. Feeling him smile against my skin, I imagine the dimple appearing in his cheek and smile myself. Light fingertips run the centerline of my chest and circle my navel before drifting upward to my breasts as he kisses my lips again.

My body begins to respond to his gentle touch. Closing my eyes, I give in to sensation, melting further with each caress. Suddenly I'm imaging I'm with Hayes. Gasping, my eyes fly open as my body tenses.

"You OK?" Jerome asks, stopping immediately.

Recovering from the shock, I relax back into his arms. "Yeah, sorry. Carry on." Closing my eyes, I run my hands over his smooth skin. He kisses me again and I work my fingers into his short hair. His lips move lower, teasing each nipple in turn. My tender skin relishes the rough feel of his unshaven jaw and I emit a low moan as I recall my fireside moments with Hayes. Swearing, I sit up.

Forced back, Jerome collects himself. "Is something wrong?"

"No," I say, quickly followed by, "Yes."

"What did I do?" Sounding worried, he backs off a little more.

"Nothing. I'm fine, I just… I can't do this, Jerome. I'm sorry." Sitting up, I feel around for something to put on. "I wanted to. It felt good, but I can't. It's not fair to you."

"What?"

"Can I borrow a shirt or something?" I ask scrabbling for his pack.

"Here," he says, pushing his shirt into my searching hands. "Talk to me, Rori. What's not fair?"

"Dreams. The future. I want to, yet I don't want to. I don't want to lose you as a friend." Words pour from my mouth without thought. Pulling his shirt over my head, I pull it down to cover as much of myself as possible, feeling stupid even while I do it. It's pitch black, and it's *Jerome*. He's seen me naked on countless occasions. Hell, we've run naked in the rain! I don't know what I'm doing. His words interrupt my madness.

"There's more you're not saying," he says shrewdly.

Sighing at my silence, he turns toward me. "You can't ruin our friendship, Twiglet. We're two peas. There are no obstacles we can't overcome. We jump any hurdles and carry on. Now tell me what you meant. Why isn't it fair to me if we're together? Because, I kinda feel like I'd be getting a good deal," he says, trying to lighten the mood.

"You wouldn't be," I correct him, fidgeting with the blankets and wondering if I should brave the rain and the dark.

"I know you don't think that poorly of yourself, Rori. Be straight with me."

Taking a deep breath, I let it out in a rush. "You'd be getting a bum deal, Jerome. Every time I was with you I'd be wanting it to be someone else." Wincing as the words leave my mouth, I can't believe I've just said them out loud. I should have lied. A lie would be less hurtful and less terrifying.

"Oh."

"I'm sorry. I'm a mess. I should go," I say, rushing my words again as I make for the tent flaps.

"Don't be daft!" he says, pulling me back. "Rori, I knew there was a chance your answer would be no. I was hoping it wouldn't be, but I knew things had changed when I got back from the mountains. I didn't want to admit it to myself until I knew for sure, but it's better to know the truth. At least that's what I've been told," he says, making light of his obvious disappointment. "Thanks for being honest with me." Taking his hand off me, he slips into silence.

I wonder if I would be that understanding if the roles were reversed.

"You're a good friend, Jerome. I would have really liked for things to be different," I say honestly.

"Me too." Patting around in the dark, he finds my hand and gives it a squeeze.

I squeeze back. "It would've been nice, I think. Easy."

"Not really your style to take the easy road," he says,

chuckling a little.

"I'm so screwed."

"Pretty much," he says, a warm smile in his voice. "Let's get some sleep, eh?" Climbing back under the covers, he pauses before pulling them up. "Coming?"

Climbing in, I nestle into his shoulder as he tucks us back in. His fingers trace patterns on my back as he sinks into thought.

"I love you, Twiglet."

"I love you too, Jerome Marshall."

Sighing, I close my eyes again, listening to the rain and Jerome's beating heart.

STAYING AWAY

The muster went off without a hitch. After the overnight rain, the sun came out with the last of autumn's warmth and dried out most of my clothes as we traveled down. I was able to change back into them before I had to do any precarious work, Jerome's shirt was far too loose to wear for that. He and I were put to use, scaling rock faces to shoo out stragglers in the gullies. It was a challenging and exhilarating process and although I was glad to get back onto Mickey each time for a rest, the rock climbing was my favorite part of the job.

Following the muster, I settled into my new life. Bill appreciated my help around the farm and he and Liza even went for a weekend getaway in the village for the first time in years, while I babysat the girls (and Grannie). It was tough doing crafting stuff all weekend, but Bill and Liza came back much restored. It was cute how they had managed to rekindle a bit of a spark between them. Even Grannie couldn't help but give a toothless grin at them when they brushed up against each other in the kitchen or tried to steal a secret smile.

Sharing a room with Grannie proves to be hard work. No wonder the Johnson's accepted me so readily! She needs help with just about everything except sitting next to the fire crafting. I can't believe how often she needs to pee in the middle of the night. Now that it's me helping her up, the Johnson's must be getting the best sleep they've ever had!

I feel more tired than ever before. Up for training at the crack of dawn to run the volunteers through their lessons, helping out with the farm chores and watching the girls has me almost at my limits. I crash pretty hard after dinner. If I stay up any later I feel like I'm dying. Living with Grannie is like having an over-sized newborn. Worse still, the weather has turned consistently cold and she's developed a hideous, hacking cough.

Lying in bed now, I don't know if I will ever get to sleep. I suppose when my body is too tired to stay awake it'll happen. Maybe I can sneak out later and sleep by the fire. Shuddering, I think about the last time I tried that. I'd almost interrupted Bill and Liza's 'alone time'. They didn't see me - thank goodness, but now I'm petrified of a repeat visual scarring.

Sighing, I turn on the little lamp. Grannie mumbles something and coughs, but remains asleep. Pulling out my gear, I rummage for the book I stashed in there. I take my cloak out, thinking an extra layer on my bed would be nice. Forgetting my train of thought, the night at the cottage floods my mind. I press the cloak to my face, blocking out the room.

Drawing the cloak back, I look at it in disbelief. Unrolling it a little, I bring it back to my nose. Hayes. Masculine and salty with a hint of citrus. Closing my eyes, I lie back down, just breathing him in, astounded that my cloak should smell of him, and that he's held it close enough for that to happen. Maybe he did what I'm doing now, trying to get back something that's gone. The thought keeps coming into my head and I chase it away. Idiocy.

It doesn't matter. Just turn off the light and go to sleep.

I shake open my cloak and lay it over my blanket. Brushing out the wrinkles, my hand flicks something firm where the inner pocket is. I run my hand over it more carefully, thinking I've imagined it, but there's definitely something there. Flipping the cloak over, I search the pocket. My hand withdraws, trembling.

Holding the paper to my nose, checking, I smell paper, ink and a hint of Hayes. It drops to my lap as I sit stunned, unable to breathe. Grannie's cough snaps me out of it and I reach down with clumsy fingers to unfold the letter.

Rori,

I feel a coward to write these words, but after the way I acted, I can only assume you'll never want to see me again.

I am so sorry. I feel sick to my stomach when I think about what I did. I hope you were right – that you can defend yourself and that I haven't hurt you. Hurting you is the worst thing I can imagine.

I owe you some explanation, though nothing could ever excuse what I did. I've never told anyone else, not even my family - especially not my family. I need to be strong for them. If I can tell you though, maybe you'll at least consider my apology sincere.

The day I got the scar on my face, was the day my father was killed before my eyes, while I could do nothing to help him. No matter how hard I try to forget, it has a way of ambushing me and throwing me into the past, forcing me to remember. The memories I keep locked away come flooding back, unleashing every sense as it was that day. Strongest and most damaging are the hurt and the rage I felt at being powerless to stop it from happening. By the time I find the present again, I've usually broken everything and everyone around me.

When I came to this time, I saw you running into the night. The look on your face when you looked back is one that will haunt me for the rest of my days.

I enjoyed every second of our time together before I ruined it (even when you were yelling at me), but it was wrong of me. I've put you at risk with every encounter. I was selfish and I sincerely regret my weakness.

I have no control over my dark side and I should never have let you get close enough to put you in danger like that. I hope you can forgive me. I will do my best to keep you safe, by staying away from you. Always.
Morrison.

I read it over and over. Each time finding a different meaning. Folding it back up, I slide it back into the pocket. Turning off the lamp, I pull the cloak up to my face, so I can breathe it in. I don't know what to think.

Every time I'm trying to move on, I get pushed back into emotional turmoil; upset by his past, by my present, by our lack of future. As much as I know it has to be this way, it hurts to see it written. Staying away. Always. Life is cruel.

Hayes got a chance to apologize in a letter, but there's nothing I can do to atone for my behavior. I was the cause of his distress, and he couldn't even seek sanctuary in his own home, taking a beating for my involvement as soon as he got there. If anyone needs to be kept safe it's him, from me. At least we agree that staying apart is the best option.

I touch the letter through the fabric of the cloak. It crinkles softly, speaking to me. He cares. Even the words that hurt me when I read them, are there to comfort me. I wish he had something to comfort him. It must be exhausting to be constantly on guard, ensuring everyone else's needs are met before your own.

Balling the cloak up again, I try to trap his smell inside it. Hugging it to my chest, I steady my breathing and enjoy the gentle wafts of Hayes that reach me. Reality prevents me from being near him again, but I know anything can happen while I sleep. Dreams are free.

***

All through the next week, my days felt long and dull. Occasionally Jerome would visit and rescue me from myself. He could tell I was unhappy, even though I put on a brave face at trainings. It's obvious I'm homesick. I'm spending too much time trying to stay close to my family when they're there.

Even Frankie is getting sick of me. I keep asking how Riley is going as an apprentice mason. (She'd agreed to take him on) She was so annoyed yesterday, she told me that if I didn't leave her alone, she would drop him.

I just miss them all. I'm tired of being nice all the time. The Johnson girls are too sensitive. I tried to tease Lucy the other day and she cried for two hours. These kids are weird. I miss the roguish MacGregors and being able to say what I think without fear of damaging them.

Sometimes I feel like all I do is sigh. Sighing again I touch my fingers to my head, tentatively pushing a rag-twisted section out of my sight as I finish the dishes. The girls have been fascinated by my long, straight hair and I have been subjected to a new hairstyle every day. Tonight they have ragged my hair, promising that tomorrow I will have a head of curls. I could barely contain my sarcasm as I told them how pleased that made me.

Pulling the plug, I excuse myself to bed. Bill and Liza wave goodnight and chuckle to each other about my appearance. Checking out the girls' handiwork in the bathroom mirror, I can't help laughing myself. I look like Medusa, with my hair sectioned and snaking in various directions. I start to take them out, but then I think about how upset the girls will be. Leaving them in, I sigh at my reflection.

I open the door to the room I share with Grannie, and am smacked in the face by the smell of the infirm. Her cough has gotten worse and she has spent today and most of yesterday in bed. I try to leave the window open to air it out, but every time I come back in it's closed, trapping the germs and the smell. She lets out another phlegm soaked splutter and I cringe, thankful that she can't see my expression in the dark.

"Grannie, your cough sounds worse than ever. Have

you been taking your medicine?" Sitting next to her on the bed, I help her to sit.

I rub her back as her body is racked by another episode. "Had the last of it yesterday, Dear. I'll be better tomor-" Her words are killed by another moist, wheezing hack.

"You sound awful," I say, trying to keep the disgust from my voice. "I'll see if there's anything else for you."

Glad to leave the room, I head back to the kitchen. Averting my eyes as I approach the living area, I walk straight to the bench, speaking loudly as I go.

"Have we got any elixir left for Grannie? She sounds terrible. She's hardly been up at all today and I'm worried she'll develop pneumonia, if she hasn't already."

"I think she had the last of it yesterday. Is she really that bad?" Liza asks, her voice full of worry as she comes into the kitchen buttoning her shirt.

Avoiding eye contact and wanting to be anywhere in the world but this house, I take a deep breath. "You know what? I'll just take Mickey to the surgery and get a new batch."

"Rori it's dark. Just wait and we'll get it in the morning," Bill says, coming up behind his wife.

"Really, it's fine. I can't sleep with her like that," I say honestly, fearing another sleepless night. I soften my tone a little with concern. "She's really unwell. I'll ask Freya to visit her tomorrow while I'm there."

Not waiting for a response, I run to get my hat and coat. Bidding Grannie farewell, I race back through the kitchen and out the door. I barely even slow enough to put a bridle on Mickey. He doesn't always need one. He is trained to respond to the subtle movements of his rider, but the bridle does allow more control, which is for the best in the dark.

Jumping on his bare back, I send him forward with a soft but urgent kick. He springs into action and soon we're out the front gate, heading toward the lights of the village in the distance. As soon as I feel the road below us, I begin to relax, realizing how badly I've been wanting to get away, and how much I hate feeling trapped.

As we get closer to the village, I can see a lot of lights. Too many. Even the Great Hall is lit. I realize my mistake. During my time with the Johnson's and in my rush to escape them, I have lost track of the calendar. It's Train Day and I should be anywhere but the village.

I pull Mickey to a stop. His feet dance on the road as I try to think, not wanting to go back to the Johnson's empty handed. I don't want to go back at all, but if I have to sleep in that house, I need to stop the noise coming from Grannie or I'll go insane. I could stop and ask at the first house I come to, but the chance of them having what I need is slim, even if they're home, which is unlikely. Most people will be at the Gathering.

The surgery isn't close to the hall. Maybe I can sneak in, get what I need and sneak back out. No-one even need see me. I'll stay off the road and go to the back door through the fields. I am a thief of skill after all. Smiling to myself at the hint of adventure I've been missing from my daily routine, I give Mickey a kick and press on toward the village.

We turn down the first alley and move beyond the houses, into the back fields, walking along in the dim light of a crescent moon, until we get to the surgery. The light is on inside and I wonder if maybe Freya has come home early from the Gathering with Ezra. It would be good to see her, or any curly blond relative right now.

Tethering Mickey by the trough, I pull my coat tight as a gust of wind blasts cold at me. I knock on the door as I open it, not wanting to wait in the frigid air.

"Freya? You in?" I call, shutting the door behind me and shivering in the foyer between her house and the clinic.

"Rori?"

Freya's surprised voice calls from the surgery. Relieved

she's already working, I walk into the back room that she calls 'the lab', where she mixes up her potions.

"I'm glad you're here," I call through to her, when I realize she's in the other room. Looking through the bottles on the shelves for Freya's miracle cough syrup, I can't find what I'm looking for.

"You got any cough syrup made up? Grannie Johnson has been hacking her lungs out and I swear, if the cough doesn't kill her I'm liable to smother her with her pillow just to get some sleep! *Dammit* - that feels so good to say out loud!" It's warm in the surgery and I shrug out of my coat, still trying to spy the right potion.

"It's been a busy week for coughs, Rori. Just go back now, you know it's Train Day," Freya calls back, her tone admonishing. She hates it when people talk meanly about the sick or the elderly, and she must know I'm meant to be out of town. Sighing audibly, she attempts to reason with me. "How about I make some up and bring it out tomorrow. I can check her when I'm there. Just go."

"I only remembered it was Train Day on the way here, that's how sleep deprived I am. I'm so desperate for sleep I snuck in anyway. I can make it up myself if you're busy. If I go back with nothing, I'll have to sleep with Mickey and he farts more than Grannie Johnson! C'mon Freya, take pity on your darling little sister," I beg, desperate not to be turned out. "I'll show you something that will make you pee your pants! I swear, you'll never guess what those brats did to my hair," I say, walking into the next room, pulling off my hat to show her.

"Rori!"

Her voice is drowned out by deep laughter that turns into a hacking cough and cries of pain as Hayes rolls back on the bed, clutching a pillow to his body. Glancing at Freya's angry, red face I understand all too well now why she wanted me to leave. I can't make my feet move.

"Please!" he gasps between fits of laughter and coughing. "Put your hat back on!"

I pull it back over my head immediately, but my feet still won't move. I can't stop staring at him. He has shrunk. His gaunt face shows more angles than I knew were there and his sunken eyes are emphasized by dark circles. The shoulders that were broad and strong are hunched, the muscles wasting.

My feet start moving, but not away from him.

"Hayes!? You're skin and bones!" I stare at him struggling to sit and rush to help him.

"You two know each other?" Freya asks uneasily. I suppose Da has kept her somewhat out of the loop. That's a relief.

"Yeah, we've met," I admit, turning to Hayes. "You were twice the size last time I saw you though."

"Just a bit run down," he says, dismissing my concern. "I think I just took the last of the cough syrup you needed, sorry." He cautiously releases the pillow he's been clutching. It lowers slightly and I catch a glimpse of the bruising over his chest. My fault. Seeing something in my reaction, he quickly covers himself with the pillow again.

"I should go," I say, feeling my color rising with the lump in my throat. "I shouldn't be here. I'm sorry to interrupt you like this." Looking deeply in his hurt, hollowed eyes, I try to express what I can't say in front of Freya. "I'm so, so sorry."

"Don't be silly," Freya says, missing my intent. "You're here now, you might as well take back what you need. Grannie Johnson's no spring chicken. She'll probably break *her* ribs if she's coughing as bad as you say and the complications arising from that, well…" Freya looks Hayes up and down and gives a small sigh. "Her prognosis wouldn't be nearly as good as a usually healthy young soldier. I'll whip up a quick relief for tonight and bring out a bottle of the good stuff tomorrow when I've brewed some more." Scanning the materials set in front of her, she nods to herself.

"Rori, you can handle Mr. Hayes here while I make it

up. You're always looking to practice your skills. I was going to apply a fresh poultice to the angry mark on his back before making a vitamin rich infusion and I can make that while I make the elixir you need. Here, you know what to do. You don't mind do you Mr. Hayes? Rori is a competent healer in her own right. She often helps in the surgery."

Hayes nods his agreement, a smile creeping onto his face as Freya leaves to the lab.

I step closer and keep my voice low. "Not doing a very good job of staying away from each other are we?"

"Life does seem to keep throwing us together," he replies, just as quietly. "So you're training to be a doctor?"

"Hardly. People's bodies are gross. Most people's," I correct myself, avoiding his eyes. "Da insists I train for 'real jobs' in case he ever gets to keep me in the Valley. Medicine is just one of the things I agreed to. Selfishly. I thought it might be useful in thieving scenarios." My eyes are drawn to the bones beneath his skin; too close to the surface.

"I'm so sorry Hayes. This is all my fault. I shouldn't have pulled my knife, and if I'd never been out, you wouldn't be sitting here broken. You didn't hurt me at all. The only one hurting is you, and it's all my fault." My voice breaks on the last word and I move behind him to hide. Going to the sink, I wash my hands in preparation for what Freya has asked me to do.

With a shaky hand, I remove the used dressing, letting out a small gasp as it comes away. Running parallel to one healed stripe, is a second oozing welt, the skin around it red and hot to the touch. I trace a finger around the edge of the inflammation. Hayes reaches a hand over his shoulder, grabbing mine. I'm forced to step forward as he pulls it to his mouth and presses his lips to it. He turns his head to meet my eyes, holding me in his gaze.

"You did none of this to me. Understand? This is not your fault. I would gladly take it again if that was the price for stopping Reg from hurting you, but this is his doing, *not* yours." Releasing my hand, he turns away again.

Re-washing my hands, I apply the onion poultice Freya has prepared to ease the inflammation. I work in awkward silence, applying the cloth dressing under and over the pulpy mass, strapping it in place. Relishing the sensation of putting my arms around him to retrieve the bandage each time I wrap it, I get closer than I really need to, brushing his skin with my own.

When I have it secured I step around in front of him again running my eyes over his face. I pull the pillow down to reveal his chest and the extent of his bruising. Bruising I understand. The marks on his back I do not. His lack of condition I do not. Replacing the pillow, I raise a questioning eyebrow at him.

"It would be healed by now if I didn't get a cold. It feels like my ribs are re-breaking every time I cough."

Unconvinced by his excuse, I cross my arms over my chest, my eyebrow still raised. "Why aren't you eating?"

"I eat," he says, cagily.

"Not enough. Why not?"

Seeing my resolve, he sighs. "I've only just started back at work. I've been on cut rations. You probably know how much we need to eat to maintain muscle mass. I can't heal fast enough. I'm no good to anyone and I hate it," he says through gritted teeth.

"Freya will help." I rest a reassuring hand on his arm and try not to let it wander. "How were you allowed to come here? I know Da would want to help you, but isn't he meant to be treating you as scum for attacking his daughter in the Village streets? What golden yarn has he spun this time?"

Hayes is looking at my hand resting on his arm. Taking it away, I keep it busy, moving Freya's empty dressing containers on the trolley next to the bed.

"He accused me of harboring disease and insisted I be quarantined in the surgery until it's time to leave tomorrow," he says, taking my hand back and squeezing it gently. "You always seem to know what people are thinking and how they will act."

"I don't know that I do," I say, hesitantly, unable to take my eyes from my hand inside his. My cheeks begin to heat. "Observation is a large part of my job. I watch and I listen to pick up the clues to read people." Shrugging, I pull my hand back as I hear Freya's footsteps coming nearer.

"That looks good Rori," she says, checking my work. "I told you, you were in good hands, didn't I?" she says to Hayes as she hands him a glass of foul-looking liquid. "Drink this. You'll feel better by morning."

Hayes looks at my face over the top of the concoction nervously. Unscrunching my nose, I clear my throat, trying not to laugh.

"Be a good boy and take your medicine, Morrison," I tease, daring him with my eyes. "Freya, has Mr. Hayes eaten this evening?"

"Of course he has," she says irritably. "Look at the state of him! The first thing I did was feed him. Can I see you in the lab a minute please?"

I follow her toward the lab, making a face at Hayes before I leave.

"What are you doing?" Her low volume does not eliminate her disapproving tone.

"What?"

"Don't play the innocent with me, Rori Lauren MacGregor. You're flirting with him! He's a *Citizen*!"

"Like I hadn't noticed? I'm not flirting," I say defensively. "He just looks so unwell, I'm trying to cheer him up."

Freya's face is unconvinced. A blond curl has strayed from her bun. This is Freya unhinged. I hold my hands up in protest.

"Fine I'll stop."

"Damn right you will," she agrees, tucking the rogue

curl back in. "Imagine what Da would say!" She returns to Hayes and I follow sheepishly in her wake.

"Can I do anything else to help?" I ask, trying to appease Freya and gain precious, guilty seconds with Hayes.

Freya shoots me a warning look. "Grannie Johnson's tonic will be ready in fifteen minutes. Maybe you could wait in the lab until then? Mr. Hayes is about to get uncomfortable."

"I am?" Hayes asks, eying her warily.

"Yes, we need to address your ribs."

"Oh," he says, visibly paling.

"I could stay?" I offer. "Help distract him from the pain?"

Freya shoots me another look, a dangerous one. I've overstepped the mark and she's going to burn me.

"I'm not sure how Jerome would feel about you being another man's distraction. Rumor has it you kids are back together?"

Hayes visibly stiffens and I feel my cheeks burning. I want to pull off Freya's bun and shove it in her stupid mouth.

"Rumor is exactly what that is Freya. Where did you hear that trash?"

"From Tessa, after the muster. She said you shared his tiny tent and were wearing his shirt in the morning."

"Because she knocked me in the river, the stupid cow. I would have frozen to death if it wasn't for Jerome, but we are *not* back together. You are being so unfair and so unprofessional. I can't believe I was excited about seeing you!" Storming out to the foyer, I throw on my coat.

"I have to go," I say, returning to the doorway and addressing only Hayes. "I'll be back in fifteen minutes. Will you still be here?"

"Of course he will be. He's quarantined," Freya says as though I'm an idiot.

Ignoring her, I await an answer from Hayes. Unable to

ask him outright, I'm waiting for his permission to see him again. After a moment of thought he looks at Freya and back to me. A wounded expression on his face, he closes his eyes and nods once.

"Good." I give Freya such a severe look, she gasps. Slamming the surgery door behind me, I move into the shadows.

About fifteen minutes later I'm back, carrying cargo.

"What the hell is in there?" Freya points at the sack slung over my shoulder.

I swing it down next to the bed. "Medicine."

Hayes is lying on his back, with what looks like a comfrey compress covering the bruising down his side. He looks at me briefly with curiosity, before looking away.

"I've got everything I need Rori," Freya says, trying to get rid of me again.

"I know you have all you need. This is what Hayes needs," I say, opening the bag to allow her to look inside. Overcome by curiosity himself, Hayes peers into the sack too, his eyes widening.

"Rori!" Freya scolds. "There must be half a cattle beast in there! What did you do? Steal Harry's jerky supply?!"

"Not all of it," I say defensively. "And don't act so surprised. I'm a thief."

Freya's eyes widen and she looks worriedly at Hayes. He is staring at me with a judgmental eyebrow raised, but there is no shock on his face.

"You know!?" Freya accuses him.

Shrugging, he looks away again.

"I don't know what's going on here." Freya steps back, confused. "I don't know how you two know each other and I don't know what you're playing at Rori." She keeps walking backwards, away from the unknown.

"There's a lot you don't know, Freya. There's a whole world outside of the Valley you know nothing about. Hayes is one of the good guys. Why else do you think Da made an excuse to get him here so you could help him?"

247

Rubbing my forehead, I step slowly towards her stricken form. "There is a lot you do know, Freya and you need to do what you can for Hayes before he leaves," I say, shoving empty herb dishes in her hands and focusing her back on her comfort zone.

"This is for after he leaves," I say, pointing to the sack at my feet. "He needs protein to regain his strength, and he won't have enough. He needs to be as strong as he can, as fast as he can. He has people who need his protection, and he can't even defend himself like this. Do you want to be an accomplice to the death of his little brothers and sisters?"

Freya looks even more shocked. Her gaze shifts continuously between Hayes and myself. Hayes however, is just staring at me, communicating silently that I should shut my mouth. I shake my head. No.

"Freya, go and make the best damn medicine you know how. You have until midday tomorrow to do all you can." I turn to Hayes and ignore Freya as she opens and closes her mouth like a trout. She stumbles back to the lab, where the clang of metal dishes and clinking of glass bottles informs me of her assistance.

Hayes is still staring at me.

"Where is your bag?" I ask, looking around the room.

"Under the bed," he says. "Leave it there. What are you doing, Rori?"

"Helping," I snap at him, pulling out the bag.

"I said leave it," he says sternly, as he tries to rise onto an elbow to stop me, wincing in the process. "You know, for a pocket-sized person you are infuriatingly bossy and pig-headed. You have a terribly unsettling way of bending people to your will and getting what you want."

"Exactly, so lie back down and quit fighting the inevitable," I reply, giving him a fierce look. Glaring at me, he reluctantly lies back down.

Ignoring him, I look through Freya's cupboards for more bandages. "You smell like herb 'n' onion soup."

"Thanks, I'm trying a new line of fragrances. You like it?" he replies sarcastically.

Surprised by his tone, I steal a glance at him and find he's watching me. I tuck a loose hair snake back under my hat. "Well, it's no salty, citrus musk, but it'll work for what we need."

There is a hush and color rises in his cheeks at my description of his scent. I smile, feeling somewhat stupid at being relieved by that response.

"And for what is it that we need herb 'n' onion soup smells?" he asks, recovering himself.

"Masking the meat smell. I'm presuming you're prohibited from carting in your own supply of goods. Derrick decides who gets what, right?"

"Right," he says slowly, following my meaning. One eyebrow raises in disbelief. "You want me to smuggle half a cow under my shirt?"

"It's not half a cow! … And yes."

Taking the sack to the bench, I leave the room, before Hayes has a chance to dispute my proposal. Coming back in with a knife from Freya's kitchen, I proceed to cut strips off the main bulk of meat. I take a few strips over to the bed and press them into his hand.

"You should eat some now. You still look hungry and I can hear your stomach from across the room."

He looks up at me, about to say something, but changes his mind and does what he's told. Satisfied, I return to my carving.

"You shouldn't have stolen for me. I can manage on my own," he says to my back.

I stop slicing and turn around. Taking a strip of jerky for myself, I walk back to the bed, chewing slowly.

"I know you can manage on your own," I say softly, pulling in a stool. "This is my way of saying that you're not alone and you can do more than just manage."

My hand reaches out to his, but he pulls away. I stare at his face as he avoids my eyes. Taking another bite of jerky,

I linger, keeping my eyes on him, hoping they make him uncomfortable. He refuses to look at me. Fed up, I grab his hand before he can pull it away again and squeeze it tightly, keeping it in mine as I lean towards his ear.

"Accepting help does not make you weak, but being unable to take it when you need it does." I throw his hand back to him and return to the meat on the bench.

No response.

"I can tell by your silence that you know I'm right," I say, rubbing it in to make my point. "And I left a note. Harry and I will work it out later. That's not the same as stealing."

Putting the knife down, I assess my work. I have large flat portions of dried beef that can be strapped to Hayes' torso under bandages. The rest lies before me in strips. Tidying them into small bundles, I wrap them in bandages. When they're all wrapped, they look like rolled bandages themselves. Collecting them, I take them to the foot of the bed where I have left his bag.

"May I?" I ask, nodding at his bag, challenging him to say no. Intense eyes stare at me angrily, cornered. He is weak if he declines, and if he lets me put them in his bag, I have got what I wanted. He gives a small and stiff nod.

I try to hide my smile. "If anyone asks, they're fresh bandages for your continued treatment. The other bits, Freya will strap to you under your clothes. It's cold enough that nobody will expect you to be without your jacket, and that will hide any extra bulk."

Returning to the bench, I wrap more bandages around the flaps of jerky, covering them. Looking at them, the cloth bandages could easily house medicinal properties. They won't look out of place strapped to the body of an injured person. Stacking them, I leave them on the bench for Freya. Looking back to Hayes, I'm surprised to see him waiting for me to turn.

Walking back to sit on the stool again, I hand him another strip of dried beef. Putting one in my own mouth,

I chew it slowly, watching him. He puts his own piece in his mouth and watches me right back. We both know I should be going. Hayes swallows his first, and I wait for him to speak as I keep chewing.

"I don't have little brothers and sisters," he says lightly.

"Well don't tell Freya, or she'll stop doing her best for you," I joke, trying to stay light-hearted too. "Clearly I don't know you very well."

"I think you might know me better than you think," he says, looking at me as though that thought frightens him a little. "I have one sister. She's nearly sixteen. And my Mom is…troubled. I'm all they have," he says quietly.

"I'm sorry about your father," I say, opening my hand near his, in invitation. He looks down the bed at it, hesitant. My heart stills as I wait for him to make up his mind. At last, his hand moves, hovering over mine. One finger tenderly traces the lines of my palm. I close my eyes, not wanting him to see them begging. Eventually, his warm hand slides into mine and gives a gentle, testing squeeze.

Squeezing back, I open my eyes. A tear tickles my cheek and I brush it away with my spare hand. Despite Freya's efforts, I know he has received what I wanted him to. The message that even if I'm not with him, he isn't alone.

"Please don't cry," he says. "You know I'm a sucker for a damsel in distress."

I smile, laughing a little and nodding in agreement as I stand up from the stool, getting ready to leave. Getting ready to say goodbye again.

"And you know you don't need to worry about me. Just get better, OK?" I wipe away another tear and sniff. "You'd think I'd be better at saying goodbye to you after the practice we've had," I say, laughing at myself.

Hayes pulls my hand up to his mouth again. Kissing it, he holds it there, the heat from his breath warming my skin. It's almost too much to bear, but I can't seem to pull my hand back.

With difficulty, he suddenly clasps his other hand onto my arm, pulling me down to his face. Single-minded lips seek mine and I lean in readily, not wanting to leave. Wanting to be left alone with him. Wanting to be next to him for as long as I choose, not as it's dictated by the world around us.

Reluctantly, I pull back. Swallowing my emotions and setting my jaw. I keep my eyes shut. If I make eye contact I will lose my strength. Squeezing his hand once more, I draw away.

"Sorry," he says, his voice sounding strained. "I had to kiss you one more time."

Barely able to breathe, I fight the lump in my throat for the right to speak. I won't leave without saying goodbye. Not again. I open my eyes, but I can't raise them from the floor to meet his.

"Take care of yourself, Hayes. If life is as cruel as it seems to be, maybe we can say goodbye again another day."

I walk out of the room without looking back, pausing briefly in the hall to calm myself before entering the lab to talk to Freya.

Explaining what I want her to do with the wrapped meat in the clinic takes little time. Convincing her to actually do it takes a little longer, but she eventually agrees. Luckily, she gives me the cough syrup for Grannie Johnson; I'd forgotten all about it. Thanking her, I leave in a daze.

Untying Mickey, I climb onto his back and turn him back through the fields. There are few lights on in the village now and it's just light enough to see the obstacles around us. Once we're beyond the village and on the open road again, I give Mickey a kick and we race back into the night again.

BREATHING SPACE

Winter is dragging.

The train came and went again and I stayed away. I've thrown myself into training and farm work, avoiding the village as much as I can. Sometimes it's still necessary. We use the Great Hall for trainings when the weather is bad out. Mostly I keep away.

Life goes on around me. Grannie Johnson recovers from her disgusting cough. The Johnson women spend an inordinate amount of time indoors, out of the cold. The crafting overwhelms every available space, suffocating me. I find myself following Bill's lead and escaping outside whenever I can.

The snows came and the train stopped coming. Jerome can't get to the City either so we live in quiet isolation. The quiet is as stifling as the crafting. No news of Hayes' welfare leaves my imagination boundless. I try to starve my pointless affection, but without distraction, my thoughts are full of him.

I'm trying to use the distance to regain some inner stability. Each day I take time away from the Johnsons. Sometimes I walk, sometimes I take Mickey, but every day I find space to work through my thoughts.

My favorite places to go are up high. When I look down at the frosted white world, my problems don't seem so insurmountable. I climb above them and they shrink behind me. If I climb high enough, I can see above the cliffs at the far end of the Valley. Gazing at the horizon, possibilities seem endless and I feel stronger. With each day, my guilt over Jerome, my anger at City injustice and my disappointment at an impossible future with Hayes, are replaced by acceptance and peace.

The passion of our people every morning at training is also uplifting. We've had to alter our lessons for the smaller space, but it has brought out the best in people, highlighting their strengths in surprising ways. After we complete our daily series of body strengthening drills, we do everything from sparring to football games and dancing.

Jerome and Ari suggested the dance workout. It's the first time I've really danced since I was younger. I didn't know I could like it. It was just another thing I had avoided. People danced at Gatherings, and I guess I had thought it was part of the show. Just an act, showing the meek and submissive natures of our people, as they dance listlessly to somber tunes. That all changed the day Ava and her band brought their instruments and dance was incorporated into training. It turns out dancing can actually make you feel legitimately happy. It's a revelation to me.

"I've never seen you dance before, Twiglet," says Jerome, climbing down to me after the first dance workout. While he's led the exercise, I have been on the floor with the masses, learning some moves. "You look so happy. It's nice to see." Winking, he wipes the sweat off his forehead before moving off to help a group work on their skills for evasion.

I can't help but smile after him. I feel happy. Jerome and I have settled back into our usual groove and it's definitely helped me to have that normalcy again. Rounding up a group to work on balance, I hustle my father along with them. Trainings are the only time I've been spending with my family and I try to work with them as much as I can.

My group is laughing constantly as they topple sideways, trying to save themselves by grabbing someone else and falling like dominoes in the effort. I hear a few skeptical people muttering about the use of balance in a fight and I smile to myself. If they only knew how many times good balance has saved my life.

Da does as he is told without second guessing me, and his example catches on. Watching Da stand on one leg is both impressive and hilarious. He stands a head above most of the others and they all stand well back, giving him room should he fall. He is surprisingly stable, but looks like a giant about to stomp on the villagers.

I partner with Da for the partnered exercises, partly because I want to spend time with him and partly because I want to prove a point. He eyes me warily.

"You have pretty good balance, and you're twice the size of me. Don't look so worried, Da."

"Big feet give me a solid foundation, but I know you. I look as worried as I should look."

"Are you ready?" I ask, with a teasing smile. He nods, bracing himself.

I let him get comfortable on one leg, before thrusting him sideways. He manages not to fall and comes after me instead. Letting him, I pull him further than he means to go, landing him on the ground.

Helping him back up, I face the group. "No matter how big or small your opponent is, do not underestimate them. You can use balance to dodge an attack and you can use it to your advantage when under attack. Practice now. Feel how your opponent moves through your connection and search for a weakness. It may be they lean to the right - push them further. It may be they pull back. Instead of resisting, try pushing them the way they're already going. Be conscious of both your movement, and that of your opponent. If you can tip the scales in your favor, do it."

The group approach the task with more focus and I turn back to Da to continue his training.

"Sorry to make an example of you," I apologize. "Let's see if you can get me back before we switch activity."

A look of determination sets on his face as he takes up the challenge. "You may look like your mother, but I see more of myself in you than you would believe."

I topple him again. "I believe it."

Pulling him back up I can see he's assessing the best way to attack me.

"Now you're thinking," I encourage him.

Da steadies himself as I come for him again. Grabbing me around the middle, he slings me up on his shoulder, still balancing on one leg. He wobbles as I wriggle, laughing.

"I could escape this, cheater! I just don't want to hurt you."

"I was thinking I would just take you home for lunch. Kidnapping you seems the only way I can get you there these days. What do you say? The kids would love to see you."

"That's a cheap trick. Did you have to bring them into it?" I say, elbowing him playfully in the shoulder. "I'd love to come. Look there's Frankie. We can ask if she and Ava want to come too. Will Lena be there?"

"If you are, I'm sure she will be. We all miss you too, you know."

"Good," I say, glad I haven't been forgotten.

***

Lunch is the usual MacGregor chaos. The influx of bodies and personalities come together in a shambolic, but heartwarming manner. The kids are all showing off and vying for my attention, which leads to copious amounts of sighing and eye-rolling from their parents. Warmth, sarcasm, teasing and laughter; it's nice to be home.

It's everything I've been missing while staying with the Johnsons. Being home is like slipping back into a comfortable pair of shoes. I wonder if I should talk to Da about moving back. My heart lifts at the thought, but I scold myself for being selfish. My reasons for leaving are still valid.

Jerome has tagged along to lunch. For the entertainment, he says. From the look on his face throughout the madness of the meal, he has spoken truthfully. After lunch we are going to ride the tracks and make our way to the lookout to check the snow levels beyond the Valley. We haven't had fresh snow inside the Valley in a week, and the white blanket over the Valley floor has started turning brown and slushy.

As soon as the snow on the tracks outside the Valley has melted, the train will come back. The timing of post-snow Train Days are unpredictable. Dependent on the weather, they can't be arranged in advance as is normally the case. As soon as the snow has gone, the citizens will be hungry for more, having had to ration their winter supply indefinitely.

The novelty of having me home wears off as the afternoon wears on. I love my family, but I'm starting to crave my maglev board more. It's been weeks since I last rode the tracks. Jerome waits by the door as I say my goodbyes and make promises to come again soon.

Reaching the door, I feel a pull to stay and turn back to watch my family disperse into their various activities. Jerome grabs my hand and pulls me out the door.

"If you don't leave now, you know you won't be able to drag yourself away. We'll have to strap you screaming to Mickey. You're still staying away, right?"

"Right." I nod. "Thanks."

"That good to be home, huh?"

"I didn't think it would be like that," I admit. "I thought I was over my homesick phase. But seeing them like that, all 'madhouse' like the old Sunday dinners, I just… Yeah. It was nice to be home."

Jerome looks sideways at me and laughs, messing my hair.

"Your house is crazy and so are you!"

"Thanks. It's nice to know I belong somewhere. You wanna race to the tunnel?"

"Already on my way!" he calls back over his shoulder as he sprints off through the slush, spraying up water in his wake.

By the time I catch up, he's holding open the people sized door that's set into the large rolling gate at the mouth of the tunnel. His bootlaces are tied together and his boots are strung around the back of his neck, the tip of a woolly sock poking out the top of each one. I wave up at Malik, the runner on tunnel-guard duty as he waves out from his post hidden in the cliff face. Stepping through the door and into the tunnel where the ground is dry, I take off my own boots, while Jerome does his victory dance.

With a boot hanging over each of my own shoulders, I set my board on a rail, flicking two switches before I stand on the metallic pads. Once I'm standing on my board, it rises from the track and a light comes on, illuminating the tunnel ahead. Jerome closes the door on the light of day and sets up on the opposite rail. The dimness brightens as the light from his board joins mine. We grin at each other and crouch down on our boards, ready to flick the last switch.

"3-2-1-Go!"

We are immediately propelled forward. Gaining speed until we hit the best speed for tunnel riding, I set the dial on the side of my board. We always have to go a bit slower in the tunnel. The blasted rock walls aren't uniform and the combination of wind and speed can create occasional turbulences that can upset your balance and dismount you. Dismounting into a rock wall at speed is not fun.

Jerome lets out a whooping noise as he rises into a standing position. I join him, setting my feet on their pads and pushing up through my legs, maintaining my balance on the slim board with barely a wobble. Rising up on the move is the trickiest part of track riding, but once you're up, it feels like flying.

We zoom along in the artificial light with our arms outstretched like wings. I see the daylight of the exit in the distance and brace myself to slow. We don't know how much snow is on the other side, and I don't want to hit a lump of it on the tracks without notice. Jerome slows too, as cautious as I am. We have both had our fair share of bad dismounts.

Pulling to a stop in the mouth of the tunnel, we assess the glistening white blanket before us. Stepping off our boards, we put our socks and boots back on. Leaving the boards in the tunnel, we step out into the daylight to explore. The snow is pristine here, without the traffic of people disturbing it. It's beautiful.

My harmonious thoughts are rudely interrupted by a snowball hitting the back of my head. I dance around maniacally to the music of Jerome's belly-deep laughter, as I try to shake out the freezing chunk that has slipped inside my collar and down my back.

"Jerome Marshall! You had better run!" I yell, still dancing.

"Run from what? Your cute little ballet steps?" he teases, pelting me with another handful before prancing away making mock impersonations of my movements.

Scowling at him I gather my own arsenal of tightly packed snowballs, storing them in my hat. I chase after him, bombarding him from behind with small but stinging snow missiles.

"Ow!" he howls, holding his ear and turning around to face me. "That one really hurt! It's like you're throwing rocks!"

"That one was a rock!"

The look on his face loses its jovial glow and turns serious.

"You're throwing rocks at me?"

"C'mon. Of course I'm not throwing rocks at you! See?" I say whipping another stinger at his head. He blanches at the impact and brushes away the crumbling remnants stuck to his hair. "Snow."

His eyes narrow and he charges, tackling me into the powder. "I'll show *you* snow!"

Pinning me down with one arm, he shovels the frozen powder into my face as I try to wrestle free. All I can see is white, and all I can hear is Jerome laughing like a madman. I manage to get my leg under him and kick him away, but when I open my mouth to laugh victoriously, I choke on the snow caked on my face.

Jerome pulls me free of the cold mess and whacks me on the back. When I can breathe properly again, I suggest we try the lookout to see how the rest of the grasslands look. Jerome agrees and pulls me up from the ground as a gesture of truce. As soon as I'm up, I push him over and keep walking, smiling back at him over my shoulder. Shaking his head at me, he stands back up and brushes himself off before following my deep tracks in the snow.

The lookout is treacherous in places, so we don't go all the way to the top. From halfway up, we can see the snow-line anyway. It's patchy above the halfway house and only becomes an issue for the tracks as the rocks close in and block sun from melting it.

"Probably only a few weeks more," Jerome says, squinting at the bright snow.

Nodding my agreement, I look out toward the City. It looks so small from this far away. There are stormy looking clouds rolling in from the sea, casting shadows and sun rays across the tiny buildings.

"I'm sure he's doing much better," he says, guessing where my thoughts are. I look at him, about to deny it, but he knows me too well. Shrugging, I turn back to the moody cityscape.

"I hope so," I say quietly. "We'll never beat the system

without support in the City and he's our only ally there at the moment."

Jerome doesn't take his eyes off my face as I look out over the land.

"Yeah, I'm sure that's the only reason you can't stop thinking about him."

"Does it matter?" I ask, still refusing to meet his eyes.

"Not unless we win, I guess. Then it might matter quite a bit." He smiles as I turn to him in surprise, his face both sympathetic and heartening. "I hope we win, Rori. Then you win too, right?"

"Or we could all die horrible, painful deaths and trap any surviving Daltons in an even worse position forever," I say in a glum monotone.

"That's the spirit!" He laughs. "Geez Twiglet, you need to spend some more time with Ava! That girl is all kinds of positive. Hey," he says nudging me. "Maybe she got your portion! When you were born they must have been scraping the barrel for optimism."

"Shut up. I can be a cynic with intermittent episodes of optimism. The world isn't all sweetness and light, but that doesn't mean I don't think some things are!" Crossing my arms over my chest, I kick his shin.

"Yeah," he says, rubbing his shin. "You're a shining example of sweetness!"

"Thank you."

When he stands back up, Jerome looks out to the City too.

"Do you ever wonder what kind of kid Patrick is now?" he asks, suddenly serious. Before I can answer, he lightens his tone again. "I mean, if they were running out of sweetness and light with you, what chance did he ever have of getting some?"

I kick him again, in the same spot. Not hard, but causing enough pain for him to scrunch his face at me. I laugh under my breath and the dimple makes an appearance in his cheek.

"He never had a chance. Period. I'm sure he's never seen a single scrap of the sweetness and light he was entitled to. C'mon. Let's go back down, I want to ride my board at the snow and flip into it. You keen?"

"Only always!" he says, already on the move. "There's nothing quite like flying through the air, don't you think? I mean track-riding is ultra-fantastic, and 'chuting from the Split is a huge rush, but there's nothing like the freedom of unattached flight."

I laugh. "Ultra-fantastic?"

"I dunno, it just came out!" he laughs back.

We walk back to our boards and remove our boots again, taking turns charging at the snow and making the most of the soft landing. Using our momentum, we manage to achieve some pretty awesome and creative dismounts. By the time we get back through the tunnel, we are tired, wet and cold. Putting our boots back on, we wade through the slush back to the MacGregor house to stand by the fire and dry out.

Rae feeds us, and I start losing the ability to leave again. Jerome senses my longing and excuses us, pushing me out the door before I can get more attached.

"Thanks again," I say, as I mount Mickey.

Jerome takes the rein under Mickey's chin and walks through the village with me.

"You're welcome. You looked like you needed help to leave. And hey," he says looking up at me. "What are friends for if not to help?"

We walk in silence a while. As we approach his house on the way out of town, he turns to say goodbye.

"A few of us are getting together for a drink later. Ava and the band are going to be playing in the hall. It could be pretty good fun if you wanna come?"

"She did mention it, but I think I should go back to the Johnsons," I say carefully, torn but not conceding. "I've had an 'ultra-fantastic' day, but we both know I can't pry myself away if I stay any longer - I miss everyone too much. I need to stay away. I don't want anyone else to be hurt because of me. It doesn't seem to matter what time it is or if a train is in or not. My actions come and bite someone in the ass. I won't risk it."

"I understand Rori. We just miss having you around is all. See you at training?" he asks in an upbeat tone that doesn't quite mask his disappointment.

"See you at training," I confirm, nodding. "I really enjoyed the dancing. Maybe you can do it again?"

"Of course," he says, the smile in his voice undeniable. "But only because dancing is enjoyable, effective cardio. Not because I love watching you when you do it."

"Good. Enjoyable, effective cardio is all I'm asking for," I say, staring at his cheeky dimple. "See ya later, Jerome." Waving, I turn Mickey onto the muddy road and ride away.

THE THAW

As he rode the train for the first time since the snows had fallen, Hayes felt fighting fit. The Dalton medicine and Rori's supplementary protein had seen him heal more quickly than he'd expected. With more down time in the City over the winter, he had been able to spend a lot of time in the gym, rebuilding his strength and endurance. He felt better than he had in a long time, both physically and mentally.

Sharing part of himself with Rori, difficult as it had been, had liberated him from the burdens of secrecy and isolation. His heart felt less heavy and a true sense of hope had blossomed there. Knowing it could lead to his demise, he was careful to maintain Smiler's usual outward impression in public, keeping his hope hidden from watchful eyes.

Hayes watched the empty grassland going by as it got progressively rockier. He hadn't seen Rori on his last trip, and was unlikely to see her this time either, but it didn't stop him from craving the chance to catch even a glimpse of her. He looked down to his boots, lest his face show signs of his inward desire.

Ambassador Malcolm was on board. Hayes wondered

what situation Owen Mac would create this time to be able to have a word alone. The escorts had teased him relentlessly for his stint as a contagion sent to infect the Daltons, but the ploy to isolate him from them, had worked well.

Hayes definitely needed to talk. Training the Citizen women was proving to be more difficult than he'd thought. He couldn't spend enough time with them to plan and go over technique without drawing too much attention. Able to meet with them singularly under the premise of 'dating', he couldn't allow himself to spend much more time than that with them, for fear they would be assumed valued by him. Like his family, they would be at risk, should the Director want to manipulate Hayes or vice versa.

As much as he could offer the girls during their brief times together in the private rooms, Hayes knew it was not enough. He needed advice. The women couldn't risk being seen practicing such things, and there wasn't much space for them to use that wasn't out in the open. Hayes needed fresh ideas.

The train went dark as they entered the tunnel. The external light could only stay on if the internal lights cut out. The engineer never traveled into the tunnel without seeing ahead of him. Hayes didn't see the big deal. They'd stay on the tracks until they reached the other side. He couldn't decide if the engineer was scared of fallen rocks hidden in the dark, or scared that the Daltons wouldn't have the door open. It didn't take him long to decide it was definitely paranoia, because the engineer did the same thing going the other way, and there was nothing to block that opening. The poor man probably knew he'd be killed if he damaged Derrick's precious train.

Soon they were back in the daylight and the train lowered onto the tracks as it powered down. Hayes looked around the faces of his regular companions. They knew their orders. Supervise, intimidate and dominate. Nodding to the crew, he opened the door. They filed out and assumed their positions. Disembarking after Ambassador Malcolm, Hayes followed him to the MacGregors.

Owen MacGregor answered the door in person, blocking the entrance with his bulk and appraising the men before him.

"Ambassador Malcolm. You look well," he said by way of greeting. He peered past to Hayes with a disgusted, yet reluctantly approving expression on his face. "Mr. Hayes, you look much improved since your last appearance. I thought for certain you'd die over the winter," he said in a tone that suggested it might have been better if he had. "Our doctors tried hard to convince me you weren't contagious, but I have to say, until seeing you now I've had my doubts." Removing his imposing bulk from the doorway, he allowed them to enter.

A brief smiling wink behind the Ambassador's back, was the Chief's only break in character. Hayes maintained his own blank expression, but felt internally warmed by Owen Mac's gesture of appreciation for his improved health.

"I am well again, thank you. Shall we proceed with business?" he said coolly.

"Let's." The Chief closed the door and led the way to the study.

After the usual business, Hayes found himself leaving the study without a clue of how he was going to talk with the Daltons. Disappointed, he continued his usual activities of surly, passive aggression with his men as Liam Malcolm retired to the Ambassador's cottage.

Hayes continued to remain baffled until he excused himself to the bathroom during the Gathering that evening. As he was peering into the strange, waterless Dalton toilet, he heard someone enter behind him. Buttoning his fly as he turned around, he came face to face with Jerome Marshall. Tilting his head in greeting, he checked the other stall was empty, as the Dalton placed himself strategically at the door to prevent anyone entering by surprise.

Jerome leaned into the door. "Looks like you wintered well."

Hayes nodded, choosing his words carefully. Jerome had a flair for rubbing him up the wrong way. Hayes didn't know if it was the tone in his voice or his ease and casualness that annoyed him the most, but the Dalton seemed to chronically provoke him into a defensive state.

"I had help."

"I know. She can be intimidating, but she has a soft spot for those in need," said Jerome, his tone warming to a friendlier quality. "She'll be pleased you're well."

"You'll pass on my thanks to Freya?"

"Sure. Her too." Jerome smiled knowingly. "Anything else?"

"Yeah, actually. I'm having more difficulty than I thought. I can't gain enough access to the women without drawing attention. I need a few ideas on how they can get up to speed on their own, in an inconspicuous way. I can do some training privately, but mostly, there's no cover. Any ideas?"

Jerome looked thoughtful for a moment.

"You need something that will look natural," he mused, itching his clipped whiskers. "Why don't you try games? They hang out with their kids a lot, so it wouldn't seem out of place.

"Games?" Hayes asked sceptically. "Like hide and seek?"

"Sure. Knowing how to hide well is very important," Jerome said with a secretive smile. "I meant fun, more active games though."

"We don't play a lot of games in the City."

Jerome smiled. "That makes a lot of sense, now that you mention it." He wore that judging look that Hayes disliked, but it faded quickly. "Try boosting fitness and confidence with football or something. Introduce a bit of healthy competition to bring out the fighter within. We've also been adding dance into our program. It's been good exercise and it's been helping a lot with balance and coordination."

"That would be perfect," Hayes replied, surprised. "Dancing they know how to do already, but what's football?"

"You don't play football? Soccer?" Jerome asked, his face showing disbelief as Hayes failed to recognize the subject. "Man, you guys are missing out! I don't think I'll have time to explain right now, but we can give you a demonstration tomorrow. Check out your library for a book. That should help. I'll meet you in the City in a week or two?"

Jerome jerked suddenly as someone tried to enter the bathroom, meeting his resistance. Without missing a beat, he yanked open the door to Griggs' hulking form and scowled at him.

"Can't a guy pee without running into one of you monsters? You're everywhere and you're giants! Don't you come in regular sizes? Honestly! Have a lovely evening feasting on our bounty gentlemen!" he called, raising his hands in fake cheer as he pushed past Griggs.

Martin Griggs turned his wide eyes from Jerome's back to Hayes. Shaking his hands dry over the basin, Hayes just shrugged.

"Penis envy," he said, slipping on an arrogant smile as he walked past Griggs and back to the hall. The door closed on Griggs' laughter and Hayes exhaled in relief.

***

True to his word, Jerome made an appearance the next morning. Hayes saw him and several others cross the tracks to the flat field beyond the train. He noticed Jerome was kicking a round ball in front of him as he walked, occasionally kicking it to a friend, who would return it the same way. That seemed simple enough, Hayes thought to himself. He knew where he could find a few balls that size. It didn't seem like very strenuous exercise though.

Hayes wondered how Jerome expected him to create a band of fighters by kicking a ball around. There must be more to it. Grabbing a loaf of bread and a jug of water from the well-stocked 'Citizens Only' snack table, he found a seat where he could eat and watch, without looking too obvious.

Half of the people on the field removed their shirts. Hayes noted there were a few women on the field, but they kept their shirts on. He was not surprised to see that the Daltons were lean and muscular. Jerome's physique was particularly impressive. Hayes had presumed the man would be well defined, given the strength it required to move the way he did, but he was impressed none-the-less.

It was cold out, and the removal of clothes drew attention. Griggs and Grayson joined him with their own morning tea, watching the proceedings curiously. Soon they were joined by Benno and Liam Malcolm.

The group on the field split into two sides; those with shirts and those without. The ball was put on the ground between them and a woman on the sideline put her fingers in her mouth and let out a shrill whistle. That was when the action started! Jerome charged the ball and skillfully flicked it behind him to a waiting team mate. The bodies dispersed around the field, with the main focus on the ball.

They fought over the ball up and down the field, but no one just picked it up and took it. The different teams pushed each other around, used fancy footwork to steal the ball and worked together to move it to the opposite side of the field, between two sticks plugged into the dirt. The crowd that had gathered to watch all cheered when the ball found its target. Then it all started again with the ball back in the center. The energy was spreading and Hayes found he wasn't the only Citizen smiling as he watched. It was perfect.

They had long finished their snacks when the game

came to a close. The players' bodies were covered with sweat and mud, and their faces were equally plastered with enjoyment. Crossing back over the tracks, they made their way back through the village.

"Hey, you!" Griggs called after the last player to leave. "What *was* that?"

Jerome turned around, his face still red from the exertion. Putting the ball on the ground, he pulled his shirt back on over his mud-striped torso.

"That, my foreign friend, was a bit of fun we like to call football!" Laughing, he waved a hand at them and waltzed off down the lane, the ball tucked under his wing.

The Citizen spectators turned to each other, their expressions ranging from surprise to disbelief.

"Football?" Benno looked to the others questioningly.

They shrugged at him, as new to the concept as he was. Gathering their gear, they readied the train for departure, double checking that the supplies were secure. The train rose up and slid back into the blackness of the tunnel and Hayes smiled freely in the dark, inspired.

***

As spring arrived and the weather warmed, Hayes carried on his Enforcer's duties in the City. Patrolling the streets with his men, he tried not to focus on how he kept order within the City by intimidation; how he helped keep the population imprisoned within the inner grid. He preferred instead, to think of the successful introduction of football to the City.

As Jerome suggested, Hayes had checked the library, finding a book on the game and the skills required for it. Reading it through, he put his knowledge into practice when he found a couple of balls in one of the store warehouses. Benno had inadvertently helped him practice, as they showed some of the other guys what they had seen in the Valley. The craze caught on and before he knew it, he was seeing guys playing in the training yard in their downtime and more importantly, kids playing in the street with their mothers joining in.

Hayes had decided to introduce it as a fun activity to the men first. Hoping to make it popular. Also, they were trained to fight, but he hoped they would benefit from a positive outlet for some of their energy outside of joyously maiming each other and their rough treatment of the women in the service pool.

He had passed on the book to Grace, for her to read and share with the others. By mid-spring, football was an established activity in the City. He expressed as much to Jerome, who was just as pleased, and offered more tips.

Hayes had come to enjoy his visits with the Dalton. Though he still felt uncomfortable at times, they seemed to leave each meeting on friendlier terms and he enjoyed being able to unload his treasonous thoughts without dire repercussions. It was a slice of freedom to express such things.

Jerome visited frequently and tended to combine his informant jaunts with his other business; thievery. He never spoke of what he was taking, and Hayes was more than curious.

"What are you getting today?" he finally asked one day, after a discussion with Jerome, who had once again slid expertly into the library in his mottled-gray outfit. It was similar to the one Rori had worn when he'd first met her. Jerome had called it a gopher-suit when he'd asked about it.

"You mean apart from essential information, an ego boost and a workout? What more could I need?" Jerome replied, laughing.

"I can't even begin to guess," Hayes said, laughing back. "That's why I'm asking."

"I take things we need, but don't have. Things we can't make ourselves. That much you've probably guessed. Am I right?" His eyes danced with the secret.

"Yes," sighed Hayes, waiting impatiently to be

enlightened.

"Today I need electrical bits and pieces," Jerome said elusively, apparently enjoying himself by creating suspense. Hayes drummed his fingers on the table, an unimpressed eyebrow raised.

"Current amplifiers mainly. We only need a few more to complete a project."

"What kind of project? Am I allowed to know?" Hayes asked, hoping he had proved trustworthy by now.

"I wouldn't think so," the Dalton teased. "You're better off not knowing. It's the kind of project that could cause a lot of problems for a soldier like yourself. That's all I'm going to say."

"A soldier like *myself* has an endless list of problems already, but other soldiers might appreciate the attention. I'm hoping that's what you meant," he said sociably, acknowledging that no more would be shared on the matter.

"Of course." Jerome smiled. "You've got enough trouble already. A regular turkey in the river."

"Huh?"

"Turkeys don't swim."

"Oh. Wait, I'm drowning in trouble?"

Hayes frowned at the thought. He had a lot of things to juggle right now, but thought he was managing so far. He was definitely seeing positive progress anyway, and wouldn't describe his troubles as overwhelming enough to drown him.

"You fell in love with a Dalton. I'd say that's pretty troublesome," Jerome said, staring at him pointedly. "And because of the one you fell for, you're in way over your head. Don't you think?"

Hayes stood in stunned silence. Although they had both alluded to his feelings for Rori, Jerome had never openly confronted him about it. He didn't know how to deal with it, but honesty seemed best at this point.

"Way, way over my head. Beyond reach," he agreed,

slumping into the chair behind him.

Hayes ran his hand through his hair, his eyes downcast under Jerome's intense scrutiny. He had been doing his best to put aside his feelings, had tried to stop letting her enter his mind. Grateful for the distraction afforded him by his duties as an Enforcer and his secret life, Hayes had managed to keep thoughts of Rori to a minimum during the daytime. Jerome's direct manner had ambushed him and Rori filled his head.

"That was rude of me," Jerome said apologetically, making Hayes look up. "I just felt like we should clear the air. We seem to skirt around the words, but never have the conversation."

"We do," Hayes said, nodding. It was time. "I know you and she were …" He paused, trying to suppress the host of unwelcome mental images he'd been envisioning since he had learned of their history. He wondered if he could utter the words allowed without unleashing a tidal wave of jealous rage. Jutting out his jaw, he avoided looking at the Dalton. "That you were… an item."

"Were." Jerome's tone was concrete. "I ruined it a long time ago in a drunken moment of weakness - Orla didn't even know Rori and I were together at the time. Anyway, I lost her and she moved on. She has made it clear that she will only refer to 'us' in past tense. Romantically speaking of course," he said, clarifying.

Jerome looked as comfortable as he always did when speaking of uncomfortable topics and it irritated Hayes. He himself felt overly sensitive and exposed.

"Why are you telling me this?" he asked uncertainly, wondering if Jerome was trying to derail him for some reason.

Jerome lapsed into thought, as he leaned casually against the bookshelf. His blue eyes stared into space as he contemplated his response.

"Because I want her to be happy. She likes you too, and if this all pans out one day, you guys might have a chance."

Jerome looked at Hayes again. "I can see why she likes you, but I can see things she won't like too. I want you to know that if you ever hurt her, I will not take it well." He was so fierce, that Hayes actually straightened in his chair.

"None of us will take it well," he continued. "In fact, imagine how *she* will take it." He paused, checking to see that Hayes was indeed imagining it.

Picturing Rori scorned and angry at him, Hayes could almost feel how bad it would be inside his skin. Swallowing hard, he nodded.

"Now amplify that by the *entire* Dalton population. We love that girl. She says and does what we all wish we were brave enough to do. No matter how much is demanded of her, she lives with a spirit of freedom the rest of us only dream of. She is a slave to no-one but herself, and she is what we all aspire to. You treat her wrong, and vengeance will rain down on you with such fury that you will wish you'd never seen her beautiful face. Understood?"

"Got it," Hayes confirmed, browbeaten. "Thanks for the pep talk."

"You're welcome." Jerome smiled sweetly, a dimple forming in his cheek, visible through his gray concealer. "Now get back to work. The sooner we win, the sooner you can get your girl," he said encouragingly. Not waiting for Hayes to come out of shock, Jerome leapt from chair, to table, to shelf top and made his way back to his usual exit.

"See ya next time, Romeo," he called back as he left.

FORCED HAND

Eventually Hayes found his legs again and left the library. Bumping into a few people, he walked the streets unseeing, in the direction of the training compound. Just when he thought he'd subdued his thoughts of Rori, Jerome had brought them crashing back into the forefront.

Ducking into a doorway, he feigned a loose boot-lace and bent down to re-tie his perfectly fine laces. If he didn't process some of his thoughts, he couldn't put Rori aside. He needed badly to put her aside. People were expecting him to be in form at combat training and patrol following that. Right now he felt a mess.

Hayes couldn't quite make sense of the encounter. Rori liked him, but they both knew pursuing it was out of the question. Then comes Jerome, giving his blessing? None of it mattered. It wasn't a possibility unless they could change the world as they knew it.

Another thought climbed into the mix. Jerome was Owen Mac's spokesperson. There was a possibility that he was passing on approval from the Chief to pursue Rori if they were victorious. Was he being baited? They clearly knew his weakness if Rori was the bait they were using. Were they trying to keep him motivated? Maybe they wanted more from him.

He was doing all he could.

The wind gusted down the street, blasting the dust with it and making him choke. Pulling his faded bandanna from his pocket, he covered his face, grateful for the disguise. He carefully pulled out his soldier-issue sunglasses and polished their aging lenses before putting them on and stepping back into the street.

Hayes decided it didn't matter why Jerome had said those things. He was already set on succeeding in his tasks and he had already imagined pursuing Rori when it was all over. At this stage he didn't care if he had permission or not. The conversation *had* cleared the air between Jerome and himself, which was positive.

The only thought that still had him reeling was the depth of Rori's feelings for him. Hayes opened the doors to the compound and shoved his thoughts away. He could ponder that one while he lay awake at night, hoping.

Smiler ran his men through their paces for an hour and marched back out with them. They were patrolling the sector to the south this afternoon. It included a large portion of derelict buildings and Hayes kicked himself for not asking Jerome where he was headed after the library, though he felt reasonably sure the Dalton would be gone by now. The thieves seemed to have a vast knowledge of the general patrol schedule.

The soldiers walked down the street, taking an alley every now and then only to rejoin formation further down the street. Citizens carried out their usual business around them. They walked by, carting fish, or vegetables to the central market, or toting children along on other errands. None made eye contact. Most of them purposely looked down and moved away, cowering from potential wrath. They all lived in fear.

It sickened Hayes.

He hated being a part of something that made people feel that way. In his private life things were different, but that couldn't be displayed in public. Whenever he saw any of the service girls, while on patrol, he couldn't smile in recognition. He just stared straight ahead. They wouldn't try to approach him either. In public they turned and cowered like the rest.

As his unit left the inner grid and moved into the abandoned neighborhoods, the people disappeared. Anyone loitering in these areas was instantly viewed with suspicion. It was illegal to loot the deserted buildings. Any and all contents were owned by the City and only the City Director could order the removal, use or gifting of such items.

It was for this reason, that Hayes was shocked when Indi's boy, Toby, came running through an alley, straight towards him.

"Toby! What are you doing here?" Hayes asked as he caught the boy and crouched to him, purposely placing his body between Toby and the soldiers. "You know you're not meant to be over here."

"I know Mr. Hayes! I didn't take anything, I swear!" The boy looked at him pleading, tears welling in his eyes. Hayes felt his heart ache at the sight of him.

"Then why are you here, Toby?" Hayes asked, knowing very well he would have been looking for something to take. Toby thought for a moment, not wanting to confess. Hayes saw something in the boy's eyes he couldn't identify. Reluctantly, the kid offered up the only excuse that could save him from a sound beating.

"I saw one, Mr. Hayes. I saw a flying man!"

Hayes stiffened and he looked at the buildings around him. Jerome? Surely not. Toby was a smart kid. He knew what words would keep him safe.

"And you followed him in here so you could tell us?" Hayes asked, prompting the boy to complete his tale, hoping that it was a tall one.

Toby nodded, jumping at the excuse for his presence in a restricted area.

"Good boy. Where did you last see him, Toby? Which way did he go?"

He watched as Toby looked up at a building halfway down the block, then back down the alley he'd come from. Hayes swallowed hard, realizing there was more truth to Toby's words than he'd thought.

"I saw him in the block behind this one," he answered confidently, his eyes betraying him with the truth. "Swinging up high."

Holding Toby by the shoulder, Hayes stood up and barked orders to his men, dividing the unit into two groups.

"You lot set up a perimeter around that block, now!" he commanded, turning to the second group as the first ran to position themselves. "You six, search each building in the block, all the way to the roof. Report back with your findings. I'll be watching for movement from this building," he said pointing to the one Toby had looked at, the tallest building on the street.

His men broke off as ordered and Hayes bent a knee to be at Toby's level. Looking the small boy in the eye, he gave his shoulder a gentle squeeze.

"Good work, Toby. Now run home and don't ever get caught down here again, OK? Next time it might not be me."

Toby nodded, tears spilling over in relief. He turned to go, but hesitated, biting his lip, a look of indecision and concern on his face.

"What is it Toby? You can tell me."

"I think he's hurt, Mr. Hayes," he said, his bottom lip quivering.

"Run home, Toby," Hayes managed to say as his innards turned to ice.

The boy ran and so did Hayes. He ran to the building and jumped for the metal fire escape bolted to its side. Pulling himself up the ladder to the first landing, he got to his feet again and ran up the steps. Around and around the rectangular structure every step creaked, until Hayes arrived dizzy at the roof.

Trying to clear his head and his vision as the world swayed, he staggered forward, sweeping his eyes over the space. No-one was there. The world settled around him and he walked toward the stair access enclosure and tested the door. It wouldn't open. Maybe Jerome had gone inside and barred it. He hoped so.

"Jerome?" he whispered, not wanting to raise his voice, lest it carry. He waited for an answer, but heard none. Relieved, he exhaled and looked about the roof. It was an open space, bordered by a low wall. Apart from the bulk of the stairwell, there was nowhere to hide. Jerome wasn't here, but maybe he had been.

Hayes dropped down to inspect a small, rust colored circle. He wiped a finger over it. The blood was fresh. Walking back to the locked door, he looked for any sign of his friend. At the foot of the door was a smudge he hadn't noticed earlier. He stared at it, trying to decide if it meant the source had gone through the door, but it was smeared the wrong way. Hayes followed its direction back where he had come from and found another drop further away. The drop had a tail. The person it had come from had been moving towards the edge.

Hayes walked to the wall to gauge the distance to the next building. Maybe he'd jumped over. The next building was only a thin alleyway distance from where he stood, but was a floor lower. Scanning that roof, he saw a carelessly large blood smattering, but nothing else. If Jerome was there, he was too hurt to clean up after himself, which meant he might be too hurt to move from there too.

Damn!

Running his hands through his hair, Hayes spun around, racking his brain for his next move. He needed to help Jerome, but he couldn't risk running down the fire escape of one building only to fly up the next. That would draw more attention than he wanted. He needed time. His men would be done with their search soon enough and would be coming to report to him.

Hayes walked back to the low wall. Could he make that jump? He'd seen Rori do further than that with ease, but he wasn't trained like her. She seemed to roll away on landing and come up running. Hayes felt like a sack of bricks when he landed from any height.

Searching his mind for any of the tips Jerome had been discussing with him, he tried to come up with something useful. If he could land like they did, the jump was easy. Looking to the street below, he wished he hadn't. It must be ten floors down. It was a long way to fall if he missed the landing.

Jogging to the other side of the roof, he checked on the progress of his men. Still searching. He waved as Paulie turned to him from a lower rooftop three buildings over. Paulie gave an emphasized shrug to display his empty hands and continued with his search. Hayes went back and stared at the blood on the next roof. It beckoned to him; conjuring up all the potential situations. It wasn't that far away. He had to try.

Walking backwards, he pictured the optimal landing in his mind. Taking a deep breath and begging Rori to help him, he ran at the low wall, pushing off it as he left. He ran in mid-air for what seemed longer than humanly possible, but all too soon, time sped up again and the neighboring roof came up to meet him. He kept his legs bent and running as he touched down, rolling immediately on impact.

Surprised and very relieved, he pulled himself up to standing and dusted himself off, unscathed. Putting aside thoughts of himself, he began a search of his new position. This roof had an access structure too, and a few ventilation caps. The caps weren't big enough to hide a person, so Hayes headed straight for the door of the enclosure.

He found blood smears on the door, and could clearly read what had happened there. About shoulder height, was a pressed smudge, with several red, closed fists stamped next to it. Below that, was a larger stain that had been dragged down the door by someone sliding down it. Hayes tested the door, to confirm the story. Locked.

An all too familiar sensation of dread crept over his shoulders like a chilling cloak. Cursing violently, he moved around the enclosure, following the giveaway trail painted in flecks and sweeping brush strokes of red.

"Jerome?"

He called again quietly. Hoping for an answer. Hoping for no answer. He didn't know what he was hoping for, other than Jerome's return to the Valley. Every moment he felt it less likely to happen.

"Romeo? You kiss your mother with that mouth?" a voice croaked from behind the ducting attached to the stair block.

Hayes closed his eyes and swallowed. It didn't sound good. He followed the voice, his heart sinking. Jerome leaned heavily against the enclosure, his legs in front of him. Hayes sank down to him, unable to ignore the horrid angle of the Dalton's right leg, or the gash to his head that had turned the top half of his gray suit to a dark crimson.

"Oh shit Jerome!" Pulling his bandanna out, he pressed it to the Dalton's head. "Shit," he uttered, more quietly, trying to free his canteen.

"I'm done." Jerome batted Hayes' hand away from his head, letting the blood flow again. "Lose Brick. Stupid mistake. Fell bad, hit my head. Tried to get it straight, but had to move. Axed the landing. Made it all worse. So much worse. Stupid. I'm well and truly done now."

"Shut up!" Hayes hissed, putting pressure back on the wound. "I'm gonna get you out. We don't have much time. Can you stand?"

Putting his arm around the Dalton, Hayes started hauling him up. Jerome's face contorted with pain, and Hayes lowered him back down to reassess.

"There is no way out. Tried. I can't do it. Too broken."

Jerome melted back into the wall behind him, defeated.

"Well I'm not gonna leave you here for those bastards, so harden up!"

Jerome laughed at him.

"I'm saving my strength for the last fight. Look at me," he said, wincing as he gestured to himself. "We both know I'm not leaving the City alive. Even if I did, I'd never be the same," he said sadly, looking at his leg. "I can't live as a cripple."

Hayes looked at Jerome, restraining himself from shaking the life from him now, for giving up.

"Quit your whining, baby! I'll carry you. Freya can fix you. She's a miracle worker." Hayes made to pick him up again, but Jerome fended him off.

"I love your optimism, but just stop," he said, hands still up.

Hayes stopped and crouched next to the broken man. Jerome rested his head back against the wall and took a long breath. After a moment he opened his eyes and fumbled with a pocket on the leg of his suit. He drew out a slightly curved rectangular object the length of his thigh.

"I need you to hide something," he said, staring at Hayes seriously. "Don't let them get it."

"What is it?" Hayes asked, taking the strange item from him.

Turning it over in his hands, he marveled at the different diagonal, metal stripes and the dial and switches. It was like nothing he'd ever seen and he knew it was a technology far advanced from that in the City. Dalton-made. No wonder Jerome wanted to hide it. Opening the front flap of his jacket, Hayes tucked it inside the torn lining under his armpit. It felt firm under his arm as he lowered it. Fitting snugly, it held secure.

"Get her to show you how it works when she trusts you again," Jerome said, a smile in his voice as he pulled a small, leather looting bag from another pocket and tossed it at Hayes' feet. "You'll like it, I think."

"What?" asked Hayes, snapping out of his bewilderment at the previous object and automatically pocketing the bag. "Why won't she trust me? I'm going to get you out of here. You'll see." He immediately doubted his ability to do any such thing. How much time? he thought, looking around.

"You're going to get me out alright, just not the way you think," Jerome muttered, trying to sit up a bit. "She's not going to like you very much after you 'off' her best friend, but she'll come around eventually."

"What?! I'm not going to *off* you! Now hurry up. We have to get you downstairs before my patrol get up here. I'll get you to the basement and we can get you out through the sewers." The plan sounded even less plausible out loud than it had in his head.

"Hayes!" Jerome snapped at him. "Look at me! I'm broken. I can't get home like this and I sure as hell ain't hanging around to get processed!" He visibly shuddered at the thought. "How many floors up are we? Eight? Eight should be plenty. Throw me off the roof. I want to fly one more time before I die."

"Are you crazy?"

"Flying is my life. It's my dying wish." His eyes locked on Hayes with conviction. In the distance they both heard the sound of boots on metal traveling up from the nearby fire escape.

"They're coming. Hurry! Make it look like a fight and toss me."

"Shut up!" Hayes heaved the Dalton onto his shoulder, beyond caring if it hurt him. He kicked at the door to the internal stair. It wouldn't budge. Even a locked door has some give. Hayes knew this one must be barred to be staying solid.

Kicking up and down the door, Hayes searched desperately for a weak spot, but it held firm. Panting, he whirled around for another exit. There was none. Paulie's voice was calling for him from the roof of the other building.

Out of time.

He ducked around the other side of the stairwell, breathing hard. Jerome was still dangling from his shoulder, the blood from his head still running. Hayes stared at it staining his shirt and khakis making them cling to his skin beneath with a sickening warmth.

"Don't make me beg, Romeo."

Hayes shook his head. He didn't want to. Didn't want to kill his friend. Didn't want Rori to hate him.

"Do it!" Jerome hammered Hayes' stomach with his fists, pleading with him as forcefully as he dared with the enemy so close. "Don't throw everything away. If you're caught with me, it's all over. The whole damn thing. Now throw me!"

Hayes knew he was right. If seen, he would need to hand Jerome in for processing and he couldn't protect the Dalton without revealing himself as a traitor. If that was revealed, he and his family were dead. There was no guarantee that Jerome would be able to keep his secrets if he was processed either, though Hayes did not want that end for the man. Moving to the roof's edge, he raised Jerome above his head.

"Please forgive me," he whispered, bracing himself.

"She will. She loves you."

Finding the strength just as Paulie's head appeared over the side of the neighboring building, Hayes heaved with all his might. The angry ache of injustice in his gut supplied the extra power needed to send Jerome Marshall out onto the breeze for his final, courageous flight.

Unable to watch, Hayes ran to the fire escape and began his descent. The noise of Paulie's shouts, drowned out any sound of impact. For that, Hayes was thankful. Hidden by the building as he climbed down, he wiped his eyes and set his mask. Smiler would have some explaining to do.

WAITING

Jerome isn't at training. I knew he had been to the City the day before, but expected him back by now. I don't feel too worried; more curious as to what is keeping him. Da looks a bit concerned and I try to appease him. It's not unusual to be delayed sometimes. Occasionally things can't be helped. Sometimes the way is blocked or there are too many Citizens around. Sometimes you'll be stuck in a spot waiting for the right gap to make a break for it. I say as much to Da, thinking of how many times he might have worried for me like this.

Anything can happen between here and the City. It's a risky job, but we're trained to survive it. I wonder again what might have happened, hoping he's alright. If he's not at training tomorrow, I'll worry then. Ari and I carry on with the program as usual, knowing that everyone is looking to us to gauge our concern in regards to Jerome's whereabouts. We calmly reassure the group and resume practice.

Standing in for Jerome, I teach combat skills, while Ari takes the group for weapon use and his son Neeko joins us to cover evasive maneuvers. My thoughts slip frequently from my work and turn to Jerome. I find myself having to repeatedly apologize to my opponents as I forget their learner status and have to pull them from the ground.

For their safety, I trade places with Ari at target practice, getting people to alternate between longbows and Horse's recently invented wrist-bows - a small, easy to load cross-bow strapped to your wrist. More portable, it's not as easy to aim. I distract my thinking away from Jerome's absence, trying to master its use and offering assistance to the others.

After training, Da approaches and puts an arm around my shoulder.

"I'm sure you're right. He's probably just running late, but if you want to wait at home until he gets in, you're welcome to," he says in a comforting tone, looking down at me with sympathetic eyes.

For some reason that makes me feel annoyed. Shrugging him off, I pull on my jersey.

"I'll be fine, Da. He'll be home later, you'll see." I tidy my sweaty hair, wondering if I should brave the cold spring river to cool off. "Bill needs me in the shearing sheds. It'll be a long, day, so I won't be back until tomorrow. I'll just see you at training in the morning." Waving goodbye, I fetch Mickey and leave.

My stomach feels unsettled, but I ignore it. There is no point in worrying when you know only time will give answers. It'll be better to keep busy until he's back and I'm looking forward to a hard day's labor in the woolshed. Working with the wool always leaves my calloused hands feeling soft and pampered.

During the day's tea breaks, I find myself looking in the direction of the Village, wondering if Jerome's sitting there, downing ale and sharing his story. When I'm not looking to the village, I scan the skies, wanting to catch a glimpse of a rainbow parachute. Each time I return to the shed disappointed by the empty blue sky.

***

He's still not here. Ari and I have run another session without Jerome. No-one is talking about it today, but we're all thinking it. He should be back. If he's taking this long to get back to the Valley, he must be injured, or worse. If it's worse, he won't be back for three more days.

Sometimes Gophers don't come back on their own. Sometimes they're returned on the train. Derrick sends them back after the processing and parades their mangled, abused bodies through the village to show us all what will happen to those who try to steal from him. I've never been allowed to see, but I've heard the stories. That's more than enough.

Da doesn't ask today, just waits for me and we walk home together. Aiden and Orla have gone on ahead, leaving us alone.

"It might still be nothing," he says, not looking at me.

"It might not be," I reply, avoiding his face too.

We walk in silence. Each of us lost in our own thoughts. I look at him, about to ask a question, but change my mind.

"Just ask."

"I already know the answer," I say, shifting my shoulder dismissively. I kick a loose pebble from the road and it skitters between two houses. "Hayes will help him if he can," I say firmly, believing it with all I'm worth.

"If he can," Da replies, just as definite.

Instead of relief at his agreement, my anxiety ramps at the words unspoken. *What if he can't?* The words eat away at me. My family swarm about with good intentions as I sit amongst them, mute and restless. The more I fidget, the more they give me space.

My own bed, in my old room provides nothing but a sleepless night. I can't even enjoy being home. My mind won't stop working and my legs won't stop moving, unable to get comfortable. The waiting gnaws at me with every passing moment. As soon as he's back, Jerome will come here. He'll know we've all been worrying and he'll stop here first. For me.

The sky begins to lighten. Jerome is still not home and I can't stand it any longer. Dressing warmly, I pack a bag with food and drink.

"Please don't go after him," Da says from the armchair in the dark corner, causing me to jump in alarm. He's probably been sitting there all night, waiting for me to leave. "Just wait, Rori. If things have gone wrong, there will be more heat in the City than you can handle. I won't lose you because you're not thinking straight."

"I am thinking straight," I answer in a steady voice. "I know what the City will be like. I'm not going there. I just can't wait here any longer."

Da rises from his chair and walks toward me. "Then where are you going?"

"To the lookout. He might be late because he's hurt. If I can see him coming, I can help him. I'm taking Mickey." I pause, waiting for Da to tell me not to or to ask what I'll do if I don't see him. He stays quiet.

"If I can't see him, I'll take Mick up to the Split and see if he went that way. If I can't find him," I break off, not wanting to admit it's an option. "I'll stay at the lookout until I see the train leave the City. Then I will come back and learn what happened with the rest of you."

A tear rolls down my cheek and Da wipes it away, pulling me close. Folding me into his huge arms, he pulls me off the ground. Pressed into his chest, I let loose a shuddering sob. He holds me until it subsides before placing me gently back on the floor.

"I really hope you find him, Baby. I know what he means to you." Kissing the top of my head, he takes a step back. "Stay safe and make sure you get back before the train," he warns, his own voice shaking.

BAD NEWS

With his gut writhing like a bundle of snakes, Hayes looked out the window. The train had left the City with a larger than normal cargo. Nestled into its own crate of salt, was the barely recognizable, pulped body of Jerome Marshall. Liam Malcolm had opted out of this delivery, choosing to avoid the disturbing task. It was a small mercy that Hayes could visit alone with the Dalton Chief to explain what had happened, but it was over-shadowed by the more gruesome duty of parading the corpse in front of the villagers.

Derrick had insisted Hayes do so himself, whilst explaining why in a proud and hearty manner. The Director had been enraged that he hadn't had a chance to question and torture Jerome. Hayes had used his history of mental instability to explain throwing the Dalton off the roof instead of turning him over. He'd reported a loss of control as the intruder was attacking him, knowing the excuse would be accepted. It had happened before. Not with a Dalton, and not on a roof, but still, it had happened.

The Escort crew left him alone during the trip. Hayes figured they were fearful of retaliation should they say something wrong, and knew he was projecting an unapproachable demeanor. Reg appeared to be taking pleasure in his discomfort. That was usual. As Hayes looked out the window, he wondered again what he would say to Owen Mac.

Hard as it would be, Hayes hoped Rori would be there, to hear it from him and to make sure she stayed inside. He couldn't have her out in the street when he had to display Jerome's body and talk gleefully of his death. Not knowing if he was even capable of such callousness, Hayes knew for certain that he couldn't do it if she was watching.

The week had passed in a storm of emotion as he tried to keep up appearances without falling apart. Smiler walked the streets by day and Hayes lay awake at nights, unable to get the incident out of his head. Jerome's face haunted him. Being helpless yet again, haunted him. The sickening shame of inadequacy had him crippled inside. Retreating into his room at any opportunity, Hayes would shut the door on his outward life. Safely hidden from view, he would crumble. Alone.

The world went dark around him as the tunnel consumed the train. Nearly there. The serpentine disquiet in his stomach threatened to escape. Swallowing hard, Hayes forced it down, needing to be strong. He had a responsibility to the MacGregors, to explain Jerome's death and the impending public spectacle. If he didn't pull that off convincingly, he'd be in even more trouble when he got back to the City.

Light chased away the dark and the train rested on its tracks. Reaching for his bag, Hayes nodded to his practiced crew. Walking from the platform to the MacGregors' without knowing how he put one foot in front of the other, he knocked on the door. He took a steadying breath, but it caught on the way in and he almost turned to leave. Obligation made him stay. Jerome had died by his hands.

Owen Mac answered the door. He took one look at Hayes and slumped. Stepping back, he held the door open.

There were two other people in the room. Aiden wore a similar expression to his father. Slightly behind him, stood Rori, looking like she hadn't slept in days. His heart wrenching, Hayes met her eyes.

"No." She said it quietly, but it rang screaming through his head.

"I'm sorry," he uttered uselessly.

"No." Shaking her head, Rori leaned on the counter for support. "No."

Each time barely more than a whisper, her echoes of objection resonated loudly within him. Each time stabbing him in the heart with renewed intensity. Hayes longed to comfort her. He took a step toward her, wanting nothing more than to clutch her to his chest and stroke her hair.

At his approach, Rori immediately backed up, her eyes wild. She stood a moment, staring at him. Before he knew what had hit him, she'd launched herself at him. Hayes stood and took her abuse, feeling deserving of it. Aiden tried to pull her off, but was sent reeling when she turned on him. Hayes watched stunned as Aiden pulled himself back up, touching a hand to his bleeding head where it had collided with the counter.

Hayes turned his eyes back to Rori in disbelief. She was unaware of her impact. As soon as she was free of Aiden, she directed her rage back at Hayes in a full frontal assault. Again he stood and took it. Owen Mac watched from the hallway door, a conflicted look on his face. Hayes shook his head just slightly, hoping the man would stay back a little longer.

Numb, he hardly felt it as she pummeled him, waiting patiently for her to tire. As she hysterically swung her final blow, he wrapped an arm around her. Pulling her into him, he closed his other arm around her heaving shoulders. Resting his lips on the top of her head, he inhaled the scent of her hair, wishing he could stay that way forever. Time was never on his side.

Raising his eyes, he met the Chief's gaze. It was time.

Nodding a recovered Aiden over, he transferred a trembling Rori into his arms. Giving her shoulder a final squeeze, he followed the Chief to the study to attend to business and to deliver the rest of the story.

Hayes handed over his documents and filed those the Chief gave him, before recounting his tale. He described the last hours of Jerome's life as best he could. The chief didn't interrupt, just sat behind his desk, hands folded under his chin, listening. As Hayes told him of the final moments, when he'd had no choice but to do as Jerome had asked, his voice broke and tears welled uncontrollably in his eyes. As soon as he had finished, Hayes reached into his bag and placed a small, bloodstained bag of electrical components on the Chief's desk, and stood to leave, unable to stay in the small room any longer.

"Morrison," Owen Mac called softly from behind him, before he could open the door. Taking his hand off the knob, he turned slowly around. Before he knew what was happening, Hayes found himself curled tightly inside the Chief's strong arms, shaking with grief and shock.

"It's not your fault, son. Accidents happen. Jerome couldn't carry on like that, and he wouldn't want to. The death you gave him was the kindest thing you could have done. If you hadn't been there to do that for him, he would have died tortured and alone. You saved him from that and you saved our plans from being discovered. I know it feels wrong, but you did the right thing," the Chief said, holding him back so he could look Hayes in the eyes. "She will understand too."

Hayes felt his legs give way, and grabbed the chair by the door, sinking into it. He hadn't been hugged like that in years. Not since he was a child, had he felt anything like Owen Mac's warmth and forgiveness from another man. Wiping his eyes, he sniffed, trying to regain his composure.

"I'll get us some water. You'll need to wait a while before leaving. If you go out looking like that, they'll eat you alive. I presume Derrick wasn't happy you ruined his chances for inflicting pain on a Dalton thief?"

Hayes could only nod. Like Rori, her father had a knack for reading a situation and seeing the truths within it.

"You're leading the parade, aren't you?" It was a statement more than a question.

Hayes confirmed it with another nod. Taking a deep breath, he found his voice again.

"I don't know how I'm going to do it. Will his family be there? Please don't let Rori watch." He ran his hands through his hair, as the snakes in his belly squirmed again.

"You'll be fine. I'll see they're kept away and I'll tell them the truth. As for the display, just pretend you're talking about killing Derrick instead. That's bound to make you feel more cheerful. Wait here."

Owen Mac returned with two jugs and two glasses. He poured a water for Hayes, who downed it rapidly. The sweet, spirit smell of whiskey filled the room as the Chief poured them both a drink. Their eyes met over their glasses.

"To Jerome," said Hayes.

"To a good death," said the Chief.

It was a potent brew and it burnt on the way down. Hayes let it singe the snakes and felt heartened by it. Drinking more of both water and whiskey, he stood to leave, stopping at the door with his eyebrows raised in question to Owen Mac.

"You'll do." The Chief pulled himself up and clapped a hand on Hayes' shoulder, squeezing it lightly. "No one will be coming to the City for a time, but don't feel like you're on your own. We'll talk on Train Days. For now, let's just take each day as it comes."

***

Staring at the jug of ale set before him, Hayes fought the urge to down it, followed by a dozen more. He had managed to uphold a convincingly evil front during the parade, but now he sat in the midst of what was clearly one of the smallest Gatherings in history. The Daltons couldn't stand to be in the same room as him. Those present were only there out of obligation or necessity.

Hayes could feel every set of hateful eyes penetrating his jacket. His skin crawled. If he drank more, he'd feel less, but he was also very aware of being a minority in a hostile environment. He needed to keep his sobriety and his wits about him.

Taking a long sip, he reluctantly put the ale back on the table. The small crowd was quiet. There was no music today. Even the MacGregors across the table were tight-lipped. The main noise came from Reg, who had no such qualms about withholding his drink. He appeared to be enjoying the uncomfortable atmosphere, eating heartily and making frequent toasts.

Poking the food about his plate, Hayes' own appetite was far from voracious. Trying to block out the surroundings, he focused on just getting through the evening until he could escape to the Ambassadors cottage to be alone. He had almost managed to fade Reg's voice into the noise of dishes clunking in the kitchen area, when he snapped to attention.

"Isn't that your daughter clearing plates, Chiefy?" Reg asked as he pointed to Rori leaving the side kitchen of the Great Hall. "Why do you keep her out the back doing dishes? Invite her to sit with us," he demanded. "I insist."

The Chief looked to Rori, who'd witnessed the exchange. Before Owen Mac could open his mouth, she came to the table and sat in her chair; the chair that had been empty for years. Red-rimmed eyes overwhelmed her pale face. Holding her head high, she fixed Reg with a hardened glare.

"It was a mistake to ask me here," she said coldly, not shifting her gaze.

Reg laughed and looked at the Chief, his eyebrows raised in disbelief.

Owen Mac looked at Rori and cleared his throat, before turning his displeased frown to Reg.

"Rori does not usually attend gatherings Mr. Derrick. She can behave recklessly in public, as I'm sure some of your more experienced Escorts may recall. Am I right Mr. Grayson?" he asked the older soldier, without taking his eyes from Reg.

Grayson coughed, choking on the potato he'd been chewing. He nodded as he cleared his throat.

"I haven't seen her at a gathering since the potato incident several years ago. It is as MacGregor says," said Grayson, trying to shrink into his chair.

Reg looked amused, his eyes dancing over his cup as he took another drink. Hayes risked a brief glance at Rori, not knowing if he could look at her without announcing to the world, his every hidden emotion. Erect in her chair, her own gaze did not shift from Reg's face. Hayes wondered if the hatred he saw there was as plain to everyone. He looked back at his plate, hurting for her.

"And yet tonight you felt she could grace us with her presence? MacGregor, what are you playing at?" Reg probed, the amusement in his voice obvious as he challenged the Dalton Chief.

Owen Mac lessened the ferocity of his glare, but held it firmly on Reg.

"My daughter was particularly fond of the young man you returned to the Valley today. I would rather she was reckless here, where I can see her than reckless at home alone. She chose to stay in the kitchen to minimize her impact. Now you have invited her to our table. May I suggest her return to the kitchen?"

Reg laughed outrageously, slapping his knee and thumping the table in an emphasized display of hilarity.

"So your youngest kid is a crazy, suicidal nutter that you can't control!"

"I'm not his youngest." Rori stood from the table. "And you should be careful how you speak to the unhinged," she warned, her eyes narrowed.

Hayes watched as she withdrew her eyes from Reg and her features mellowed. Turning, she smiled graciously to the rest of the table.

"Please excuse me dear family, I appear to have forgotten my manners. Treasured Citizen guests, please enjoy the rest of your meal without fear that someone has spat in it. I have been dutiful in the kitchen all evening."

Giving a dramatic flourish of a curtsy, she strode back into the kitchen, slamming the door behind her. A stunned silence fell upon the room, broken only by the sound of cutlery being dropped to plates, as the soldiers stared at their half-eaten meals in disgust. Hayes felt laughter bubble up inside him and bit his tongue. Instead, he picked up his ale and held it high.

"It appears dinner is over for tonight," he said to his men and downed the contents of the jug. Smiler looked to the Chief as he moved his chair back.

"I can see why you've been keeping that one hidden away! Mad, fiery *and* poor taste in men!" he said, motioning to his men to leave the table.

"A father's nightmare at times," Owen Mac conceded honestly. Pulling himself up from the table, he bowed diplomatically to the departing guests as they filed out of the hall.

Seeing his men to the bunk-room, Hayes warned them to lay low. Despite the overall power the City had over the Daltons, they were outnumbered here and it was clear that today they were unwelcome. The men seemed to accept this. Only Reg wanted to push the boundaries. Hayes ignored him. Without back up, Reg was powerless. Eventually he'd get bored with trying to talk the men into causing trouble and he'd fall asleep. With as much booze as he had on-board, it wouldn't take long.

Hayes backtracked through the village, risking separating from his group for the promise of peace at the cottage. He craved solitude. This trip was half over and the hardest parts were done. Depressingly, he still had to get through tomorrow morning and many future Train Days. They would be excruciating until time distanced Jerome's passing.

The hairs on his neck began to prickle as he walked. Continuing with his eyes ahead, he pretended to be unaware of company joining him on the road. Once he reached a decent place, where no-one could sneak up on him, he stopped. Turning around slowly, he counted six of them. The looks on their faces told him they were intent on harm.

"I can see you're riled, but I'm not looking for a fight," he said firmly. Six would be difficult, but not impossible. He could work through that number seriously injuring whoever came within his grasp if he needed to. They were young and cocky, and although they looked like they would put up a reasonable fight, they were no match for him.

"Not so tough on your own are ya, Big Guy?" said the tallest of the group. "I bet Jerome took out a dozen of you assholes in his blaze of glory. How many of you did it take to bring him down?"

They were Jerome fans. Hayes had figured as much. They all wanted to be just like him. He'd have to show them they didn't want to be *just* like him. Drawing himself up tall, he towered over them.

"Just one asshole," he replied coolly. "This one. Still want to dance?"

As indecision crossed their faces, Morrison heard a light thud behind him. He saw hope light the faces in front of him and inhaled cautiously. Seven might change things, depending on who it was. She stepped in front of him, facing the group, hands on her hips.

"You're out of your depth and you're out of order. Go home before I let the Chief deal with you!" she growled at them. They looked at her unsure.

"But Jerome!" the tall one tried.

"Was *my* best friend. This one is *mine*. Go."

The group lingered, not wanting to leave her alone in the presence of the looming monster.

"Now!" she ordered, with such severity that they almost fell over each other in their rush to leave. Soon they were alone in the lane. Hayes was rendered speechless by the experience.

"Close your mouth," she said as she walked away. "I'll escort you to the cottage."

Catching up to her in three long strides, he fell easily into step with her brisk pace. "I was about to scare them off. Where did you come from?"

"I thought that might happen, so I followed you from the rooftops. And if *I* scare them off, they get home less broken."

It was true, but her words stung him. He thought of how broken Jerome had been when he came home. Hanging his head, he saw that she no longer cared for him.

"So you came to save them, not me?"

Stopping, she looked up at him with tired, sad eyes; her dark lashes emphasizing their pain.

"You don't look like a damsel in distress," she muttered and kept moving. Her carelessly tied ponytail swung limply as she walked and her clothes were crumpled and unlaundered.

You do, he thought, wanting to bundle her into his arms. By the time he caught up to her again, they were at the door of the cottage. He opened it and she pushed past him, walking a circuit of the small house before returning to the door.

"Would you stay a while?" he asked, hopefully. "I'd like to talk to you." As much as he wanted to comfort her, he wanted just as much for her to hold him and tell him it would be alright. That he'd had no choice. That she understood. That in time his pain would lessen and his guilt would fade.

Rori shook her head and fought back tears.

"I can't," she said, choking back emotion and looking at the ground. "I can't be near you without thinking about him. Goodbye Hayes."

She walked away into the darkness and his eyes followed her, trying helplessly to pull her back into the hole she was leaving in his chest. She disappeared and he closed the cottage door, sliding down to rest against it.

She'd said before that life was cruel. He had known as much, but had not imagined the extent he felt presently was possible. Staring blankly at the room, he leaned back into the solid wood with the finality of her last words ringing in his head.

MORE BAD NEWS

A few weeks went by before Hayes saw the Valley again. The weeks had felt more like years as he'd trudged through his routines, not looking forward to his return. Liam Malcolm had decided to avoid the flak and remain in the City until the spectacle of Jerome's death had lost its impact. Knowing how highly regarded the Dalton was, Hayes thought that might be a while yet.

Hayes' reception in the Valley had been icy. Beyond the Chief's study, he remained hyper-vigilant, lest he be approached in the dark again. There would be no way to avoid violence if he was. There was no Rori to come to his defense.

When he'd asked after her, Owen Mac had told him that she'd disappeared before the train had left last time. He'd said she must want to process Jerome's death on her own; that she was up the mountain at the end of the Valley, taking it out on the rocks. When Morrison had asked how he knew she was even alive, the Chief had laughed at him.

"I see the smoke from her fire every evening before the sun goes down. Believe me, I'm checking!" he'd said. "She's tough. She'll get through it."

Hayes envied her options. Having the time and space to think was a dream to him. He had only his bedroom at night, and that felt suffocatingly inadequate. Looking toward the mountain before he boarded the train to leave, he tried to picture the slight, graceful figure sitting by a pool at the base of the impressive waterfall that ran down the cliff. Did she throw rocks into it until her arm was sore? Did she sit beneath the falls letting the water sting her skin? Or did she just stare, unseeing? Alone and numb.

Leaving the Valley again, Hayes felt just as miserable as he had on arrival. Needing a way to cut himself off from feeling, he ached to be numb. It was becoming difficult to maintain Smiler's upbeat character. Flat, Hayes did his job, unable to bring any smile to his face, even the arrogant smile of his protective guise.

The punching bags in the gym bore the brunt of his frustrations. No-one would spar with him. It was obvious he was in no mood for mercy. When combined with his reputation as a prime fighter and his recent 'loss of control' with the intruder, he was a fight best avoided.

At the club, he drank his week's ration in one sitting. When Grace approached him, he didn't even noticed her until she shook him and called his name. Blinking eventually brought her into focus.

"Come on," she said, trying to pull him up.

She was dressed flirtatiously. Working tonight, Hayes realized. His eyes traveled from her ankles to her face. Pretty. Smiling sadly at her, he knocked over the chair as he stood, holding the table to steady himself. He couldn't let her down. If he didn't take her back to a room, she'd have to take someone else.

"Water," he slurred at her as she righted the chair under the watchful eyes of the crowd. Swaying as she left to get some, Hayes sat down again. Grace returned with a large jug of water and two glasses. She poured, he drank. He began to feel vaguely more alert as he emptied the jug, but his bladder was full.

"Back in a minute." He staggered off to the restrooms.

Arriving back, he wiped an arm across his face, collecting the water that still dripped from where he'd splashed it to sober himself. Grace was sitting at the table looking uncomfortable. A man stood over her, his back to Hayes. Bristling possessively, Hayes strode over to the man and grabbed him by the collar, flinging him backwards and out of the way. He held a hand out to a wide-eyed Grace. Taking it, she pulled him hastily to the back of the club, where the private rooms were.

Once inside she shut the door and leaned against it, staring at him.

"Morrison, I've never seen you like this," she said, still bug-eyed and breathing hard. Hayes felt his eyes drawn to her chest as it moved up and down. Scolding himself, he moved away from her.

"Is this about what happened with the Dalton guy? Did you know him?" she asked, her tone as soft as the hand that reached out to touch his back in support.

Sighing, he walked away from her and checked the room as he always did, looking for spy holes. Finding it clear, he turned to find her staring at him, still waiting for an answer. He nodded, his shoulders sagging with the weight of his burden.

"Oh Morrison." She wrapped her arms around him and he melted into her. It felt good to share his pain. She leaned back, her eyes demanding to be met. Returning her gaze briefly, he couldn't handle his reflection in her eyes. He closed his own to escape the pitiful image of himself. Her lips touched his.

Surprised, his eyes flew open and locked on hers as she shed her clothes and unbuttoned his shirt. A voice inside told him to stop, but it was dulled by drink and overpowered by the urge to feel something, anything other than misery. She kissed him again, and hating himself, he kissed her back. Grace worked his belt loose as his own hands ran over her body, greedy for human comfort.

Hayes walked her against the wall for support, pants dropping as he moved. Grabbing below her round cheeks, he lifted her and she wrapped her long legs around him. His lips broke away from her face and kissed the length of her neck, his hands stroking her sides and finding her firm breasts. Grace gasped and he met her eyes to see if he'd hurt her, but she nodded him onward. A look of wanting had replaced the pity he had seen earlier and she reached a hand down to guide him.

The door next to them swung open and Fat Elmo forced his way into the room, followed closely by Eddie, the Bouncer.

"Occupied!" yelled Hayes, fuming as he stood on the brink of insertion for the first time in over seven years, knowing the prospect was escaping out the door with the stench of vinegar. He hadn't realized how badly he'd wanted to be inside a woman again.

"Ahem." Standing behind him, they waited.

Lowering Grace to the floor, Hayes pulled his pants up awkwardly as he sheltered her exposed body with his own. Turning to face them, he puffed air and held his pants up with white knuckled hands, trying to keep his temper from exploding.

"Boss wants to see you," Elmerson grunted in his deep rumble.

"Now?!"

"Unless you want to risk keeping him waiting." He chuckled, leaving the room.

Hayes stared at Eddie, his shoulders rising with each exasperated breath. Eddie put his palms up and shrugged.

"I don't want any trouble, Smiler. The Boss gets what the Boss wants," he said, stepping cautiously to the side and gesturing to Grace over Hayes' shoulder. "You can go home, Honey. I've got you marked down with Smiler here, so you're done for the night." Eddie smiled uncomfortably as he backed out the open door.

Hayes slammed it after him and tried to collect himself

as he gathered Grace's clothes from the floor. Handing them to her, he couldn't meet her eyes.

"That was probably for the best," he said, breathlessly as he buttoned his shirt. "Sorry, Grace. I shouldn't have put you in that position. I wasn't thinking." Hayes suddenly felt extremely sober.

"I happened to like the position you put me in," she said sadly. "In case you didn't notice, I initiated it. I know your rule, and I wanted to break it to make you feel better. It's me who should apologize." Grace dressed herself, avoiding his gaze just as much. Her cheeks blazed with shame as she buttoned the front of her dress.

Hayes watched her fumble with her buttons, her words echoing in his ears. For a long time, he'd suspected she liked him, and as he looked at her, he only felt relief that they had been interrupted.

"I appreciate what you were offering, Grace, but I would have done anything with anybody to have felt better and you deserve better than that. I can't give you what you want from me, and I won't hurt you by pretending I can." Hugging her, he tried to wordlessly communicate his meaning. "I think we would have lost our friendship, had we actually finished what we started here."

Grace nodded agreement as she leaned into him. Testing himself, he breathed in her hair. His nostrils stung with the acidic scent of the room and again he felt relief. He found no comfort in her scent. Releasing her, he opened the door and left her standing alone in the unsympathetic room. Not looking back, he ran to the elevator to face the next problem Derrick had to throw at him.

***

Cynthia waved him through, barely looking up from her paperwork. That struck Hayes as unusual. Something was going on. Feeling continually on edge about his secrets, he wondered if this would be the moment he was going to be found out. He was surprised that the feeling in his stomach scarcely registered as nervous. Had he become that accustomed to living in perpetual chaos? Taking a deep breath, he set his face and Smiler pushed open the door to Derrick's office to find out what was wrong this time.

"Ah, Smiler. Elmo informs me, the timing might have been somewhat inconvenient for you," Luther Derrick said with a slimy smile.

"I can complete that business another time, Sir," Smiler replied, looking straight ahead, but smiling in his own sleazy way. "How can I be of service, to *you*?"

Derrick laughed a little to himself and studied Hayes carefully for a moment. There was no Reg in the office today, just Elmerson and Beaumont. That didn't give Hayes any clue to his reason for being there.

"Reginald tells me the Daltons are still quite upset with you for killing that intruder. You must have done a good job rubbing their hillbilly noses in it. They must have liked that one a lot." He paused, waiting for Hayes to say something.

"Yes Sir. It appears that way. Visits have been particularly uncomfortable."

"A shame we didn't get to find out what information he had isn't it?" Derrick asked, his irritation as clear and present now as it had been when Hayes had originally explained why processing the intruder was impossible.

"Yes Sir. Apologies for that Sir. I was overcome by the urge to kill the Dalton scum." Hayes spoke in little more than monotone, going for a look of nonchalance. Inwardly, he was just happy his voice didn't break.

"Yes, well," Derrick began another lecture. Hayes had heard it three times already this week. "While I admire your Dalton-hating spirit, I remain disappointed by my loss. I rather enjoy inflicting pain on the smug shits myself." The frown he wore eased at the edges slightly. "I'm glad visits have been *uncomfortable* for you. Next time you get your hands on one, make sure you hand him over still screaming, or I will not be so lenient. You are a marvelous specimen Smiler, and it would be a shame for your genes to go to waste, but you have a habit of really pissing me off. One of these days, I'm going to cut my losses."

"Yes Sir."

"That being said, I'm sure you are wondering what you are doing here." Not expecting an answer, Derrick continued. "I feel like you're not quite suffering enough for depriving me of a creative outlet." Hayes froze. *What now?* Staring straight ahead, he waited, praying his family would be left out of whatever punishment the Director saw to inflict this time.

"There is a delicate matter to discuss with the Dalton Chief, requiring great diplomacy. Fitting for the Ambassador's apprentice, no?"

"Sir?"

"We have some more bad news to deliver to the Valley," Derrick said. Hayes kept his face blank while his mind raced. What news? Was Rori safe? Please don't let her be in the City, he thought. *Please don't let her be on route for processing.* Derrick kept talking and Hayes tried to focus.

"Because they hate you so much already, I can think of no better person to deliver the message to them. It can't wait until Train Day. When Train Day comes, you must return with Owen MacGregor, and he will need notice before then. As much as I'd like to spring it on him, I need him to be in the mood to negotiate an increase in supply."

"Sir?" Hayes asked again, not understanding what was happening.

"His son, the hostage. The Doctor doesn't think he'll last. A week, tops. We need a new hostage." Derrick steepled his fingers beneath his chin as he watched Hayes.

Hayes stayed silent. Initially he was relieved the news wasn't about Rori, but then the reality started to sink in. After taking her best friend, he now had to report her brother's impending death and take another member of her family. Now she would certainly hate him. He'd be the typical Enforcer she despised, bringing nothing but pain.

He definitely felt punished, if that was what Derrick was intending. But Derrick didn't know he pined for Rori. He was hoping the Daltons would attack the messenger. Train Day was three days away. The tunnel gate would remain closed until then. Derrick wouldn't break the rules of engagement and risk the train traveling before that. Hayes would deliver the message on foot and enter through the door, unannounced. Alone.

"Am I to understand, Sir, that you're asking me to walk into a hostile mob without prior arrangement?" Hayes felt his voice waver as the words left his mouth.

"I'm not asking. Is there a problem?" he challenged.

"No Sir," Hayes replied immediately. "I am simply concerned that perhaps the message might not make it through, if I should be ... met inhospitably before I can deliver it. Will I have men to accompany me?"

Derrick looked him over appraisingly as he considered the question.

"I'm sure you'll manage on your own," he said after his assessment. "You have quite the reputation as a fighter and even if they overcome you, I'm sure they'll drag you to their Chief before they kill you. You can tell him then."

"Yes Sir. When would you like me to leave?" he asked, resigned and unsurprised by his apparent lack of worth.

"First thing tomorrow," Derrick replied, smiling. "I'm not a monster, Smiler. I'll let you say goodbye to your family if you think you might need to." Dismissing Hayes with a flick of his hand, the Director leaned back in his chair laughing, apparently impressed by his own wickedness.

"Yes Sir. Thank you Sir." Hayes bowed his head slightly and left, his hands balling themselves into tight fists as he went through the door.

Arriving home, Hayes didn't remember the walk there. It was late. Lu-Belle and Iris were already in bed. Moving through the apartment in the dark, he thought about what lay ahead. He didn't need to wake them. Finding a pen and paper, he sat down to write his family a note, keeping it brief.

My Dearest Girls,

Have been sent out of town for a few days on important business. Will be back on the train. Stay safe.

Love Morrison.

Leaving it on the table, where they would see it, he looked toward their rooms. They would worry about why he was gone, but he needn't make it worse with details. Although Derrick seemed to think he was on route to his death, Hayes knew he would return to the City. Owen Mac wouldn't have him killed.

For a brief, elated moment, Hayes fantasized about being put to death in the Valley. Not actually killed, but faking his death, so he could live there forever. He had dreamed of escaping to the Valley for most of his adult life. The elation was quickly replaced by a sense of doom.

It would not be pleasant to be stuck there if Rori could never forgive him, and he had his family to think of. What would become of them if he abandoned them? Without him to provide for them, they'd be forced out of their home. No-one would take on Lu-Belle's troubles. Iris would end up in the service pool. Hayes sighed, trapped either way.

Closing the door to his room, he lay on the bed. The room was too stuffy. He opened the glass door to the balcony and the breeze ruffled his hair as he watched the City below going to bed, the lights blinking out one by one. Quiet tonight. It was too dark to see them, but he could hear the waves crashing on the beach. The repetitive sound soothed him a little. Leaving the door open, he flopped back down on his bed.

How would the Daltons take the news? Who would Owen Mac send to the City? He only had one other son. If Aiden was to be Chief one day, would it be one of his young sons instead? It didn't matter. Rori would be close to them all. They lived in the same house.

Hayes had often watched the older members of the MacGregor family interact as they ate together at the Gatherings. They were all so similar looking, but so different in personality. Despite their differences, it was obvious they were a close, loving family. Hayes could only imagine that Rori cared deeply for them all, and they her. He'd seen proof enough when Freya had been tending to his injuries. Despite Rori's bristly communications with her sister, Freya had done exactly as she'd asked. In fact, she had exceeded her previous efforts, which had already impressed Hayes.

Sighing, Hayes knew he wouldn't sleep. Waiting was too difficult. Getting up, he packed his bag. Giving himself a tentative sniff, he decided on a shower. As he caught the scent of Grace and the back room, a new wave of shame and guilt washed over him. The guilt clung to him worse than the smell did. Standing under the water, he began to feel that he'd spent too many showers lately, trying to wash away things that couldn't be cleansed with mere water. Jerome's voice came back to him.

She won't like you much after you off her best friend. How would she feel when he broke apart her family? *She loves you.*

Hayes couldn't allow himself to believe it. It hadn't come from her and there were too many obstacles to overcome for it to be likely. Things had changed. Finding the way to 'happy ever after' was too difficult. Nothing but a struggle at every conceivable turn. Romeo indeed.

Hayes hadn't thought too much about the names Jerome had called him, dismissing it as teasing. Now he could see what Jerome had seen. Two young fools kept apart by the feuding relationship of their people, overcoming the odds to be together, only to be doomed in the end anyway. Charming, he thought. Thanks Jerome.

Turning off the water, he wrapped a towel around his

waist. He chose tidy, but comfortable clothing. It would be a long walk and he'd need to give a reasonable impression when he got there. In the kitchen, he found the glass lantern and a candle they kept for power outages and put them in his bag. He would arrive in daylight, but the tunnel would be pitch black.

Walking into his closet, Hayes turned around. He reached above the door and firmly pushed the wall panel, gliding it upward with his fingertips. Sliding it out of the groove in the door frame, he pulled the panel out and placed it at his feet. Taking down the thing Jerome had given him to hide, he ran his fingers over the smooth surfaces of the metal plates set into the polished wood. There was a slight curve to the board and he recalled that Jerome had taken it from his thigh. Hayes hadn't even noticed anything there until the Dalton had removed it.

Holding it to his own thigh, he wondered again what it did. While it didn't sit well, it definitely followed the shape of his leg. He was much bigger than Jerome and Hayes felt that was probably why it wasn't quite right on him.

Why would he keep it on his thigh? It was hard. Maybe it was a thin type of armor. Too brittle, he thought, and it didn't make sense to wear armor only on one leg.

Hayes brought it back up for a closer look. Flicking the switches, he spun the dial curiously, but nothing happened. He turned them back the other way; still nothing. Giving up, he took it to his bag. Whatever it was, it would be safest back in the Valley.

About to close his bag, Hayes had another thought. Would it be safe if he met an angry mob in the Valley? If he had to fight, he might not be able to keep it from breaking. He sat next to the bag, staring at the thin board. The light reflected from its gleaming mixture of surfaces. It was beautifully crafted and thin enough to be breakable. Taking it out, he stroked it thoughtfully.

Jerome had told him to hide it. He'd said Hayes would like it and that Rori would show him what it did when she trusted him again. When would that be? Probably never. Hayes pushed the thought aside, but kept hold of the mysterious object. Jerome had given the board to *him*, to keep safe. He wondered if it might somehow be the key to regaining Rori's trust. A small but undeniable spark of hope rose in the back of his mind.

Taking the board to the closet, he set it back into the framework. Refitting the missing panel back over it, Hayes double checked it was secure and cast his eyes over it, ensuring it lay flush. Satisfied it looked natural and untampered with, he closed the closet door.

In one smooth movement, he grabbed his bag, swinging it over his shoulder. Closing his door quietly, he crept down the hall to the front door. Leaving the apartment, he began the long trip down fifteen flights of stairs and through the sleeping City. Stopping briefly at the guarded border, he followed the tracks out into the open wasteland beyond.

THE MESSENGER

As he drew closer to the Valley, Hayes started to feel he had imagined every possible reception he might get. Most of them made him nervous. Most of them included Rori. Many of them ended violently. It began to dawn on him that traveling alone offered him what he had been craving for weeks; solitude. He had plenty of time for thinking. Too much time perhaps.

The halfway house came into view by mid-morning. He thought back to when he'd seen Rori there, covered in the fallen autumn leaves. It was late spring now and the tops of the trees rose green and lush above the high walls of its garden. Veering away from the tracks, he walked uphill to the beckoning landmark.

The haunting sockets of the empty windows stared blankly at him as he walked past the decrepit house. Approaching the stone wall, he wrestled with its thorny guardian as he tried to enter the hidden sanctuary. The rose was covered in glossy green, and he saw hundreds of developing buds promising a spectacular show. Life surrounded by ruin.

He walked down to the spring on the bottom level, having to force his way through the new growth. Filling his canteen, he drank, looking at his surroundings. The garden was beautiful. All around him were beautiful blossoms and emerald leaves. The fragrance of life was intoxicating.

The sun shone down on him as he sat on the soft, cool moss and thought of how best to approach the Valley. Pulling a withered, unappealing apple from his bag, he ate while he thought. He would make it into the Valley by early evening. Hopefully the streets would be empty as people went home for their dinner. The light would be fading. Maybe he could slip in and sneak to the Chief's house unnoticed.

Then again, if he was noticed sneaking, he would be in more danger. Honesty had always proved to be the best approach with the Daltons he knew. He would just have to walk in openly and let them know he needed to talk with the Chief. If they gave him the chance to explain, that is.

His approach would have to be as non-threatening as possible. Scratching his jawline, he regretted not shaving recently. He looked down at himself. It was hard to appear non-threatening when you were his height and built like a machine. A fighting machine. Standing up, he removed his belt, with its baton and knives, and thrust it into his bag. It was a start, but they might assume he had hidden weapons too.

He removed his shirt. If he went bare-chested, they'd see he had nothing to hide. Hayes looked down at himself again. His chiseled physique in plain sight might be more intimidating. The only way he could make himself look more vulnerable was if he went completely naked, and even that might not do it. Nor would it give the right impression.

Sighing, he dug into his bag for a tank top. Pulling it over his head, he checked again. Tight enough, it was clear he wasn't concealing anything, and it covered him enough that people wouldn't be freaked out by his muscles. It was as good as he could manage. He tried to tidy his wayward hair, but that was fairly pointless. It never stayed that way for long.

Closing his bag, he swung it back over his shoulder and had another long drink. Mind set on the task ahead, he moved toward the rose. His eye was drawn to a tiny hint of color at the top and he reached up to the stem below it.

The opening bud stayed just out of his reach. Trying again, he pricked his thumb on a thorn. Shrugging his bag off, he pulled out a knife. It extended his arm just enough. With a subtle flick of the blade, the pale pink head fell into his waiting hand.

Hayes stared at it a while and decided he would give it to Rori if he got the chance. Putting it carefully into his bag, he made sure it was protected.

Pushing his way behind the rose, he left the oasis. The sun beat down on him as he walked back to the tracks and followed them up into the rocks. As he passed the rocks he had been climbing when he'd seen her flying across the grasslands on her spotted horse, Hayes glanced up, but saw nobody. He walked on until he came to the mouth of the tunnel.

Kneeling to light the candle, he put on his jacket. Inside the tunnel, the temperature dropped significantly. He would take his jacket off again when he reached the other side. It was too much a symbol of his role as an Enforcer - definitely not what he needed for a peaceful entry into the Valley.

Shouldering his bag, he walked into the gaping tunnel. There was nothing but darkness all around the glow of the lantern. Hayes eyed the rock walls and imagined the men that had blasted and picked their way through solid stone a century ago. They had paved the way for the train and carted their looted food back to Citizens on the brink of survival. Shuddering at how little had changed, he stared at the tracks instead.

Eventually, the glow of candlelight illuminated the huge door made of wood and steel. Set into it, was a smaller, man-sized door. Taking off his jacket, Hayes put it back in his bag. He carried its strap in hand, ready to drop it should he need to.

Taking a deep breath, he stepped through into the fading light of the evening. It was clear. Closing the door, he began walking the tracks next to the platform. Before rounding the store shed at the end, by the bunkhouse, he froze. Turning, he saw no-one, but the sound of someone running away was distinct.

Shit.

It wouldn't be long before they showed up. He kept walking, wondering when he would be confronted.

They came toward him, blocking his path. Stopping, Hayes put his bag on the ground beside him, nudging it away with his foot as he raised his hands high for them to see.

"I mean you no harm. I've come to see the Chief," he said clearly, hoping they would let him pass. Judging by the stances they assumed, he was doubtful. He heard movement behind him. Without looking, he felt there were two of them. That made six all together. He recognized the tall youth from the previous lane experience and knew there would be a fight.

"Harm is all you ever bring," said a man from the group in front of him. He spat on the ground at Hayes' feet.

Hayes looked at their faces. They had a right to their anger and their suspicions. He didn't want to fight them. He tried again.

"I am alone and unarmed, and I must speak with MacGregor. Please let me pass," he asked the resolute faces. "I mean harm to no one, but I will defend myself in order to deliver my message to the Chief."

Another man joined the group. If Hayes didn't get through them soon, it was going to get very messy.

"Please," he said again, but caught the flicker of eye contact from one in front to one behind and knew it was decided.

He placed his feet carefully into position. Something came at him. He didn't realize what it was until he saw the knife pierce his left shoulder. Without hesitating, Hayes grabbed it and threw it so forcefully into the foot of the man approaching him from behind, that he was stopped in his tracks, the knife pinning him to the road while he screamed.

What followed was a blur of bodies. Hayes turned into the automatic fighter he was trained to be, dealing with each blow as it came. Defending himself, he threw them off as he was able, trying not to hurt them. Consumed within a mass of writhing bodies and surrounded by the noises of effort and pain, Hayes began to falter.

There were too many. More arrived to take the place of those he discarded. Hayes couldn't keep them off without hurting them any longer, and he couldn't give in. The message must get through. Gritting his teeth, he began his assault. Shaking off whoever he could, he grabbed at those who still clung to him, knocking them back with brutal force. A primal scream escaped him as he pulled himself to full height.

Gaining ground, Hayes was intent on making it to the MacGregor's, but still they charged at him. He dispatched them as best he could. Another rear assault saw him kick a man clear across the lane into the side of a building. They started to slow down, stepping back as he staggered forward. There was a thudding sound behind them, around the corner. Hayes hoped it wasn't more villagers running to join the attack.

"STOP!" roared a deep voice. Hayes recognized it immediately and sank to his knees in relief.

Owen MacGregor pushed his way between the remaining men and stopped short in front of Hayes, viewing the kneeling, bloodied man and the carnage that lay in his wake.

"Aiden, run to Freya and warn her. She and Eldon will be busy all night," he said, amazement in his voice.

"Anyone left standing, help the wounded to the clinic." No one moved. "Now!" People jumped into action, supporting each other as they cleared the street.

Hayes stayed put, his breathing labored and body trembling as the fight left his system. He didn't want to meet the Chief's eyes, afraid of what he might read there. Owen Mac's large boot stepped into his vision.

"Get up, Morrison."

Hayes found his feet and stood, swaying slightly. He met the chief's gaze.

"What's happened? Are there more of you? Why are you here out of terms, injuring my people?"

"I'm sorry for that," Hayes apologized quickly, not wanting Owen Mac to think him a traitor. "I tried to pass peacefully," he managed before falling back to one knee, reaching a hand to the ground to steady himself. "I'm alone. I have news from the Director. Bad news."

"Come and we'll talk about it inside. You're hurt. Can you walk?"

Hayes nodded, his head light. Willing his body back under control, he stood. Not as steady as he would have liked, he wished he'd eaten more today. MacGregor turned and walked back to his home, leaving Hayes to follow. Returning for his bag, he trailed after the Chief.

When Hayes got in the door, the house was a blur of movement and crying. Children were being shooed from the dinner table, their plates unfinished. They didn't seem scared of him, more upset by the way he looked.

"Take them to Lena's. They can stay there tonight," Owen Mac advised Rae. "Why don't you stay there a while too? We have things to discuss."

A look of fear flashed across Rae's face as she looked from Hayes to her children, then back to the Chief. On the verge of tears, she kept them from spilling. Nodding to her father-in-law, she hustled the children out the door.

Hayes was alone with the Chief and a table full of food.

"Have you eaten?" Owen Mac asked, as he rummaged

in a drawer in the kitchen.

Hayes shook his head. The Chief gestured for him to sit, so he lowered himself into a chair and waited, not wanting to seem too forward in the already strained scenario. The chief walked toward him with something in his hands. As he approached, Hayes realized it was cloth.

The Chief pressed the wadded cloth into Hayes' shoulder that he now noticed had a steady stream of blood running from it. He took over the pressure and Owen Mac wrapped a strip around it, tying it tightly over the stab wound. Taking stock of the rest of his body, Hayes decided his other injuries weren't of major concern.

The Chief sat opposite him and poured two tall glasses of amber liquid, handing one to Hayes, who nodded his thanks. Owen Mac drank deeply and set the glass on the table. Hayes did the same, waiting for him to speak first, signaling his readiness to hear the dreaded message.

"It's Patrick?" he asked, looking more vulnerable than should have been possible for such a large and powerful man.

Hayes nodded respectfully. "He is dying. The doctors don't think he will survive another week. They have been doing all they can, but as you know, it was always a matter of time. I'm very sorry."

The Chief inhaled and looked to the ceiling, a tear escaping from the corner of his eye. Hayes averted his eyes sympathetically and scratched his whiskers. His stomach growled and he tried not to look at the food either. He looked up as Owen Mac began to move, heaping food onto a plate. Sliding it in front of Hayes, he passed him a set of cutlery.

"Eat. I'm sorry for the welcome party. It's a bad time to be a Citizen alone in the Valley. You in particular, are very unpopular. I'm afraid your parade was particularly difficult for people. We were all very affected by Jerome's death," he explained.

"I understand. I knew it would be dangerous. So did

Derrick, I think he hoped you'd kill me." Hayes picked up a fork and poked his food. He wanted to ask if Rori had come home yet. Probably not. She wouldn't miss the evening's action if she was nearby.

"She's still away," the Chief confirmed, watching him through perceptive eyes.

Hayes looked at him quizzically. She definitely got it from him then; the gift of intuition. He shoved a potato in his mouth so he wouldn't have to admit anything aloud. Owen Mac sat in silence as Hayes ate. After a huge meal and a jug of water, Hayes felt much steadier. Sipping his whiskey, he sank into his own thoughts.

"Could we do it now?" he asked, not really thinking it was an option, but he didn't know what the Daltons had been working on in the Valley. Jerome had alluded to something, and they clearly had the technological skill to create something powerful.

"Not yet," the Chief replied sadly. "We're not ready. The timing is all wrong." He took another slug of whiskey.

Hayes sat quietly a moment, staring at his own glass. "Derrick said he wanted you in the mood to negotiate. He wants more of something, so that gives you *some* power, right? I'm sorry I can't be more help in this situation. I could be helpful to your boy in the City, if you'd like to include that in your terms somehow. It's the least I can do."

Aiden arrived home at that moment, with Orla in tow. They sat at the table next to their father, wary of the grim tension. Owen Mac watched them a while before he spoke.

"Thank you Morrison," he said, "I think I need to talk with my son." Getting up from the table, he was about to excuse them when he must have realized Hayes needed somewhere to go. "We have a few spare beds here tonight if you'd prefer to stay, or you are welcome to the cottage?"

Hayes looked at the MacGregors' anxious faces and thought of the news that was about to be shared with them.

"Thank you, Sir. I believe I'll stay at the cottage and give your family some space." Standing immediately, he put his chair in.

"I appreciate your thoughts, though be wary in the streets until I can spread the word to respect your presence. Orla will come by shortly with some supplies."

Orla didn't look overly impressed to hear that, but looked Hayes up and down and gave a curt nod. Hayes bowed his own head lightly to Owen Mac, grabbed his bag and left. Message delivered, all he wanted to do now was have a hot bath and go to sleep.

RAISED EMOTIONS

As Mickey and I saunter back into the village, I can tell that something is wrong. No-one is about. Even though it's early evening, the curtains are pulled in every window. The evening is cool, but not cold enough to demand such vigilance. Putting Mickey in the stables, I approach cautiously on foot. After weeks on my own, I'm not sure I'm ready for people, let alone those in unknown situations. All I want is a hot bath and my bed.

Stealing through the back gardens, I head to the one house openly blazing its lights; mine. Through the window, I spy Aiden trying to comfort a crying Rae, Orla packing a box and Da sitting at the table with Horse and a nearly empty bottle of Whiskey. The table is still set with half-eaten meals. What the hell is going on?

It's obviously serious and I don't want to just walk in unannounced after having been missing for weeks. I need information. Slinging my bag over a shoulder, I climb up the outside of the house to reach my room. Fiddling the latch, I let myself in, dropping my bag quietly to the floor. Checking the landing is clear, I tip toe downstairs to listen.

"I thought we'd have more time," Da says to Horse. "I thought he would live long enough for us to bring him home."

My heart skips a beat. Who? Who's dead? Rae's Dad? He's been sick.

Horse puts down his glass, turning it in slow circles. "We've been working hard to get to the City, but you can't fight a clock, Mac."

Lowering myself onto a stair, my thoughts begin spiraling. It's Patrick. Rae is crying, because she will lose a husband or a son.

Patrick is dead. They've killed him like they did Uncle Alex! Something has been leaked and he's sent another warning! Stress has brought out the whiskey and we can't fight a clock. We're not ready. It's happened again.

I feel unreal. A ghost sitting on a step, watching other people experiencing the crap life serves up. I can't go in there. Not yet. I need to think.

"I'm going to the cottage now," Orla calls from the kitchen. "If I'm not back in twenty minutes, send a search party."

"Don't be so dramatic Orla," Da scolds. "Hayes is on our side. He isn't going to hurt you. Just take him the damn bandages!"

Hayes? Of course. It's not Train Day. How else would they get news? He must have walked in. And he needs bandages? My mind rolls back to the dark lane and the angry mob. Dammit.

As Orla leaves out the front door, I silently climb the stairs and slide back out my window. Following in the shadows, I watch as she makes her way to the cottage. She knocks on the door and waits, adjusting the box in her arms. After a while, the door opens and a dripping Hayes stands before her, a towel held around his hips.

He looks a bloody mess in every sense of the phrase. Diluted blood drips down his torso to be collected by the towel. A rugged beard has stolen half his face and there are dark circles under his eyes that have nothing to do with physical injury. I watch as Orla gives his body a once over with her eyes and changes her posture. Flipping her blond locks over her shoulder, she holds out the box.

"Do you need some help to clean up your... cuts?" she asks, swiveling slightly in front of him.

"Pardon?" Hayes asks as he takes the box. Taking a second look at her, his expression is a mixture of shock and disgust. "Oh. Ah, no. Thank you Orla. Goodnight." He shuts the door in her face before she can protest. Huffing a little, she turns and heads for home. Despite everything going through my head, I can barely contain my laughter as she walks by me, unaware.

Once she has gone, I step to the door and knock gently. It swings open and a disgruntled Hayes growls at me.

"I said no thank you Or-" He stares at me, round eyed, still dripping. "Rori?"

"May I come in?"

Hayes opens the door wide and I step through, turning to see him check the lane before he closes it. A walking mass of welts, bumps and lacerations, he has seen better days. The pressure bandage on his shoulder is soaked through, but most others things look to be relatively superficial.

"I'd hate to see what the other guy looks like," I say lightly.

What am I *doing* here? I'm trying to work it out when Hayes asks the same thing.

"What are you doing here, Rori? You should be with your family."

Avoiding his eyes while I think, I poke about the box that Orla brought.

"They don't know I'm back. I know what's happened and I just can't face that right now," I say, knowing it's the truth. "So I'm hiding, OK? I don't want to talk about anything that's happening. Go get back in the bath before you get cold. I'll help you with that shoulder when you're clean and if you don't want me to hide here after that, I'll find somewhere else."

Looking at me a long time, he nods and returns to the bathroom, not bothering to close its door.

I jump as someone bangs loudly on the front door.

"I'll get this one," I call to the bathroom.

Yanking open the door, I scowl at Connor Martin. His eyes are swollen with the shadows of new bruising and his nose is twice the width it should be. With fresh stitches in his eyebrow and one arm in a sling, he looks very surprised to see me.

"Rori?"

"You must be the other guy, or one of them," I say, laughing at him. "I said you weren't ready. What do you want?"

"I just came to warn the parasite that we're watching him! You better not try anything else Freak!" he calls to the space behind me.

"Or what? You'll get a sling for your other arm? Grow up Connor! As you can see, he's already under guard." I gesture to myself and smile demurely. "So you can go home and sleep off your ego."

"But you're tiny! What are *you* gonna do if he tries anything?"

"Probably the same thing I'll do to you in two seconds if you don't get out of my face, Connor Martin! Up for it?" He knows I could take him. I did it twice in one training session a month ago. Backing down, he frowns at the ground, before kicking at the dirt and walking away.

"I'll be here all night Connor, so don't even *think* about burning the house down or I swear, I will rise from the ashes and kick you so hard in the nuts they'll explode into your mouth!" I slam the door to punctuate my threat.

A peal of laughter comes from the bathroom, bringing a smile to my own lips.

"Quiet you," I warn, digging in the box for what I need. Putting the kettle on, I take the honey and bandages with me.

"Are you decent?" I ask, stopping outside the door.

"No," he says, still laughing a little. "*And* I'm still in the bath."

"Funny. Probably best you stay there. Cover your junk, I'm coming in."

"What?" he cries, splashing about hurriedly to keep his dignity as I walk in. "Honestly, all I wanted was a hot bath and a good night's sleep."

"Me too," I say indifferently. "Life is so obliging, isn't it? Now sit still while I clean out the gash on the back of your head."

He doesn't even flinch, just sits patiently and quietly, even when I get a bit rough to get some gravel out. By the time I'm finished, the bath water is rust-colored. I've managed to patch most things, but the wound in his shoulder needs stitches. Waiting for him to dry off, I thread up a suture needle and make some willow bark tea.

"You don't have to do that," he says, nodding at my needle as he comes out of the bathroom with his towel tucked tightly around his hips.

"It's not going to stop bleeding unless it's stitched."

Craning his neck to study the wound, he sighs as a fresh rivulet of blood escapes it, proving my point.

"Fine. I'll do it," he says, holding out a hand for the needle.

"At that angle? I'm sure you'll do a really good job. Here." I offer him the needle.

He looks at me, knowing I'm right, but not wanting to admit it. I raise an eyebrow at him and he drops his hand.

"Shall I get it started for you?" I ask, gesturing to the chair in front of me.

Narrowing his eyes at me, he sits and waits silently. Wiping away the blood, I push the tissue together and begin. Setting his jaw, he sits perfectly still while I stitch him neatly back together. Smothering it in honey, I put a clean dressing on the wound.

Walking around him, I admire my handiwork, sucking

honey off my knuckle. Warm, hazel eyes watch me. Feeling heat prickling my cheeks, I rinse my sticky hands in the sink, fetching us each a cup of tea when I'm done. Putting his on the table in front of him, I sit in the armchair by the fire and put my feet up on the hearthstones.

Behind me, he sighs as he gets up. Rummaging in his bag, he heads back to the bathroom to get dressed. Watching the fire, I sip my tea, lost in thought as I stare at the flames.

The next thing I know, Hayes is kneeling next to me, a worried look on his face. His whiskers have gone.

"Sorry?" I ask unsure, realizing he must have been talking to me.

"Your turn," he says, taking the cold tea from my hands and placing it on the hearth. He is wearing a pair of soldier issue, khaki slacks and no shirt. Even battered and bruised, he is mesmerizing. Taking my hand, he pulls me from the chair, leading me to the bathroom. A fresh bath awaits and he's put out a dry towel.

"It's not very deep. Sorry. I used most of the hot water on the first bath."

"I don't have any clean clothes," I say, the words sounding meaningless and strange, as though someone else has said them. He disappears. When he returns, he puts one of his shirts next to the towel and places something gently on top. The new bud of a pink rose. Meeting his eyes, a tear rolls down my cheek.

"Thank you," I breathe.

Hayes steps to me, holding my face in his hands. His thumb brushes my tear away as I stare into his achingly beautiful eyes. They display an undeniable sheen. Rubbing his cheek on his unscathed shoulder, he turns me toward the bath.

"Hop in before it gets cold." His voice is strained and he retreats to the door. "I'll make you a fresh tea." The door closes behind him.

The bath is bliss. Being out of my poorly laundered

mountain clothes is a refreshing change. The heat seeps into my bones and drains away the pains of living rough. I sink down in the water, dragging my hair under. Scrubbing myself all over with soap and cloth, I remove weeks of built up grime. The water is a disgusting gray-brown color as I get out. I must have looked dreadful.

Wrapping my hair in the towel, I shrug on Hayes' shirt. It's soft and worn and far too big. Buttoning it, I roll up the sleeves. It comes nearly to my knees.

I quickly wash my clothes in the sink, so I'll have something to wear in the morning. I definitely can't go outside in *his* shirt. Wringing them out as much as I can, I unwrap my hair, put the clothes in the towel and take them out to hang by the fire.

Braiding my hair to one side, I smile as Hayes puts a new cup of tea on the hearth at my feet. Thanking him, I blow on it as the heat from the fire warms the backs of my legs. I watch him as he moves around the room, adjusting the furniture.

"What are you doing?"

"Making a bit more room, so you can hide here," he answers. "I'll sleep by the fire. You have the bed." Pulling a cushion from the chair, he drops it to the floor and shakes out a blanket.

"Don't be stupid," I say in disbelief. "You're injured and you look like you haven't slept in weeks. Take the bed."

"You don't look like you've slept in weeks either," he counters, challenging my logic just as stubbornly. "Do you want a good night's sleep or not?"

I really do. My eyes dart between him and the bed. "You take it."

With grumpy brows, he grunts at me as he walks past and flops onto the bed, lounging exaggeratedly.

"Is this what you want?" he asks condescendingly.

Frowning at him, I say nothing. Finishing my tea, I put the cup in the sink and turn out the main light. Hesitantly,

I walk over to the bed and look down at him. Already under the blankets, he sees my face and his attitude melts away.

"I think what I really want... is to be held," I say quietly, my voice breaking.

Without pause, he pulls back the covers and I slide in next to him. Reaching over to turn off the bedside lamp, he lies on his side, inviting me into the crook of his arm. Curling my back into him, I lay my head on the muscular pillow as his other arm folds over me, pulling me into him. Kissing my hair, he rests his cheek on my head. Tender arms tighten around me, as I unleash a shuddering sob.

"I'm so sorry I couldn't save him, Rori," he whispers into my hair as his body tenses with the guilt.

I battle myself for the ability to speak.

"I want to thank you," I manage to say. "You did what Jerome asked of you, even though it was..." Squeezing my eyes tight shut, I try not to imagine it. "It's what he would have wanted and you saved him from worse. You have nothing to be sorry for."

His tense body eases as he exhales behind me. I wrap my arm over his, cupping his massive knuckles in my small hand. Letting out a relieving sigh of my own, I relax back against him, feeling comforted by his solid presence.

"Let's just get some sleep," I say, my breathing becoming more regular as the emotion fades and my mind turns to my family situation. Hayes nestles against me, his own breathing getting slower and deeper. Hypnotized by its rhythm, I fade into sleep.

TAKING COMMAND

Hayes felt a strong sense of belonging, as he lay wrapped around Rori's small frame. Her words had released him from blame and he had willed his love to her as she lay sleeping in his arms. Following her into slumber, he'd felt more peace than he'd ever thought was possible.

Roused from sleep, he noticed the room was lightened by the morning sun, but didn't think it was the sun that had woken him. Rori still lay in his arms asleep. Closing his eyes again, he enjoyed the feel of her body against his. She moved and his eyes shot open at the sound that escaped her lips. He lay, stunned and motionless. It happened again.

This time her neck extended as her hips nudged into him. The low moan that followed sent shivers down his spine and awakened other things. His body responded of its own accord, rising like his pulse as she moved against him.

Cautiously, he repositioned himself in order to see her face. Still asleep. Was she dreaming? Her long dark lashes fluttered against her cheeks as a small gasp slipped her lips. So damn beautiful. Hayes gulped, longing to stroke the curve of her sweet, round behind and trail his fingers down her bare thigh.

Her body moved into his again, more forcefully this time. It was too much for him to stay where he was. Rolling over, he sat on the edge of the bed with his heart racing and the seam of his khakis under pressure.

"Hayes?" she asked breathlessly, wrenched awake by his movement.

"I'm here," he said shakily, his back still towards her, screening her from the view of his lust.

"You OK?"

"Yeah, fine. I'm just..." He paused thinking how he would finish that sentence. Keeping myself away from you? In case you don't want me. In case I lose control and I can't keep myself from taking you.

"...scared," he said, finding the right word.

He felt her sit up behind him, felt her looking at him.

"Scared of what?"

Looking at the ceiling, he took a deep breath, releasing it slowly through pursed lips.

"Scared of the noises you make in your sleep. Scared of what they make me want to do to you. Scared of what your father would do to me if I did. Lots of things. I just feel safer over here, that's all."

"Oh," she said before falling silent.

Moving slowly closer, she pressed up against his back, her lips resting by his ear.

"If it's any consolation, you already did those things to me in my sleep, but I won't tell him if you don't." The smile in her voice made him want to turn around and pin her to the bed, but he would likely run her through.

"Not helping," he warned, gripping the bedsheets.

"You were good too," she teased, her breath tickling his ear.

Hayes launched himself off the bed, looking for somewhere to hide in the tiny cottage. Hastily shutting himself in the bathroom, he splashed cold water on his face and looked at his reflection as her laughter subsided.

At least it was better than her crying, he supposed. It was worth the indignity if it made her happy.

A loud knock sounded at the door. Rushing from the bathroom, Hayes looked to Rori. She shrugged. Pointing at her, he shot her a look of insistence. Raising an eyebrow at him, she promptly rolled off the bed, hidden if viewed from the door.

Approaching the door warily, he was grateful that his trousers had resumed their regular shape. Hayes opened the door to look directly into the ominous eyes of Owen MacGregor.

"Good morning Sir," he managed to stumble out. Looking down at his bare chest, he wished he'd pulled on a shirt.

"Hayes." MacGregor took in his bruised torso, his eyes lingering at the stitches in his shoulder. "Thought you might like to come by for breakfast this morning. I doubt Orla thought to put anything edible in the box she brought you." His tone conveyed less warmth than his words suggested.

"Thank you for the invitation, Sir," Hayes replied as evenly as he could. "I'll be along shortly, after I dress."

"Good," said the Chief, turning to go. "You should come too Rori," he called over his shoulder.

The Chief kept walking and Hayes shut the door slowly and stood, staring at the wood, too shocked to move. Rori came and stood in his vision, an amused look on her face.

"This is not funny," he cautioned her. "He thinks we just spent the night together."

"We did spend the night together," she said matter-of-factly.

"You know what I mean," Hayes said impatiently. "He thinks we slept together!"

She nodded. "There was sleeping." She continued to smile laughingly at him.

"Rori!" He ran his hands through his hair before settling them on his hips. "He's going to kill me. Can't you even pretend to care?"

Threading her arms though his and around his waist, she pulled herself into him, leaning her forehead into his chest a moment. It was oddly soothing and arousing at the same time.

"He wouldn't kill you even if you had made my dreams come true, so stop worrying about it. I'm a grown up. I can do as I please."

"You're seventeen."

"Exactly. I've been an adult for ages. We grow up fast in the Valley. Lena was *married* at my age." She paused when his eyebrows raised. "Is my age a problem for you? Should I have asked your consent before I let you enter my fantasies?" she asked, giving him a strange look.

Hayes couldn't answer that. Overwhelmed by the morning's events in the bed and the Chief's assumed knowledge of it, he was shaken. He wanted to sit down. Rori seemed to recognize this and led him to the armchair by the fireplace. His fingers tapped the chairs wooden arms as he stared at the ashes of last night's fire.

"You know, it's a shame that I'm the only one who enjoyed myself. If you think he's going to kill you anyway, you might want to think about actually doing the deed," she said calmly.

His eyes snapped to her as if she was crazy and she laughed.

"I'm kidding!" She tossed him his bag, smiling cheekily at him. "Get dressed before you hurt yourself."

"This isn't funny, and you're wearing my only clean shirt."

"It is a *little* funny," she said, looking at him. Hayes could only stare at her as she gathered her clothes from their various fireside locations. Pulling her underwear tantalizingly up her legs, she unbuttoned his shirt. Hayes swallowed hard as he viewed her curves and navel through the thin gap that opened down the front. Turning her back to him slightly, she slipped out of it, throwing it over his face as she donned her own shirt. Pulling a cropped corset type article over top, she pulled its strings tight so it hugged her ample bosom snuggly.

"Damn it, Rori!" he grumbled, removing himself to the bathroom again.

When he finally came out again, he was calmer, certain he could face her again without bursting his seams; for a while at least. He got dressed, ready to face the MacGregors. Helpfully, she had put her pants on, but not her big woolen jumper that had hidden her shape so well the day before.

"It's still wet," she said apologetically, seeming to know his thoughts. She had undone her braid and was raking fingers through her long, now wavy hair. Flicking it over her shoulder, she motioned to him. "Shall we?"

Nodding, he opened the door, waiting for her to walk out before him. It was warm for a spring morning. The sun was already blazing. Hayes watched her appreciatively as she walked slightly ahead of him, the sun picking out the fiery highlights in her hair as it swayed with the movement of her hips. The hairs on his own head tingled as he felt an inkling lower down. Damn her sweet behind. Increasing his stride, he walked beside her, looking down the lane instead.

***

Rori smiled up at him and elbowed him in the side. Hayes smiled back.

"It's nice to see you smiling," he said as they arrived at her doorstep.

"I have a few things to smile about," she said, secretively. "Just remember, it doesn't matter what he says. It's not you that he's angry at."

"What?" Hayes asked, confused, but she'd already opened the door and gone in, leaving him alone on the doorstep. Walking slowly inside, he blinked as his eyes adjusted to the change in light. The faces of all the adult

MacGregors watched him from the dining table, leaving him extremely self-conscious.

Rori walked right past the table and down the hall. Pushing back his chair, Owen Mac followed her without saying a word. Lena stood and pulled out the chair next to her, smiling at Hayes kindly.

"Have a seat. They'll be a while," she said, sitting back down.

"Ah, thanks." Still looking down the hall as he moved toward the table, Hayes lowered himself hesitantly into the awaiting chair. The eyes still watched him. He sighed and they all burst into laughter.

"Nothing happened," he said defensively, reaching for the milk jug and pouring himself a glass.

"It's not your fault Hayes," said Lena in a caring voice. "If Rori makes up her mind about something, it will happen whether you like it or not. She's gifted."

Hayes looked at her, considering the comment.

"I can't say I disagree," he said, "But nothing happened."

Nobody spoke, but they all smiled knowingly into their breakfast. Hayes buttered a piece of toast and chewed it thoughtfully as he looked in the direction of the study.

"You'll hear them soon enough," Aiden said, reaching for a piece of toast himself.

As if on cue, raised voices came from down the hall. Hayes moved his chair back, wondering if he should interject. Lena put a hand on his and shook her head.

"It's between them," she said, removing her hand. "They'll be done soon, then it will be your turn. Better you eat now, while you can."

Hayes didn't know what to make of that, but the others seemed to nod in agreement. Taking an apple, he bit into it sullenly.

The study door opened and angry footsteps neared.

"You!" He pointed at Hayes, who rose instinctively from his chair to meet the Chief's blazing eyes. "This is all *your* fault! We had a deal. Leave her out of it! That's what we agreed!" He was all but frothing at the mouth.

Hayes put his hands up defensively.

"Nothing happened, I swear," he said truthfully.

"What?" Owen Mac looked him up and down and shook his head. "I'm not talking about that, you idiot! I'm talking about her being the next hostage!"

"What?!" Hayes roared, trying to see around the colossal man to his conniving minx of a daughter. "What the hell Rori? No! No way. Not happening. He's right, we had a deal. You are *not* going!"

Rori stepped boldly forward to defend herself.

"Stop it, both of you! It's *my* choice and I'm not making it lightly. I'm not being the hot-headed, reckless child you all think I am!" She turned to her father, not intimidated in the least by his size or his furious eyes. "It makes sense Da, and you know it. Aiden's needed here. He has his work, his family and will be chief one day. I promised the boys neither of them would be going and I meant it. I am the best pick of the girls. Lena's got her girls. Freya's got family and the clinic to run. You can't send Ava. You know Derrick would make her life *very* difficult once he found out she has a girlfriend. He might even kill her. And we all know you can't send Orla, for obvious reasons."

"What reasons?" demands Orla.

"You're just too pretty," Rori said dismissively. "It'd be too dangerous." Turning back to her father she counted off her attributes on her fingers as she stated them.

"I'm young, I'm strong and I can defend myself. I'm smart enough to deal with difficult situations and stubborn enough to live with my decisions. I'm resilient. I have no specific job besides being a thief and I have no dependents. I can solve Hayes' problem of training the women in the City and I can help scout and recruit other talent. If all goes well, I'll be back in the Valley in no time. I'm the perfect candidate and you know it."

There was silence as everyone processed what was being discussed. Rori used the lull to casually pick over the selection of food. Finishing Hayes' glass of milk for him, she put a strip of bacon in her mouth. It hung out like a wrinkly, salted tongue as she buttered a slice of toast and jammed an apple in her pocket. Hayes just watched her, through eyes glazed like those of a stunned mullet.

"Think it over," she said to no one and everyone. "I'm the best hostage we could have. I'll see you all later. The sun is shining and it's a beautiful day." Walking to the door, she hesitated on the step. "You coming?" she called over her shoulder.

All eyes turned to Hayes, who couldn't move. His innards were somersaulting. Lena gave him a nudge.

"You should go," she urged. "The train will come tomorrow, so you'll only have the freedom to enjoy the Valley and its treasures today."

Lena shoved him toward the door until his feet started moving on their own and he found himself chasing Rori out into the sunshine. She glanced up into his bewildered face as he fell in beside her. Smiling sweetly, she took a bite of her apple, not breaking eye contact. About to speak, he instead raised his own apple to his mouth, powerlessly trapped in her gaze. Taking a bite and chewing, he marveled at the might of the young woman beside him.

They walked wordlessly along the lane in the vague direction of the Ambassador's cottage. Fighting the pull of her eyes, Hayes stared ahead trying to straighten his thoughts. Rori was an expert at getting her own way and he would have to fortify his argument if he were to convince her to stay in the Valley.

"Can you talk yet?" she asked, disrupting his flow of ideas.

He glowered at her and she raised her eyebrows, unimpressed. Hayes shook his head in disbelief.

"I can't decide if I want to kick you or kiss you. So no.

I can't talk yet."

"I know which I'd prefer, but you can't do either in public," she stated calmly. "You're an Enforcer in the Valley. You have an image to uphold."

"That's why I'm walking to the cottage."

She stopped and looked about.

"Or we could stay in public," she said quietly.

"*Now* you're scared?" he teased as he kept walking, hearing her sigh and follow.

"I just don't know if there will be enough room in the cottage for the discussion you want to have," she said to his back.

Opening the door, he held it for her, trying not to soften his stern expression when he saw her uncharacteristically timid behavior.

"If you don't come in now, you'll give me more time to think. You are a force of nature Rori MacGregor, but I can cause just as much damage given the chance to prepare. Is that what you want?" He met her eyes, daring her.

Resigned, she walked in and he closed the door. Glancing around, she pulled herself backwards to sit on the tall kitchen counter.

"You don't want to sit in a chair?"

Shaking her head, she gestured to the armchair.

"Too low. I want you to look me in the eye when you talk to me and I know you'll be pacing," she said shrewdly. "The table might have worked, but I don't trust your repairs." She nodded at the leg that rested askew. "And on the off chance you did want to kiss me, this is a good level." Her cheeks blushed a little with her last comment.

Hayes loved that color as it crept into the background of her freckles. Smiling, he ran his eyes over her body and her blush deepened. Nudging her dangling legs apart, he stood between them and pulled her forward.

Tilting her jaw upward, he ran his thumb lightly over her lips, before meeting their soft, parted welcome. Hayes kissed her with all the passion he felt for her, his hands moving into her silky hair. Rori came to him willingly and he felt his resolve challenged. Breaking away, he looked into her eyes.

"You like that?" he asked hoarsely.

The blush still in her cheeks, her eyes tried to escape his by darting sideways. It didn't matter, her mouth gave away her answer as she bit her lower lip.

"Do you think if you come to the City we can be together? That I can kiss you like that, and we can save the world together?"

Rori continued to avoid his eyes.

"Do you think that if I see you in the City streets, I can speak nicely to you and ask you how your day was? Do you think I'll be able to help you if you need me to? Like I could help Jerome?!" Hayes stopped a moment, chewing his lip and gripping the counter. "Do you think if I see you in trouble, I'll be strong enough to leave you? I won't be able to help myself, and I'll give us up in a second! I can't deny whatever this is between us, Rori. Can you? If we let that show, it's all over." Hayes wondered how he was going to make her understand when she wouldn't even look at him.

"If I show even a hint of leniency, let alone actual care for you, it's over. I will be made to suffer for it and I will be made to make others suffer. I might be made to make *you* suffer. Do you think I can do that? Do you even have any idea how dangerous the City is for a young woman?!" Hayes felt his anxiety spike at that and changed tack to avoid the thought. "If Derrick looks on the Valley with suspicion, that means more security, more examples being made of your people to keep them under control *and* a failed rebellion. Can't you see that?"

Finally, Rori met his eyes. He could see she knew the truth, but worse, he could see there was no surprise in her expression. She had known it all already; had made her decision knowing it. Hayes stepped back from her. He'd underestimated her again. Running a hand through his hair, he began pacing, just as she'd said he would. It hurt to look at her.

"We'll just have to work on hiding our feelings then," she said quietly. Slipping down from the counter-top, she straightened her clothes.

"I'd hoped we could enjoy the one day we have to be free together, but I know I might have screwed that up. I'll give you some time."

As she moved to the door, Hayes sank to the floor and stared after her with pleading eyes.

"What do you want from me, Rori? I'll give you anything I have, just change your mind. Please."

Walking back, she knelt before him, her eyes sadly meeting his own.

"There isn't a price, Hayes. I have to go, to protect my family, just as you protect yours. Maybe one day things will be different, but not today. What would you have me do? Send a child in my place? So that I can stay in the Valley and see you sometimes? Sneak a moment with you when you get to spend a night in the cottage? That's a life you think I could live?"

Holding his face, she forced him to meet her eyes. They both knew the answer.

"Exactly," she said, planting a soft kiss on his lips before releasing him.

Standing abruptly, Hayes walked to the door.

"Where are you going?" she asked, taken aback by his sudden movement.

"To talk to your father." Her footsteps followed him and he paused. "You don't have to come."

"I'm your bodyguard," she replied, in a tone that illustrated she was less than enthusiastic about the job. "Until your friends get here tomorrow, anyway."

"I have no friends," he muttered under his breath, increasing his pace.

Hayes stopped as he approached the MacGregor house and turned to face her. He didn't want her to watch him beg her father.

"I'm not going in with you," she sighed. "I'll be in my room. Give me a yell when you're leaving." With that she launched herself up the side of the house and climbed into a window on the top level.

Shaking his head at her, he knocked on the door and waited. Rae answered the door and held it open as he walked in. Hayes saw Aiden and the Chief at the table and decided he would do as Rori had done. Walking straight past, he went down the hall to the study where he waited for Owen Mac to join him.

The tall, broad man stood in the door-frame as he viewed Hayes. It had only been one day, but the Chief looked older than he had when Hayes had given him the news of Patrick's impending demise. Sighing, Rori's father closed the door and sat behind his desk.

"I know why you're here, but I can do as little about it as you can."

"You're the Chief. Of course there's something you can do about it!" Hayes snapped at him.

"Watch how you talk to me, boy," he warned. "She has made up her mind and as you heard her explain, it is technically the best option. You think because I'm her father or her Chief that she will do as I say? If I forbid her, she will run straight to Derrick and offer herself before anyone had a chance to stop her. And how would we stop her? By locking her up for the rest of her life?"

Hayes knew the Chief spoke the truth, but couldn't curb his anger at the situation.

"She has always had a will of steel. You think I like her line of work? That I encouraged her to put herself at such risk? I let her do those things because she knows who she is and what she is capable of. If I deny her, I lose her. Is it easy? Not even remotely. The only thing I can do is support her as best I can."

"And how do you do that when she is trapped in the City?"

"By negotiating the best terms I can to keep her safe while she is there," said the Chief wearily. "I need her back here one day, Hayes. Regardless of how things play out. She was right about her being the best choice at the moment. She was right about everything this morning, except for one thing. Everyone assumes that it's Aiden who will be Chief one day, but it's her that has the strength and the will. It's *her* the people follow. She doesn't see it, but I know it."

Again, Hayes knew the Chief was right.

"Tell her. Maybe then she'll pay more attention to self-preservation. Why are you telling me?" Hayes asked.

"She wouldn't believe me if I told her. She is blind to my faith in her and words won't convince her otherwise. She's been fighting me so long, she still thinks she has to prove herself." MacGregor took a deep breath and stared irritably at the ceiling before meeting Hayes' eyes again. "I'm telling you, because I need your help to keep her safe until it's time for her to come back. I need you to do whatever is necessary to protect her from harm."

Hayes could feel the pressure of the man's request. Of course he wanted to do that, but what power did he have?

"I would love to, Sir. I will do all I can. But my powers are limited. Should I step out of line in Rori's defense at the wrong moment, she will be left with no-one on her side. I can barely keep my own family safe from Derrick." Hayes floundered for a while, trying to explain the severity of the situation.

"We have a common interest." Owen Mac spoke soberly. "I know how you feel about her. I knew it that first time we talked, when I asked you to keep her out of it and you did. I know that you would defend her as best you can and I have seen an example of your prowess in my own streets. If I can get Derrick to agree to it, you could be her designated protector, making it your approved job to defend her. Would you accept the position? Knowing that you could never let him know of your feelings?"

Hayes let the words settle.

"I will do anything to keep her safe. Anything. If there are no repercussions for defending her, if it is my sworn duty and cannot be perceived as an act of love, I can do it easily. Furthermore, I will hide my feelings, emitting discontent or at most indifference towards her, which shouldn't be too difficult, given the general frustration she continually makes me feel." Standing, he thrust his hand out to the Chief, who shook it firmly. "If you can get Luther to agree to your terms, then you can trust my mask. For her protection, I will also ensure that she treats me with disdain. Thank you, Sir."

"Thank you, Morrison," Owen Mac replied. "I know you will do all you can for her. Now sit down and tell me what else you need to live a safe and comfortable life in the City."

"Sir, what you're describing is enough," said Hayes, unsure if the Chief thought he needed extra incentive to protect Rori.

"You could do better for your family, surely. It would help her if you did," he said. "Tell me what you want so I can work it into my negotiations."

FRIENDS

Changing my clothes, I poke about my room, waiting for Hayes and Da to accept the inevitable. It's taken all of five minutes to sort my gear for packing and now there is only time to think. Mostly I've been thinking about how I can salvage the day. There are so many things I'd like to show Hayes here in the Valley. The front door shuts and I watch through the window as Hayes starts down the lane. Shimmying out the window and down the side of the house, I run to catch him as he strides angrily away. He and Da know it *will* happen then.

"You were meant to call for me when you were ready to leave," I say moodily. "You're still pretty banged up. Are you sure you're ready for round two?"

"Can't hurt much more than it does," he replies not talking about the bruises on his skin. Moving at his fierce pace, we reach the cottage quickly. Hayes opens the door and pauses in the frame so I can't follow.

"Can I come in?" I'm forced to ask.

"Why?" he asks, not turning to face me. "You only have two days left in the Valley. Shouldn't you be packing or saying goodbye to your friends?"

Hayes walks into the cottage, leaving the door open.

My decision. Stepping in, I close the door behind me. I can tell from his body language and the way he is staring at the wall that he is too frustrated to look at me.

"I don't have any friends either," I say quietly to his back as I take a step closer to him.

He turns his head to the side, but doesn't look over his shoulder to me.

"You're wrong, Rori. Don't talk to me about being lonely." Moving as far away from me as possible, he sits on the edge of the bed, looking out the window.

"I don't have close friends. The few I let in end up hurt, or dead. Are you sure I'm wrong?" I ask, my voice catching on the words.

Hayes puts his head in his hands and doesn't answer. Inching closer, as I would to an injured animal, I try not to spook him.

"I'm not doing this to hurt you. I'm doing it because it's the right thing to do."

Slowly climbing onto the bed, I crawl toward him in his distant corner and place a tentative hand to his back. He baulks at my touch. I try again, firmer this time and he sits stiffly under my hand as I move closer. He turns his head away.

"Talk to me," I whisper. "*I'm* your friend."

"You're my friend now," he says quietly, before correcting himself, "*Maybe*. In the City, you'll hate me."

"Only for show. Not truly."

"Urgh!" he cries, breaking free of my hold and pushing to his feet. "You don't get it!"

"Why are you yelling at me?"

"Because I'm angry! At you! You're a manipulator and you think you've got your own way again!" Hayes paces the room, firing irate words at me. "Everyone always does what Rori wants! Rori MacGregor, back in the game! Out-foxing the City from the inside! It's what you've always wanted and nothing else matters!"

"You think I wanted it to happen this way!?" I yell

back, hurt by his words and their undeniable tones of truth. "My whole reason for wanting to breach the City in the first place was to bring Patrick home! You think you're angry? I'm fucking livid! I took too long and now my brother is dead! They took him!" Breathing hard, I try to fend off the guilt I've been holding back for years. My failure manifests in my knees as they fold beneath me. "I didn't even get to tell him how sorry I was," I whisper to the floor.

"What are you *talking* about?" Hayes stops pacing to look at me. Wiping my eyes, I pull myself off the floor and stand tall.

"Forget it. The killing ends here. All that matters is to take Luther Derrick down so he can't do it again."

Hayes squints at me and scratches his jaw. "You think *Derrick* killed your brother?"

"Wouldn't be the first time he's killed a young hostage."

Hayes regards me oddly and I fold my arms over my chest.

"What? Why are you looking at me like that?"

He closes his eyes slowly. "You didn't talk to your father about this before you volunteered?"

"About what?"

Hayes wets his lips and rubs his forehead as he sighs at me. "Rori, Patrick isn't dead. He's sick. Very sick. He's been sick for years. Derrick's been keeping him alive, fulfilling his part of the hostage bargain."

"What?" Unstable knees take me to the fireside chair and I slump into it. Kept in the dark by my father again.

"You didn't know?" Hayes asks softly. Pointlessly. I shake my head.

"What else don't I know, Hayes?" I ask heatedly as I stare at the cold ashes in the fireplace.

"You don't know anything," he says coldly, forcing me to look up in alarm.

"I know some," I start defensively.

"You *think* you know, but you don't," he says, his tone raising the hairs on my neck. "Living in the City is different from your thieving 'skirt around the outside and take a peek' kind of day-trip. You'll see. Five minutes off the train and you'll be wishing you were back in the Valley."

"Several thousand *other* people live there, so I'm sure I'll manage," I say, folding my arms in front of my chest again.

"They have shit lives, but even *they* have other people, family to support them. You'll have no-one."

"And not you?"

"No-one," he confirms harshly. "I'm the last person you'll want near you. I'm an Enforcer. Unpleasant by occupation. How do you think I got that high in rank? By being nice? You might think I'm a nice guy trapped in a bad situation, but I'm just a bad guy. I don't have friends, because they're a burden. I'm a bully. I hurt people and exploit their weaknesses to further my own agenda, just like Derrick."

Narrowing my eyes at him, I study his face. Holding his jaw stiffly, he meets my gaze defiantly.

"You're just saying this to make me angry at you!" I say, catching him out.

"Yes," he admits openly, still intent on provoking me. "Say goodbye to nice feelings, Rori. They don't exist in the City! Why do you think we all want to leave? You've had it sweet, and now you're throwing it all away!"

"You think Valley life is a piece of cake? We're *slaves*!"

"You're the freest fucking slaves I've ever heard of! So you have to work really hard and bad guys come and take your shit - you have no idea what life is like in the City. It's ten times the level of 'eat shit and smile!' You and your feelings are insignificant. Sound good?" Hayes starts pacing again, fists clenching at his sides. "You're so young and naïve," he says, needling my insecurities. "You think you're so damn amazing because you know patrol routes and where to find wires. None of that means shit! *You* don't mean shit!"

Taking a deep breath, he meets my eyes and lowers his tone. "To survive in the City you have to be a horrible person. It's use or be used, and for all your roaring, you're nothing but a pussycat."

"If you're trying to insult me by telling me I've got a big mouth and a soft heart, I've heard it all before. I don't scare easily, so don't bother. You're trying to make me hate you, but it's not going to work. I understand we can't interact in the City, and I'll leave you the fuck alone, OK? Can we just stop this? You don't use people like Derrick does. You're making yourself sound worse than you are."

"Am I?" he challenges, still vying for the role of biggest jerk.

"You never used me."

"You don't think so?"

"I think I would have noticed," I say, sighing at the time we're wasting fighting. "You didn't even use my body." Watching him closely, I lean suggestively back on the bed, baiting him. "You could have. *Easily.*"

His eyes grow wider as they travel my body and I watch the struggle on his face before he masks it with an arrogant sneer and looks away. It's the same look I've seen plastered on his face when he's with the other soldiers.

"The funny thing is," he says, looking much more relaxed than he did a few moments ago. "I once thought that I'd need to blackmail you to get your assistance. But, after I realized you were hell-bent on the track to rebellion already, I didn't need to bother. Now I have an alliance with the Dalton Chief! Tell me I didn't get what I wanted," he says, snickering.

"Fine," I concede. "So you didn't need to blackmail me. I'm a total pushover when it comes to fighting for what's right." Standing up, I step right to him, sick of his bullshit. "What about the sex? If you're such a nasty, exploiting asshole, why am I still feeling so fucking virtuous?"

Pausing for only the slightest moment, he laughs at me. Not expecting that response, I lose some of my nerve.

"I'm an Enforcer. I get women served on a platter any night of the week. I don't need you! I left your 'virtue' intact on purpose, not wanting to jeopardize things with your father." He laughs again, until he sees my face.

"Don't believe me? Jerome used to call me Cassanova. Hell, I was with a woman when they interrupted us to send me here!"

His words ring true and his face isn't lying as I stare at him, my mouth agape.

"Tell me," he says, putting a finger under my chin and closing my mouth for me. "If I'd fucked you, and you'd found out about the rest, would you do nothing?"

Staying quiet, I swallow with difficulty and avoid his eyes.

"Exactly," he says smugly. "You would have blown it for me with the Chief and it would all be over. But not this way. I've broken no rules, broken no trust."

"Yeah," I reply quietly, tears welling. "You're a real 'stand-up' guy."

"I tried to tell you," he says. There is almost a hint of apology detectable in his voice, but his face remains the cruel mask of an Enforcer.

Nodding, I hold back the threatening tears for all I'm worth; not giving him the satisfaction of seeing them fall. "You did try to tell me. Oddly, I didn't trust you, but I believe you now. Happy?"

He brings his face directly in front of mine and jabs a finger at his chin. "Do I fucking *look* happy?!" he snarls through his teeth.

"Hard to tell with your stupid face, *Smiler*!" I yell at his excruciatingly handsome face with its smiling scar. Breathing hard we stare at each other. Looking slightly wounded, he quickly recovers his smirk and stands tall. I try to get round him, but he blocks me.

"Let me leave," I say evenly, burning a hole in his chest with my eyes.

"Not until you look me in the eye and tell me you'll keep your mouth shut. It won't be safe to progress unless you realize this rebellion is bigger than you and your pathetic little feelings."

Staring at him, I feel the strong urge to thump him in the mouth. "Still worried you won't be safe in the City? Worry about the present, if you keep standing in my way."

Leaning down to peer into my face again, his eyes laugh at me. "Are you threatening me, Pussycat?"

Quick as a flash, I ram my palm into his nose for the second time since we met.

"Meow."

Blood gushes through the inadequate dam of his fingers. Stepping around him, I walk as calmly as I can to the door.

Once outside, I run. Angry tears spill down my cheeks. On the bridge in no time, I jump onto the rail and stare at the water moving quickly below. It's swollen from the melting snows; running high and fast. The sun bears down on me forcefully and I think briefly of diving in. Walking along the rail, I focus on balancing my emotions.

The fury within needs to be let out before I can go home. And I need to go home. It will be my last real evening with Da. He'll be off to the City tomorrow to negotiate the terms of my contract. Then it will be my turn to leave.

Flipping off the end of the rail, I run down the river track to the rocky cliff above the cave. Not slowing my pace at all, I hurl myself up the rocks until I'm forced to climb vertically. I keep moving up, trying to climb out of my shitty, self-imposed life. Forced to stop in shock as I lose a grip, I look up. I'm closer to the top of the cliff than I have ever been without ropes. Breathing heavily, I look back down and try to decide my safest course. Edging my way back down cautiously, I double check each hold. It would do no good to fall now. I'm destined for the City; have insisted it be me, in order to preserve my family. It'd be foolish of me to risk further inattention. I now need to be on full alert indefinitely.

When I touch back down to earth, my body is shaking from the effort, but my mind is clearer. Determined. Surprisingly, Da is waiting at the bottom. Walking towards me, he pulls me into a hug. My legs collapse. Picking me up as he did when I was a child, he throws me over his shoulder. My father carries me home like an animal carcass, and I let him, feeling uncomfortably close to being just that.

HOSTAGE NEGOTIATIONS

Hayes scratched his nose gingerly. Freya had reset it for him and had stuck some sort of dressing over it that itched mercilessly. He wondered if she'd done so on purpose, to repay him for treating her sister poorly. He deserved it. It was awful to do that to her, but he had to be sure she wouldn't betray herself in the City. If negotiations went well today, they'd be forced into each other's company and the only way to safely move forward was to have her despise him.

Standing on the doorstep of the MacGregor house, he dared not enter, for fear of having to look her in the eye. Eventually he would, but he wasn't ready yet. If she saw him now, she'd see right through him. Knocking again, he waited to escort Owen Mac to the train now that it had arrived, and on to the City.

The other escorts had said little about his injuries when they'd arrived. They knew what his reception would have been, and knew of his skills as a fighter. None seemed surprised to see him alive. Reg appeared to be disappointed, but not surprised.

The Chief arrived at the door and they left together.

The lane was quiet. The Daltons were hiding from the domineering presence of the soldiers. Owen Mac walked tall, shoulder to shoulder with Hayes. Looking about, Hayes made sure they were alone.

"Will she be OK?"

"You did her a favor. What she doesn't know, can't hurt her. Best you put it out of your mind. You should be thinking like an asshole," the Chief warned.

Hayes nodded, slipping into character as they approached the train. Walking with more confidence, he gave a Dalton worker at the platform an aggressive shove. The escorts waiting for him laughed at the entertainment.

From his side, the Chief looked at him with an admonishing glower and the escorts took their stifled chuckles aboard the train. Owen Mac watched them turn their backs.

"Better."

They took their seats in the uncomfortably tense atmosphere inside the carriage. It was a notable day in history. It wasn't often that a new hostage was needed and it was a big deal for the Chief to leave the Valley. They rode through the darkness of the tunnel in silence and as they re-entered the light, most of the men averted their eyes, looking respectfully out the window with apparent interest at the same boring scenery they'd seen countless times before.

All but Reg. He twisted in his seat to eyeball the Chief. Owen Mac dismissed him with a raised eyebrow, turning his own gaze out to the grasslands.

"So which one are we getting old man? Your little boy or his little boy?"

Hayes watched Owen Mac consider Reg a while, his expression unimpressed, as though he were examining a pull in his woolen sweater.

"I will inform the Director at the appropriate time. I don't discuss business with mere pawns," he said slowly and deliberately before turning back to the window.

Reg sat in shock. No-one talked to him like that. Owen Mac had just illustrated how pathetic and worthless he truly was. Inside, Hayes was laughing at Reg, but Smiler needed to gain back some of his sway.

"The *Daltons* are the pawns, *Mac*," he said in a condescending tone. "Now everyone shut your faces."

Hayes watched Reg smirk and knew his comments had hit the mark. If Reg had an excuse not to try the Chief again, he'd be saved from repeat humiliation. Hayes scratched his nose again, wincing.

They pulled into the station and the escorts disembarked, lining up outside to form a wall leading to the elevator. Owen Mac walked along the human wall with his head high. Smiler gave him a slight push in the direction of the elevator and the Chief swung around and glared at him.

"Don't push me, *Boy!*" he growled. "Or I'll re-break your nose for you!"

"Try it, *Old man*," Smiler sneered back, taking a step closer. "You'll only get one shot."

The Chief considered, then walked to the elevator.

"Damn straight," muttered Reg.

Hayes, Reg and the Chief boarded the elevator and rode up to Derrick's office in silence. The doors opened into the reception area and Cynthia eyed up Owen Mac with an obvious sense of approval. Asking them to wait, she glided over to Derrick's door to notify him of their arrival. Hayes noticed the extra effort she was putting into swaying her hips and was embarrassed for her.

"Mr. Derrick will see you now," she said, fluttering her eyelashes shamelessly at Owen Mac as she held the door open for him. He looked as disgusted by her behavior as Hayes felt.

"Of course he will, you poor, mindless girl. He wants something from me." Walking past the speechless, high-heeled dimwit, the Dalton Chief entered Derrick's office.

"Owen MacGregor! I always forget how big you are! My, you're as big as Smiler! Please, have a seat." He gestured to the chair opposite.

Reg moved around behind his father and Luther Derrick looked at Hayes.

"You made it back. Not as pretty, I see. Which one got close enough to break your nose?"

"That would be a MacGregor," the Chief said proudly.

Luther chuckled. "Well, I think we can do without you here, Smiler," he said shooing a hand at Hayes.

"He stays," the Chief said firmly.

Luther raised his eyebrows at Owen Mac. "And why is that?"

"Asshole pissed me off. I'd like to repay him in kind."

Derrick chuckled again and looked at Reg who grinned while he shrugged agreement.

"He does have a talent for that. Fine. He stays," the Director said. "Let's get down to business then."

"How is Patrick? Is he still alive? I want to see him."

"For now. You can see him after we talk. Don't be surprised if he doesn't recognize you." Luther said, stifling a laugh.

"He was a baby when he last saw me. Of course I don't expect him to know who I am!" MacGregor responded, his color rising. "But, I *will* see him."

"You are understandably angry at the hand life has dealt you MacGregor, but I have tried to make it easier for you. I sent Smiler here to warn you of the situation so you'd have some time to prepare. Was that not kinder than thrusting the decisions upon you? I think for that show of diplomacy, I deserve civil interactions, and likely, an increase in your co-operation." Luther set a level gaze at the Chief, who fed it right back to him.

"I gathered you wanted more. How much you get will depend on you meeting *my* demands," Owen Mac bargained.

"You'd better tell me who we're getting first. Taking on Patrick turned out to be quite demanding."

"Your next hostage will be my next youngest child. My daughter, Rori."

Hayes watched as the Chief spoke of her without emotion and moved his gaze to the Derricks to gauge their responses. They both looked surprised.

"A girl? The one that resembles your wife? Ooh hoo hoo! That's gotta hurt. You're sure?"

"The wild one?" Reg cried. "Of course you want to get rid of the wild one! Dad, make him give us the hot one. She'll be more useful."

All eyes turned to Reg. The Director looked momentarily stunned before his face began to turn an angry shade of red.

"Leave!" he ordered, grabbing the desk with white knuckles.

"But-"

At Reg's protest, his father rose from his seat, staring straight ahead. "Go." The low volume of his voice was more threatening than if he had yelled. "Before I have you beaten and branded."

Everyone stayed quiet as Reg weighed up his options and stormed out of the room.

The Director lowered himself back into his chair. "Apologies MacGregor. My son often speaks before his brain is engaged. No hostage will suffer from molestation. As has been agreed for generations, a hostage shall be kept safe unless found to be colluding against the City. Though I will ask again, are you sure of your choice? She will be the first female Dalton to take such a role. I typically believe women to be less resilient than men. If she is indeed unstable, you may need to supply another hostage sooner than expected."

"She is not unstable. She is spirited. There is a

355

difference," the Chief stated, reigning in his disgust at Reg's outburst. "I believe she can handle the adjustment, and she is the only one I can spare at present. She has no set role within the Valley as yet, and the others are indispensable."

Luther nodded, following the Chief's explanation.

"How old is she?"

"Seventeen."

"Ah. So young and sweet. You're certain you want the City life for her? What if she wants to marry some City man? Her children will belong to me, you understand."

"What life I *want* for her is of no consequence. She will be your hostage under no volition of my own," the Chief argued with Derrick. "And I can't imagine she'd want to marry any of these cretins," he said eying the Citizens present. "She'd rather live a spinster. I fear not for her future children. She would rather have none."

"I see. You must know that goes against City regulation. All fertile women are expected to reproduce at some time in their life. If she is to become a Citizen, she must obey our laws."

The Chief scowled at the Director.

"A compromise then. If she does happen to choose a husband in the City, she can be expected to have children at some stage."

"Deal. What else? I have other terms to discuss, you understand." Luther leaned back in his chair and put his feet up on the desk, gesturing for Owen to go on.

"Indeed," Owen Mac said warily. "I want her to be able to choose her profession. She'll need some time to find a suitable one. She has many talents and will be an asset to your systems, I have no doubt. She is not to be forced into an occupation in any way, or you will find her stubbornly refusing, as will be her right."

The Director frowned. "She's only seventeen. Surely you'll want her to finish school before she finds a job."

"She hasn't been in a classroom since she was twelve. I don't think your education system would be beneficial for her."

"Twelve? Is she thick?"

"It would be foolish to assume so. As I said, she has many talents. Do we have an understanding or not?" Owen paused, awaiting Derrick's agreement or otherwise. The Director appeared perplexed, but waved him on, nodding.

"I want her to live in a family situation. She has always done so and it will make her transition easier. She has lived a long time without a mother, and may benefit from time with a woman of that nature. She needs to live away from Derrick Towers so she isn't constantly intimidated. And I want her to live with someone I already know. I won't have her subjected to some horrid lifestyle I can only imagine."

Derrick put his feet carefully on the floor and sat up, studying the Chief through his narrow, menacing eyes.

"That is a tall order. Your options there are limited. I can think of only one household that meets your criteria." He looked in Hayes' direction.

Hayes shook his head rapidly. "No."

Derrick stared at him and rose from his seat. He gave the slightest movement of face and Elmerson and Beaumont moved next to Hayes.

"I don't remember asking for your opinion on this, Smiler," he said coldly and gave a quick nod before sitting back down. Fat Elmo seized Morrison's arms and Beaumont thumped him in the stomach hard enough to make him drop to his knees, winded. The Henchmen took a step back and Derrick addressed the Chief again.

"I must say, I'm happy to oblige, but I don't think you'll be pleased to know that Smiler here is part of that household. Didn't he have some sort of scuffle with one of your daughters?"

"I am aware of that, yes. I also saw he was punished accordingly for that and it brings me to my next demand. I have seen this man in action recently, and although he appears to be an arrogant asshole, he is one hell of a fighter. My daughter is quite small and may not always be able to defend herself. I want her to have a sworn protector to see no harm comes to her. You say she won't be molested, but I need to see how you plan to keep that from happening. If Mr. Hayes here were to defend her from such things, I think I could come to terms with the living arrangements. It would make sense actually."

Luther leaned forward and looked from the Chief to Smiler, still kneeling on the floor.

"And if Smiler himself should try to molest your daughter?"

"Then you should eliminate him and send me the pieces before negotiating compensation and another protector."

"That seems fair. He clearly dislikes the notion, so that makes it all the more appealing. Smiler's mother is a very likable woman, and his little sister is almost the same age as your daughter. I'm sure Rori will make a delightful addition to his hen-house. I have no doubt he will control himself. He has other resources through which he can expend such energies and I already monitor his regular use of them. You will control yourself, won't you, Smiler?"

Hayes looked from Derrick to Owen Mac, feeling as helpless as he always did in this office.

"But I -"

"Answer the question, Smiler. Only the question," Derrick warned. "Will you protect the Chief's daughter against all harm, including from yourself? Be careful with your answer. I have my own requests of the Chief and I will be sorely disappointed if your answer should compromise those negotiations."

Hayes slumped his shoulders. Always damned, no

matter the 'choice'. Taking a deep breath, he climbed to his feet to face both leaders.

"I will. I swear it," he replied, in a resigned tone.

"Good that's settled then. Was that all, MacGregor?"

"Not quite," MacGregor said, adjusting himself in his chair. "I want my daughter to live a happy and healthy life. I want her to have as much food as she requests. She has a very healthy appetite despite her appearance. She will need full access to any medical care she should require during her life in the City. In fact, for her health, anyone in the household should be treated as needed. I've already had to quarantine Smiler because he was rife with disease. I don't want my daughter exposed to that unnecessarily."

Luther rumbled with laughter under his breath.

"We did enjoy a good laugh over that. As you wish, though I can't promise she will never be sick."

"I accept that possibility," Owen Mac sighed. "I also expect correspondence in her own hand to be sure of her welfare, and delivery of mine to her, including gifts. I want too, a verbal report from Ambassador Malcolm. I like to see a man's face to know he speaks truth."

"Yes, yes," Derrick waved him off as if those terms were assumed, but then he refocused. "Smiler here is one of my Ambassadors. If he is watching your girl, I lose an Ambassador."

"Then I suggest you train another. Though I am sure Rori could stay safely home while Hayes is away on business, until you find his replacement. Actually, seeing the truth on *his* face might mean more than Malcolm's. Perhaps he could visit intermittently to be assessed by me. Monthly perhaps. You work out that detail, that's your jurisdiction. I reserve the right to renegotiate should my terms be broken. Is that understood?"

"Yes, yes. Are you done? Because I feel like you're asking for quite a lot, and I have my own conditions," Luther leaned back in his chair, overacting a tired boredom.

MacGregor raised an eyebrow and gave him a measured look.

"One more thing," he said, looking at each of the citizens in the room, including Hayes. "Should someone approach Rori with intent to harm her, she may protect herself by any means necessary. She will not be punished under any circumstances for such behavior, nor will she be persecuted for any perceived misbehavior committed prior to her commencement as hostage."

Hayes kept his expression blank as Derrick scanned the Chief's face and then his, appearing quite perplexed.

"I'm afraid I don't understand. Is your daughter a troublemaker you want to be rid of? If so, you should lax on the negotiations and let the City mold her into a model Citizen. And if you think Smiler here isn't enough to stop an attack, what do you think your girl is going to be able to do about it?"

"I will clarify. She is a small, but good-hearted girl, with big opinions. She knows what is expected of her in the City, and she will act accordingly. However, in recent times she may have done things to upset a few of your men, and I don't think she should be subjected to poor treatment from those who may have taken offense to her, ah ... efforts. She should get a clean slate as she moves to the City. As for the self-defense clause I was thinking should Smiler be absent, or if she should need protection from Smiler himself, she should be able to defend herself without fear of punishment."

"I see," said Derrick thoughtfully. "I'm curious as to what kind of things she has been doing? I recall a potato incident a while back, and my son told me of another recent incident involving dinner sabotage. Is that what you're talking about? The men were annoyed, but I'm sure they wouldn't take it out on her physically."

The Chief sighed and rubbed his forehead.

"There's a bit more, but yes. She hasn't gone out of her way to be friendly toward visiting escorts."

"More like what? Why haven't I been told?" Luther sat up straight in his chair, staring at Smiler angrily.

"Maybe you have been told, but didn't realize it was Rori," Owen Mac intercepted. "There was an apple throwing incident a few months back. That was her. Another example was very recent. Smiler here hasn't had the opportunity to tell you which MacGregor broke his nose," he said, laughter in his voice.

Derrick's eyes shot wide in disbelief as he too joined the Chief in laughter. They enjoyed the joke a while, looking intermittently at Smiler's bandaged face only to erupt into further hilarity at his expense. Hayes stood patiently and awaited his inevitable dismissal from the room. The Chief had made all his necessary requests, and Derrick seemed to be responding to them positively enough. They didn't need him here anymore, and there would be much to do before returning to the Valley to collect Rori.

"I can see now why he was so reluctant to share his apartment! Ha! I haven't laughed like that in years! Bested by a little girl. Well Smiler, I think you should go and organize accommodation for your new house-mate! I have always so enjoyed watching you squirm," he said, still chuckling as he nodded Elmo over to shoo Smiler from the room. "Be back at the station by fifteen hundred hours. The Chief should get back for one last night with his girl before you whisk her away forever. Patrick will be dead in a day or two. There's no point in wasting time traveling to and fro. She comes tomorrow."

Hayes nodded cordially to the leaders as he departed, hoping the rest of MacGregor's negotiations would go as well. He knew the man was worried about the price of his terms, but Hayes felt that Derrick had been surprised and excited about exploiting the Hayes household further, and thought it would work in the Chief's favor.

Turning his thoughts to home as he walked, he thought about how his family would take the news. A lot had happened in three days. They would have been worried by his note, but would be glad to have him back, no matter the cost. He thought about sleeping arrangements and wondered how it would work.

The apartment had three small bedrooms and the white room. No-one would want to sleep in the white room. For what it symbolized to the Hayes family, it was not a place any of them would go voluntarily. It would be just as much a nightmare for Rori, given the fact that it was such a small space, with no windows. She would need as much space as possible to prevent her anger from consuming them all.

Maybe his Mom could share a room with Iris. He couldn't share a room with her after how she'd been acting toward him. Perhaps Rori and Iris could share? They were only a few years difference in age. If they got on alright, maybe. Rori would probably be best with a room of her own if possible.

Scratching his nose again, Hayes swore, determined to remove the dressing as soon as he could. He wondered how Rori would take the news when her father told her about his conditions for her hostage stint. Likely she'd be very motivated to revolt as soon as possible, just to escape him. Hayes tried to decide if that counted as thinking optimistically.

Sighing, he dreaded how hard it would be to live with her after what he'd done. At least he could do everything to protect her now. True to his word, the Chief had seen to that. Hayes could still work towards freedom for them all. That hadn't changed. If one day, their people could live in peace and if she could ever trust him again, maybe then his only request to the Chief would be possible.

TICKET TO RIDE

The neatly printed writing on my copy of the contract bends in my white-knuckled grasp. The walls seem to grow closer in my father's study. Unable to take it sitting down, I rise off my chair and begin to pace. Heat builds within me as the words sink in and when I open my mouth, the steam pours forth.

"You can't do this to me!" I yell at him as he sits calmly at his desk with his own copy. "I'd rather live in Derrick's closet being his personal footstool than be subjected to this cruelty! You're punishing me for volunteering! I'm the right choice and you know it!" Kicking my chair over, I screw the paper up and throw it at my father. Expertly dodging the projectile without looking up, he sighs, putting down his pen.

"You *are* the right choice," he agrees, meeting my eyes. "For now. But I need you to come home safe one day and this is the only way I can ensure that will happen. I'm not trying to punish you. I'm trying to help you," he says in a calm and rational manner, making me even more irate.

"I can't live with him! He got off easy with a broken nose! He doesn't care about my safety and well-being! He used me to get your support! That's alright though is it?"

Staring at him, I still can't believe my father is selling me out. Whether he admits it or not, he's using me to strengthen his alliance with that asshole, Smiler. Keeping us linked in a do or die contract, he gets to keep tabs on us both and be the puppet-master.

"Rori," he says standing up and towering over me as he does when he really wants to make his point. Staring at the wall, I wait for the impending 'I am your Father and your Chief' line with a scowl so deep I feel it penetrating the bones of my face.

"I love you."

My scowl turns up to see his face and loses its intensity. His eyes are fierce with love and I look away, not wanting it to overpower me.

"Funny way of showing it. Didn't know you liked torturing people as much as Derrick does," I mutter, righting my chair and slumping into it.

"You think it's going to be any less torturous for him? He won't get away with what he's done, because he won't be able to get away from you. He'll have to face you every day. Not only that, he will have to do his utmost to keep you from harm, or he will not get what he wants. And if he ever hurts you, he will be killed. Does that not sound even remotely reasonable?"

Snorting a little, I look at the floor to hide my smile.

"When you put it like that it does look pretty grim for him. Fine. I'll live with it, but I'm not happy about it. When I get back here, you all better be working hard to make it up to me."

Da smiles and scratches his beard thoughtfully. "What would you like done?"

"I want my own place. Somewhere high, like in a tree or something. With a deep bath and a garden already growing. With a plum tree."

"Anything else, my sweet?" he asks, laughing. "A

personal chef and masseur perhaps?"

"I'll settle for a weekly delivery of Rae Rae's oatmeal cookies and a cat."

"Done."

His eyes watch me intensely, as if he's trying to lock my image into his memory. Maybe trying to update a memory of her. Feeling tears creeping in, I stand to leave.

"I gotta pack." I open the door to make my escape. "See you at dinner." Pausing in the door frame, I look back at him. His own eyes are wet now.

"I love you too, Da."

Rushing from the study, I head upstairs.

I knew it would be a difficult path when I opted to be the hostage. The reality of the situation is getting more complicated daily. My life for the next few months or years or however long it will take for me to come home again, is almost unimaginable. The big 'what if?' questions hang ominously over my head. What if I ruin things, like I always seem to? If we fail and die? Or worse, what if we fail and I have to live in that hell forever.

Probably best not to have any solid expectations. I wonder what the Hayes family will be like, and if they will be as manipulative as all Citizens seem to be. He'd convinced me he was different, but I should have known better. How am I going to face him every day, knowing I was just the means to an end? I shake my head. Too much. One day at a time.

Packing my one bag again, I look about my room and consider leaving it for good. I fold the quilt Mama made for me. I'm taking it with me this time. There's a gentle knock on the door. Sniffing, I quickly wipe my eyes.

"Come in," I croak, clearing my throat as the door swings in and Orla enters, carrying a large, ornately carved, wooden box. It's so big she needs three attempts to find the best way to get it through the door. Setting it at my feet, she looks at me with her pretty green eyes. Staring at her, I wonder why on earth she would lug something so awkward and heavy up two flights of stairs. I will miss the way her brain works. It has entertained me over the years.

"I made you something," she says, stepping close to dab a remnant tear with her sleeve.

"You made a box?" I ask, sniffing again.

"No, Silly," she replies, tucking loose hairs behind my ear. "Aiden made the box. And Ava did the carving."

She lifts the lid of the box to reveal its contents. As it opens, the smell of Rae's floral soaps greet me with a rush of summer fragrance. My hands tremble as I kneel beside the box, looking at its treasures. Inside are packages of herbs that I know will be from Freya. There are pictures from the children and a small toolkit that will be from Horse. I see a sheathed knife, with a note tucked under the handle, written in Ari's hand. There are books from Da's library and a bottle of whiskey cushioned by a large package wrapped in supple leather.

Orla carefully removes the package and unties the cord that holds it together, spreading the soft fabric so I can see. Arranging the neatly folded items so they can all be seen at once, she begins pointing them out, explaining what each is meant for. She has created me a new range of supportive underwear and exercise gear.

"And these two," she declares, as a beautiful, straight smile graces her face, "Are for when you want to wear something less sporty. I think the colors suit you perfectly, and Lena told me what designs she thought you'd be happy with. This one will be lovely for hot days, because it's so light," she says, stroking a pale yellow sun-dress.

"Thank you Orla, I love them. They're beautiful and practical and just what I needed. My wardrobe has been in a right state since the farm," I say, hugging her tightly.

Stroking the soft fabrics myself as I bundle them back together, I place them carefully back in the box. Putting my mother's quilt on top, I close the lid. My fingers trace the carvings and run over the smooth surface, buffed to a shine with beeswax. Securing the latch, I look at Orla, shaking my head.

"Why on earth did you carry it up here? I could have come down."

She shrugs as if it was no big deal. "I wanted you to see that we all love you, and we'll be thinking about you every day. Including this one."

Hugging her, I try to keep more tears at bay. "I love you too. Let's go to dinner. I can smell Rae's pies from here and I'm already drooling."

We race down the stairs as we did when we were younger and I smile fondly at the memory. The whole family are already there. They've been hanging around since it was decided. Making my way around the room, I thank everyone for their kind and thoughtful gifts. Lena evades me.

I've chased her halfway around the house before I finally get my hands on her and pull her into my arms. She has always been my mainstay. The one who I felt understood me, always.

"You can't escape me Lena," I whisper into her ear. "I'm leaving and you have to say goodbye. You're strong enough. And I'm going to come back if it's the last thing I do, so don't you dare say goodbye forever. Don't even think it."

Lena disintegrates. "I can't think about losing you too," she utters between sobs.

"You're not losing me. You'll know exactly where I am. And I will be back to see how great your girls are turning out, because they have the best mother in the world. Now stop being a crybaby and let's have some dinner."

Giving her another squeeze, I take her hand to lead her back to the dining room. Stopped short by her inertia, I turn back to see why she won't come. Keeping hold of my hand, she reaches into her pocket, pulling out a small fabric bag. Pressing the bag into my palm, she closes my fingers over the top.

"I didn't want to put it in the box."

Opening my hand, I look from the bag back to her as she wipes her eyes. I untie the drawstring and gently shake the tarnished silver chain into my hand. It's much shorter than I remember it being. I look at her, shaking my head.

"Stefan gave you this as a wedding gift. I know how much this means to you, Lena. I can't take it." I try to give it back to her, but she moves out of reach.

"I want you to have it. So you know how much *you* mean to me." Rolling up her sleeve, she reveals an identical silver chain around her wrist. "Two of a kind," she sniffs. "Maybe when you get back, we can give them to the girls?"

"Of course," I agree, nodding as she helps me put it on. Touching it gently, I give Lena another fierce embrace. Our hands lock together, the bracelets touching at our wrists. I smile at her beautiful, loving face and kiss her cheek. This time when I lead, she follows.

***

The morning comes all too soon and I hide in my room for as long as I dare, reluctant to leave its sanctuary. When I finally arrive downstairs, my gear is stacked at the door, the table is laden and the place is buzzing with people. Bodies fill every space, breathing all the air that I can't seem to find.

They've come to pay their respects; to say goodbye to the Chief's daughter. I wonder what they must be thinking. Thank goodness it's not us? One more MacGregor pacifying the parasites? Lucky there's more where she came from? After ten minutes I can't stand it. I walk to Da's study.

"Too much?" he asks as he comes in behind me.

"Much too much." My chest tightens further and I wring my sweaty hands. "Can't they just wait by the train and wave or something? They've only come out of guilt. Feeling bad that they're relieved it's not any of them. I don't need it."

"Alright," he says haltingly, a strange look on his face. "I don't think that's why they're here, but I can ask them to leave. If you like?"

Nodding rapidly, I close my eyes and enjoy the air that fills my lungs.

"Stay here. I'll come and get you when it's clear."

"Thank you." I sigh gratefully, plonking down in my usual seat.

Soon the house becomes quieter and I sneak down the hall a little, my stomach rumbling and impatient to eat. Stopping abruptly as I hear Da greet Hayes at the door, I press myself into the wall.

Dammit. He's early.

"Quite a crowd," I hear him say. "I didn't even know there were that many people in the Valley. Does she know how many have come to see her off?"

"She has no idea. The few she has seen, I had to chase away. She thinks they've come to alleviate their guilt. It hasn't occurred to her that they all love her. Or that she is worthy of their love. She thinks people are nice to her because she gets them things or because I told them they had to be. Believe me, I've never had to do any such thing. For some reason she believes her only value stems from being my daughter and being a thief."

"Well, she is a very good thief," Hayes says, the smile in his voice big enough to be heard from my hiding place down the hall. "How did she take the news?"

"About how we thought. You'll be in for a rough ride. You should prepare yourself."

"I don't think Rori is something I can prepare for. I feel awful for hurting her, but I'll keep doing what needs to be done. Hopefully without causing any more damage," he says, sighing. Still hidden, I listen uncomprehendingly.

369

"The train is stocked. Is she nearly ready?"

"She hasn't eaten yet. She's hiding in the study waiting for everyone to clear out. Brace yourself and I'll get her now."

I'm sitting in my chair when Da arrives in the study. My posture is rigid and still. The antithesis of what is happening inside my head. A tangle of doubt, I'm trying to understand what I've heard. What is the truth?

"Rori?" Da asks, as he walks around to see my face. He looks down at me, concern wrinkling his forehead. "You've gone pale. Are you feeling alright?"

Rubbing color into my cheeks, I tidy my hair. Letting out the breath I've been holding, I stand up and straighten my clothes.

"Just nervous I think. Same as before I jump from the Split. I just never know if my 'chute is going to open until it does. I'll be OK. Everyone gone?"

Da looks guiltily out to the hall.

"Not *everyone*. Hayes has arrived," he says reluctantly. "You still have an appetite?"

I feign surprise at the information. Sighing, I pretend to be annoyed at his presence; pretend to be thinking over whether or not Hayes will prevent me from eating. I'm always hungry, so of course I'll eat. All I really want to do is read his face and find the truth.

"Have you ever known anything to keep me from food?"

"Only your appendix," Da smiles, offering me his elbow. Sliding my arm under it, I rest my hand on his thick forearm.

"I'm ready."

Hayes is sitting at the kitchen counter with his back to us. His shoulders tense as he hears us approaching. Swiveling on his stool, he stands to meet us, but doesn't meet my eyes.

"Morning Rori. Would you mind if I wait while you

eat? If I have to wade through the mob again, I might not make it back to collect you before dark."

My eyes examine him while I consider my answer. He is dressed in his Enforcer garb with the jacket that accentuates his shape. Freya has done a good job resetting his nose. It looks straight again and the swelling isn't too bad. The curved, crimson bruising below his eyes actually makes them look greener, and maybe more appealing. I sigh, more at myself than anything else.

"That depends," I say slowly, walking closer and not taking my eyes off him. "Do you plan on avoiding my eyes forever?"

Hayes sets his jaw and his practiced smirk. Smiler the Enforcer meets my eyes. I get a sour taste in my mouth as I look at his protective, arrogant persona.

"Well?" he asks with more attitude than I care for.

"Hayes is welcome to stay, but Smiler can get the fuck out of my house." I catch the slight twitch in his face and know I've got it right. Turning my back on him, I sit down at the table, loading up my plate with what might be the last decent meal I have for years.

I'm halfway through my tower of food when Hayes sits down sheepishly at the far end of the table. I ignore him.

He clears his throat gently. "In the interest of peace, can we agree to be civil? I imagine living together will be hard enough without adding blind hatred to the mix."

"Blind? I can see through you perfectly well."

Inhaling sharply, he turns his head away.

"You should be ashamed of yourself." Taking another bite of toast, I regard him as I chew. "I can be civil, but don't think I forgive easily. You've done a lot of damage."

"I understand," he says seriously. Looking out the window, he runs a hand through his wayward hair. When he turns back to watch me, the tension is gone from his shoulders. Raising an eyebrow at my plate as I reach for another piece of bacon, he looks back out the window to hide his smile.

"I'm hungry. Shut up."

"She's always hungry," Da says, coming to sit at the table too. "I wasn't kidding when I negotiated those extra rations. You'll need it all."

I kick him under the table and he chuckles. Smiling, I close my eyes, trying to commit the sound to memory. When I open them, both men are looking at me with identical expressions. Hayes quickly looks back out the window and I drink the last of the water in my glass, wondering.

"Let's go," I say, rising from the table. "It's not going to get any easier."

They look at each other and rise. Something goes unspoken and I see Hayes nod ever so slightly.

We walk out the door into the hordes of people. They see me and part down the center of the lane, leaving a clear path. Music plays from the direction of the train. I walk tall, acknowledging the familiar faces as I walk by them. A strong voice rings out in melody and is joined by more. Voices rise all around me, sending me off with promises of their love and support, despite the distance. Tears threaten, but I hold them back and choke down the lump in my throat, determined not to cry.

My choice is made and I stand by it.

Embracing my family on the platform, I try not to think of the things I'll miss most about them. Dragging myself away, I board the train. The doors close, severing our ties for now. For all I know, this could be the last time I see them, or they me.

Sitting rigidly in a seat, I try to project an image of strength, though I'm crumbling inside. Hayes stands in the aisle at my shoulder, on guard. The train rises and I watch the long faces disappear as the dark tunnel swallows us.

The bottled-up tears fall and I feel his hand on my shoulder. It rests there in the darkness, until with a final, gentle squeeze it is gone. Removed before we re-emerge into the light. Despite his hand's absence, its warmth remains; invisible to those who would use it against us. United, we ride the familiar tracks, toward an uncertain future.

MOIRA KAY

THE STORY CONTINUES IN
TRACKS BOOK TWO

DERAILED

MOIRA KAY

MOIRA KAY

A WELCOME

As I step from the train onto the platform, the reality of my decision hits me. The Enforcers filed out before us and formed a human wall, making it clear that there was only one direction we could move in. I look up at Morrison Hayes, hoping for a friendly, encouraging smile, only to see 'Smiler's' arrogant sneer and aggressive nod toward the elevator. Forced to endure my co-conspirator's personality paradox, I take a deep breath, set my jaw and walk forward.

When I had volunteered to be the new hostage, I had been thinking of protecting the rest of my family. Between the train on my right, the barrier of muscle on my left and the constant supervision from the inconsistent man at my shoulder, I am trapped. Any freedom I thought I once had, has been lost; left behind in the Valley.

I try not to think of the true impact that moving to the City might have. My hand reaches to my thigh as the urge to race home overwhelms me. Stopping myself before I reveal my secret cargo, I swing my hand upwards to wipe fresh beads of anxious sweat from my forehead. I don't feel well.

Followed by my protector, I step inside the metal cube. The elevator doors close and I grab the handrail as the vertical movement of the box catches me off-guard. I adjust to the odd machine and wipe my sweaty hands on my trousers. I'm breathing way too fast and my heart is banging on my chest wall, as if desperate to get out. I know the feeling.

"You OK?"

His tone sounds concerned, but I can't see him with my eyes shut tight. I shake my head. No.

"Just breathe. We're nearly there. The doors will open soon."

Hayes thinks I'm freaking out about being in the elevator.

"I'm right here with you. Open your eyes."

Prying them open, I meet his kind eyes. He is stooped on one knee, looking up at my face. The hilarity of him being down on bended knee in a City elevator causes a half-strangled laugh to escape my throat. He looks at me oddly and I shake my head.

"I'm OK," I say, finding a regular rhythm to my breathing again. "Thanks."

Hayes stands back up as the doors open into the shiniest room I've ever seen. We step out into the white, gloss-tiled reception area of Luther Derrick's office. Two very attractive women look up from behind a buffed, wooden bench. Both stare at me; overly curious. I stare right back. One has the decency to blush and return her eyes to her paperwork. The other stands and comes around the desk for a closer look.

The clip-clop noise she makes draws my attention to her shoes. They add at least two inches to her height. I wonder if she wears them for the height or for the way they make her hips move as she walks. It's very suggestive. I feel a little embarrassed for her. Coming to a stop, she towers above me. Looking beyond me to my shadow, she flashes him a smile as she swishes her hair over her shoulder. My eyes roll.

"This is our new Citizen, is it Smiler?" she asks, ignoring me and talking directly to Hayes.

"Rori MacGregor, meet Cynthia Kirk, Mr. Derrick's Personal Assistant," he says without emotion.

"She doesn't look like any MacGregor I've ever seen," she says, assessing me. "Are you sure this is a legitimate offering?"

"Not really your business, is it Sweet Cheeks?" Smiler's tone rings clear around the room and I focus on keeping a straight face. "The Director ready to meet her? I think *he'd* like to ask the first questions of the new MacGregor, don't you?"

Flustered, Cynthia pouts and turns away, walking toward a set of glass doors further down the wall. She disappears through them, leaving us standing awkwardly in the middle of the room. I clear a bubble of laughter from my throat and tuck a stray lock behind my ear, avoiding eye contact with Hayes. These are some of the most bizarre interactions I've ever been privy to. On my previous visits to the City, I have purely been an observer in the shadows, unable to make my presence known. I have never before seen the inner workings of such a place, and I don't yet know what to make of what I am seeing.

Cynthia returns and gives Hayes a cool nod.

"Mr. Derrick will see you now."

"Thank you, Cynthia," he responds in a tone oozing gratitude.

Nudging me toward the door, he strides around me and holds it open. Glancing briefly at his face, I catch him winking at Cynthia over my head. Letting out a disgruntled sigh, I raise an eyebrow at him, before turning into the office to face the enemy.

It seems strange to me that the man sitting behind the large desk is human. I've pictured Luther Derrick, the oppressive City Director in my head many times over the years and not once did he look like a regular man. He stands politely and moves around the desk to offer his hand for shaking. My hand automatically comes up to accept it, despite my brain recoiling at the thought. Again I'm surprised that his hand is just a hand; just bone, muscle and skin; like mine. We study each other a moment in silence as we shake. He releases my hand and gestures to a chair, before returning to his own.

"Welcome to the City, Rori," he says as I sit down. "I trust the ride on the tracks was a new and exciting experience for you?"

It takes a moment for me to recover from finding a man instead of a monster. His words repeat in my head as I prepare an answer. I've ridden the tracks hundreds of times, to steal things from the City and take them back to the Valley to help our people, but he doesn't know that. He can't know that. I'm the Chief's daughter. If the Chief were to be connected to City intrusion and theft, it would have dangerous repercussions for us all.

"I've never traveled by train. It was an experience I'll not forget."

He considers me a while.

"I've made the trip myself. It's been a while since my last trip though." He pauses, watching me.

I fidget under his constant gaze. Looking around, I see two over-sized thugs standing patiently on either side of the room. I wonder if they have to stand there all day or if they are allowed to sit. There doesn't seem to be any chairs for them. Derrick interrupts my musings.

"I met you then, though you probably don't remember. You were busy playing. I knew then, that you were very precious to your father. Do you still feel precious?"

I shrug, not sure what he wants from me.

There is a quiet knock on the glass door. The meeker woman from the front desk enters quietly and places a sheet of paper on the desk in front of Derrick. He reads the note and dismisses her with a nod. As she retreats to the door, he calls out to her.

"Bernice? That other item we discussed earlier, did that get delivered?"

"Yes Sir," she says quietly, glancing briefly at Hayes.

"Good. Thank you Bernice." He waits for the door to close behind her before he looks back to me.

"It seems your arrival was well timed. Your brother, Patrick has just passed. We will pack him in salt and send him back to your father on the next train."

"May I see him? Before you salt him?" I have always wondered about the little brother we lost to the City.

"Why? He's dead." Derrick looks at me as if I'm mad, then sighs. "He couldn't have advised you about life in the City, if that's what you were hoping. He was bedridden for the last few years."

Da hadn't even told us Patrick had been sick. He probably didn't want us to worry. That is my father's way, but it makes me wonder what else he has kept from me. Looking Derrick in the eye, I keep my tone neutral.

"I understand he is dead. I would still like to see him."

Derrick leans back in his chair and sighs warily as he scratches his silvering head.

"Very well," he sighs. "You'd best go now before they pack him. You will dine with me this evening. Be at my door at 1700hrs." He shifts his gaze to Hayes. "Smiler, see that she is on time. I'm anxious to learn more of you, Rori. I've had mixed reports and wish to make my own assessment." He waves a dismissive hand at us, as though shooing away flies. Taking the hint, I stand and walk back to the door. My shadow follows.

***

Hayes silently guides me to a medical wing on a lower floor of the same building. Distracted by all the new sights, I do my best to keep up. Down a hallway of doors, he begins to slow. I can see where we are heading. An open door at the end of the hall has a steady stream of people leaving it, pushing machines and cleaning equipment, like ants moving things about their colony. I rush past Hayes and dodge traffic until I get inside the room. There, I stop short.

Still more people are in the room, tidying cables and machines around a centralized, mechanical bed. A plain white sheet covers the still form atop the bed. I stare at the sheet and at the people ignoring it. Looking behind me I find Hayes watching me closely. He looks at those working around the room and clears his throat.

"Leave," he says, firmly.

Faces turn to him, pulled from their activity by authority. They stop what they're doing and vacate the room promptly, some glaring at me on their way out. He closes the door behind them and turns back to me. I give him a grateful half-smile and turn back to the bed. Staring a moment longer, I cross to it.

This will be my first real meeting with Patrick. I was too young to remember him clearly, when he was taken as a baby. I've often wondered what he looked like as he grew. Reaching out with a tentative hand, I rest it on the covered chest, feeling nothing but lifeless flesh beneath it. Withdrawing my hand quickly, I summon the courage to pull down the sheet.

Unable to suppress a gasp as I pull the sheet back to reveal his head, I gaze upon the pale angel before me. His eyes are closed, his features slack and his golden curls have been tidied from his brow. Patrick. A tear trickles down my cheek as I stroke a warm finger down his cooling face. Brushing the tear away, I gaze at this smaller, younger version of my other brother Aiden, and my father. He is a MacGregor. I move the sheet at the side to reveal his hand and squeeze it gently as I lean in close and whisper my apologies to the brother that gave me precious freedom. The little brother I blamed for things I shouldn't have. The brother I couldn't save in time.

I stay close to him, my forehead bent to his unheeding ear as I tell him quiet stories and stroke his soft curls. I tell him of the Valley he never got to know and the people who never stopped thinking of him. I tell him he'll be going home again. I cry for him and for my family, who will see him soon.

I continue to stroke his hair, silently communicating my love to his departed soul.

Hayes gently touches my shoulder and I jump. I'd forgotten him.

"It's time to go," he says softly, handing me a glass of water. "I'm sorry, Rori."

Nodding my understanding, I take a sip. The water catches in my throat and I hand the glass back to Hayes. With a final look at Patrick's innocent face, I pull the sheet back over him and place my hand back onto his chest in final farewell. I follow Hayes' boots out the door, blind to everything else.

***

We come out of the elevator at a new level. Apart from the large Henchman positioned off to the side, this one is more like a home, with a lived-in atmosphere, recognizable furniture and plants in pots. A small, plump woman greets us. She ushers us through the space to an intimate and attractively set dinner table. My stomach rumbles loudly at the sight of food and Hayes raises an eyebrow at me.

Luther Derrick arrives from another door, wiping his hands on a dishcloth and casually slinging it over his shoulder when he's done. I still can't get over how normal he seems. It's unsettling.

"Thank you, Marcy. I'll take it from here," he says dismissively. "Please, have a seat Rori. You sit too, Smiler. You might as well eat and enjoy the perks of being a bodyguard. I have no intention of harming our new guest."

We do as we're told and Derrick sits across from us smiling benevolently.

"Help yourself. Marcy is an excellent cook, so you're in for a treat."

I load my plate as he watches me, fascinated. His scrutiny makes me feel uncomfortable, but after this dinner and assessment are over, I expect he'll be bored with me. I don't feel like talking and that's usually what gets me into trouble.

"Would you care for a drink, Rori? We have water, ale, wine and whiskey this evening."

My thoughts go to the foul water Hayes had offered me in Patrick's room.

"Ale, please."

Derrick smiles and fills a large glass in front of me. An eyebrow and nod exchanged sees Hayes' glass filled too. Derrick pours one for himself and sits.

"Welcome," he says, raising his glass. I raise mine in response, but remain silent. He stares at me and I break the eye contact by sipping my beer. It slides down refreshingly and I realize how thirsty I am. Before I know it, my glass is empty. Derrick fills it again and nods to my full plate.

"Your father said you had a healthy appetite. Difficult to say where you find room for it."

"Mm," I agree flatly, having heard the same thing all my life. When you're small, people like to point it out to you as if you didn't already know.

He continues to watch me, surveying me with his eyes and barely touching his own meal. Hayes eats silently, carefully watching us both without being too obvious, as if he is trying to blend into the patterned walls around us; trying to be invisible.

"You're very pretty. Did you leave any broken hearts in the Valley?"

I choke on my mouthful and grab for my glass to wash it down.

"Only my Father's," I reply, when I can manage.

"Interesting. How old are you again? Eighteen?"

"I'll be eighteen in about a month," I confirm, feeling more than a little uncomfortable at his line of questioning and his blatant, lecherous attentions.

"I see." He fills my glass again and I try to focus on the food. Marcy *is* a good cook. I decide to change the subject to something less personal.

"Please give Marcy my compliments. She is a talented woman."

"Isn't she just," he says, smiling proudly, as though the praise were for him. "What is your special talent, Rori? Your father said you had no specific role in the Valley, but you might like to decide before too long how to occupy yourself here in the City."

I poke a potato around my plate with a fork, thinking about how the best lies are those closest to the truth.

"I guess the main thing I am is a courier. I run or ride, delivering things or messages, but I do a lot of different things. I help where help is needed. I have no talent or many talents, depending on how you look at it."

"Interesting. I'm not sure we need more runners in the City. It's usually a boy's job anyway. Do you cook?"

I shake my head and fill my mouth with ale before I start an argument with him about the part gender plays in running or cooking. He looks at me expectantly, waiting for me to expand on 'no'. Looking at the appealing spread before me, I sigh at my own lack of culinary ability.

"Nothing edible. I've tried cooking, many times, but always unsuccessfully. I was banned from the kitchen, to prevent the wastage," I say, my cheeks burning. It's Hayes' turn to choke on his food and he reaches for his drink as I had done. Ignoring him, I return to eating.

Derrick gives Hayes a warning look before regarding me again.

"So what kind of help did you mean then? What sort of things have you helped with lately?"

I wash down my mouthful and recall my last few months in the Valley. It seems a long time ago already.

"Apart from running? I've been working with the animals and crops, shoveling shit, babysitting, cleaning, teaching, nursing, fixing broken things and just being a spare pair of hands in general. Obviously you don't have animals in the City, but I'm sure after I have a look around, I'll find somewhere I can be useful."

"No doubt you will, with that mix of skills," he says thoughtfully. "Smiler here will see to your orientation. I look forward to hearing of your decision as to what role you'll play in our wonderful City."

Wonderful City? I find myself wondering if he is deluded, or if his privileged perspective keeps him blind to those beneath him. Tasting blood in my mouth, I realize I have literally bitten my tongue to keep from responding. I wash the taste away and Derrick fills my glass again. He makes to fill Hayes' again too, but Hayes declines loudly, saying he's had enough. His words resonate with me as I put my now half empty glass back on the table. My cheeks are hot and panic flares on the border of fuzzy thoughts. I stare at the beer and curse myself for being an idiot.

"I must say," Luther Derrick begins, as he smiles knowingly at me. "I'm a little disappointed. My men have painted a picture of an angry girl with a sharp tongue to accompany her aggressive fists. But you seem rather delightful. Have I been misinformed?"

"About my being angry, or delightful?" I ask impolitely. I take a steadying breath and try to clear my head. "I could be both."

"You could be." He smiles and bites into a slice of bread, chewing over my statement as he does the crust. "But are you more one than the other? You can answer honestly."

Pressure is applied to my foot under the table by a much larger one; warning. I ignore Hayes.

"Angry."

"I thought so. I'm glad we can be open like this. What

is it that you're most angry about?"

I glare at him. I look at the table, filled with food from the Valley, that he has had no hand in producing, yet feasts upon as if it were his right. I look at Hayes, who purposely avoids my eyes, his jaw set resolutely.

"Everything," I say slowly and clearly. "Everything that you and your City have done to me and my people. We do the best we can to move forward, but you keep us back. You're parasites, always wanting more."

The pressure on my foot is painful now. Derrick's eyebrows rise with amusement at my accusations.

"Those are strong words for a victim. Surely you can see the reasoning behind it all?"

"Your reasoning is false. You're set in your power-hungry ways; too resistant to change because it would be too much like hard work."

Hayes clears his throat and moves uncomfortably in his chair. Luther holds a hand up to still him.

"Are you suggesting we're lazy, here in the City?"

"I'm not suggesting." I take another drink. Too far gone for redemption, I might as well enjoy it. Derrick laughs out loud.

"My dear girl! You are a treasure! It's been too long since I had such a frank discussion, and I am enjoying it immensely. I like to think we have inspired your people into innovation. But I can assure you, we have not been sitting idle while you Daltons find new ways to turn one pumpkin into two or two lambs into three. We have our own systems developed to ensure our ongoing position of power. Have you not noticed how we tower above you?"

"Everyone towers above me," I snap. "Are you trying to claim my pitiful height as your achievement?"

Again, laughter escapes his lips. He looks cruel when he

laughs.

"Not *your* height, no. Ours. Smiler here is a marvelous specimen. Don't you think?"

"Specimen?" I ask, looking Hayes up and down as a sickening sensation grows in my stomach. "Of what? A really *big* parasite?"

This time he bangs the table with his hand as his head rears back in hilarity. I risk a quick glance at Hayes. His eyes are downcast, his brow furrowed.

"You are just precious! It wouldn't have been my exact description, but essentially, you've hit the nail on the head. In the Valley, you breed meat stock. In the City, we breed really big parasites. That way we can always get what we want. Isn't that clever?"

"Breed?" I look at Derrick in disbelief. He is busy chuckling at my response. I turn to look at Hayes, unable to keep myself from doing so. He stares at his plate, his square jaw clamped firmly shut. My chair falls as I scrape it backwards in haste.

"Bathroom!?"

"Down the hall. Third door on the left!" he calls after me, still chuckling as I race away with my hand clasped over my mouth.

Eventually I return to the table, unable to hide in the bathroom any longer. My stomach is empty and my appetite has gone. I sit stiffly and silently. Derrick attempts to pick the conversation back up again, but I'm too disgusted to participate.

"I think I've had all I can take for one day, Director. Would you mind if we continued this another time?"

He studies me again with interest.

"I have very much enjoyed meeting you, Miss MacGregor. Another time indeed. Welcome again to the

City. I hope you'll find your accommodation acceptable. Be sure to let me know if Smiler here becomes inadequate in his duties and we can make new arrangements."

"Thank you. Excuse me."

I can't walk to the door fast enough. I wait outside the elevator, jabbing repeatedly at the button with the downward arrow, as Hayes catches up. The doors close as he pushes a button and my stomach lurches with the movement of the lift. I move to the back corner and press my head against the cool metal, feeling dirty and sick.

"I tried to warn you."

"Don't! Please!"

The doors open and the platform appears before me again. Relieved to see it's empty now, I stumble out of the lift and drop to my knees, gulping the fresh air that flows in through the large arches of the station. My mind is filled with images of a human breeding program. Slowly, I get back on my feet. My eyes travel to the tracks that head out of the station; back to the Valley. My hand wanders to my thigh, where my board rests snuggly against my leg, ready to take me home on those tracks. I want to go so badly, but I can't leave. Helplessly, I look back to Hayes. His eyes move from my thigh to my face and he starts to say something, but stops, looking around as though people are watching us. Sighing loudly, he moves to a door at the side of the platform. Fetching a set of keys from his pocket, he opens what appears to be a storage cupboard. My gear is stacked inside. He pockets the keys and throws me my satchel as he swings my big pack over his shoulder. Picking up my large wooden chest and an overloaded box of food as if they were nothing, he kicks the door shut again.

"You ready? Our building is a ten minute walk from here."

"Our building?"

"Mine, yours and about a hundred and eighty other people. You'll see. Come on." He starts walking away.

"A hundred and eighty?"

Hayes waits for me to catch up, an impatient look on his face.

"This is a big adjustment for you, I know. But your questions have to wait. I'll answer when I can." He turns and keeps walking.

Annoyed, I follow. I don't sulk for long, distracted by the sights and sounds around me. I haven't ventured this far into the heart of the inner grid before. The buildings tower around us, lights shining from their windows into the growing dark of the evening. The air is filled with the noises of people and strange music that escapes from well-lit doors as people walk through them. There are people everywhere. I hurry to keep up with Hayes, fearful of being lost in the chaos.

Spying me at his elbow, he laughs silently to himself.

"That one," he says before long, tilting his head at the tallest building.

My eyes travel up the impressive height of the ugly building. "That one?"

"Do you plan on turning everything I say into a question?"

"What floor?" I say, screwing my eyes up at him.

"Fifteenth."

Counting the lit windows up the side, I realize level fifteen is only one floor from the top.

"Who lives on sixteen? Friend or foe?"

"Don't kid yourself. We're all foes here."

Glancing around again, I shudder at the thought of so many adversaries. Looking back to the building ahead, I try to imagine a sanctuary within.

"Looks like a death trap," I say under my breath.

"Huh?" Hayes looks down at me again, moving the boxes to the side so he can see me better. "You say something?"

"Your building looks like a fire hazard."

"*Our* building. And don't worry about it. Life in the City might be different, but we have our own systems. Our building has two separate stairwells, fire doors, external fire escapes and a sprinkler system. In the event of a fire, water rains down from above to extinguish it, while you move safely to an available exit. Simple, see? There's a lot to learn, but you'll pick it up."

Hayes turns around and uses the back of his shoulder to push through a heavy set of doors into the building. Using himself as a doorstop, he waits for me to follow him in. I walk through, looking at the panels of wood nailed to the door segments. The top rectangle on the left door holds a properly inserted glass panel, suggesting that once, all the panels had been glass.

I walk through into the beige lobby and can't help but see the cracks in the floor and the mirrored glass walls and the obvious paths worn into the once shiny tiles. The place is a dump. With a hundred and eighty people living in it, I would've expected someone to take pride in their home and keep it maintained. The elevator sits dormant, with one door opened to the lobby. The other metal door is dented to such a degree that it has been bent inward, as though someone very strong has kicked it.

"I guess we're taking the stairs?"

"Think of it as exercise."

"Fine with me." I hold the door to the stairwell open for him. "I was wondering how I was going to stay in shape without giving myself away."

We climb a few floors in silence. I build up the nerve to ask the questions I don't really want to hear the answers to.

"So how does it all work then?"

"How does all what work?" Hayes asks as if he's only half paying attention, but I can see he's just avoiding the question. Frowning at his back as he keeps climbing, I stomp persistently after him.

"A breeding program, for starters. We're alone in here. Can you answer questions yet?"

"I can, but I don't want to."

"Why not? I need to know how this place functions and that means I need to know about all of Derrick's schemes; no matter how... disturbing they might be."

Hayes remains silent as we continue to trudge upwards. We pass a landing with a big, brown number seven painted on the wall.

"Tell me."

"I'm sure you can imagine. It's fairly self-explanatory."

He increases his pace and I keep up, glaring at the back of his head in frustration. Irritated by his avoidance, I try a different tack. Climbing onto the central hand rail, I jump the gap between rises, grabbing the bottom rail on the other side and swinging myself up and over it. Now I'm on the stairs above him, blocking his path.

"Rori! Don't do that! Shit!"

"I wouldn't have to if you'd just answer the damn question!"

"I told you. It speaks for itself."

"So what happens? Women just volunteer to line up and be impregnated by big, burly men and then nine months later big, burly babies are born?!"

Hayes shuffles his load uncomfortably and avoids my eyes, seeking a way past me. Sighing at me as I move into every gap, forcing him to stop, he looks at the stairs and speaks.

"It's not exactly voluntary, no."

Taking advantage of my stunned, frozen state, he slips past me and keeps climbing.

Jogging to catch up, I try to comprehend.

"What do you mean? The women are forced? Rape?"

"Coerced. Not all women are involved. Only unwed women between eighteen and thirty must join the Service Pool. If they want to eat, they participate. It's a way of life in the City; been that way for several generations. Initially they said it was to maximize birth rates in a sometimes sterile population. Derrick didn't think it up."

His explanation barely registers, because I still can't believe what I've heard. "If they want to eat?! What about the men? Are they forced too?"

Silence.

"Hayes!"

"Yes and no. It's complicated," he says, avoiding my eyes.

"Tell me!" I growl, my tolerance spent.

"Well, there are obvious perks for a man if he participates, and there are added bonuses regarding rations and rank. They're encouraged, rather than coerced, but it's not exactly optional. There are assumptions made if you don't participate and those assumptions can be deadly."

His pace increases again and it's level thirteen before I can catch him.

"Do *you* participate?"

He stops dead in the middle of the stairs. I can't get around him to see his face. Jumping the rail, I leap the gap again. Walking slowly back down the stairs to where he stands, I try to read his face. His expression is wracked with indecision.

"Just tell me the truth."

He looks me in the eye. "I don't want you to be hurt."

"Since when did you care about my feelings? The truth, Hayes! That's what matters to me."

"It's complicated," he say, averting his eyes again.

"It's a yes/no answer Hayes! It doesn't get any simpler! Do you participate?!"

His eyes close and his jaw clenches as he takes a deep breath; the indecision is gone.

"Yes."

"But, *why*?" I utter, moving away from him in disbelief and disgust.

"Many reasons - none of which I want to discuss with you. Let's go."

He pushes past me as my mind struggles to file this information alongside the Hayes I had found myself falling in love with only a few short months ago. Angry with myself, I begin to climb again. At floor fifteen, he's playing doorstop again and looking down the hall with a worried look on his face.

"What *now*?"

He looks back at me, a little surprised. "I can hear music."

"And?"

"And I shouldn't," he says anxiously, trying to juggle the boxes as he walks to his door. "Can you get my keys? They're in my pocket."

Scowling at him and then at his trouser pocket as I think about sliding my hand in there, I knock on the door.

ACKNOWLEDGMENTS

A huge thank you to:

Lonnie, my incredibly tolerant husband and our daughters Molly and Yve. You so often gave me the grace of 'just five more minutes!'
My mother, whose feedback was critical to the adventure. Thank you for the love of stories, for your interest, and for being there. Dad, you were dragged along too; sorry.
My precious test subjects, Keel, Ruth, Stacey, Chrissy, Donna, Jac, Janice, Kathryn, Rosanna and Dave! You were all part of the final product and your honest feedback and unwavering support is appreciated beyond measure.
Special thanks to Nyria, for being such a joyful sounding board over many a cup of tea!
The Kapiti Indie Publishing group! Your regular support, assistance and shared enthusiasm has helped shape my writing. Special thanks to Leeann and Diana, for your generosity in sharing both your abundant knowledge and your precious time; for pioneering and holding our hands when we try to follow.
Jade Saunders at Hue Design, for your endless patience and amazing eye.
Toro Hill, for your immediate support and heroic actions in the jungle of the interweb.
All the friends and family (particularly those from the 9Bhive - you know who you are!), your belief in me fortified my own. Thank you for always asking when I see you, and thank you more for listening.

ABOUT THE AUTHOR

Moira Kay lives with her family in New Zealand. When not writing, she can be found in the garden, reading, re-watching any of her favorite TV series, or climbing trees with her children. Find out more at moirakay.com

Printed in Great Britain
by Amazon